Praise for *Forbidden*

"At its core, this is a romance, with all the push and pull that goes along with impossible love, and Little elevates the story by creating a perilous landscape, both outward and inward, as Jayden must deal with the hardship of desert life as well as her own desires." —ALA *Booklist* (starred review)

"Lush, lyrical, romantic. *Forbidden* transports readers into a vividly imagined place and time." —Claudia Gray, *New York Times* bestselling author

"The harsh beauty of the deserts of ancient Mesopotamia come to life in *Forbidden*, with beautiful descriptions that will make you crave water and check for sand in your clothes. Your heart will break as you root for Jayden to triumph over the many struggles that threaten to tear her world apart, and the ending will leave you thirsting for more!" —Sara B. Larson, author of *Defy*

"A fast-paced, entertaining choice that will appeal to fans of historical fiction and romance." —*SLJ*

"Rich historical details are deftly woven into Jayden's narration, and the dynamics of Jayden's tribe are vividly drawn. Jayden's story becomes as much about finding herself as it is about finding love." —*BCCB*

Also by Kimberley Griffiths Little
Banished

Forbidden

KIMBERLEY GRIFFITHS LITTLE

HARPER

An Imprint of HarperCollinsPublishers

Library of Congress Catalog Card Number: 2014942413
ISBN 978-0-06-219499-2

Typography by Torborg Davern
15 16 17 18 19   PC/RRDH   10 9 8 7 6 5 4 3 2 1
❖
First paperback edition, 2015

For my mother,
whose enduring faith sustains her in all things—
and inspires me.

1

1759 BC

THE DESERTS OF MESOPOTAMIA

Tonight was the night of my betrothal ceremony, and a cold, sharp moon hung low in the eastern sky. I yanked back the heavy panel doors of the tent and peered into the darkness, a lump of dread sitting like curdled camel's milk in my belly.

Dozens of small torches bobbed and weaved along the paths. Held aloft by the approaching women, they emerged as drops of frozen fire against the blackness. I shivered at the sight of so many guests imminently arriving. A year ago we had celebrated my older sister Leila's betrothal to Zenos, and now, at sixteen, it was my turn to perform the betrothal dance before my family and the women of my tribe.

As I scanned the path for my sister, nerves raced along my skin. I kicked my bare toes at Aunt Judith's tapestry rug in her back bedroom, ready to tear the frayed edges into shreds. Leila had promised to dress and perfume me, so I was waiting here, alone. Of course, she was nowhere to be seen. All was darkness and starlight.

"Leila, where are you?" I muttered, snapping the panel doors again.

I chewed my fingernails, then glanced down at my dusty clothes. Two hours ago, the sun had burned my face, the wind had whipped at my cheeks, and I'd savored my last hours of freedom.

Now I swiped a comb through the collection of particularly nasty knots in my hair—a consequence of an impulsive camel ride out to the desert. It was a desperate attempt to escape my fate, but my father had quietly hauled me back after my mother's wild search had proved fruitless.

Mother had stood at the camel pens, her brow creased with worry, her eyes hunting the open desert. Even though she had been upset, she had folded me in her arms when I returned and held me close, whispering words of reassurance.

Through the crack in the tent's doorway, I finally spotted a small flame advancing on the curve of the path and darted outside.

"Where have you been?" I grabbed for Leila as she came within reach, but she spun away, holding up the lantern.

Her dark hair floated like silk over her shoulders. The jewel in her navel winked green in the shadows, accenting the pleated white linen skirt that hung low, slung around her sensuous hips. A sheer crimson drape crossed her bare shoulder, emphasizing the shape of her chest. My sister was the picture of beauty. An Egyptian princess. The way I should look tonight, and I envied her.

"*Where* did you get that dress?" I asked.

A hint of a smile twitched at Leila's lips. "It's a secret."

"Tell me!" I begged. "Are you going to wear that dress tonight with all of our cousins and friends watching?" My eyes traveled the length of her slim torso. "You can see practically everything!"

"Oh, Jayden, you're such a prude!" Laughing softly, Leila twirled around on her toes. "What does it matter if the dress makes us beautiful?" When she lifted her arms, she looked like a jeweled white column from the goddess temple in Tadmur— the Temple of Ashtoreth.

"Leila, you know the goddess dresses are forbidden. It's as though you enjoy shaming our family." I stared at the flowing, revealing garment. I'd never seen anything so evocative, so sensuous.

Leila came closer, a shrewd look in her eye. "Deep down, you probably wish you were wearing this dress."

She was right, although I wouldn't admit it to her. A part of me wished I were as bold and as stunningly beautiful as my sister. A hot sensation of envy and irritation crept up my neck. "Are you trying to sabotage my betrothal ceremony? You'll be the center of all the attention."

"You worry too much, Jayden. I'm not doing anything wrong, just having some fun. Now try to focus on *tonight*, your night," Leila added with a grin. "And your dance before the women of the tribe, in preparation for Horeb." She raised an eyebrow and the twisted nerves in my gut roiled like scorpions. "Think of how much Horeb wishes he had permission to watch you."

I looked down, embarrassed. That was the problem. Eventually he would.

"You are terrible!" I snapped, unable to express my true feelings. This night didn't mean to me what it meant to Leila. She had been in love with Zenos, Horeb's older brother and heir to the tribal throne. I was only engaged to Horeb because our fathers had arranged it when we were children. But after losing Zenos in the terrible raid by the Maachathite tribe last year, Horeb had automatically become the eldest son, which changed my fate, too.

"Remember, Jayden, you'll get your womanly jewelry tonight," Leila said softly, as though trying to make amends.

I smiled despite my frustration. "I hope so. That's the only good thing about tonight's ceremony."

My father had lost too many camels this year, and had never been a rich man, but I held out hope that my parents had the means for me to receive my betrothal jewelry. The childish beads I wore around my neck looked hideously plain next to Leila's shimmering jewelry.

"What are you two doing out here?" A curt female voice cut through the darkness before I could haul Leila inside. "Can't you hear everyone inside already?"

It was Dinah, our haughty neighbor, standing with her hands on her hips, a fierce expression on her face.

Quickly, I stepped in front of my half-dressed sister to hide her.

Dinah eyed me with silent disapproval. "I would think you'd be ready by now." She stepped closer and touched my messy, tangled hair, pursing her lips. "You're a disgrace, Jayden. You don't deserve the honor of a betrothal ceremony. Under Horeb's family tent, no less."

Dinah's presence was impervious. Her dress lay in perfect folds. Her hair had not a strand out of place. "Any other girl would be counting her blessings every morning. Horeb is a prize and the girl who marries him will be the richest woman of the tribe." She glared at me. "You don't deserve him at all."

I took a ragged breath, upset at her demeaning words, but before I could form a retort, Dinah whirled around and marched to the front doors of Aunt Judith's tent.

"Come on," Leila said, grabbing my arm and hauling me inside the back dressing room. "Ignore her. Dinah just wishes she were sixteen again and could fight you for Horeb. Here, look at yourself." She thrust Aunt Judith's piece of copper at me so I could check my reflection as she threw one of her modest dresses over her alluring costume to cover it up before we entered the party. Terrified eyes stared back at me in the mirror, and my hair was worse than I thought.

I ran my fingers through it, trying to untangle the knots. I wanted to crawl under a stack of blankets and curl up into a ball. "Maybe I could hide in Aunt Judith's largest cooking pot."

"Don't even think it, Jayden," Leila warned.

"Or we could postpone the ceremony until next month. What does a few weeks matter?" I swallowed, my heart screaming that I needed more time.

"What's wrong with you?" Leila rolled her eyes, bending to fix the belt at my waist and ignoring my suggestion. "Jayden, will you stop fidgeting? That kohl along your eyelids is smudged, too," she added.

"I'm always getting it crooked!" I looked again in the copper plate and dabbed at my eyes, knowing I was just making it worse.

Not a moment later, our mother stepped around the rug partition, her belly swollen under her dress with a growing new baby. She slipped her hand into mine and kissed my cheek. "I know you're anxious," she whispered. "By the time of your wedding next year, you'll be a strong, beautiful woman and so very capable."

I heard my mother say the words, but I was having a hard time accepting them. Married. My own household. And babies. All within a year. I pictured Horeb under the wedding canopy, in the marriage tent, undressing me, touching me, and felt queasy.

"Every girl gets nervous," my mother added. "Right before Leila's betrothal ceremony, your sister hurtled spoons and jars of yogurt all over the tent."

"I did not!" Leila protested.

I gazed at Leila with new admiration. She never seemed out of control. And yet, I couldn't stop imagining my sister's sheer sultry dress caressing my own skin, floating against my body with its fine softness. I shook my head to banish the temptation. Leila's heart and beliefs were drifting away from our family, ever since Zenos was killed only a month after their engagement last summer.

My mother's face grew thoughtful. "There are times, Jayden, when a woman's emotions run higher and fuller than the waves on the Gulf of Akabah, threatening to drag her to the bottom and drown her."

"And what does she do to stop it?" I whispered.

"She prays and smiles and greets it with a strong heart."

"I think I need a lot more practice."

My mother pulled me close with a soft laugh. "You can do this, Jayden. A betrothal ceremony only happens once in a girl's life, so enjoy every moment."

That was the problem. I was dreading every moment of my life from this point forward. But I couldn't tell her that.

"Where are the male cousins?" Leila asked, peering over the tent partition panels. "Aren't they invited?"

"What?" I whirled to grab her arm. "The men are coming to the party, too?"

Mother sighed. "Oh, Leila, stop teasing her. You know the men are never invited. And Jayden is true to Horeb and looks at no one else," she added.

I glanced away, taking a strand of my loose hair and twisting until my scalp burned. I bit back the words I desperately wanted to blurt out. Words I could never, ever say out loud.

Mother put her arms around me and dropped a kiss on my hair. "My beautiful daughter, so lucky to become our tribe's princess next year. I'm so proud of you."

Over my mother's shoulders, I caught Leila's eyes and saw her chin drop as she turned away from us. *She* was supposed to have been the tribe princess with Zenos. My eyes swam with tears every time I reflected on her loss.

My mother turned to Leila, lifting her chin with gentle fingers. "You have shown great courage this year, daughter," she said quietly. "Now, girls, hurry and finish dressing! The night awaits!" She disappeared through the tent partition into the big room, where the chatter and greetings were rising in volume.

"Let's fix your hair," Leila said, sitting me down on the rug to brush out my knots and tangles. "This is going to take forever, your hair is so long and thick. Next time you run away on a camel fasten it up inside the hood of your cloak!" Expertly, she pulled my hair up into a loose whorl, fastening it to the top of my head with a bone clip. "There, you look presentable now."

We stared at each other for a moment, and a fresh set of nerves prickled at my skin. The time was upon me, and there was no getting out of it. "Is it selfish to want to be as beautiful as you are, Leila?"

She laughed. "Jayden, you're more beautiful than you realize. Sometimes *I'm* envious of *you*."

It was all I could do not to fall over in shock.

"Come." Leila pulled my hand toward the main room. "Everyone is waiting."

I tugged back, hesitating, scared to leave this last, quiet moment. "Leila, what do you think Horeb sees in me?"

She gazed into my face. "Even though you can be as awkward as a newborn camel, Horeb sees what Mother and Father and everyone else sees in you . . . your heart."

Her words overwhelmed me. Was that true? At this moment, there were bigger things to worry about. In the next room, the guests of my aunt and mother, our friends and family were gathered, ready for my performance.

"Were you afraid to dance in front of everyone last year?" I asked.

"You know it's going to happen your whole life," Leila said, her tender tone surprising me. "But it doesn't seem real until it's actually here. And yes," she added with her lazy smile, "I was scared, too."

My sister left to give me one last moment to collect myself before I entered the room full of waiting guests. I wanted to stop time, to hang on to this moment forever. I didn't want to face the women and dance the first dance of my adult life. After tonight, my betrothal to Horeb would be official, binding. And final.

I took a deep, shaking breath and slipped into the main room. Happy cries of welcome greeted me. Each guest had already added her torch to the center fire. Now the women chatted in clusters, wearing their finest embroidered dresses. Necklaces, earrings, pendants, ankle chains—all made a marvelous jingling sound.

The room grew noisier as the hot flames of the fire licked at the pile of dried camel dung. My mind spun, like I was being swept into a canyon river after a torrential rain.

As the festivities began, Leila poured tea and I passed around the small, delicate cups trying to act like an adult, smiling at each person even though I wanted to gallop away into the desert again.

My mother's voice rose and fell as she greeted each neighbor and cousin, despite the heat and her swollen belly. We were all hopeful that she'd give birth to the brother my parents had always wanted. I watched her closely, realizing for the first time that my mother was a favorite with everyone. She had a way of making each person feel loved and important.

"Jayden," Aunt Judith said to me as I placed a teacup in her hands. "You're going to be a beauty like your mother. We've been predicting it for years."

"You have lines on your forehead, Jayden!" my cousin Hakak teased. "You're not supposed to be frowning."

"Or getting so grown-up," said another voice, wobbly with age. The sea of women parted as my grandmother entered the tent. "Grandmother!" I exclaimed. Setting down my tray, I ran to her, burying my face in the folds of her neck.

She took my hands in her frail, thin ones, black eyes almost hidden in pleats of drooping skin. "I have lived to see all my granddaughters to womanhood. Now I can die in peace."

I clutched her fingers. "No, don't say that!"

Her lips cracked into a wicked grin and she gave me a quick, hard embrace. "Don't worry, child, I'll be here to wash and dress your first babe after your marriage."

The tent engulfed me with laughter, the serious moment dissolving into giggles. Then, without any more waiting, my grandmother untied the clasp from her neck and let her white hair cascade to her knees. She shook it out like she was sixteen again. I'd never seen my grandmother act like this before.

"Tonight we celebrate womanhood and Jayden's betrothal to Horeb," she announced, commanding the guests' attention. "Our divine connection to the Earth and the heavens as we create life for our families. We have a power men will never possess, and that is why they revere and adore us. Inside us is the gift of life, the seed of all people. Our men forever cling to the hope of unraveling the mystery of our feminine secrets."

I hated this kind of talk—men and babies. I'd been dreading this, and right now I wanted to melt into the sand.

"My brother Horeb will adore Jayden," Hakak said. "Moving day is tomorrow—which means their wedding is getting closer."

My face went hot as I ran a finger down the red threads of my dress. "Just because you've got marriage to Laham on the mind doesn't mean mine is happening this year, too!" I told her, trying to keep my voice light.

Our tribe was readying to make our annual migration to the summer lands, where water would be plentiful and the heat not so brutal. Once we were there, my wedding would be a focus and preparations would begin.

Hakak leaned over to kiss my cheek. "You'll change your mind after the journey to the oasis and we won't have to move for a few months. There will be nothing to do but sew your wedding dresses and plan the ceremony."

"You'll be a beautiful bride, Jayden," someone called out.

"Technically Leila should marry first," I heard my mother say across the room.

"Oh, of course," said my cousin Timnath, joining the chatter. "But who will she choose?"

A conversation to my left speculated about the various unmarried boys of the tribe and who Leila might choose since Zenos's death.

Aunt Judith's strained face watched me across the fire. I felt her grief flare with the talk around us. Zenos had been her eldest son, set to inherit leadership of the clan and become tribal chief.

Brasia, my father's cousin, leaned into my side to speak quietly. "Does it bother Leila that you're getting married?"

I studied my sister across the fire, her graceful fingers on the teapot. "I don't know. She never speaks of it—of Zenos, I mean," I admitted, realizing it myself for the first time.

"Her grief must be terrible," Brasia went on, shaking her head. "To lose her beloved before they ever had a chance to wed."

My stomach dropped as I realized that only weeks after that fateful raid that claimed Zenos's life, Leila had dragged me to the Temple of Ashtoreth in Tadmur. Had Leila ever wept over Zenos? I wasn't sure.

"She keeps her feelings close to her heart," I said, struggling for the right words. Aunt Judith had taken to her bed for a month after Zenos's burial, but Leila wasn't the sort of girl to weep or talk of lost dreams. Or were there secrets she didn't dare divulge?

In my secret dreams, I wished that Leila had been betrothed to Horeb. I would hand him over without a second thought!

Brasia sipped at her tea. "Judith must be so grateful to have Horeb. The clan leadership will remain intact even with Zenos gone. Especially when your father has no sons that could come forward for Abimelech to adopt for tribal prince. But at least there are daughters like you to unite with Horeb and keep the families and the tribe together. As long as the Maachathites and the Ammonites don't join together to destroy us."

I nodded, my lips straining to keep up my smile. I'd never paid much attention to tribal politics, but with my new position, I supposed I'd have to learn.

"Listen to me talking such gloom!" Brasia said with a laugh. "Not on your special night, Jayden. And Horeb is so handsome," she added. "Truly, he inherited all the looks in his family. I've always thought so."

"So do all the girls!" another girl interrupted, listening to our talk.

I flinched, knowing I needed to be careful of every ear in the room and what I said—or didn't say.

Hands and arms squeezed me, happy and envious as their fingers pressed into mine. A giggle came from behind. "I wish my father was a relative of Horeb. It's just pure chance that out of all the girls you will get him for yourself."

I gave a faint laugh, my face beginning to hurt. "Yes, lucky me."

"That's the problem with betrothals when we're children," someone else added. "Nobody gets to chase the most coveted man in the tribe."

I shifted my legs and rose, unable to listen anymore. "I'll

get some more hot tea."

"Sit down, Jayden," Hakak told me from the other side of the circle. "*We* are the ones to wait on *you*, like the princess you are. You only get a betrothal celebration once in your lifetime."

"But I love to serve, and I need to stretch my legs," I said, moving quickly out of the room. When I passed my mother, her eyes flickered to me, and I wondered if she sensed that I was ill at ease.

"It's time to give my gift to Jayden," she announced, gazing at me as though relaying a message. "But I was in such a rush I left it back at our tent. Jayden, would you please retrieve my alabaster box? The chest is beside the baskets I packed this morning."

I smiled and nodded. A rush of love for my mother spread through my heart. She knew my discomfort and was sending me out for a moment of relief. "Of course, Mother. I'll be right back."

Before anyone could stop me, I set down the tea tray and flew through Aunt Judith's door into the night.

2

*L*aughter followed me as I ran along the path back to my own family's tent. I breathed in the cool, clean air as I jumped over saltbushes and skirted around a small hillock of sand, passing several black-and-white goat-hair tents. Hobbled camels muttered to one another in the distance.

Close to my tent, I slowed, taking in the night, which was starkly beautiful under a canopy of jeweled stars. I savored my moments of freedom, which were marred by the realization that it was dripping away day by day.

A moment later, I spied the clansmen seated around the hearth fire. My toes curled into the dirt when I realized I had to go directly past them to get back to the safety of the women's quarters. While the women had their celebration, the men gathered at another tent to talk and drink their own strong coffee. I remembered the days when I was small and I'd curl up under my father's cloak to rest my head on his knee and fall asleep to the sound of their deep voices.

The sizzle of coffee beans roasting in the skillet floated across the still air. Cups clinked on a tray as my father passed them around the circle. The aroma of roasted brew spiced with cardamom seeped into the night.

As I tried to slip past, Horeb's eyes caught mine. Firelight flickered over his face, outlining his jaw and wind-tangled black hair. He was devastatingly handsome just as all the girls said, but his lips curled into a smile that sent shudders down my spine.

Horeb's glance lingered on my body, settling not on my face, but lower, as if he was undressing me right there on the dirt path.

His eyes locking onto mine, Horeb rose from the circle of men. I jerked around, breaking off his stare. Walking faster, I turned the corner of the tent just as his arm reached out to stop me.

"So, little cousin," Horeb said. "Have you been enjoying the betrothal ceremony? Tell me, are the women recounting stories of marital relations?"

My breath caught like a thorn in my throat. The women's ceremonies were not discussed with any male—only inside the privacy of a marriage bed.

"You shouldn't be saying these things to me."

Running his fingers down my arm, Horeb continued to study me. "There are so many things I'd like to say to you, Jayden. Do to you."

There used to be a time when my throat pounded every time Horeb turned in my direction. A time when he was growing into those big, dark eyes and that hard, muscular body. Moments when I wanted to touch his thick, black hair, or run my finger along his jaw to discover what a boy's skin felt like with a newly growing beard. But now that I was sixteen, and he twenty, his stares made me uneasy. My heart still pounded, but not from love. And I wasn't sure what it was or what to call it.

Wary of the strength in Horeb's hands, I bit my lips. The fire crackled behind me, and I could hear the men's low murmurs. My father and Uncle Abimelech wouldn't mind Horeb talking to me, but they wouldn't let it go on too long.

"Better to get to know each other before the wedding day," my father always said. "As long as you're in sight of other members of your family."

I lifted my chin, pretending I was Leila, who never worried about what to say. "You used to call me a whipping stick."

"I did? You were probably only nine years old."

"And you said my nose was big enough to scare a scorpion."

He laughed now, as if pleased with his creative insults—and still his gaze did not leave me. "A few months from now we will be wed," he said, his voice dropping. "You will be queen of our tribe. How fortunate for you and me."

"What are you saying? Our fortunes have only grown because Zenos was killed. An event we all still mourn."

"Zenos was never a great warrior." His voice grew stony. "A daydreamer who empathized with our enemies when we needed to make sure they didn't return to their wives and children."

A cold chill seeped through my bones. "How can you speak so cavalierly about your own brother? Zenos died a hero."

His face steeled, an expression I'd seen more often since that tragic war with the Maachathites. "You are ignorant, Jayden. What do you know of war and raids?" he hissed.

Questions ran unheeded through my mind. "But didn't you say upon your return that Zenos died while you were scouting ahead as spies?" As soon as I spoke the words, I wanted to take them back. I was questioning his skill as a warrior and his courage.

Horeb's voice was low and fierce. "I barely managed to escape certain death myself on that ill-fated raid. Which was fortunate. What if my parents had lost both of us? I did what I had to do."

There was something he wasn't admitting. "Tell me what happened that day, Horeb," I urged. Perhaps it was evil on my part to suspect that Horeb ran away and left Zenos to die. That he was a coward. War was harsh. Who was I to judge?

Horeb bent over me, his expression hardening. "I advise you never to speak of it. As my wife and queen, you are expected to fully support my decisions—in *everything*."

We stared at each other and I couldn't stop myself from remembering the many times Horeb insisted on winning over Zenos in their games and warrior training while growing up. There was also the particular incident when Zenos had pinned him to the ground and Horeb, at twelve, had actually burst out in tears.

I was the only witness that day, accidentally coming upon the brothers as I was delivering sewing items to Aunt Judith.

Horeb told me he would slit my throat if I ever told another person.

My eyes flickered and Horeb grabbed my arm as though seeing the memory in my face. I swallowed hard, wondering if he'd hurt me now. To deflect him, I quickly added, "Zenos was like an older brother, kind and thoughtful. I deeply regret his untimely death."

"Let's not speak of the dead any longer," Horeb said, softening his voice. "Our tribe is moving forward, moving toward our marriage and a new leadership." Before I could speak again, Horeb bent over me and ran his hand down my neck, not stopping when his fingers reached my chest.

I jerked backward, stunned. "What are you doing?"

His eyes were black and intense on mine. "A little taste before the wedding, Jayden?"

"You're mad. And rude." Pushing him away, I raced for the back door of my tent, hearing his laughter and hoping he wouldn't follow me.

When I yanked the door in place, I sank to my knees before the wooden chest in the corner, trying to catch my breath. Was Horeb's behavior normal for a betrothed couple? Perhaps I was the rude one by not allowing him to touch me, since tonight it was official? Nobody had talked about this part of betrothal. I'd always assumed any physical affection was strictly for the marriage bed. For a moment, I tried to picture kissing Horeb and then stopped, not wanting to imagine it. I realized more and more that I did not want him, and the knowledge left a bitter taste in my mouth.

I lifted the lid of my mother's chest and found the green, luminescent box lying underneath a stack of white linen. The box was the most beautiful thing my mother owned. A wedding gift from my father, purchased from a merchant in the grand city of Akabah. Holding it close, I ran back to Aunt Judith's tent, careful to stay as far from the men's circle as possible.

The scent of perfume and sugared sweets was even stronger now and the chatter of the women at high volume. I clenched my shaking hands and banished Horeb's encounter from my mind. Besides, I still had to dance my solo and that was more than enough to terrify me.

My mother pressed a hand to her belly as if the baby kicked her. "Yes, yes, Jayden, bring it quickly." Lifting the lid, she took out a small package wrapped in thick cloth and gave it to me. "A gift, my daughter, to celebrate the crossing of this important threshold."

Sitting at her feet, I unfolded the corners of the linen cloth. Stunning jewelry glittered in the fire's light—silver armbands, earrings, and a matching necklace with intricate workings like lace. My cousins and aunt crowded closer and I heard *ooh*s and *ahh*s echoing around the fire.

"Oh, Mother, where did you get this?"

She smiled. "A year ago I found a silversmith in the seaside market and purchased them, waiting for your special day."

The necklace was a delicate drapery of silver strands and coins. Two bracelets, one for each arm, boasted etchings of flowers and leaves and stars. The earrings were hanging domes of needle-thin strands of silver, with tiny blue and amber beads woven throughout.

"Your next jewelry will be the gifts your husband gives you on your wedding day."

I must have scowled because my mother laughed and smoothed my brow with her finger. "When the time comes, you'll be ready, my sweet daughter." She gazed at me more closely, gently cupping my chin and speaking softly. "You will be happy, Jayden. I promise. There's nothing to be afraid of."

My throat tightened with tears and I willed my eyes not to spill over. I couldn't disappoint my parents. I wanted to do what was right, but inside I was miserable. I couldn't please my family and find happiness and love with Horeb, too. I couldn't do both.

My mother whispered, her dark eyes looking deep into mine, "Shall we talk more tomorrow?"

I swallowed hard and nodded, clinging to the chance to tell her my feelings.

Next to me, Leila reached out to examine the jewelry, picking each piece up in her fingers. "Hurry up and put them on!"

I slapped her hand away. "Don't touch them."

She sniffed. "Aren't you selfish tonight?"

Hakak spoke, her voice light. "Jayden gets to be wonderfully selfish. It's her special night."

My mother smiled at me again, and I looked into her black eyes: pools of still, shining water. I'd heard stories of my mother's beauty as a young girl and the bride price my father had paid for her. He'd once told me that I was favoring her more each passing day, but that wasn't completely true. I hadn't inherited my mother's beautiful, womanly body. I was thinner and taller, and my aunts said I had skinny arms. Just like Horeb had always told me. But when I peeked at myself in a piece of shiny copper or the oasis waters, my eyes were as black and deep as my mother's, and I had the same high cheekbones.

My mother picked up the necklace and wrapped it around my neck, fastening the clasp. "Here is the symbol of the evening star hugging a full moon, the sign of our clan. Your father and I had these made especially for you."

The necklace was a small weight against my breastbone, its layers of finely wrought chain lavish against my skin. My mother reached out to tuck my hair behind my ears while she inserted the earrings. Swinging my head, I felt them brush my neck. Last of all, she slipped the silver bracelets onto my arms. They fit perfectly.

"Oh, Mother," I said, overwhelmed. I embraced her and breathed in the smell of her clean hair and milky skin. "I'll treasure this gift always, and never take them off."

She kissed me on both cheeks. "Tonight we celebrate you, Jayden."

My grandmother's face turned sober. "From the beginning of time we have been taught about the God and Goddess. Divine, heavenly parents who created us and then passed along the seeds of creation to us."

Aunt Judith spoke up next. "We inherited the ability to give life and bring forth our own bounty—children."

"Rebekah will soon be blessed with another precious baby," my grandmother said, nodding toward my mother. "Creating life is a dangerous journey for a woman, one fraught with potential perils. Our Goddess Mother knew she needed to give us safety between this earth and the invisible world of the dead. If not, a woman could die each time she tried to bring a new soul into the world. So our Mother gave us a dance to use—that would help save our lives."

My mother gave my hand a squeeze. "The dances of fertility and labor help us bring our babies safely from the spirit world into mortality. A physical gift to give our bodies strength to become mothers as she is our Mother."

"If we had a Mother Goddess so long ago," Leila asked, "why do we only speak of the true and living God now?"

I leaned over to pinch her. My sister absolutely could *not* keep her mouth shut.

"That's very simple," my grandmother said. Her face glowed with the power of her wise soul and the many decades she had lived. "Because She is sacred. We celebrate Her divinity and purity and modesty. *Our* pureness must not be spoiled and dishonored."

My mother put an arm around me. "We also know that She once existed, and perhaps She still exists in a place we cannot see, but a realm where we will meet Her after death. To maintain this fragile relationship is the reason the daughters of the desert do not associate with the Temple of Ashtoreth. For all her claims of divinity, Ashtoreth is not our Mother Goddess. She is merely a symbol, and her likeness simply inanimate stone or marble. The temples are a place where womanhood and marriage have become desecrated."

"So true," Aunt Judith murmured with a hard look at Leila. "Any desert woman whose daughter runs away to become a temple priestess is to be pitied."

"But aren't any of you curious to see inside the temples?" Leila asked. "To know what they do when they dance?"

Mother looked at Leila pointedly as though to shush her, but my sister ignored her and tossed her hair. Someone else snickered.

"It's what happens *after* they dance that tribal girls shun," Hakak said demurely.

"Everyone speaks in riddles," Leila said defensively, staring around the tent. "Just come out and tell us."

My sister's questions were my own. I wondered what happened there, too. "How is the dance turned into something wrong at the temples?" I asked softly, afraid the women would laugh at me for my ignorance.

Dinah pushed into the conversation with her loud, insufferable voice. "It's what the dance leads up to. First, they wear dresses so sheer it shows off their naked bodies underneath, just to lure men in off the streets. Then the temple priestesses perform the Sacred Marriage Rite. They offer their bodies to the priests of Ba'al and the men of Tadmur so they can partake of divinity with the Goddess."

I gulped and Leila hid a smile behind her hand.

"Is that true?" I asked, comprehension dawning on me as the room tittered with nervous laughter.

"That's enough, Dinah," my grandmother said firmly, her eyes roaming the room, aware of the younger girls who sat in their mothers' laps.

"It's a sham," Dinah went on. "For gold and jewels, the women of the temple pretend they're married for one night—with the priests or even strangers in the city—"

My mother quickly interrupted her. "There now, we've had a marvelous lesson on our eternal and sacred Goddess roots. It's time to welcome my precious Jayden into the circle of women."

She kissed the top of my head, causing the new earrings to jingle in the sudden quiet. Bursts of relieved laughter broke the tension. Beads of sweat had broken out across my mother's forehead and her face drooped with exhaustion. Perhaps she was just sitting too close to the fire.

"And now, Jayden, we'll help you prepare for the day you will take your husband. He will adore you as you care for the babies you will have together."

"Mother," I said, and the tent burst into laughter. My cheeks burned, but a cold dread pushed deep into my belly.

A low thumping on the drum sounded when Nalla, Brasia's mother, began playing. I nibbled at my favorite sweet bread, sick with nerves. The steady beat pulsed and Brasia began to sing in the language of the ancient fathers. Stars and desert moonlight slipped from her lips as she sang words of beautiful women and the men who loved them.

The air hummed when Aunt Judith rose from her spot. Taking the scarf from her shoulders, she knotted it around her hips. Then my aunt began to create circles with her hips, first to the right, then to the left as if she were tracing a large coin in the air. The beaded tassels sewn into the material created a soft swishing sound as they clicked together. Her arms rose to the roof of the tent, palms and fingers rolling like gentle ocean waves.

Aunt Judith smiled at the watching women. Isolating one hip, she lifted it in a sharp, staccato movement. Up, up, up with each beat of the drum. Judith's hip twitched, first to the right, then to the left.

Even after bearing three sons and three daughters, Aunt Judith's body was beautiful to watch. I loved how gracefully she could swivel her hips, flowing effortlessly like a snake slithering across the desert sands. A moment later, her daughter Hakak rose and she and my aunt mirrored each other's hip circles, arms crossing in the air.

Aunt Judith moved out of the firelight, extending her hand to Timnath, her oldest married daughter, so that she could dance next. Falail, who was the same age as Leila, also rose and joined them.

The drum pounded faster, and then a second drum joined with a syncopated rhythm underneath the steady pulse. My cousins moved around the fire, the beads and coins on their scarves jangling. Their hips moved faster, intricate and spectacular, and I wanted nothing more than to dance like that one day.

Next, my grandmother rose to her feet, a mischievous smile on her lips. She yanked her hips to the right and left in tiny, quick snaps. Arms snaked through the air, the fingers sometimes fluid and graceful, sometimes poised at the hip to accent the move. She held out her hands to my mother. "Dance with me, Rebekah."

With her round, swollen belly, my mother was slower rising to her feet, but each morning she took a few moments to dance and loosen her muscles before the day's work began. The dance made her strong for childbirth.

Her eyes caught mine and we smiled at each other. When I was just a little girl, my mother chased me around the tent while I giggled, catching me up in her arms before patiently teaching me the hip circles and dips, how to dig my feet into the sand to anchor myself with the Earth.

Leila stood up next, calmly flinging off her outer dress to reveal the close-fitting white linen skirt and the thin layers of silk that barely covered her chest.

Gasps filled the room, but Leila just smiled, unaffected by the sudden attention until Dinah rose to her feet.

"That dress is blasphemous!" the woman cried. "She shouldn't be allowed to wear it!"

"Dinah, please sit down," my mother said calmly. She pursed her lips meaningfully at Leila. "This celebration is for Jayden, and I will not allow you to interrupt it."

There were whispers around the room, but nobody said anything else about Leila's daring clothing.

I couldn't help feeling proud of my sister when she ignored everyone, turned around, and performed a series of intricate hip circles that proceeded to outshine everyone before her.

I was so caught up in her dance I wasn't ready when she and my mother twirled toward me and pulled me to my feet. "Oh!" I cried out, but it was too late to run away.

My mother tied a scarf of beads around my hips, and gave me a quick kiss on the cheek. "It's your turn, Jayden."

My throat was so tight I could barely speak. "I'm not ready—I can't!"

My mother smiled serenely and faded into the firelight. I was alone in the circle. The trills and clapping quieted, waiting for me to begin. I could hear my heart in my ears.

Nalla proceeded to give me loud, steady beats on the drum to follow. Copying my grandmother, I untied the clasp of bone from my head to shake out the braids and whorls Leila had created earlier. My hair now hung thick and loose and soft about my waist.

"Go on, Daughter," my grandmother whispered from beyond the firelight.

Letting out a shaky breath, I turned on the tips of my toes. I wanted to shrink back into the circle of women and disappear, but finally I threw back my arms and began to spin. The tent's four walls merged and the women blended into a whirl of colorful dresses and dark, beautiful eyes.

Before I toppled over with dizziness, I stopped, holding out my arms to keep my balance. I curved my arms and hands, then lifted my right hip in a slow, exaggerated arch, bringing it down with a thump of my heel to the soft sand.

I wasn't like the swaying, large-hipped women who were so beautiful when they danced, but the jangling scarf accented each of my hip drops. My hair swished like water when I moved into the larger hip circles. Reaching overhead, I brought my hands down, fluttering my fingertips to mimic raindrops. Sighs of admiration filled the tent and I felt my lips curve upward in delight.

I continued dancing, trying the various steps and movements my mother had taught me over the years. The ancient dance filled me with a pleasure I'd never known before. Time seemed to stand still, and I knew that the universe was watching this moment. My moment.

When the drumbeats grew louder and faster, the other women all rose to their feet to join me in the final moments of the music. I watched their hips and my own become loose and flowing, moving into rapid, frenzied shimmying.

I could have sworn my body started to glow as if light were shooting from my fingertips and each strand of hair. The throbbing shimmy spread through my hips and thighs. I trembled with the power of it as though something mysterious and unearthly was happening to me.

Nalla gave the drum a final blow and the tent vibrated from the lingering echo. An instant later the room exploded with ecstatic, high-pitched trilling and laughter and happiness.

I sank to my knees, perspiration pouring off my face and body. I wasn't as accomplished as Aunt Judith, or as sensuous as my sister, but I'd passed the test of womanhood. I'd crossed the doorway into a new world, *their* world. Hugs and kisses rained like dew on my neck and cheeks.

My grandmother slipped an arm around my waist. "You

do have the gift of dance, my dear. Your beauty tonight was enchanting."

Her praise poured over me like warm, silky water.

"Always remember the sacred purpose," she went on in a low voice. "You have the Goddess within you, but you must use it wisely, not freely."

As Leila poured fresh cups of tea, I stole out the tent door. The sweat on my skin evaporated in the cool air, and I gulped to catch my breath, throwing my head back to stare at the shimmering night sky.

Never had the power of the dance been so intense. I didn't know why I'd been so afraid. My body had responded and I felt a thrill deep in my soul.

Tonight something powerful and magical had happened, just like my grandmother and mother had said. I had changed.

And I knew that my life would never be the same again.

3

I awoke the next morning with the sound of the drum still beating in my throat. Lying in my bed, eyes closed, I relived the ceremony, my wild, intoxicating dance when time seemed to stand still and the stars fell from the heavens just for me.

Last year when I stood in the circle of women and couldn't move a single toe, I'd burst into tears and raced outside to hide with the camels. Mother had laughed at my silliness and stroked my hair. But now it was different. The strange magic of last night's dancing, the power of my shaking hips, the clapping and laughing and cheers of the women of my tribe—I wanted to do it all over again.

Rolling over slowly, I lifted the bottom edge of the tent and saw a dusty haze drifting through the valley. The sea of camels kicked up enough dirt to create a brown cloud. Today was moving day—the day our tribe would relocate to the northern summer lands to weather the harsh heat—and I'd overslept. Eagerness overwhelmed me, because this was our last move for the year. No more chasing after rain clouds and small patches of green for our animals, only to pick up and move camp again. In a few weeks we'd pitch our tent at Tadmur oasis and stay for months.

The bright sun made me squint. Our camels grumbled, the females begging to be milked, and I could see my father out in the distant desert rounding up the males. Shiz, our best milk-white camel, lumbered over and bumped her nose into my face through the bottom of the tent, the beaded tassels on her forehead tickling as she nibbled on my cheek.

I reached out to stroke her neck. "Yes, yes, I will pet you, silly girl." Ducking back under, I scrambled to my feet. Dust danced lazily in slivers of light as I searched for my mother.

I took a step and nearly stumbled over Leila, who still slept beside me. With my toe I nudged her. "Get up; half the valley has already left! We're going to be the last ones to leave!"

"Go away," Leila muttered into her pillow.

I grabbed the wooden milking bowl as the unexpected sound of moans came from the other side of the partition.

"Mother?" I hurried past the hanging panels and found her crouched in a corner, a stick clamped between her teeth, sweat pouring off her face. "Mother! What's wrong? Why didn't you call for me?"

She spit out the stick. "Began at dawn," she gasped. "I hoped it would stop." Her face clenched in another spasm. "I can't have this baby now."

The baby.

My mind raced. The oasis midwife was three hundred miles away and the caravan procession of families and pack camels was already leaving. "How long since the pains began?"

My mother's eyes rose to meet mine. "Two hours and they're coming faster and harder. We need to prepare. I'm getting older, so there's no predicting what will happen." She gave me a wan smile as if trying to alleviate my fears. "All will be well. I'm looking forward to my first son."

My thoughts ran in circles. No midwife. No preparations. "What—"

"Go. Ask your father to fetch Judith and Timnath," my mother suggested.

I nodded and grabbed a leather skin of cool water and held it to her lips. Then I dipped a piece of cloth in the water and laid it over her forehead.

Leaping over the pile of rolled rugs, I kicked my sister again. "Get up! Our baby brother is about to arrive."

Leila groaned and blinked her eyes.

"If you're not ill, I swear I'm going to scream!"

Leila got up on one elbow, her hair rumpled, eyes rimmed with streaks of black, messy kohl. "I went with Falail to the caves in the hills after your ceremony, and we didn't get home until dawn."

I halted in midstep. "The caves? What were you doing there?"

Leila began to pack up her bed, not looking at me. "We

watched the women dance."

"What women?"

"Not *our* clan, of course. We don't do anything that's not completely dull and boring. But there was a girl—she danced like a goddess. As if she were Ashtoreth herself."

I was so startled I couldn't even react. I was also so curious I wanted to ask her a hundred questions, but there was no time. "Right now you need to help Mother while I get Father to find Aunt Judith."

"I think Aunt Judith is already gone," Leila said, yawning. "Uncle Abimelech's tent was to lead off—which means your beloved Horeb is officially in training as tribal prince."

I gulped. The oasis by Tadmur was the place of weddings and births. With Horeb officially being trained as tribal leader, that meant our wedding . . . It was all happening much too fast.

"But I could be wrong," Leila added with a grin.

"For once, I hope you're right. I mean wrong." I let out a choked laugh as I heard another moan. "Where's Grandmother?"

"She's traveling with Abimelech's tent. We'll see her when we reach Tadmur. Didn't you pay any attention to the gossip last night?"

Parting the tent doors, I stumbled into the hot sunshine, trying not to panic as I stared out across the desert, which was quickly emptying.

All I could see for miles was the long, winding train of camels and litters, moving slowly out of the valley. The nearest tent was at least half a mile away, but familiar landmarks shifted on moving day. As I shielded my eyes, the doors of one of the last-standing tents parted and Horeb emerged, regal in his finest cloak. A blue headdress sat on the crown of his head, the tail end of it swathed across his face for traveling. His bearing was majestic, as though he had already slipped into his role as tribal prince.

The world around me seemed to tilt. A trickle of sweat dripped down my spine. Memories floated to the surface of my mind, images of Horeb when he was younger, trying to steal kisses from the other girls in the tribe. Those old memories still stung, like lemon juice on a cut.

From the tent, my mother's moans grew more intense, taking me out of my worries. I had to get somebody now, and Horeb was the only one who could lead me to Aunt Judith or my grandmother. And yet, it could take hours to find them. Time my mother didn't have.

"Horeb!" I called out to him. Keeping my eyes on the tent, I headed for the white horizontal stripes that marked the women's quarters. The tent flaps closed and Horeb strode toward his camel, a massive animal so tall I barely reached its girth.

"Horeb, please help us. My mother—the baby is coming!"

He swung into the saddle of his camel as I ran up to him, dust flying into my eyes, dirt in my mouth.

"The camel train is ready to go," he said, his fist resting on the hilt of his sword. "I'm already late."

"What?" I wanted to scream at him. Instead I clutched at the hem of his trousers. "You can't leave us alone! I need Judith. Or my grandmother. Or—please ride into the gully and find my father—something!"

Horeb jerked his chin toward the procession and I could feel the ground shake from the movement of hundreds of camels. "My mother is a mile from here in that sea of camels. I won't see her until tonight."

"But you have to—"

His camel began to dance on the sand, eager to run. "If you want to be married to a tribal chief, you have to get used to doing things on your own. And you have to run the camp without me."

I grabbed at his halter, trying to stop him, but the leather slipped from my fists, burning the skin of my palms. "Zenos would have stayed and helped—even if he was the tribal prince!" I spat out.

Horeb shrugged, unmoved by my words. "I'm not Zenos, am I?" Digging his heels into his camel, the animal galloped off, leaving me standing there. I wanted to let loose a string of curses and take my cousin's smug smile and grind it into the dirt.

The tent Horeb had emerged from suddenly crumpled to the ground in great waves of panels, ready for rolling and packing. Silently, the women began the work of preparing the tent for loading onto their camels. I noticed one particularly pretty girl on her knees folding over the edges of a panel and wondered whether Horeb had been visiting her.

Turning away, I scanned the desert. I couldn't worry about Horeb right now. Another tent was still standing off to my right. The last one besides our own. "Please," I prayed, "let someone help me."

I took off running again, shouting when I got close. "Women of the tent, it is Jayden, daughter of Pharez!"

The rear flap opened and Nalla ran out. "Is someone ill?"

"My mother. The baby is coming," I gasped.

Nalla's face turned sober. "Where is your family on the trail? Is your mother inside the camel litter?"

"No, we aren't even loaded, and her pains are getting worse."

Behind Nalla's shoulder, I watched her daughters, Dinah and Brasia, pull the inner poles down, collapsing the tent.

Nalla called to them to follow us as soon as the tent was finished. Gripping my hand, she ran with me back home.

My father had returned with the rest of the herd and I was so glad to see him I wanted to cry. Shouting commands, he kept the camels from knocking over the tent as they milled about the yard, then he grabbed the bowls to finish the milk-ing—usually a woman's job, mine. He nodded as Nalla and I came into the campsite, and his solemn, worried eyes told me that he knew the baby was coming early.

Ducking inside our tent, Nalla pressed her hands against my mother's abdomen and she gave a groan. "The baby is large, but I think it's in the right position. It's just going to take time. Leila, bring more water to keep her cool. And Jayden, you need to make the preparations so your mother can deliver the child when it's time."

Slowly I nodded, sinking to the floor on my knees to pre-pare the birthing hole as Leila hurried to the water pots to refresh the cold cloths.

"Roll back the carpets and dig a hole the length of two hands and just as deep," Nalla told me. "This way the baby will have a place to land when he's born."

Moments later, Dinah and Brasia arrived with hair pulled back and tense faces.

"Form a circle around Rebekah," Nalla said. "We're going to do the birthing dance to help her breathe through the pains and to help the baby move more easily."

My heart was lodged in my throat, thick and painful. "I don't know how to do that dance," I said, still kneeling beside the freshly dug hole in the floor.

"Just follow us," Brasia replied, pulling me into the circle.

Perspiration drenched my mother's face as she let out a grunt and rose to her feet.

"Fetch a piece of camel hide to put in the hole," Nalla instructed me. "It will give the baby a softer spot to lie in."

I scurried to find some soft, tanned hide and patted it down into the hole, forming a small bowl. "Done."

My mother bent over, clinging to the tent pole. "Sharp pains. Down low."

Nalla soothed her. "It's been so long, you've forgotten what they're like."

My mother's eyes were bright and glassy, her face flushed as she shook her head. "Something isn't right. I don't want to lose my baby, not again."

"Stay strong, Rebekah, and you'll do well." As she rubbed my mother's neck and shoulders to ease the tension, Nalla signaled for the rest of us to begin dancing.

The older girls began to roll their stomachs in undulating waves. Copying them, I realized that the rolling movement mimicked the labor contraction, the muscles squeezing to push the baby down.

I felt my own body responding to the strong, powerful undulation. My chest rolled backward then forward as my hips pushed in and out. I danced and sang for what seemed an eternity as my mother breathed through each pain, watching my sister and Brasia and Dinah so I would know what to do. Finally, my mother dropped to the floor over the hole in the earth, her expression filled with intense focus.

Nalla crouched next to her. "Your son is coming, Rebekah. Keep pushing. You can rest after he's born, and hold him in the camel litter your husband has ready."

My mother bore down with all her strength, sweat streaming along her face. She gave a gasp and then I heard a soft thump. When she lifted her dress, I saw a tiny infant lying in the hollow.

"It's a girl," I breathed, staring in wonder. "Another daughter!"

I watched my mother suddenly strain again, her eyes tightly closed.

"What's happening?" I asked.

Nalla placed her hands on my mother's belly. "There is another child," she whispered.

Tears stung my eyelids. We were having twins—no wonder my mother had grown so large and uncomfortable. Two babies!

A few moments later I heard a second child drop into the soft hole.

My mother toppled backward on her heels. As her dress swept away from the birthing hole I saw a small, perfect baby and a thatch of wiry, dark hair.

"A boy!" Leila burst out next to me. "Our brother, a son at last!"

"I can't wait to tell Father!" I exclaimed, but Leila was faster. She ran out the tent door and I heard her cry out the news, but I didn't mind. It was a wonderful day, and my sister was as excited as I was.

Quickly Nalla and Dinah worked together to cut the babies' cords and clean them.

The infants' startled cries filled the tent and I laughed in delight at the sheer wonder of the sound.

I knelt beside my mother, who was finally lying quietly after the hard labor. "Mother, you have twins, a daughter and a son—it truly is a blessed day!"

She moved her lips, but I had to bend close to hear the words. "My babies," she whispered. "I want to see them."

"Here she is," Nalla said, bringing over the girl baby. The pink mouth mewed plaintive cries, tiny as a newborn kitten. Her black hair was wet and dewy.

"She's beautiful," I said, reaching out to touch the soft, pink skin. My new sister was so delicate, so small and beautiful, I was sure I was witnessing a miracle. I'd never seen anything quite so perfect.

My mother tried to move her head as I placed the baby on

her chest. She attempted to lift her hands to hold her close, but her strength was gone and her arms fell limply to her sides.

"I can't," she whispered, and her voice was so weak I felt a prick of alarm in the center of my chest. "I want to name her Sahmril," my mother added hoarsely. "She will be—a ray of sunshine when my eyes grow dim."

"She's already a thousand rays of sunshine," I said, taking one of my sister's tiny fists in my own giant palm. "She's perfect."

"Where's my other baby?" my mother asked. Her mouth clamped down as a spasm of pain crossed her face when Nalla knelt to massage her belly. "My son," my mother called again, staring up at the tent's ceiling. "I want to see him."

Nalla had given the wrapped bundle that held Sahmril's twin brother to her younger daughter, Brasia. I watched as Brasia rocked him and crooned, tears running down her face.

"Mother," Brasia whispered to Nalla, her eyes dropping to stare down at the ground.

I followed the young woman's gaze to the floor of the tent, watching in horror as my mother's blood began to fill the hollow in the floor.

I may never have witnessed a birth before, but I didn't need to be told that something was terribly wrong.

"Dear God in heaven!" Nalla said. "There's too much blood! I need rags, cloth, or camel's hide. Turmeric and henna—quickly!"

There was a roaring in my ears as I jumped up to retrieve the container from the kitchen supplies. My hands shook as I searched the baskets. A fear, deeper than any I had ever known, shot through my gut as I added water and mixed the herb. Every moment felt like a hundred.

Finally, I thrust the bowl of thick, reddish liquid at Nalla, who was working feverishly.

"Jayden!" my mother cried out, her fingers fumbling for my sleeve.

"I'm here," I said, shocked at how cold her hands were in mine. "You have two beautiful children," I told her, trying to distract her from the pain. "Sahmril, your daughter, and a handsome, big son. But you need to name him. What will be his name?"

My mother's lips parted. Her breath came in shallow, rapid bursts. I placed a cool towel against her sweat-soaked skin. "I—Isaac. He will be Isaac," she said, so faintly I barely heard the words.

"Isaac is the perfect name," I told her softly. "Just rest now. We'll take care of everything."

My mother's eyes widened and she choked out another breath, as if every word was more painful than the last. "Be sure my babies—Isaac—Sahmril—are raised here. Desert children."

"Of course they will be," I told her.

"Promise me." Her voice grew even fainter and I watched my mother's dry, cracked lips mouth the words. "Promise."

I leaned close to her ear so she would be sure to hear. "Mother, I promise with all my heart."

There was no response. "Leila!" I called out. "More water!

She's parched dry as a stone."

My mother continued to stare upward as if she saw something heavenly and wondrous etched into the tent ceiling. I kept talking to her, gripping her hands to give her warmth and assurance, but after a moment I noticed that her eyes had stopped moving.

I stared at my mother's motionless face, trying to tell myself that she was in shock, that she was just terribly ill and weak.

"No," I whispered, bringing my mother's cold hands to my chest. I clutched them fiercely, my eyes filling with scalding tears. This wasn't happening; she was merely resting.

Dinah suddenly sat back, her words coming out in jerks. "She's not moving. Because she is dead."

Her words slammed into me as though I'd been pelted with a stack of mud bricks. "No," I whispered again. It couldn't be true. But then I heard sobs all around me. The other women looked so far away I couldn't seem to bring their faces into focus.

Then I heard Leila begin to wail, followed by the sound of feeble screeching as the babies cried for milk. Already I recognized Sahmril's tiny voice, and it pierced me to the core of my being.

But there was only one cry, I realized with sudden awareness.

"Let me see him," I said, not letting go of my mother's hand. "Isaac—bring him here." If there was any way to give my mother strength or renew her life, I would do it, even if I had to breathe into her mouth or give her my own blood.

I stared hard at Brasia again. "Let my mother see her son.

The sight of Isaac will give her the will to live."

Brasia's glance darted first to Dinah and then to Nalla, who gave a silent nod. She shuffled forward, unable to meet my eyes.

When I peered past the folds of the blanket, my little brother appeared to be sleeping. His miniature lips were puckered into a solemn bud, his hair black and thick like Sahmril's. But my brother was cold, and now I knew why Brasia was so reluctant to let me see him. Isaac had never lived at all.

"No!" I clasped his small, stiff body to my chest and buried my face into my brother's tiny form, grief roaring in my head.

"Where's my father?" I screamed. "Let him come and bless our mother back to life."

Nalla put a hand on my shoulder, tears falling down her face. "Please. It's too late, Jayden. But Brasia has run to fetch your father. He is almost here."

Before I could speak again, the back door of the tent was thrust aside and Leila let out a sudden, piercing scream. "Look," she said hoarsely. She held aside the tapestry draperies so we could see the expansive view of the desert campsites. All the tents were gone.

Nalla's face went pale.

My heart shattered into a thousand pieces.

The valley was completely empty.

4

I touched my mother's eyelids with my fingertips, and then leaned down to softly kiss each of her cheeks. For an hour, Leila had been sobbing noisily, tearing at her hair and clothes. Now she stood silently on the far side of the main tent, nose swollen, her face wet with smeared kohl.

My eyes burned with the fire of unshed tears. I wanted to lie on the floor and cry for days, but I didn't have that luxury. It was midday already, and we had to catch up with the rest of the tribe. We were already hours late. My family might get lost or attacked without the safety of the rest of our clan. But first Leila and I had to perform the burial for our mother. And right now my sister was useless.

"As the oldest daughter I should be dressing her," Leila told me, handing over the silver coins that would be placed on my mother's closed eyes when we laid her in the ground.

I bit my lips. "You've said that three times now, but you've made no attempt to help me."

"I can't touch her!" Leila cried. "Her dead body scares me. What if there are evil spirits lurking about, waiting to take us to the land of the dead, too?"

I stared at her. "Where would you get an idea like that?"

She turned away from me. "Nowhere."

"Is that something you've heard people say in the caves or cypress groves where Ashtoreth's priestesses meet?"

"You know nothing about it!" Leila turned on her heel and threw herself on a pillow.

I tried not to scream with impatience.

Taking off the small knife I kept strapped to my leg, I cut strips of linen for washing my mother's body. Over and over, I had to wipe my eyes, my face, in order to see more clearly. One moment grief threatened to drown me. The next I was so angry I wanted to bite Leila's head off.

Last night my family had celebrated one of the most important events of my life. Today, less than twelve hours later, my mother and my little brother were dead. And my new sister, as perfect and sweet as she was, would soon die as well without my mother's milk.

I tried to steady myself, even as hatred rose in my chest. Dinah had a toddler whom she was still nursing, and I'd hoped she would volunteer to become a wet nurse for Sahmril. But then I overheard the quick burst of words between Dinah and her mother.

"There's no point in my feeding her," Dinah had said.

"The baby will die without a wet nurse, and I don't intend to do it. Besides, we depart for the city of Mari halfway along the journey. I might be able to keep the baby alive for ten days, but after that she would surely die."

"Hush!" Nalla had hissed, darting a glance behind her.

I sagged against the tent door. Dinah and her husband had been keeping their plans to leave the tribe a secret. The news just added another dose of misery. I couldn't understand how anyone would willingly leave the freedom of the desert to live in a city far from family and friends, or to walk on crowded, dirty streets each day.

This news also meant my family would travel alone. We'd never survive, not without a group. Sickness, running out of food and water—all meant death. Not to mention a raiding tribe who might take what we had and leave us to die.

"Nurse the child, at least for a few days," Nalla urged. "The girls will be grief-stricken and unable to make the journey if the babe dies now. They're already burying two this day."

Nalla's husband, Shem, arrived at the tent just as Dinah strode away, clearly unhappy with her mother's advice. The conversation between Shem and my father had gone no better.

"We can travel together for the first half of the journey north to Tadmur," Shem had said. "But we've made arrangements at the crossroads to meet my brothers who will take us to Mari in the East, across the barren desert."

Watching from the doorway, I saw my father's face fall as he studied Shem astride his camel. "Why would you want to leave the tribe, Shem?"

"We've had news that Nalla's mother in Mari is ill. And there are signs that the Tadmur oasis is shrinking. It's a good time to move to a city. Come east with us and we can travel together. Mari is still a free city, and far enough away that Babylon's grasp will never reach it. A walled city with farms and plenty of grazing by the great river."

My father shook his head. "I don't trust the land of Mari any longer. Haven't you heard that King Hammurabi of Babylon has taken over that part of the world? It's not safe."

"This is no time to discuss the politics of Mari," Shem replied with impatience. "I suggest you bury your wife as fast as you can and get your camels moving before we all die out here." He wheeled around and galloped off in a cloud of dust.

"I hate him," I said from behind the tent door. "He feels nothing. And his daughter, Dinah, is just like him."

My father heard my words and silently wrapped his arms around me. He held me for several moments, and when he released me my hair was damp where his own tears had fallen. My eyes fell to his cloak, which hung in two jagged pieces. My father had torn the cloth in half the moment he saw my mother's dead body. Then he'd banished everyone from the tent for so long I began to fear he'd died of grief right over my mother's body.

"Shem's right," he whispered. "We must leave immediately. If we hurry there's still a chance we can reach the tribe's first stop by nightfall."

"But, Father," I began.

"We have no other choice, Jayden. There will be time to

mourn your mother when we rest at the oasis."

I now stumbled about the tent as the burden of a hundred tasks weighed me down.

I leaned over my mother's freshly washed body. I'd dressed her in her favorite embroidered gown and then washed and combed her dark hair. Now it lay drying, falling in silky waves across her shoulders. I applied fresh kohl to her eyelids and the henna dye to her hands.

The last step was to put my mother's jewelry around her neck, the bracelets on her wrists, rings on her fingers and in her ears. I took my time, slipping on each ornament and jewel slowly, wanting it to last, not ready to say good-bye.

When I was finished I kissed my mother's forehead and held her hands. I would do anything to turn back time and talk to her once more. Ask her all the questions that would never be answered. I was alone now, despite my sister being here. Leila could never take my mother's place.

"Good-bye, my dear mother," I whispered, staring at her face, memorizing every feature so I could remember her lovely beauty the rest of my life.

Behind me, Leila's voice rose. "How can you be so calm?"

I wondered myself how I could remain so composed. I wasn't wailing and tearing my clothing. Somehow, deep inside of me, I knew that if I did, there would be no hope for my family.

My legs were shaking as I went over to Leila and pulled her to me for a brief moment, stroking her long hair, feeling her sobs against my chest. Then I forced myself to drop my arms and walk to the tent doorway.

"I'm finished," I said to my father. "It's time."

It was strange to be moving around the tent, empty now of our personal belongings. Usually the bustle of packing and the collapse of the tent were so quick, there was no time to walk the empty spaces, to linger and reflect and remember. The tent, no matter where it was, would never be the same again without my mother's voice and laughter.

Taking a bit of water on a rag, I watched my father wipe the dust from his hands before kneeling next to my mother. He stroked the line of her cheek, touched her hair, and bent to kiss her lips.

That was the kind of love I'd hoped to have one day, and I couldn't help wondering if it would ever happen. I'd known Horeb my whole life, traveled together, played games, tended camels, but he was distant now, changing each day into someone I didn't recognize. A boy distracted by his goal to become tribal prince and groom our many family clans into a fierce and powerful tribe. These things were important for our safety and survival. I just wished he seemed a little more interested in courting me and talking about our future life together.

I was becoming surer every day that I didn't matter to him. Horeb probably didn't give me a moment's thought when I was out of his sight. Our marriage was merely a stepping-stone to his goal of status and riches.

Watching my father weep over my mother, I had a sudden, desperate urge to ask my father to break the betrothal, but I could never do that. Horeb's father was his oldest friend. Every one of my father's older brothers had died over the years from raids or illness or accidents. He and Abimelech had known each other since childhood, protected each other, and had become brothers in every sense of the word without actually sharing blood.

Clutching the wall partition in my fists, my gut ached with the knowledge that the only possible way to break the promise to Horeb and his father would have been through my mother. She could have pleaded for my happiness and tried to negotiate another betrothal. And now, with her death, that chance was gone.

I wiped away fresh tears, hot and grimy and miserable. My whole body ached as I bent down to feel Sahmril's breath against my cheek. She was sleeping so quietly and yet she was so vulnerable. She'd never survive the long, hot journey through the desert. Losing her would tear my heart to shreds. I'd do whatever I had to do to keep her alive.

Finally I lifted Isaac's tiny, stiff body into my arms and waited for my father outside the door. I could hear his whispers as he said good-bye, and I glanced away, not wanting to eavesdrop.

I found myself rocking my brother back and forth, just like I saw mothers around the camp comforting a whimpering child. Only I wanted someone to comfort me. As my father lifted my mother's body from the rug, I wished I could hold this final moment forever, all of us here together, for the last time.

We walked silently through the empty desert—our only listeners the rocks and ravines and a flaming ball of orange overhead. Half a mile away, nestled below the buttress of a cliff, my father had chosen a shaded spot for the grave, protected from the worst of the hot winds. Slowly, he lowered my mother's body into the hole he'd been digging while I dressed her for burial. Staring down at her lying in the shadow of that hollow, he ripped another section of his cloak, letting out a wail as he flung his head back to stare up at the expanse of empty sky. I followed his gaze and saw a cloudless, sharp blue. A cutting brilliance that hurt as if designed to hack at my heart.

He dropped to his knees beside the open grave, his face in his hands. My chest tightened into a hard knot as I knelt beside him and put Isaac into his arms. Tears streamed down my father's sunburned skin as he pressed the baby to his face, not wanting to let go of his only son. Finally, he placed Isaac into my mother's arms, arranging the folds of the blankets with tender hands.

Taking the last of our silver coins from my pocket, I placed them on top of my mother's closed eyelids. A silk shawl went over her head to cover her face and I knotted the ends with shaking hands. A shiver ran down my neck despite the brutal sun. Imagining dirt and scorpions seeping in through my mother's mouth and ears and nose was too awful to contemplate.

When my father threw the first scoop of dirt into the grave, Leila ran screaming back to the tent, seizing Sahmril to her chest. I winced, but it was just as well. There was nothing Leila could do here and it was a relief to have her gone.

Tiny shards of gravel covered my mother's feet, then her

knees and hands and arms, obscuring the threads of red, violet, and yellow that she had painstakingly sewn into the dress she'd made last year for Brasia's wedding. Could we have ever dreamed that it would become her burial gown? Sitting beside my father as he shoveled dirt, I felt as though I'd aged ten years.

And yet, only a few hours ago we'd danced and celebrated and laughed. Only hours ago, my mother had held my hands and kissed me and assured me I'd have a good life. She'd beamed at my first solo dance. We'd rejoiced that new life was coming, and made plans for my wedding.

When the soil began to cover Isaac, I glanced at my father, worried, but didn't speak. A never-ending stream of grief flowed over his cheeks like so many precious raindrops.

I turned my head toward the vacant desert, noticing that our tent was not visible from here.

After my father packed down the dirt, we rose to gather rocks, not speaking, just piling the biggest stones we could find on top of the grave to ensure its protection from wolves or hyenas.

When we were finished, he put his arms around my shoulders and kissed the top of my head. "The sun is at the zenith," he said quietly. "We must leave within the hour."

"I'm coming," I answered, but I couldn't seem to take a step to follow him. The burial felt unfinished; it was all happening too fast. "Father!" I called to his retreating figure.

He looked back at me, his figure stooped as though he carried the weight of all sorrow upon his shoulders.

"Will we forget where they're buried?" The hot breeze

snatched at my shaky voice. "This bluff, this spot?"

My father shook his head, giving me a sad smile. "Don't fear, Jayden. I know the desert like I know my own hands. And I could never forget where your mother is."

He turned, and as he disappeared over the sandy rise that hid our camp, I was all at once aware of what I needed to do. There were no other women or neighbors to share this enormous, battering grief, but I had to do something. I couldn't leave my mother alone under the brutal sands with only wolves and beetles for company.

Raising my arms, I slowly clapped my hands to a silent drumbeat, swaying my body in the flowing hip circles. The noises of the desert, hot wind and shifting sand, the soft drone of insects and rustling lizards filled my ears like familiar music. The heat and pulse of the earth rose through my toes.

Digging my heels into the dirt clinging to the edge of the grave, I sensed my mother's sudden presence. In my mind, I could see her hands kneading a lump of dough beside the hearth.

Hands stripping milk from a camel's udder.

Fingers gliding a needle through a piece of fabric.

Palms caressing her rounded belly in eternal hope of a new child.

My mother's proud smile as I opened the gift of jewelry she had purchased for me so many months before.

Memories swept through me and I danced in remembrance of all the many things my mother had done for me. If her spirit still lingered, I hoped she would see me dancing all the love I held for her. Sobs spilled out my throat. How could I bear this crushing burden laid on my soul?

My body dripped with sweat, but I couldn't stop dancing. I wanted to dance forever, to never leave this moment in time. Why couldn't last night's celebration have stretched out forever so that *this* day would never come?

I raised my arms to the sky, my palms opened in prayer as I danced and danced.

Tears finally dried on my cheeks as my hips slowed. My spirit began to calm, and I felt a strange moment of comfort.

All at once, an eerie, prickling sensation ran down my legs and arms. A wild thought jolted through my mind. I had the distinct feeling that I was being watched.

Lowering my arms, I flickered my eyelids against the harsh sunlight.

Up above, on the crest of the bluff, a young man squatted on the rocky shale, staring straight at me, as if the desert had conjured him out of thin air.

His robes were made of a fine, dark-brown material. A cream-colored head scarf had been wrapped about his lower face, exposing only his eyes and the straight, dark hair that fell past his shoulders. The stranger's left arm hung casually over his crouched knee, his right hand gripping the sword at his belt. I knew instantly that he was not from my tribe. The cloth of his cloak was much too rich and the patterns were all wrong.

Fresh fear rolled over me. He'd been watching me for some time. And strangers in the desert were never a good sign.

I reached through the folds of my dress to retrieve the small kitchen knife on my right leg, the one I used to cut twine and dig splinters out of youngsters' hands.

But the knife wasn't there. I'd left the weapon lying next to the bag of linens when I prepared my mother's body for burial. My stomach plummeted straight into the sands.

Perhaps I would die before I ever got a chance to leave the valley at all.

5

I was too far from camp to scream for help. The wind would merely fling my cries across the emptiness and my father would never hear me. I wavered on my feet, exhausted, the midday sun burning me up from my toes to the top of my head. My insides were torn asunder from all the tears and grief. Why did we bury Mother and Isaac so far from camp? All was wrong with this day. Half my family dead, the tribe vanished into the desert like a mirage.

I scanned the hills where the boy crouched, wondering if he was a scout for a raiding party. If our camels were taken, we'd never be able to make the journey north.

There would be only one thing to do. Dig fresh burial holes, lie down, and wait for death. Or perhaps I could just scratch my way through the dirt of my mother's new grave, and crawl down into the earth to lie beside her and my tiny brother.

The stranger rose from his crouched position and I backed up against the rocks and sand, my heart an anvil against my ribs. A whimper rose in my throat and I choked it back.

As he stood on the cliff's edge, his robes swirled around his legs, the color and fabric exquisite. I knew the marks of all the surrounding tribes, friend or enemy. My father had taught me these things when I was small. These facts meant survival. But I'd never seen clothing such as his before in my life.

The stranger straightened, tall and magnificent. Imposing. Then he began to scramble down the bluff. I had mere seconds to make my escape, but trying to run was not an option. He would cut me down before I'd gone a few steps. I would not die with my back to my enemy. I thrust my hand down my leg, pretending to grab a knife. Then I held my arm behind my back. "Come no closer!" I cried.

As he strode nearer, I noticed he was younger than he'd appeared from his perch on the ledge. Perhaps no more than eighteen or nineteen, nearly the same age as Horeb.

I stepped backward, uneasy at his proximity. The stranger's black eyes studied my face. I couldn't see the lower half of his face, but I could have sworn he was smiling at me.

"How wicked to laugh at one's intended prey," I cried in a loud voice to mask my fear. "Especially when I'm nearly half your size, and female. The least you can do is kill me with dignity before stealing our last few camels."

His cloak whipped about him in the hot wind, one hand at his knife belt as he continued to close the gap between us, silent and staring.

"You stand on the sacred ground of the dead. Be gone! I warn you that I am armed."

"I believe you are bluffing," he finally said, speaking in an unfamiliar accent. Slowly, he lowered his head scarf and I held myself rigid, terrified to have him within a foot of me, and bracing for the moment his sword sliced my throat.

I tried to take another step backward, but frozen with terror, I couldn't get my legs to move. Holding his gaze, I willed myself not to move, not to speak, in an effort to buy some more time.

His face was strong and narrow, with a straight nose and high cheekbones. The beginnings of a beard showed on his dark skin, and his eyes, so dark, but with a curious kindness and warmth brewing in them. When he spoke, I felt his breath cross my face and it had a warm, exotic smell.

I broke his gaze. "Stay back!" I shouted as I hurried to retreat, but I was too late, and he was too quick. The young man swiftly reached around and grabbed my arms. Twisting away, I tried to keep my arms hidden, but he wrenched my hands forward and peeled open my fists to reveal their emptiness.

"So I am correct. You have no knife."

I screamed and lunged to the side to flee, but he cut off my scream, clapping a hand to my mouth. Spluttering, I tried to wrestle from his grasp, but he was too strong and I couldn't move. I tried to kick him, but he caught one of my legs with his own and I was off-balance. I didn't want to fall to the ground, so I stopped struggling and hoped for a better moment of opportunity to get away.

In my ear, he growled, "I'll take my hand from your mouth if you promise not to scream."

I fixed cold eyes on him, resenting his intrusion into my life and my grief. Terrified of this stranger who shouldn't be in our lands and what he might do to me and my sister or father. I had no way to warn them. Neither of us moved for several long moments, but finally I nodded.

He lifted his hand, testing my word.

"If you intend to violate me," I spit out, "I will scream again. My father is on the other side of that ridge." Since the hillocks of sand and the ridge hid us from view of our campsite, my father was within a five-minute walk, and yet he wouldn't be able to see or hear me, but I said it anyway, hoping the stranger wouldn't know.

He nodded. "I believe you."

"Then why—" I held my tongue and stared back at him. Who was this boy? He wasn't an Amorite from the north, or from the kingdom of Babylonia to the east. I didn't sense that he was a Canaanite, or an Egyptian either. I'd heard Egyptian spoken in the marketplace at Akabah and this stranger didn't have the same accent at all.

The only places that were left were the deserts of the South. Lands I'd never seen, but had heard of through stories from neighbors or traveling merchants. But how had this boy crossed hundreds of miles of barren land by himself—an empty desert where no rivers or oases bubbled, only the sands that ate men and camels alive?

The stranger gave a slight bow, holding it for a moment,

another sign of his foreign roots.

"Tell me your name," I demanded, stalling for time.

"Are customs so different here that you demand my name before formal introductions?" He grinned, looking up at my face with a flash of his dark eyes and then standing straight again. "Take me to your father's tent and I'll explain everything."

"How do I know you don't have a band of raiders with you?"

"If I did I would never have bothered coming down the cliff to speak with you. I would have already attacked."

The obvious logic infuriated me.

"I also know that your home is just a short walk from here," he added.

"Why didn't you obey the customs and go directly to the tent?"

"To get to your father's tent I needed to cross this cliff. You were in the way."

"So instead you decided to watch me?"

His eyes widened as though surprised I would accuse him of this. Then he grimaced with a sudden spasm, but it was so fleeting I wondered if I'd imagined it. Still, I wasn't going to let him get away with his bad behavior. Evenly, I said, "You shouldn't have been watching me."

"I wasn't . . . really. I just wondered what you were doing in the desert alone, unguarded." He glanced at the fresh mound of earth where my mother and baby brother were buried.

I could still see them in my mind's eye, my mother in her beautiful red dress, cradling my baby brother, who was swaddled in the last of our white linen, their bodies buried under sand and dirt and rocks, lying in the blackness of the earth. I choked back the stone of tears in my throat, but the effort made my eyes burn.

"You've been burying someone," he whispered, and respectfully dropped his chin. "Someone you loved."

I didn't want him to see the swift rise of tears in my eyes so I pulled my scarf over my head, wishing I could hide my face from his searing stare.

"You should have turned away, Stranger!"

His eyes held something I couldn't define. Empathy, contrition? I recognized a sorrow of his own in his face, and felt a pang in my chest, which I quickly pushed away.

"You're right, and I hope that you can forgive me." He paused. "But I was compelled by a power stronger than my own."

"That's no excuse. Have you no restraint?"

"I've never found it difficult to restrain myself before now," he answered, staring at me.

His words confused me. What was he implying?

"I'm going back to my father's tent, and if you must call on your men and horses from the mountain, then you must. Only I warn you, we'll fight until our deaths!"

"That won't be necessary," he replied, unruffled by my outburst. "I am alone."

As if to prove his words, the stranger unbuckled his sword from his waist belt and handed the weapon to me. I was completely astounded. When I took the hilt in both hands, the weight of the weapon dragged at my arms. Wrenching it higher, I stared at the markings in the bronze handle, hundreds of swirls and lines in a display of unusual and intricate patterns. I'd heard of such coppersmithing in the city of Damascus to the north, but never seen it before.

"If you wish, you can now cut *my* throat." He lowered himself to his knees, turned his neck, and exposed his skin. He didn't even flinch.

"You're taunting me now—making me believe you'll let me kill you, instead of you killing me."

"I've never been more serious in my life. Death might just put me out of my misery."

"Why do you speak in jests?" I scanned his body to see if I could spy any other hidden weapons. Giving up his sword to prove his innocent intentions could just be a trap.

Still kneeling, the young man suddenly dug his fingers into the sand and scooped it up. He threw the sand into the air, showering his head and shoulders, sprays of gold shimmering in the sunlight.

Throwing sand was a sign of peace. The universal gesture of friendship and submission. A sign all desert people used when approaching an unknown tent in which they wished to lodge or if they needed help. "Have I convinced you now?" he asked. His action knocked the breath from me. If the sign of peace was ever used to deceive another person, the law of the desert was to enact justice and instantly cut the person's throat and leave them to die. Surely, he'd meant what he'd done.

"Where are you from? Where did you learn that?"

"I've spent the last five years with my uncle's household, but my father was originally a desert dweller two weeks' journey from here. South of the Midianites near the coasts of the Red Sea."

I was astonished but kept my guard up. "You can tell your story to my father, and he will know whether you speak the truth or lie." Using both hands, I lifted his magnificent sword to his chin, experimenting with the grip, startled at its weight and shining edge. He sat on his knees unmoving while I stared back at him. His eyes seemed to draw me in with a strange power, and I couldn't keep myself from touching the tip of the sharp blade to his skin ever so lightly. A tiny spot of blood appeared.

"Oh!" I cried out, not intending to cut him.

"I was going to suggest you show me the direction to your tent, and I would go and you could follow with my sword"—throwing back his head, he dabbed at the blood, then held up his finger to show the red smear—"but I think this works out better."

"What are you talking about?"

"To harm a traveler within your own borders is to create a bond of friendship that cannot be broken, isn't that correct? Or are you not aware of that custom?"

"No! I mean yes!" I said, and felt my face flush. What a fool I was to prick his skin. "Go!" I ordered, trying to cover up my careless actions. But why did I care what this stranger thought of me? He was nothing, and still a potential enemy. "That way," I added. "Quickly!"

I held the sword straight out, keeping it brandished. If he

came at me, I could run him through in two seconds. And I knew I wouldn't hesitate. I couldn't completely trust him until my father had interrogated him.

As we passed my mother's grave with its pile of rocks and stones, the stranger paused, his lips moving silently as though in prayer.

"Keep going!" I shouted. He reached inside his cloak, and I jumped back, panic lacing my nerves. Tears clouded my vision. "This place is sacred. I helped my father bury her with my own hands."

He placed a hand on his chest and his eyes shifted, taking note of my dirty fingers and palms. "I'm very sorry for your loss," he said simply.

I stared at him for a moment, and then motioned him toward my tent. As we descended the hill, the empty valley opened to view. A dust cloud marked the departure of Shem's family and I felt the urgency to leave more than ever. As soon as I saw the tent I began to shout.

Leila looked up from where she was rolling the tent's panels. My father was on Bith, his large female camel, tying the herd together for traveling. When he heard my voice and saw me with the stranger, he swung Bith around and kicked the animal into a gallop. He was at my side before I could take another step, and I was never so glad to see him in my life.

"Well, my tent has never welcomed a stranger into its midst at knifepoint," my father said in his slow way, appraising the stranger.

I watched as he took in every detail of the young man. My

arms trembled with the weight of the sword and I longed to set it down, but I gritted my teeth and steeled my muscles until my father gave me a signal.

"Father," I said quietly. "He appears alone; there was no sign of other camels or men on the ridge. He also gave the sign of peace—with the sand."

My father tugged at his beard and nodded, acknowledging my words. A traveler, especially one who was without a caravan and alone, was always welcomed with food, drink, and perhaps even a bed. Desert life was too inhospitable to do otherwise. My father would honor the desert code because his reputation as well as his own life depended on it. But this day had been the worst of our lives. Grief and urgency to get moving had made us nervous and wary.

"What is the news?" my father asked. He wouldn't inquire about the man's name directly until later. It was bad manners, until a stranger's immediate needs were taken care of.

The young man bowed his head in respect. "The news is good," he said, repeating the familiar tribal words of peace.

"Do you have any report of the rains?"

"I've been skirting the lands of the Maachathites for months, where it's been very dry, but there's talk of storm clouds to the north."

"That's why we're going north," my father said simply. "Are you Maachathite? If so, I should kill you now. You are one of our worst enemies."

The stranger looked startled. "I do not know any Maach-athite tribesmen"—his voice rose as he vigorously shook his head—"I promise you I have no affiliation with them."

My father nodded at me and I lowered the sword at last, my arms so weak, they collapsed to my sides. The weapon fell to the earth and I cringed, not meaning to show such carelessness.

The stranger didn't move a muscle or show any anger that his fine weapon was now lying on the sand. He let it lie as if to prove his word was good. I couldn't help being impressed.

"My daughter must have had her reasons for holding you hostage in such a manner."

"Please believe she never suffered any threat from me," he said, and once again I noticed a quick spasm cross his face. "My only wish is to serve you and your household."

I picked up the sword and brushed off the grains of sand clinging to the blade. "It's true, Father. He gave it to me so that I would consider myself safe as we walked back to camp. The sword's purpose is now complete, and I hope its owner will use it with mercy and justice."

The stranger shook his head, holding up one hand. "Keep it, if you need it. The weapon will help protect you and your family."

"If you would do me that honor, it would be very welcome," my father said. "You can see that we are the last of our caravan and time is critical—"

The young man's face suddenly twisted into a pained grimace. Letting out a groan, he dropped to his knees, and then crumpled face-first to the sand.

"Oh!" I cried, scrambling to fetch the leather waterskin tied to my father's camel.

My father rolled the stranger onto his back. The boy's eyes were closed, and he let out another moan before going unconscious.

Clutching Sahmril, Leila hovered closer, her eyes wide. "What is wrong with him?"

Flinging back the richly crafted cloak, my father examined him. The cotton weave of his shirt was stained a deep red, and the crusted fabric stuck to his skin. Father slowly pulled it back so as not to rip open the wound, then lifted it up to expose the young man's torso. An ugly gash had sliced the length of his right side. "Whoever he is, he's been hurt."

"That's horrible!" Leila cried, turning away.

I opened the waterskin, trying not to be sick at the sight of the oozing, ugly wound. Biting my lips, I poured water while my father dabbed at the blood. "This is several days old and has reopened," he said. "It needs to be sewn."

"How do you think he got hurt?" I asked.

"This is not the work of a wild animal," my father murmured, glancing up at me. "It's the work of a blade."

I stared at him in astonishment as he lifted the young man up in his arms. He carried him to the palm trees by the well, the only shade in the flat valley. "Try to get him to drink, Jayden. I'll ride up on the bluff and take a look."

"Do you think there's a group of raiders waiting for us— that this is all a ruse?"

My father brushed a hand against my cheek. "Do not worry. I believe he's alone. If he was part of a band of raiders, they would have already killed me and taken the camels. How he crossed so much desert without an animal is the strangest fact. No man could walk from the wells of the Maachathite to this valley."

I started to speak, but my father shook his head. "All our questions will soon be answered." He mounted Bith and galloped off before I could say another word.

My mind went crazy with a hundred new fears. What would I do if my father didn't return? Staring down at the unconscious stranger, I wondered who had wanted him dead.

"How old do you think he is?" Leila asked, inching closer again.

I looked down at his fine features, resisting the urge to stroke his brow for fever. "Perhaps nineteen?"

My sister lowered her voice. "He's very handsome."

I let out a small laugh so I wouldn't have to answer. Then I lowered my eyes to study him more closely, pretending to assess his wound instead. His features were dark and wild and beautiful all at the same time. Even more so than Horeb. There was also an unexpected gentle air about this stranger, even as he slept. No hollow cheeks from constant hunger. No lines etched into the skin around his mouth or forehead caused by stress or revenge or a hard life.

Leila nudged me again. "Well? The muscles in his chest are quite remarkable, don't you think? How broad he is—"

"I think he's quite passed out," I said, cutting her off, hiding the fact that I'd also been staring at his bare stomach and chest. "And I haven't paid the slightest bit of attention to his appearance," I added, the lie snaking out of my mouth so easily

I almost choked to hear myself say it. "I—I've been too busy staying alive."

Leila squeezed my hand. "I never knew you were so brave."

"Oh, Leila, I've been much more terrified than brave."

"His clothing is very fine, isn't it? He must come from a wealthy family."

The young man stirred and I lifted his head to give him a sip from the waterskin. He coughed, the liquid dribbling from his mouth, and fell back again.

"Will you fetch the henna and turmeric?" I asked Leila.

"You go get it," she answered, never taking her eyes off the wounded stranger. "I'll give him more water and keep Sahmril here in the shade. But hurry because she'll soon be screaming again."

"Fine," I said, too tired to argue, but annoyed with my sister for hovering so close to the stranger, as though she had been the one to find him.

At the shrinking campsite, baskets lay in piles waiting to be tied to the pack camels. Leila had finished rolling the panels of the goat-hair tent, but it would take all three of us to lift the huge rolls onto the camels.

The herd was beginning to snort and spit, impatient to begin the journey to our summer lands.

I hurriedly sorted through the kitchen baskets and found the supplies I needed. And my missing knife. Then I ran back to the palm trees, cut strips of clean cloth, and dipped one into the turmeric to clean the wound.

Lifting the stranger's shirt, I hesitated to touch him. I was looking at a boy's bare chest for the first time in my life. His skin was pale where the sun had never directly shone. A line of dark hair ran straight down from his navel, disappearing into his underclothes. I glanced away, light-headed.

Next to me, Leila fingered his finely stitched robe lying next to him. "Fit for a king," she said. "Oh, look at this!" She held up a dagger hidden inside the folds of the stranger's cloak.

"He had a second weapon all along," I whispered. "He could have swung around and killed me at any time."

Leila's eyes met mine. "But he didn't."

I didn't have time to think about the ramifications of that fact or the stranger's motives for anything. "He'll soon be ill if this isn't taken care of." I surveyed the flaming-red wound that oozed infection, completely inadequate in the skills needed to tend it properly.

A tear spilled down my cheek, and I wiped it away. Our mother would have tended to him. She always knew what to do, and managed to have gentle hands and kind words of assurance. I'd never been afraid when she was here. Since her death, I felt constantly frightened, trying not to panic every other minute.

Gritting my teeth, I finally plunged into the task, cleaning up the blood and pus while my stomach lurched.

Leila stepped back, squeamish. "Who do you think did that to him?"

"Looks like a fight," I said simply. This worried me the most, as we didn't know who was out there, or if he'd been followed. Once again I wished we were on our way and this day was finally over.

I finished up, and even though the stranger's wound was still red and swollen, it was cleaner now. I wrapped strips of cloth around his torso, enlisting Leila's help to roll him from side to side to pull it underneath. When I finished knotting the ends, the young man's eyes flew open.

"Oh!" I fell back on my knees, startled. "You're still with us, then."

His voice was weak, but his eyes came into focus. "Am I seeing a vision, or am I dead?"

I smiled. "Neither," I told him, my heart pounding at the way he was looking at me. "Lie still. Tonight my father will stitch the wound so that it will stop bleeding."

I was relieved when Leila pointed toward the bluffs. "Look, there's Father!"

"No signs of animals or men," he said as he pulled into camp and slid off Bith. "The tracks on the ridge are at least several days old. The only fresh prints belong to this stranger. If I didn't know better, I would think the desert had conjured him from the rocks."

I noticed that the boy's eyes were closed again. Had he really fallen asleep or was he listening to our conversation?

"When he wakes, we'll learn more," my father said. "For now, we must go."

"And what do we do with him?" I asked.

"He comes with us. Even if he didn't intend to travel north toward Damascus and then east to Tadmur, he has no choice now."

6

We made our final preparations and the young man stirred again as I tied the last basket of grain to our camel.

I plunged a waterskin into the well to fill it, and the stranger reached out and touched the hem of my dress. "Oh!" I jumped back, alarmed.

He held up his hands. "I'm sorry to startle you. Where's your family going, and why am I lying here?"

"You fainted," I said simply. "You miraculously survived a knife attack but you're in no shape to travel alone without a camel. You'd collapse before you managed a single day's journey. We're going north to the big oasis Tadmur, the city of palms. And you're coming with us."

He shook his head. "No, that cannot be. I must get back to my uncle in the South at—the South."

"When you say the South, where do you mean exactly? The kingdom of Akabah by the Red Sea? Or the lands of the Midianites and Moabites?"

He shook his head. "Much farther than that. Weeks and weeks beyond the Red Sea."

I gazed at him in disbelief. "Nobody lives beyond the far eastern borders of the Red Sea. There is nothing but the death trap of the Empty Sands. Not even a camel can cross that."

He just stared at me without answering, and I couldn't imagine what location or geography he was referring to. "Once you pass the Moabite nation," I continued, wondering why he wouldn't just tell me, "there are no paths or roads, only mountains and then straight east to borders guarded by vicious nomads."

He lifted an eyebrow and gave me that half smile again. "The people of the farthest southern lands are not all vicious."

I stared at him, not speaking for a moment, and then I said, "You're teasing me. Are these the people you escaped from? The ones who knifed you?"

"I do not flee my own people and my own land, but I need to return as quickly as I can."

His mild manners and teasing tongue didn't coincide with the stories I'd heard my entire life—tales of lands that bordered on mythical. "You have no camel, no food, and no water. How do you intend to get there alive?"

"If it is the will of God, I can do it." He tried to sit up, then grimaced with pain and fell back to his bed of dirt.

I didn't respond; instead I busied my hands with the

waterskins, clumsy and embarrassed. The subject of God was a topic for the men around the campfire.

The stranger looked at me. "As a daughter of Abraham, do you find it difficult to live in a land of Babylonian religion, its rites and sacrifices?" he asked softly. "The gods of the sun and moon and stars?"

I quickly retied the last of our water, hoping the old camel skins didn't drip all the way to Tadmur. "We stay away from the temples so we don't accidentally get chosen for the sacrificial table. Or dropped into a bottomless well," I said simply.

When he glanced up, surprised, I gave him a sideways smile to let him know that I was exaggerating. "It's not as bad as that," I conceded. "But there are stories of children being taken. It's the reason we don't live in the cities, only entering on market days when we need supplies."

A moment passed, and our eyes met. "Well, I'm blessed to have found a tribe that won't drop me into a bottomless well."

I let out a choked laugh. To cover up my unease, I got to my knees, wrapping up the basket of herbs and medicine.

The stranger lifted his hand to keep my attention. "Do you know where the closest well is?"

"You're sitting right next to it," I replied.

He squinted around the campsite. "I guess I meant, how far is the next one?"

"There's no water again until we reach the canyon lands, which is five more days' journey to the north."

"There are cities along the way you could stop at."

I shook my head no. "We avoid the cities until we reach

Tadmur. There are too many outlying tribes, so we pack enough water from this well to make the five-day journey to the red canyons. But as the weather is growing hotter, it's easy to run out. The last day or two becomes very difficult. With your ill health, I fear it's going to be a terrible few days for you."

He gazed into the distance, as if he could see his homeland from here. "I'd like to take water and go south alone if I can. I *need* to go south."

I looked at him and shook my head again. "Your wound has gone to your head! You couldn't begin to carry enough water with you, and on foot you would surely die before the end of the first day."

"To accompany your family takes me far out of my way. Multiply your journey many times over, and that is where my uncle awaits me. When I don't arrive on time, he will be mad with worry."

"To attempt a desert crossing alone would be mad."

He gave a small shrug, looking up through his long hair as I handed him a small roll of bread from the previous evening's meal. Even though it was nearly hard as a rock, he bit into it ravenously. "Perhaps, but I'm not completely crazy."

My face burned. "I didn't mean to imply that you're crazy."

"What did you mean to imply, then?"

"Nothing," I mumbled, heat creeping up my face. His nearness was making me flustered. I'd never felt like this with Horeb. "You have no choice but to come with us until you are healed and strong again. Otherwise, you will die. Would your uncle rather a dead nephew or a late one?"

He stared at me thoughtfully.

"Besides, you will need camels and a caravan for safety. Of which you presently have none."

He smiled faintly. "It seems you are right. I might be a little crazy. For I still insist to go."

I smiled back, raising an eyebrow. "I'm sorry, you can insist all you want, but my father won't have it any other way." I turned my back on him to tend to my chores. "You will go on with my family, until you are well. You've no other choice."

Holding a hand to his side, he tried to rise but only got as far as his knees. He sank back and sighed. "Fine. But as soon as your family is at the oasis, I'll return to my uncle."

He tried again to rise, then took a deep breath as though contemplating how to get up without asking for help. "You and your father are very kind. Thank you for taking care of me."

I turned around and smiled to myself. Then stared back at him, curious. "Will you tell me who did this to you?" I asked, nodding to the bandage wrapped around his torso. It was not a question for me to ask, but I couldn't help myself.

"I don't intend to keep my tale a secret, but it's neither heroic nor courageous," he replied cryptically.

"Were they trying to kill you?"

He didn't answer at first, but finally he nodded. "When someone puts a knife near your heart, they intend for death to follow."

I hefted the waterskin, pressing my lips together and

wondering who wanted him dead. Then I reached down to stroke Sahmril, who squirmed in her sleep in a small patch of shade. My curiosity kept rising, but I'd wait until my father asked the questions—and got the answers.

The stranger glanced between me and Sahmril as he dribbled more water into his mouth. "The babe, is she yours?"

"She's my sister," I answered, trying to keep my voice steady. "Born this morning to my mother, who is now dead."

Awareness flooded his face. "Ah, yes. The burial spot."

"The babe's twin brother lies there as well."

He looked down. "I'm truly sorry," he said quietly. "I owe you a debt for my life, and I've burdened you even further on such a day of sorrow. But I'm not sure how much longer I could have survived. I've been praying for three days that I'd find someone who would help me."

"Then it appears as though your prayers were answered," I said. Why did he have to say such kind things when I wanted to curse him for delaying us and frightening me so badly? He had caused more anguish than he would ever understand, even though his manners were impeccable. Which just annoyed me even more.

I strapped the last waterskin onto Shiz as the boy rose to his feet, keeping one hand on top of the well's wooden cover for balance when my father appeared.

"There's no time to exchange talk and news," my father said. "But if we're to travel together, please tell me your name."

"My name is Kadesh and I'm of the lineage of Dedan."

My father's eyebrows lifted in surprise. "You *are* a long way from home. I'm Pharez of the tribe of Nephish. My daughters are Leila and Jayden, and the babe is Sahmril. If we're to harbor you on our journey you must tell me your business in these lands. The well belongs to the Kedar tribe, who is friendly to us. I've traveled these lands since I could walk." Pointedly, he added, "Men of the South rarely pass through here. Usually never get this far north, but travel west to the cities of Salem and Egypt."

"You deserve an answer," Kadesh agreed, making an effort to stand straight, but I noticed from his pained expression that he was still greatly hurting. "My uncle and his brothers and cousins are building trading posts and forts along the Red Sea highway. It's getting too dangerous not to have shelter, weapons, or food on such long caravan journeys. Our goods are sold in the cities of Mesopotamia, along the Great Sea, as well as into Egypt. I've grown up learning my uncle's trade, since he has no son. He sent me north with stops at Akabah and Salem, but there were complications, and I found myself in unknown territory. Three days ago my camel collapsed and I was caught in a raid between two other tribes."

"Is that how you were wounded?"

Kadesh nodded. "The raiders mistook me for an enemy. When darkness fell, I managed to escape."

"Foolish," my father said briefly, securing the ropes on the loaded camels. "You're lucky you're not dead."

The young man helped him check the halters and ropes as they walked the small line of our camels. I followed behind, curious. "I heard about a well in this direction but it was farther than I expected, and I was slower on foot . . ." The boy's voice trailed off as his eyes took in the shade of the palm tree and the waterskins. "But I did find the well."

My father gave a quick laugh. "You're fortunate, although you're still weeks short of Damascus." He clapped his hands for Bith, who trotted over. "It's time to go. The sun is beginning to cross the sky. Take the lead and push the camels as hard as you can. I still hope to catch up to Shem's family by nightfall. I'll make sure the rear ones don't stray and drag us behind. They'll obey me, not you."

After climbing into the camel litter, I held Sahmril on my lap, listening to the creaking leather harnesses of the carriage. It was stifling inside the contraption, and cramped, but at least the sun wasn't burning our heads.

Parting the front draperies, I watched Kadesh straddle the lead camel behind the animals' large hump, lying flat on his stomach. It was obvious he was no stranger to desert journeys, since that position was the most comfortable way to ride for long hours.

Kadesh's story was curious. Mysterious wealth, surviving a raid without a camel, and the intelligence of a desert tracker. These characteristics did not usually go together. There had to be much more that he wasn't telling us. . . .

The heat of the day was now at its height and Leila immediately fell asleep. The swaying motion soon had me dozing in fits and starts. Images from the morning wouldn't leave my mind; the washing of my mother's dead body, Isaac's tiny form, his dark lashes and clenched fists. I rolled over and dreamed of handfuls of earth that fell without ceasing, clods of sand and earth that rained down until I was buried just like my mother.

I woke to Sahmril's screams.

Leila opened one eye. "Feed her, Jayden! Her screams are giving me a headache."

"What do you think I'm doing? The heat makes you so irritable. Don't you have any patience?"

"Not for crying babies. Perhaps I'll rethink motherhood."

"You'll feel differently when you have your own babies."

Leila closed her eyes again, mumbling. "I'm not so sure."

Now Sahmril was kicking her legs and fists, her screeches rising in volume. Unstopping a jar of camel milk, I dipped a small rag into it, and then squeezed the milk into her mouth. She gagged when the liquid hit her throat, but she was so hungry I finally managed to get some of the milk inside of her. After a few minutes, she fell asleep, her face scrunched against the blanket, the tiny brow lined with frowns.

"Finally." Leila sighed.

I fell against my own pillows, hoping the camel's milk wouldn't give Sahmril stomach cramps. Tucking her into a corner filled with blankets to cushion her from the jolting ride, I stretched out my legs against the wooden frame of the litter's opening. "Oh, Sahmril," I whispered, bending down to kiss her fragile eyelids. "Try hard to live. Our mother would want you to live, to be strong and beautiful."

After a few hours Father stopped to let the camels rest. He untied a waterskin from Bith and gave us each a small drink, but that would be our last one until evening.

Kadesh and my father studied the ground in both directions, then scanned the horizon and checked the sun. I watched them, mesmerized. Every desert man knew his own camel's footprints intimately. He could also identify the herds of his clan and neighbors, making it easier to track another clan's journey. My father could tell how many camels they had, the number of people in the group, and their pace and direction.

My father trotted past the carriage on his way back to the rear and I leaned out from behind the curtains. "Father, what do you see?"

"Shem's tracks. He passed only a few hours ago, and we'll be certain to catch up to him."

Good news, I thought, and sat back down next to my sleeping sisters.

We started off again, and I sat deep in reflection until the sun's long rays slanted through the curtains.

A headache pounded at my temple as the camel lurched across the desert. When I rubbed at my burning eyes, I saw that Leila was staring out between the curtains, tears silently falling down her cheeks. Her knees were pulled up underneath her chin.

"Leila," I whispered.

She stayed silent until finally she turned her face, eyes red-rimmed, looking miserable. "What are we going to do without Mother?"

I shook my head, trying to speak, tears forming in my own eyes. I'd been wondering the same thing.

"We have to do everything now," Leila said. "Take care of

the entire household, the camels, the meals, raising Sahmril—everything. I—I don't think I can, Jayden. I don't *want* to. I just feel like running away. If only we had money, we could have help. I hate being poor."

I wasn't surprised to hear my sister say these things. She'd always said she wanted to marry a rich man. A merchant or a nobleman with a big house and servants.

"I know," I managed to croak out.

"What about our weddings to plan, our trousseaus to sew? And how will I find a husband without Mother's help to negotiate an agreement between the families?"

"I wish—" I stopped abruptly. I wished Leila could marry Horeb. That the betrothal with Zenos had passed on to the next brother. They seemed better suited for each other, and she was ready now for the world of men and marriage. Leila was practiced at flirting with the boys of the tribe. But I couldn't say any of this.

"What?" Leila asked.

"Nothing." I patted Sahmril mindlessly as she began to cry again. It all felt hopeless.

Leila let out a sob and buried her face into her knees, bowing her head. "I miss her! Even traveling to Tadmur is not the same without Mother."

"I know," I agreed, and the tears threatened to overwhelm me. I bit my lips and held them in. Even so, I wanted to rip at my clothes as my father had done. Throw dirt in my hair and wail for a week as was the custom of our women. But we had a stranger with us. And a long journey ahead. I had to keep my wits about me and not give in to the mourning. "I miss her, too. We will for the rest of our lives."

A moment later, a sharp dip in the road made a hard, wooden object clatter across the litter floor. I reached down to pick it up. It was the figure of a naked woman carved from a tamarisk tree. She had large hips and a voluptuous figure. Her arms rose in a circle above her head, and her face was lifted upward, eyes closed as if in prayer.

My pulse seemed to stop for a moment; I was so shocked to see a statue from one of the goddess temples here in our belongings. "What is this doing here?"

Leila reached out to grab it from me. "Give me that!"

"Leila? Where did this come from?" I pulled the statue away from her outstretched hands. I studied the beautiful statue, the swirls of dark and light within the polished wood. The woman's face was serene, her nakedness sensuous and exotic.

"It's mine! I mean, I got it from a girl in the groves."

"You should never have accepted a gift like this. We are not idol worshippers, Leila."

"But *I* think it's beautiful. Let me have it, Jayden." Leila retrieved one of her scarves and held out her hand, challenging me.

I ignored her, running my fingers down the satiny finish. The artistry was astonishing. "It's valuable, isn't it?"

Leila's eyes flitted away and then returned, nodding slowly. "Yes, it's a woman dancing for the divine Ashtoreth, the goddess of fertility."

"What would our mother say? She would weep, you know." I broke off, thinking of her lying in that dark grave, farther away with every passing moment. "This figure is not only dancing, but she's *praying* to Ashtoreth. That is idol worship and you know that our people don't worship idols."

"It's only a wooden statue, Jayden! Dancing just like *we* dance for babies and weddings. Must you make a mountain out of a grain of dust?"

"This is no grain of sand," I told her. "Mother warned us about the goddess temples. The wealth and idleness. Our grandmother said the same thing. For the women of the desert, this is pure wickedness."

"Dancing is not wicked," Leila said evenly, tossing her hair over her shoulder. "You dance. Every woman we know dances. There's nothing wrong with this statue either. It was given to me out of friendship. Created by a master artist."

"I feel sick seeing you with this. These girls—these friends from the groves—they're trying to lure you to the Temple of Ashtoreth. Don't you see that?"

"They haven't blinded me, Jayden. I want to see behind the walls of the temple in Tadmur for myself. Not because they're bribing me or forcing me. I've heard it's the most beautiful place in all the world, and the rites of the goddess make you feel as though you've become divine, right here in this world. Think of it!"

Her words made me shudder. The dance last night had risen forcefully and mystically from deep inside my soul. My grandmother had told me that the power of women was beautiful and good and that if I used my abilities wisely, I would have joy and peace and an eternal, loving husband. I'd never pondered the idea before that I personally had the power to be beautiful and good and wise.

"Our ancient Mother Goddess gave us life, Leila. She doesn't have cold marble arms, lips made of stone, or a heart made of rock."

"Don't talk about something you know nothing of! If the activities in the groves go beyond a few friends dancing together, I'll be sure to warn you," she said sarcastically.

I stared down at the elegant torso of the dancing woman and touched her closed, praying eyelids. All at once, the wooden figurine seemed to burn my fingers. I threw it across the swaying camel carriage and let out a cry.

"What are you doing?" Leila flung herself to the floor, snatching up the carving and holding it like a child in her arms. "Don't touch my things again. Ever."

I leaned forward, pleading. "Bury the statue in the sand and forget it ever existed. Put away thoughts of the city and the temple. You are a desert girl, and you will always be a part of the desert. Stay with me, Leila. Please don't leave."

Leila stared through the draperies, her face red and splotchy from our argument.

"I need you, Leila," I added softly. "Now more than ever. I don't want to sit alone with our grief and tears."

She finally reached out her hands to me and we held on to each other. Her skin was warm against mine as we embraced. Her hot, salty tears wet my face, and I cried into her hair.

7

Late in the afternoon there were shouts from Kadesh. "Fresh tracks," he yelled. "And a dust cloud from camels up ahead."

Leila stuck her head out through the curtains, and the blinding sun cast lines of light across the floor of the carriage. "Jayden, it's them!" she cried, a wave of relief in her voice.

I looked out as we entered a valley of rising swells and definite signs of smoke from a campfire. Within the next hour, we caught up to the tribe. My father herded his camels into a circle next to Shem's campsite, and I couldn't get out of the camel litter fast enough.

As I stepped down and stood unsteadily on the ground, I saw Kadesh standing next to the camel he'd been riding. The light of the setting sun shone down on him, glinting off his dark brown hair. Despite the hardship he had suffered, he was beautiful.

I tried not to gaze at him, but I knew that, no matter what happened, years from now, I would still have a clear memory of those penetrating eyes under the rich, hooded cloak. I shivered, and yet I wasn't afraid of this mysterious stranger.

I warned myself not to be foolish. Kadesh had still looked upon me as I danced at my mother's grave, even if he'd given me profuse apologies ever since. He'd said that his was a curious and unashamed marveling as he observed my tears and heard my prayers.

I had no idea what he thought of me, and yet I suddenly, desperately wanted to know.

He glanced over at me, and I quickly looked away. "Let me take Sahmril," he offered, walking over to me and reaching out to take the sleeping bundle. It was true that she was growing heavy in my arms. "I have a younger sister," Kadesh added as though to convince me of his abilities. "And many nephews and nieces."

He looked so eager I almost laughed. "Are you going to add any of your own children to that list?"

"Not yet," Kadesh mumbled, his eyes glancing away from mine.

"She'll probably start screaming," I warned.

"I've held crying babies before."

Before I could speak again, Nalla ran up. "We've been praying all day that you would reach us. Praise God Sahmril is still with us." Then she looked at Kadesh with an appraising gape. "Who are you, young stranger?"

Rocking Sahmril in his arms, he answered, "Kadesh, of

the tribe of Dedan, from the southern lands."

Nalla took the tiny baby from his hands. "I've never heard of your tribe, but if you travel with Jayden's father, then welcome."

I felt guilty letting Nalla take over, but I was so weary from the long hours of crying and feeding. "I've been giving her camel's milk, but it's not fresh any longer. She'll probably have stomach pains all night. Is there any way Dinah would be willing . . ." I stopped, having no idea how to negotiate something as delicate as this.

Nalla shushed Sahmril, rubbing the baby's back with firm, experienced hands. "Dinah doesn't want another child so soon. Her own is still so young."

"A wet nurse is all I need," I added quickly. "I want to keep Sahmril and raise her myself."

"Do you understand what that means?" Nalla asked. "The responsibility? The years it will take to raise her?"

I nodded knowing that I couldn't count on Leila's help, especially if she married this summer, plus our father might be gone for months trying to get our missing camels back. But if I lost Sahmril it would be like losing my mother all over again.

I wondered if Horeb might break the betrothal if I was raising Sahmril. Then again, his family might pressure him to provide a home to my baby sister, and I'd be bound to the agreement more than ever.

"We have time to decide such things," Nalla said. "After such a long and grief-filled day, sleep is what you need right now."

After we settled and ate, the sun disappeared behind the mountains, and my father lifted his chin toward Kadesh. "It's time to care for that wound of yours."

"It can wait. You've had a difficult day," he added, his words threaded with an unspoken condolence.

"I've seen the wound with my own eyes," my father said firmly. "The blade went deep and soon you'll be ill with a fever and another burden on me. We must heal it, now."

"It will go well," I whispered, and my hand automatically reached out to Kadesh to reassure him. It was an impulsive gesture, and I pulled back quickly, embarrassed. I felt my face flush, and moved away to collect clean rags from the baskets.

When I returned, I instructed Kadesh to lie down so I could doctor him before the stitching. Blood had seeped through the bandage, staining the cloth bright red again. He wouldn't be able to go on like this, and I wondered how he'd managed to make it this far.

"You should have lain down in the camel carriage," I told him. "I could have ridden. I've done it my whole life. And helped my father drive the herd."

His eyes locked on to mine and he said in a low voice, "I'm sure you're very good at it, too."

I didn't respond and kept my eyes on the task of cutting the new cloth.

He gave a shudder as I pulled the old bandage from the oozing wound. "I was fine most of the day, but I think you're right. I overdid it and the wound has opened again."

I nodded, but when I picked up the turmeric to clean the

cut, he stopped me, pulling out a leather bag tucked into his waistband.

"Lie still," I told him. "The bleeding has started again."

"In my land, we use this for treating wounds," Kadesh said, glancing about as if to make sure no one could overhear. The women were cleaning up dinner and I could see my father and Shem tethering the camels for the night.

"I have turmeric and henna ready."

"What I possess is even more powerful." Opening the bag's strings, he shook out a handful of pale yellow, teardrop-shaped nuggets into his cupped hand. A strong, perfumed smell wafted through the air.

My eyes widened. "What is that?"

Kadesh dropped his voice so only I could hear him. His eyes held my gaze with such intensity I could barely breathe. "They call these frankincense tears."

I'd heard of frankincense, had even seen the expensive and rare spice in a marketplace stall from afar, but never this close. It was a luxury my family could never dream of purchasing.

"This is worth a great deal of money," I whispered. "Where did you get it?"

"I farmed this bag from my uncle's trees."

"What?" My jaw dropped in astonishment. "What are you saying? Your uncle owns frankincense—?"

"Ssh," he warned, and reached out to grasp my hand. His fingers were warm and gentle around mine and his touch created an instant, intense reaction in my belly. One by one he shook six of the teardrop nuggets into my palm. They were dense and very fragrant, but light, hardly weighing anything.

"Frankincense groves don't grow anywhere near here!" I exclaimed.

"That's true," Kadesh said, glancing up to catch my eyes.

Tingles raced up my spine as I realized what he was saying. "You don't live near the Moabite nation at all. The frankincense lands . . . Nobody knows where they are."

"Your father is correct; the travel is more than three months' journey from here."

"That's the ends of the earth! How did you get here?"

Kadesh tightened the drawstring of the bag and tucked it back into his cloak, leaving the frankincense in my hand. "With much preparation the journey can be done twice a year, but that's only part of the reason frankincense is so expensive. Frankincense is also quite rare, more so than gold or silk or the most precious gems. Every city and temple, physician and embalmer, cosmetic merchant and farmer desires it. But the trees only grow in one place on Earth, and I'm blessed that it's my homeland."

"You are fortunate, indeed. I've always thought that it must be a magical place."

"You know how difficult it is to travel these deserts, but to reach the frankincense lands takes a great deal longer. The trees grow in special forests in a range of mountains where it's very rocky, also making harvest difficult."

I swallowed past my dry throat. "What are you saying? You lied to us? You brought a caravan of frankincense up north to sell."

"No, I have not lied to you!" Kadesh tried to sit up.

I pushed him back to the ground. "Stop moving. You'll only make this wound bleed worse."

"Jayden." He gazed into my face—speaking my name in such a gentle yet firm tone that my heart raced. "What I say is true. I have not misled you or your father. I was heading north to take messages to my Dedan clan, who are building forts along the King's Highway to protect caravans and travelers. The caravan roads have grown dangerous." He glanced at his knife wound and added, "As I am a witness. We left our load of frankincense in Akabah with another company, who takes it west into Egypt. We were attacked, the frankincense stolen, and our company split apart. I escaped, lost my way, and found you—I mean, your family. If I hadn't, I'd be dead now." He stopped, his voice becoming unsteady.

"What is it?" I sensed that something even more terrible had happened.

"My friend was murdered by thieves a few months ago. They stole thirty camels laden with my family's frankincense. I had planned to stay in the north and avenge his death, but with this wound, I'm in no shape. And now, I'm afraid that my uncle will hear I've disappeared, too."

"I understand why the Dedan tribe is building fortresses," I said, a peculiar tightness rising in my chest when I pictured the precarious journeys he made each year. "Soldiers to protect travelers, as well as a place to rest and buy supplies. But you need to get well and my father can help you. Does he know about your family?"

Kadesh's breathing became more labored. "I spoke with him when we stopped to study the tracks. He needed to know the truth if he was willing to harbor me. And now I'm entrusting you with this secret."

Chills ran down my neck. Why he felt he should tell me, I did not know. "You can trust my father, and me. But if less honorable men discover you're an heir to frankincense, you will be in certain danger. There are stories of men murdering just to learn the location of the secret groves."

"The stories and rumors are true," Kadesh affirmed, his voice so quiet I barely heard the words. "We are often followed once we turn east across The Sands to get to our homeland."

"Gossip says that those who search never find the groves— or they are never heard from again."

"True on both counts."

"So you must have guards . . . with weapons . . ." I shivered in the warm evening air, and our eyes met in the dusky light. I studied him, taking note of his profile, the way his long dark hair fell and brushed my hand. He really was beautiful, and the kindness in his eyes ran deep. A kindness I hadn't seen, especially not in Horeb's eyes. "Why do you trust me?"

"My grandmother used to tell me that I'm a good judge of others."

I brushed off his words, turning my attention to his injury. "You're about to start bleeding again. I can only hold pressure on this for so long."

"Grind one of the nuggets to a powder," Kadesh said. "Then apply it to my wound."

I rose to retrieve a bowl and pestle, feeling secretive and guarded. Keeping my back to the rest of the camp, I quickly ground the nuggets. The frankincense tears were so soft, it didn't take long before they became a silky, shimmering powder. I applied it to the wound and gently pressed down with a clean cloth as my father arrived with Shem.

"Hide the bowl—quickly!" Kadesh began, and then fell back. His skin had suddenly turned ashen. Perspiration was a sheen on his face. He had lost too much blood, and was weakening.

I tucked the grinding bowl under his pillow just as Shem knelt down beside me, producing a stick from our supply of wood.

"Clench this between your teeth," he told Kadesh.

My father was prepared with thread and a sharpened camel bone. "I'm going to sew up the skin so the scar will be small."

Kadesh nodded, closing his eyes tightly.

Using tiny stitches my father sewed the flaps of skin together around the open wound. Sweat poured from Kadesh's face, but he barely made a sound.

"You're doing well," I told him when the stitching was finished. The bleeding had slowed considerably, and I wiped away the few streaks of blood with a clean, wet cloth one last time to prepare the skin for the burning.

Shem had already laid a flat disk of iron on top of the hot coals of the fire. Using tongs, he picked it up and prepared to lay it on Kadesh's side. The heated iron would burn the laceration and seal the skin together.

"Is there any way to change your mind?" Kadesh asked.

My father came forward to hold his arms down, saying briefly, "I promise you, the pain doesn't last long."

Shem straddled Kadesh's legs so that he couldn't move during the procedure. Leaning over, the older man held the fire-heated disk close to the young man's bare flesh.

"Don't look at it," I warned. I closed my eyes, saying a silent prayer, and then quickly opened them again. I was surprised to find Kadesh watching me. His hand reached out to grip mine and the touch of his fingers made me tremble.

My eyes watered as Shem positioned the scorching metal directly over Kadesh's tender, wounded side, then pressed it down, hard. The young man's entire body went rigid, and grinding his teeth against the stick, he choked down a series of screams. Within seconds, it was over and Shem stood, dropping the hot iron seal into the sand to cool it.

I looked down at the wound, and even though it was bright red, it had closed, no longer seeping blood. Kadesh released his grip on my arm, his face gray as an old dishrag. "I didn't mean to crush your hand."

I gave him a faint smile. "All my fingers are accounted for." How many times in one day had he touched me now? I remembered every single one, and only wanted more. "I'm—" I started, but the next moment Kadesh lost consciousness. I covered him with a blanket, tucking it around his form as my mother used to do, and fighting an urge to curl myself around him while he slept so he wouldn't be alone.

I bid my father and Shem good night and walked through

the camp, which had quieted at last under the milky stars. Usually there were dozens of flickering campfires to keep the wilderness at bay when the rest of the tribe camped alongside us. Now the blackness was so thick it was as though the world had been swallowed whole.

The temperature dropped and the air turned colder. As I approached our bedding, which lay on top of tarps under a shelter of scrub brush, I heard Leila crying and I crawled into bed next to her and reached out to take her hand.

"Leila," I whispered. "Are you all right?"

She didn't speak at first, her back to me. And then she rolled over, shielding Sahmril, who was fast asleep between us for extra warmth. "My thoughts are hateful and horrible. At least you'll think so."

"I would never think that."

"I can't help wishing that our mother had lived, and Sahmril had not."

I reached out to wipe away the tears that rolled down her chin. It seemed evil to wish for our mother's life instead of Sahmril's, but I didn't blame Leila for how she felt. "Perhaps it's a good thing *we* didn't have to choose between them."

There was silence between us and little comfort out here, without shelter. My baby sister would be crying again before dawn. A moment later, Leila threw the blanket over her head and fell asleep. She usually hid when life became too unbearable, just as she had disappeared while Kadesh was being doctored.

I rolled onto my back, unable to get warm. Finally I rose

and hovered over the remains of the fire, but I still felt chilled.

The camels huddled together, softly chewing their cud. I was tempted to curl up next to one, but I needed to do something first.

This day must end with my last thoughts for my mother.

Stepping around the sleeping forms of my sister and my father, I tiptoed to the perimeter of the camp toward the litter, now taken down from the back of our camel and sitting on the ground for the night. Not having a candle, I parted the curtains, using my hands to sweep under the piles of pillows and blankets. At last my fingers touched the hard piece of wood wrapped in one of Leila's scarves.

I rocked back on my heels and caressed the dark golden piece of wood. In the moonlight, the figure's polished strands of hair cut from the terebinth bark were glossy, her legs firm, her hips and breasts lovely.

"What secrets do you hold?" I whispered in the night air. "What music do you dance to? Certainly not the music of my tribe. Is this why you are forbidden, as my mother always said?"

No immediate answers came, and I finally placed the dancing woman back under the pillows so Leila wouldn't be screaming at me in the morning. Then I found a large, flat rock away from my sleeping family and sat down, shivering inside the folds of my old, worn cloak.

A shooting star dropped out of the sky, sizzling at the horizon. I wanted to hear the voice of my mother one more time. I tried to recall the sound of her laughter, the music of her singing, the vision of her dancing.

Her soul had gone somewhere else, somewhere I couldn't see. I tried to conjure her beautiful face, her strong arms, the touch of her hands stroking my hair. "I've never felt so lost in all my life," I told her softly, hoping her spirit was nearby and could hear me. "I'm afraid I will lose Leila to the desert's harshness—or the Temple of Ashtoreth. I'm afraid Sahmril will die because I don't know how to take care of her. And—" I paused, knowing I shouldn't say this out loud. "And I'm afraid to marry Horeb, even though I know you wanted me to, and it is my duty to our family and tribe."

Only last night I'd danced with my mother and sister and grandmother. Eaten sweets until my stomach ached. Laughed at the women teasing me about the marriage bed, and shivered with fear as I stood in the circle to dance by myself for the first time.

"Turn to the dance of our ancient mothers," a voice seemed to whisper to me along the wind.

With the memory of my mother's face before me, I dropped my cloak to the rock, raised my arms, and began moving them in slow half circles—first my right arm, then my left, swaying to the silent music of the desert.

I dug my toes into grains of sand still warm from the day's sun, and outlined the moon overhead with my wrists and arms, gazing at the white, perfect sphere encrusted by a galaxy of stars. Closing my eyes, I pressed my legs together to form small, tight hip circles. Four to the right, and then four to the left. With each change of direction I increased the speed of the circles until my body began to warm up and loosen all the fear and grief I'd been holding in all day.

Then I brought my arms higher and clasped my hands flat together overhead. In this position, I began a series of hip thrusts, holding the rest of myself as still as possible. My mother had once shown me how to balance on my back foot while putting my front foot forward.

I practiced hip drops, bringing my hands down and holding them at my hip bone so I could experience the movement more fully. When I ended my dance with a series of final slow circles, there was a film of sweat on my forehead. Finally, I was tired—not from stress and grief, but from physical exhaustion.

I raised my eyes and hands to the sky, hoping I could pull down the powers of heaven.

"Life for Sahmril," I whispered like a prayer. "Safe passage to the northlands. Abundant rain and life for the families of my father and Shem. A tender heart and flowing milk for Dinah."

I began to drop my hands, and then added, "And healing for the stranger, Kadesh, as well as a safe journey back to his uncle."

I picked up my cloak to return to bed, trying to get Kadesh out of my mind, and then realized I'd forgotten someone—my sister Leila. Perhaps she was the person I needed to pray for the most.

As I finished, a dark shape crossed my path. The saltbush crackled and I let out a small shriek. "Who's there?"

A male voice spoke from the darkness. "It's only me, Kadesh."

"By the god of heavens," I hissed. "You scare me again!

The second time today."

"It wasn't intended. Either time."

"You lie, sir. Jumping down from the bluff was no accident."

"That's true, but I didn't want you to run away. Blame it on
crazed thirst, or a delirious fear that I was going to die."

I took a step backward, every nerve along my skin raw and
exposed, knowing he'd watched me—again—as I danced in
the darkness. He was too close, too personal, listening to my
prayers.

His face had invaded my mind all day. His voice rang like
music in my ears; his touch stirred my emotions. And now he
was here, as if I'd called to him; as if our souls were speaking
to each other without using any words.

"What are you doing up from your bed?" I asked him.
"You need to sleep, to heal."

"The burned skin makes my sleep restless. I needed some
cool desert air."

"Let me get you a wet cloth. The first hours are the most
painful." As I turned, my arm accidentally brushed against the
soft weave of his cloak. He was closer than I realized. Too
close. "Just now, you were watching me again, weren't you?"

"I confess my shortcomings, daughter of Pharez."

"It's not right." I lowered my voice. "You know that."

A heartbeat passed, and then he asked, "What is this dance
you do when all the world is asleep?"

"A prayer for strength."

"Strength for who?"

I stared into his eyes, feeling parts of me pulled in every direction. My heart pounded so fast my face was hot, even in the chilly air. "You ask too many questions. Go back to bed. You need to heal." I needed him to leave me alone. I needed to encase my heart with stone so that he couldn't penetrate it. Emotions surged over me, mystifying, and yet powerfully real. Even as I tried to push the feelings away, I wanted to draw them close.

Perhaps the young man wasn't so dangerous to my family. Maybe Kadesh was only dangerous to me.

There was silence and I took a step toward camp, then paused. "Do the women of the southern lands dance for prayer and childbirth and celebrations?"

He frowned, and I wondered what he was thinking. "No," he finally said. "They celebrate in other ways."

I rubbed at my arms and stammered, "Please don't—don't watch me again."

"Your warning is noted. But what if I stumble upon you— or what if I can't resist?"

I took a sharp breath, noting his words and his meaning. I felt his eyes on my face in the starlight. "Restraint is a virtue," I said simply, and turned and headed back to my bed. I was proud of myself that I didn't look back.

8

The sun plowed a path over the ridge of approaching mountains, baking the earth even though it was only midmorning. I stood in the shade my camel, Shiz, provided, holding Sahmril, who Dinah had nursed that morning and would now sleep for a few hours. Nalla had helped me create a sling out of two lengths of linen and wrap it around my shoulder, making a pouch to hold the infant. The sling made walking easier, but I was already sweating from my sister's body heat as I listened to the men discuss the route north. We had been traveling for the last two days and were getting close to Edomite land and the canyon lands that lay before Tadmur and the oasis.

"The dunes here are hazardous," I heard Kadesh say. "They'll collapse under the weight of the camels."

My father stroked his beard, nodded in agreement. "We

must go around the dunes."

Shem crossed his arms, throwing Kadesh a look that wasn't quite confident. "That will take an extra day. We can't spare the time," he said abruptly.

"I doubt the main tribe crossed them either," Kadesh said. "They're probably also skirting the dunes. Here are the fresh tracks. Do you recognize them as your tribesmen?"

I squinted into the emptiness, hoping to see a line of distant camels that would indicate the tribe up ahead, but the horizon was vacant. Only the ragged range of mountains glittered in the morning heat.

"We'll avoid the line of dunes, and go north toward the mountain canyons," my father finally said decisively.

"The land of Edom lies ahead in those mountains," Shem spoke up. "We need to avoid that at all cost."

"The Edomites make no war with our tribe," my father said. "If we go too far east at this point we'll miss the line of wells completely. Besides, straight east puts us in the heart of the Assyrian desert. We must continue north, then part at the crossroads as originally planned."

Shem threw his hands in the air. "I've said my warning. Your family may be killed in their sleep if you take the path through Edomite country. Thieves lurk in those hills."

I was curious to know what my father and Kadesh's opinion was about Shem's warning. The fear of murdering thieves made my gut tighten, but I saw Kadesh quickly shake his head, as if to reassure me that the Edomite country wasn't as bad as Shem insisted.

"You should listen to Kadesh," I blurted out. "He knows this country, these people. His caravans travel through here on their way to Salem, right?"

My father and Shem gave me long, hard looks while Kadesh appeared startled that I'd vouched for his knowledge and wisdom. I should have kept my mouth shut, but the words had burst forth. There was something about Kadesh that made me bold. Awareness of his silent, unspoken language toward me rippled like a hot wave along my spine.

Muttering curses, Shem stomped off. I was glad that my father and Kadesh were in agreement. As Kadesh went past me to get the line of camels moving again, I reached out a hand to stop him.

"How is the wound after these days of healing?"

"Your father and Shem worked a small miracle with their torturous piece of hot metal. I think I'll live after all."

"That's good." I started walking back to my camel.

"Jayden," Kadesh called.

I turned, my pulse pounding in my throat.

He smiled. "Thank you for your concern." He continued to watch me as he placed his scarf around his lower face.

"I'd be worried about anyone that came so close to death," I said lightly as I turned and kept walking. But that wasn't true, and I knew it deep within my soul. With each step I felt Kadesh's eyes on my back, and I wondered if he could discern that I was not quite telling the truth. That the sight of him each morning as we ate breakfast made my heart fly into my throat. And each evening as I set up our beds and gathered firewood, pretending nonchalance, I actually hung on to his every word.

Our journey continued, and hours later we finally reached the last well before we entered the worst part of the trip—the land of desolation. With a heaviness dragging at my soul, I filled the waterskins. The well was low, the water poor and brackish. The female camels' milk had already turned watery without much to eat for a week. The animals complained and grew stubborn, slowing their pace, dragging out our journey.

Our food supply was also depleting. I had to cut back on the flour for our nightly bread. The bag of dates was growing lighter as we used up our winter stock. During the heat of the day when I was sleepy and sluggish, I dreamed of the fat, juicy dates at the oasis, of eating until my belly burst. I awoke drenched in sweat and lethargic as if I were ill.

Everyone was irritable—the desert harshness taking its toll on our little group. Sometimes I wondered if we were wandering in circles. To our left, a ridge of hills rose like the sharp, skeleton ribs of a dead animal. Slippery gravel shale caused the camels to lose their footing and our pace slowed dramatically.

The shimmering sand of the flat infinite desert to my right was a constant mirage, tricking my mind with the lust for water.

I lay against Shiz, listening to the men argue as they did each afternoon during the worst of the heat when we stopped to rest for an hour or two. And I began to wonder if we would ever catch up with our tribe's caravan, or if we would die out here.

I didn't remember the journey being so difficult before. Was it really taking longer this year? Was the desert heat fiercer than usual? Perhaps life just seemed more miserable because Mother wasn't here with her stories and songs to make our burden lighter.

Burying my face into Shiz's coarse hair, I bit back tears of misery. The camel's huge, black eyes peered at me through the dirty tassels hanging over her forehead, and I wondered if she sensed my grief and worries.

Suddenly, fresh shouts echoed in the searing temperatures. The men were arguing worse than ever, and I turned to see that Shem and his family were repacking their camels, in spite of the fact that we wouldn't be leaving for another hour, when the sun lowered a bit.

I jumped to my feet and felt my legs buckle, feverous heat sucking the little energy I had.

Shem and my father's voices took on a different quality as I flew to my father's side.

"What are you doing?" I said, sounding shrill.

"Look at the dust cloud up ahead," my father said grimly. "Those are Shem's relatives at the crossroads. It's time to part ways."

His words slammed into my mind. "I thought we'd get to the mountains before we separated."

My father shook his head with a grimace. "Shem was

determined to avoid the Edomite canyons—and now we have to go through them alone. I'm sorry, Jayden."

"We have to face the Edomites by ourselves?" I reeled on my feet. Even though the Edomites had no feud with our tribe, it was always safer to go through another tribe's territory with a large group. Since the Edomites had water and a village marketplace hidden inside their valleys, there were sure to be roving hunters or scavengers, ready to steal what we owned.

I hurried over to Nalla, who should have been happy to see her husband's family coming toward us across the plain. Instead, she was angrily throwing bundles of clothing and food jars into baskets. Sahmril was in Dinah's arms, finally asleep after crying most of the morning.

Without a word, Dinah strode over to me and placed my sister into my arms.

"What are you doing?" I said.

"Our relatives are here and I'm going with them. So here is your sister."

"But if you leave her with me, you will be dooming her to starvation! You promised to feed her."

Dinah wouldn't look at me. "Dinah," I started again, trying to keep my voice calm. "Watery camel's milk isn't enough. She'll starve. I'm begging you, please care for her."

Dinah whirled around. "What about my own child? What if I don't have enough milk for him?"

"I'll give you my best camel, anything you wish. Please keep her with you and keep her alive until we can meet again."

Snapping the baskets closed, Nalla spoke in a terse voice. "Dinah, I'm ashamed to have raised such a selfish daughter."

"We may all die before the journey's end," Dinah said, drawing herself upright.

"You're right," Nalla said, taking her daughter's hands in her own. "The desert is cruel and we live one day at a time. And if we die helping someone else, then God will reward us in the next life."

"I'm supposed to take her out of guilt?"

"Guilt is a start at being a charitable woman!"

I tried not to panic, but words I hadn't planned burst out of my mouth. "What if I came with you to help care for her?"

There was silence as my father and Leila and Kadesh all stared at me. What had I done? I didn't want to leave my family. Leave Leila—or Kadesh. But I also didn't want to leave my baby sister to Dinah either. The woman would treat her with derision or disregard. But if I went with Shem's family, I may never see my own again. Both choices were unimaginable.

"No! Jayden, you can't leave me," Leila screamed, stumbling toward me. "I need you. We can't be parted."

She clung to me and I realized how thin she was getting. Her weak fingers pawed at my arm as her eyes pleaded with me. Leila had never been very strong. The cooking, the cleaning, the dirty work, tending Sahmril—she did very little of it. Maybe she really wasn't made for this kind of life as I was. She needed attention, to be pampered and fed and admired. If I left her alone to make the rest of the journey—a single girl, even with our father—it was more likely the Edomites might kidnap her.

My heart was shredding into pieces. Both my sisters needed me for survival, but how could I part with either one of them?

"Sahmril needs Dinah's milk," Leila went on in a quieter voice. "She and Nalla can take care of her until she's weaned and we can find her again in the city of Mari. When *we* are stronger. And Father's herd is replenished—" Leila broke off, and her face turned red with shame to speak of our father's meager circumstances so plainly in front of others.

My father's expression stiffened when he stared at me. I wanted to crawl into a hole and weep for a week. None of this would be happening if we'd saved my mother. Losing her was too enormous to even comprehend, today worst of all as I watched Shem's family resolutely packing up and tying their herd together.

My father took a step forward. "Shem. Dinah. Nalla. We will do whatever you will us to do."

I bit my lips, but the tears I'd been fiercely holding back slipped out anyway.

Nalla stared hard at her married daughter and there was a terrible silence in the camp.

"Please," Leila whispered again, so softly, I swore the wind had taken her plea and stolen it.

Finally, Dinah started throwing pillows and cooking pots right and left. Her thin face flashed. "Fine. I'll take her. I will expect to see you in one year's time or less to get her back. But if my son dies because of her—I will make you pay dearly."

My legs turned weak with relief. "Thank you, Dinah, thank you," I whispered, embracing her even though she stood rigidly before me. "Always, you will be my sister for this."

She didn't answer, just turned away and kept packing.

I could hear the sounds of Shem's shouting, Nalla's frustration, Leila's weeping, but I tried to block it all out as I buried my face into Sahmril's soft, sweet neck. I didn't want to say good-bye. I wasn't sure which good-bye was more painful. Preparing my mother's body for burial and letting her spirit fly away into the empty sky—or watching Dinah take my sister and treat her as she would a slave.

It would be so easy for Dinah to leave my little sister on the desert trail to die. When we met again, months from now, all Dinah would have to say was that Sahmril had taken sick. And I'd never know the truth.

I swayed on my feet, unable to doom my baby sister to such a fate. But as my mother's face swam before my eyes, I also knew I couldn't let her down by not doing everything I could to save my family.

A moment later, my father's hand was on my shoulder. "Sometimes the desert gives no choices," he said quietly.

Impatiently, Dinah turned toward her crying toddler, who was trying to pull a piece of bread out of one of the baskets.

"Tell me, Dinah," I said, swallowing past my raw throat. "Which camel do you want? I will have my father untie the animal and bring it to you. May her milk help care for my sister and your own son, too."

Dinah pointed to the camel that still lay where I'd been

resting. "That one. With the tassels falling over its eyes."

Shiz. I felt myself choke. Dinah had picked one of our very best animals, and my favorite.

"Fine," I said, my eyes swimming. "She's yours."

"There's something else," Dinah added, and the unpleasant glare she gave me caused me to prickle with dislike. "The camel will provide milk for your sister when she's weaned, or perhaps meat if needed, but I want something for me."

"What else could you possibly want besides my beloved camel?" I swallowed the harsh words, willing myself not to be selfish. After all, Dinah would sacrifice much to care for Sahmril. She should be given a token of payment. My mother would want me to do that.

Dinah stepped closer, and her eyes were like slits of yellow in the harsh sunlight. "I want your jewelry. Your necklace and earrings and bracelets."

I sucked in a breath. *"No,"* I whispered. "It was my mother's last gift—it's all that I own."

Instantly, Nalla shuddered beside me. "Dinah!" she exclaimed. "How can you ask such a thing?"

Dinah ignored her. "They are very fine and worth much. Just like your sister Sahmril. I believe I ask for a fair trade."

I was so outraged I couldn't find any words. My jewelry was the only thing of worth that I owned. My dowry. My measure of beauty and worth as a woman. Even poor women had their blood jewelry, though it might be the only jewelry they ever owned their entire life.

"Sahmril's life for your jewelry," Dinah repeated.

I couldn't believe she was doing this—robbing me of these precious possessions. A stabbing pain throbbed behind my eyes as I unhooked the earrings. The strands of the silver necklace, the symbols of my clan, the moon and evening star, disappeared into Dinah's outstretched, grimy hands.

She didn't leave until I'd watched her clasp the necklace around her neck and laid the silver across her chest, mingling with her own jewelry. She put the bracelets alongside the two already on her wrists, and then clipped the earrings onto her ears. Swinging her head, she smiled as the fine silver strands brushed her neck.

Hatred screamed inside my head. I gripped Sahmril so tightly she began to whimper. "I'm so sorry, Sahmril," I choked out, kissing the pink, puckered lips. "You're worth more than any jewelry."

Just as I was about to faint with misery, my father pulled me to his chest, and held me and Sahmril together in his arms. I clutched at his robe, the coarse cloth against my face. I smelled the baby skin of my sister and brushed my lips against her wispy, dark hair for the last time. I tried to say good-bye, but no words existed for this terrible moment.

"I promised Mother," I told my father, my voice muffled against his clothes. "I promised her I'd care for Sahmril! I think she knew," I added. "She knew she was dying."

My father's bearded cheek pressed against mine. "I know, Jayden, but the desert breaks promises all the time. We cannot make her obey our will."

"Jayden," Nalla said, touching my hand. "Let me take her.

I'll make sure she stays well."

I nodded miserably, my eyes swollen with tears. My arms were cold and horribly empty once Nalla had taken her. I buried my face into my father's neck again. "I'm so sorry I've lost Sahmril and Shiz both."

He didn't speak, but his anguish was palpable as we watched Nalla tuck Sahmril into the crook of her arm and walk back to her own camp.

"Let's get the camels moving," my father said hoarsely. Then he released me and stiffly walked away, but I could see the added sorrow in his posture and his unsteady gait.

Lowering my head, tears ran down my face like drops of fire. For a moment I hated myself. I was losing my family one by one. What if by the time we reached Tadmur, the only person I had left was my betrothed, Horeb? I'd rather die in the desert and let the jackals tear me to pieces.

I stumbled into a rock and nearly fell face-first onto the earth, but at that moment, someone caught my arm, keeping me upright. I let out a gasp of relief as well as surprise.

When I lifted my head, Kadesh was there; his dark, unwavering eyes looked directly into mine. Concern furrowed his brow, but I didn't speak a single word. "I overheard, Jayden, and I'm so sorry. I wish there was something I could do to ease the pain."

"There is nothing. Nothing," I said, not ready to accept his kindnesses. I tugged my arm away and tried to walk on, tears strangling me. I craved the luxury of a single day to properly mourn, preferably alone. But those luxuries were not an option. Never had they been an option for me.

I glanced at Kadesh as I moved away, his gaze still steadfast. His presence was disquieting. He knew I'd just given up one sister to save another sister. He understood that the loss of my jewelry, my mother's last gift to me the night before she died, was an enormous blow. He also seemed to know that I'd give anything to save Sahmril's life. Somehow, this stranger from the mysterious southern lands knew without being told that my heart had broken, several times over.

And somehow, this boy who was creeping into my mind and my heart a little more with each passing hour seemed to see everything and know everything about me.

9

We continued on, and after seemingly endless days of thirst and swollen, tender feet, the shimmering images of my mother, Isaac, and Sahmril wavered before my eyes. Their ghosts hovered constantly, and I often woke in the middle of the night with tears on my face.

I shifted for the hundredth time on the dusty pillows while Leila studied the ragged hem of her dress. She plucked at the torn seams angrily. "I'm tired of traveling. I'm tired of being hungry and thirsty. I despise this old dress and this dirty litter we have to sit in all day, our father's lack of position, Mother's death, everything!"

I reached out and stroked the back of her hair, my hands tragically empty without my baby sister. "Leila, we can't change anything that's happened. Mother would want us to persevere."

"Persevere for *what*? More long days and nights in search

of water? Poor and wretched and begging the gods to keep us safe and bring us food?"

"Leila, please don't say these things," I begged.

Frustrated, my sister rolled over onto her back, our shoulders touching in the small space as the camel lurched beneath us. "I never want to be hungry anymore. I want roasted lamb and fruit from the oasis. And lemon juice sweetened with honey."

I didn't speak, not wanting to encourage her when I was so hungry I was ready to start eating the camel's harnesses.

"You know it's true. We have no future now without Mother here to arrange one for us. Do you really think Horeb is going to go through with his commitment to you, the way things are?" Her eyes passed over my chest, where my dowry jewelry used to be. "We'll be lucky to earn ourselves the beds of a peasant now, and you know it!" She dropped her face into her hands and sobbed. "We're doomed to travel endlessly with father, trying to win back his dignity."

"How dare you say such things about our father, who gave us life and a home, Leila." Her words tore at my heart.

"What else is there to say? Our dreams have all been shattered."

"That's always been your problem, Leila. You are nothing but a daydreamer."

"And your practicality is not a problem? Is it so bad to want to live in a city . . . to dream of riches and finery?"

I closed my eyes, fighting the urge to scold her, but dreams of my own seeped from my mouth. "Sometimes I dream of soft bread sprinkled with cinnamon," I admitted softly. She reached for my hand.

"Baked turnips with spoonfuls of butter."

"Baskets of overflowing fruit." I turned my face to her.

"Gallons of real tea not watered down!"

"Rice raining down from the skies and drowning our litter!"

We started to laugh at the image of rice coming down from the clouds and flooding the desert, the camels stuck in waves of rice like heavy sand.

Our laughter fell to silence. Both of us solemn with thoughts of hunger.

Leila pressed her hands to her sunken belly. "We've been traveling for over two weeks now. How much farther to the oasis?"

"The canyons are the halfway point. Hopefully, we're almost there." I parted the curtain and looked out into the sea of rolling sand. "The camels will need water soon."

"As will we." Leila's voice scratched as she spoke. Her lips were dry and parched.

"We can wait for water. Without the camels, we will truly die in this desert."

Leila let out a whimper and clutched my fingers tighter. "I'm not sure I can do this anymore, Jayden." She looked at me, her eyes pale and weak. "Mother would probably fall right out of heaven to hear me say this, but I don't want to live in the desert anymore and move camp over and over again to find the rains, always moving. I want to live in a real house with walls that don't shudder in the wind. With a fireplace and painted tiles and a pond in the garden. A well of cold water that never runs dry. A river to walk beside. Flowers and trees. And shade that goes on as far as I can see."

"You can't say such things, Leila—"

Her words made my throat ache. I'd known she had a secret dream to leave the desert, but I'd always believed it was a childish dream and nothing more. I believed the duties of our clan would wash the longing from her mind, but it was clear they'd been embedded far too deeply to be removed now. All at once, I was struck by a helpless betrayal.

"When we gave Sahmril to Dinah, you said you didn't want me to leave, remember? And now *you* want to leave *me*!"

Leila's eyes pulled at me. "What if we steal away together? We both go to the city?"

"And leave Father here alone!"

"It'd be a relief for him, not to have to fend for his daughters, don't you think? We'll be gone soon anyway once we're married off—" She turned her face as if she wanted to hide what she had to say next. "Besides, he won't be alone long. He's likely to remarry."

"Leila!" I snapped, though it was probably true. It was just too soon after Mother to contemplate. "What of Sahmril? Is she to never know our father?"

"What of Sahmril? Are we to base our futures on an infant we may never see again?"

I choked as she spoke, knowing it might be true. But I couldn't bear to lose Leila, along with everyone else. I reached over, taking her hands in mine. "We only have each other now. If you leave and marry a city person, I'll be completely alone. Besides, you have no idea what you're doing, Leila. City people are nothing like us. Their minds, and lifestyle, are completely different from ours. They care more about comforts and gossip and money than freedom and loyalty to their tribe and family. What you're thinking of doing would be wrong."

Leila pulled her hands away. "I don't think we're that different. I'm more like them than you realize, Jayden. Besides, you'll soon be married to Horeb and live happily in your beloved desert with as many camels as you wish. You can milk camels all day if you want to. Ride them. Play with the babies. Have your own babies. Once you're married with your own family, you won't miss me at all."

"That's ridiculous! I'll miss you every single day."

But my sister didn't stop. "You're likely to be married off this summer anyway; you know that. Like Hakak. Although she and Aunt Judith have been sewing her trousseau and making wedding plans for months already, yours is to be the wedding of the year. With the new baby coming, Mother hadn't even started your wedding clothing. But the other women will help you. They'll want to see this marriage follow through in memory of our mother."

I swallowed, turning my face away.

"You know it's true. And once you're married, what is there here in this desert life for me?"

I wiped a tear from my eye and she pulled my face around to meet hers.

"What? What is it?"

I wanted to tell her but I couldn't. I shrugged and shook my head, wondering if I could confide in her. I feared she would run and tell Aunt Judith and Hakak and Falail all my secrets. I needed to find time to speak with my father about the betrothal first.

Her face brightened in an effort to make me smile. "Not a single tribe member will miss the crowning of Horeb as prince. Don't you see how lucky you are! You'll be crowned as his princess. And one day you will be king and queen."

I tried to smile, but my mouth wouldn't cooperate. I looked deep into Leila's face. "But you were to wear the title of Queen. Does it anger you that I will have it instead?"

"No," she said thoughtfully. "I used to be angry that Zenos died, or got himself killed, but it means that now I'm free to live the life I'd rather have instead. I'm not sure I was ever that in love with him when my mourning lasted so briefly. But now I'm free from all the tribal and political problems of whether we should join another tribe, or making friends—or enemies to gain more wealth. Moving every few weeks during the winter to catch the rains. The camp bickering and noise. I'd never have made a good Queen of Nephish." She stroked my hair. "But you, my dear sister, will make a perfect one." Her eyes became dreamy and distant again. "I want to be queen in a different way."

"What are you saying?"

"Don't you see, Jayden? Now that I don't have to marry anybody I can truly leave and go live in Tadmur or Mari, or even Babylon or Nineveh."

"But how would you support yourself? Have you thought about that? You'll have no family to protect you. Those distant lands mean I might never see you again." My heart lurched at the uncertainty of her future, my future without her in it. "It's impossible. And dangerous. I can't let you do it! Mother would never have approved!"

My sister's face became impassive. She stared out the front of the camel litter. The jangling of the bells on the camel filled our silence.

"I don't care what you say. I've decided," she said quietly. "I will go to the Temple of Ashtoreth. There is work there. And girls and women who become your family. It would be a good life, everything I've always craved. Beauty and luxury and food—and baths every single day."

I blinked at her, not knowing what to say. "You would leave your family for gold and silk? For a *bath*?"

"Yes." Her lips were stark and pulled thin. "Oh, Jayden, the goddess priestesses are kind. I've seen them. They're not sacrificing girls to Moloch, or throwing them into pits or turning them into street beggars! They dance to worship life. New life in the spring. Fertility. Good harvests and the bounty of the earth. That's their biggest celebration, the one each spring as the earth wakes after the death of winter. It's the celebration of Ashtoreth and Ba'al as they unite in the Sacred Marriage Rite to end the winter and bring good crops and wealth."

"How can you have a Sacred Marriage Rite with a god and goddess made of stone or marble?" I asked. I'd been warned away from the groves and temples my whole life, but I still didn't understand exactly why.

"Ashtoreth's priestesses join with the priests of Ba'al to perform the marriage rite."

"You mean you'll marry one of them? Someone you don't even know?" I couldn't believe what I was hearing. "You could have your choice of any boy in our tribe, Leila." I was desperate to have her stay with me and not abandon our family.

She shrugged. "It's not a marriage, actually. There's no ceremony or having children together. The priest doesn't become my husband. We are united only in body and spiritual divinity so we can experience the god and goddess flowing through us."

I suddenly wished we were headed in the opposite direction. Right now we were only about a week away from Tadmur. And the Spring Festival would happen soon after our arrival.

I took a deep breath, trying not to weep with the story she was telling me. "Is it always the same man, the same priest?"

"Oh, no," Leila said, leaning back against the pillows. "It could be a different man every night of the week."

My breath rattled against my chest. "Mother would rise from her grave and shred her soul into a thousand pieces to lose you to those temple ceremonies. You can't do this, Leila!"

"But I must."

A tense and uncomfortable silence drew out between us.

A moment later, Leila brushed my hair with her fingers the way our mother used to do. "Father is getting desperate for more camels, especially since we lost Shiz to Dinah.

Your bride price will bring him only so many. Just wait, we'll be scrambling to sew your wedding clothes this summer and you'll be married before the tribe moves back to the winter lands."

I tried not to choke, knowing she was right. I would most likely be married by the end of the summer. Five or six months from now. And she would be alone. No, Leila had already made up her mind to go to the temple, and nothing I said seemed to convince her otherwise.

But if she did, the women of our tribe would banish her, and that's what I was afraid of, too.

"Let's talk about something else," I said, picturing Horeb, his too-handsome face, his condescending manner and roving eyes. I held my arms against myself as I remembered the night of the betrothal celebration and how he stopped me on the path and tried to touch me.

"Do you not want to marry, Sister?" Leila's eyes were penetrating, as though she was able to read my thoughts.

I didn't answer.

"Oh, Jayden." She moved closer.

"It's nothing—I can't explain my feelings."

"Try. Tell me."

"It's Horeb. He's different lately. He looks at me strangely."

"Because he can't wait to marry you!"

I shook my head. "It's not like that. I fear he only cares to marry me because of the title and power it will bring. Not because of *me*. He's not the same boy we've always known. Something has changed him this last year."

"He had to grow up quickly after we lost Zenos," Leila said. "He's been grieving, losing his older brother. We all adored Zenos."

"Yes, but there's something more to it. He's hard-edged—the way he speaks, his laugh—there's no real warmth in his eyes! And—I'm not in love with him."

Leila laughed. "You're breaking every girl's heart in the tribe by marrying him. You are so naive, Jayden. Marriage isn't necessarily about love. But," she conceded, "most couples do grow to love each other. Hakak and Laham already do."

"I know," I whispered. Jealousy ran through me whenever I saw Hakak and Laham together. How happy they were, how good together. "What if," I added softly, looking up at her through my long hair, "I feel nothing for him? What if our friendship has turned to dislike? Leila, I fear him, and I fear that I'm starting to dislike him more than anyone else I've ever known."

Leila didn't answer, just stared at me as though in shock.

My belly felt like a stone was lodged at its pit. "What if I told you I wanted to break the betrothal?"

My sister grabbed me by the arms. "Don't be a fool, Jayden. You *are* just nervous. I will speak with Horeb and tell him that he needs to spend some time with you. That he needs to talk to you—"

"No!" I nearly shouted. "Never speak to anyone about what I've told you. Not until I can talk to Father. Please, Leila, promise me you will keep this in confidence."

"All right, I promise," she finally agreed, and closing her

eyes, she settled back into the pillows as I wiped at my face, brushing away the tears and dirt.

Father's voice filled the silence, shouting at the camels at the front of the line. I wondered how soon it would be before he took another wife. I bent forward, craving to hear Kadesh's voice, the slight foreign accent.

Sitting up, I impulsively lifted the hem of the back drapery to where Kadesh was riding with the rear camels. I opened the curtain to find him gazing at our carriage as though hoping I would peek through the curtains. His dark brown eyes found mine, and even though he wore his scarf over most of his face to keep out the haze of dust and dirt rising from the road, I could tell he was smiling at me. I let out a gasp and let the curtain drop, my hands shaking.

"What is it? What are you doing?" Leila said sleepily.

"Nothing," I said, lying down again beside her in the afternoon heat.

But I found myself thinking about dancing for Kadesh, and the way his eyes locked on to mine each time he passed me by.

10

The next morning, we approached the jagged rock columns of the canyon lands, rising on both sides of the
path like impervious, watchful kings.

In the early-morning light, our camels slowed through the
narrow, winding terrain as if wary and uneasy. My father and
Kadesh walked up and down the line, urging the animals to
keep moving. No more wading through slippery sand as we
had for days. Everywhere I looked, layers of pink and red were
painted in splashes of color over the rock of the entire valley. I
wondered if the mirages of heat had permanently warped my
mind.

"It's beautiful, isn't it?" my father asked from his saddle as
we passed through never-ending canyon walls rising up around
us. "This sight always is."

I tried to smile, but my lips barely moved; they were

cracked so badly. "My eyes aren't playing tricks? This is always my favorite scenery of the journey. A piece of heaven, even though we're starving and about to shrink from lack of water."

My father gave me a wan smile. "Your eyes do not deceive you, Jayden."

"I want to walk," I told him. "My legs are so cramped."

Within a minute, the camel lowered the litter and I jumped out, stamping my feet. The towering stone walls shaded the glare of the sun. A perfect time to walk instead of ride.

"We are ants, small and insignificant," I said. "As if the rocks delight in glaring down at our trivial little camel train."

My father nodded at my words and trotted back to the rear of the line, Kadesh moving to the front to keep the animals firmly on the narrow road.

Sunlight played between the cone-shaped columns, creating shafts of yellow on the desert floor. The beauty was stark and wondrous, but I sensed an unspoken danger, as if dozens of eyes were watching from the cliffs.

Swiftly, I grasped the leather rope of Runa, the litter camel, and slowed her down. Standing on tiptoe, I hissed into the curtains, "Leila!"

My sister's sleepy voice floated down. "What is it?"

"Take off your jewelry and hide it!"

"I can hardly breathe in this oppressive heat, let alone move. I haven't had a drink of water in nearly two days."

"Just do it."

Leila gave a groan, but I could hear the finery coming off

piece by piece, jingling softly in the muted stillness of the walls of the canyon.

"Where did you hide it?"

"In my undergarments."

As she spoke the words, a group of horseback riders suddenly swarmed from the fissures of the stone walls as if they had been flushed out. The canyon men wore thick swaths of black over their faces, and the earth thundered with the noise of galloping horses.

Behind me, my father gave a shout, and Kadesh wheeled his camel, flew down the line, and scooped me up from my spot on the trail, shoving me brusquely into the litter. "Stay hidden and do not speak," he said swiftly, his eyes gazing sternly into mine.

I grasped Leila's hand just as the pack of riders formed a circle, completely enclosing us.

Leila moaned softly. "What will they do if they see us?"

"You don't want to know."

Sweat crawled down my back as I peered through the curtains. The men had ragged, wild hair and dusty, belted tunics that draped to their ankles. Swords and sabers dangled in plain view, and only their eyes showed above their facecloths, flinty and suspicious.

Black and chestnut horses glistened with foam. I watched my father ride past the litter, purposely slowing Bith's pace, his hand caressing her neck.

"We're on our way north to Tadmur," he said in a steady voice. "Hoping to pass through these beautiful lands peacefully."

"Peace is only for our brothers," the largest horseman

declared. The rest of the Edomites laughed, which only made our camels skittish.

"We are of the tribe of Nephish," my father said.

Ignoring him, one of the horsemen turned to stare at the litter as if he could see my face behind the curtain. I fell back, hoping he couldn't sense our presence.

Beside me, Leila was silently weeping, terrified that these strange men wouldn't honor the desert code of leaving women and children alone.

"We've traveled for many days and need water," my father continued. "My children will die of thirst."

This plea was met with stony silence.

"I'm a poor nomad with a dwindling herd," my father persisted. "After we water our animals, we'll disappear from your lands and leave you in peace."

"You're a liar, man of Nephish," the leader said, pointing to Kadesh. "This man is not poor. Look at his cloak. In fact, he's not your kin at all."

"You speak the truth," my father said quickly. "This man isn't my kin, but a blood brother indeed. He's given his loyalty to help me take my family into the north to join my tribe."

"We wish no trouble," Kadesh added. "I've passed through this canyon before and always found the Edomites welcoming and peaceful. Is there a man named Chemish here? He and I are like brothers."

The leader's face cracked with a sly grin. "Unfortunately for you, Chemish is away." He galloped off a short distance, forming a tight circle with the rest of his band as they began to confer among themselves.

My father and Kadesh give each other long, sober looks, and I didn't move an inch. After what seemed an eternity the horsemen galloped back.

"Tell us who will be drinking our water," the leader demanded.

My father sat straight, not willing to be bullied, but not ready to flee either. "My name is Pharez. The Nephish are a peaceful nation and don't war with any."

One of the men smirked. "Perhaps that's why you have so few camels! A good raid would make you a richer man."

"Perhaps," my father conceded.

"We have a well with clean, good water, man of Nephish, but it comes with a price."

"Name your price."

"Your two best camels. And the gold he carries," he said, pointing to Kadesh.

My father was visibly startled. "He carries no gold."

Kadesh didn't speak to confirm or deny the statement.

Two of the horsemen swung down from their mounts and walked the line of camels, appraising them. To lose two of our camels would be devastating. The price for water was robbery. It was well known that the Edomite well was one of the best water sources on this side of the Assyrian desert. Depths of water that nobody had ever been able to measure. There was enough for the Edomite citizens, and more to spare.

"I want this camel," one of the men shouted. "The one carrying the litter."

Before we could hide under a blanket, the man threw back the curtain. "This poor man carries more valuables than he admits."

The leader and two of his bodyguards galloped closer. He pushed aside the curtains and studied me and Leila as I clenched my sister's hand. The man's broken nose filled his face, and deep, furrowed lines ran the length of his cheeks. His teeth were cracked and poor, but he was probably no older than my father.

Fear crossed my father's face as he galloped over to the litter and pushed himself in front of the leader.

"Get aside!" one of the bodyguards yelled, shoving him over with the blunt end of a spear.

"These are girls, my daughters!" my father cried. "Not women. Not slaves. Leave them alone, or I will kill you myself."

I was stunned to hear him speak like this.

The Edomite leader laughed. "Get out of the litter and let me have a look."

Father moved in closer, a terrible expression on his face as though he might attack the man. "Don't, Father," I whispered, plucking at his sleeve. "Leila and I can't survive without you."

I cringed, shooting a quick glance at Kadesh. His face was pale under the shadows of the red rock walls and his expression had turned to stone. I could tell he was furious, but not afraid.

Leila began to weep as we climbed out of the carriage so that it could be untied from our camels. I watched, broken-hearted as the camel was led off, hissing and biting and fighting at the halter rope.

"May the men of Esau lose a finger to her temper," I muttered under my breath.

Their leader laughed as he jumped down from his horse and pressed up close to my face. "You'd better watch your tongue, girl, or I'll cut it out from your mouth."

I gave him an icy glare, and my heart thundered inside my chest.

The Edomite swaggered across the last few feet, staring at us, his eyes raking over our frames. "You call them children, but they look like women to me."

"They're unmarried, and will remain so for more than a year," my father replied.

I was surprised to hear my father say this since my marriage to Horeb was much more imminent, but immediately I realized that he was trying to make it appear as though we were younger than we were.

"You're lying, camel herder, just like you're lying about your friend over there," the man spit back, jerking a finger toward Kadesh.

"They are my daughters, and they're staying with me!" Father shouted. "How dare you break the code of the desert and defile a man's daughters in front of him."

I could hardly breathe as the filthy Edomite stuck a fat finger in my face. I shuddered at the touch of his skin as he drew it along my cheek and neck. His eyes ran up and down my body.

I wanted to spit in his face, and hurl a thousand insults. If he tried to kidnap me and take me off to one of the caves nearby, I'd kill him before he could drop his sword belt.

"It's obvious they're ready to wed. We can arrange that right now. I have several willing men." His meaning slammed into my mind with horror. I'd kill myself before I let that happen.

The next instant, my father had his knife under the man's throat. "You will die before you touch my children. *I* will gladly die—and I will kill my daughters—before I let you touch them."

Before I could take another breath, the two bodyguards had my father in their grip, a dagger to his throat and a second aimed at his heart.

His knees buckled as he crashed to the ground. "Father!" Leila screamed, and her cries echoed off the canyon walls. A second later, Kadesh was on the other side of me, his sword drawn, the tip of it poised along the Edomite's neck. "Is it your day to die?" he spit out.

The sour odor of the leader's skin scraped across my face. Dried sweat reeked on his clothes. "You touch me, stranger," he drawled, "and the rest of my men will kill you all before you've drawn your next breath."

The world turned sluggish, reeling before my vision. I saw us all brutally murdered right here on the hard rock floor. But Kadesh didn't move a muscle. "It's up to you how this turns out," he told the man.

Several moments passed, and the world swam before my eyes. I gritted my teeth, knowing our lives hung in the balance. The grief of my mother and baby brother, as well as the taxing journey, had taken its toll. My father appeared ready to succumb to our deaths. Leila's eyes rolled back in her head as she gripped Kadesh's arm with her fist.

"Don't bring shame and death to your tribe," I said slowly, holding the Edomite's gaze and digging deep into his black heart. "If we do not travel safely through these lands, our tribe will return to avenge us. And there are not enough of you to fight them. You will lose."

The leader gave a sudden bark of a laugh. "It seems we have a draw, camel herder," he spit between his fat lips.

Not trusting him, neither my father nor Kadesh moved. Finally, the two bodyguards lowered their weapons and my father cautiously did as well.

"Back off," the Edomite leader grunted to his men. "I'll let your *children* off this year, but if you come through here again, your daughters will belong to me."

I shuddered and my legs failed me. My father gripped my shoulders to keep me on my feet, but Leila crumpled to the ground beside me. Kadesh quickly put an arm around her, easing her down before she hurt herself.

I watched him press a hand to her brow as he whispered words I couldn't hear. Leila's eyelids fluttered open and she stared into Kadesh's face, whispering something in return. I strained to hear, but couldn't. Then Leila clutched at the sleeve of Kadesh's cloak and I silently begged her to rise to her feet on her own.

Finally, I turned away, unable to watch Kadesh holding my sister's hands as he lifted her up again. My heart was pierced through. I couldn't seem to draw a full breath. I was a selfish sister. I had no rights to Kadesh. He was a stranger and would be on his way home within weeks. After his departure, I'd never see him again. These starry-eyed notions of mine were silly and vain.

"Get the other camel!" the leader shouted to my father and, within moments, our second-best female, Pela, was untied from the camel train. Grimly, I watched as she was taken away. There was no recourse, no argument. We were soundly out-numbered.

Before any of us could move again, three men shoved Kadesh to the ground, holding him at knifepoint. "Don't move!" one of them yelled, his knee in Kadesh's back. "Now show us your hidden gold, or you're dead."

My mind went straight to the bag of frankincense tied to Kadesh's chest under his shirt, the last thing he'd want discov-ered.

Squatting in the dust, a sword at his neck, Kadesh began to remove his leather shoe. I held my breath, knowing it was only a matter of moments before he'd lose everything he possessed, and we would lose the security Kadesh gave my family.

He turned the first shoe over and several pieces of coin fell to the ground. It was a small pile, but even I could see that the coins were solid gold. I gasped in surprise, wondering what else Kadesh had hidden on himself.

Leila leaned in close to whisper, "Where did he get that gold!"

The tribesmen dropped from their saddles to snatch up Kadesh's other shoe. One man shook it greedily, feverishly, but nothing fell out. Kadesh held up his hands to show that they had taken everything he had.

"If it will help you more than me, then you are welcome to it," he said simply, but I could hear the strain in his voice.

The Edomite men shouted with glee and clapped him on the shoulders, flickers of respect in their eyes. I let out the breath I was holding as the search ended and Kadesh's frankincense went undiscovered.

"You've struck a fine bargain, Pharez, son of Nephish," the leader said. "The well is one mile from here, just off the main road. Use what you need, but be gone at dawn."

The riders climbed onto their horses and galloped off, dust creating a red haze as they disappeared into the canyons, our two mare camels tied to the rear horses. The loss was bitter indeed. Runa and Pela were more than riding animals, and more than pets. Our camels were life itself.

"Ride Meela, Jayden," my father told me quietly as he and Kadesh heaved some of the baggage off the younger camels and rearranged the loads. "And Leila, you ride Tazr."

We were down from ten camels to eight now. Barely enough to get us to the oasis—if nothing else happened along the trail. I climbed onto the skittish young camel, and my vengeful desires were soon replaced by another as I held a hand to my mouth and tried to swallow past my parched mouth. *One mile until water.*

Leila had begun to cough, choking on the dust left by the departing riders, but now our camels picked up their pace. Whether they sensed that water was near or wanted to be rid of the uneasy spirits in the canyons, I didn't know, but before long the well was within sight.

I let out a cry and slid down the back of Meela's haunches without waiting for her to lower her neck. Racing to the hole in the ground, I began to scrabble in the dirt, pulling off the big, flat rocks that covered the well, and trying to heave them aside. Now that it was so near, right underneath me, thirst was making me crazy.

"Easy, easy," Kadesh murmured, lifting my hands away so he could pull off the heavy stones.

Sweat poured along the inside of my dress. My arms were covered in a layer of reddish dirt, the soles of my feet hard and black. Perhaps that's why the horsemen had finally left Leila and me alone. We weren't very appealing after so long on the trail.

But now I could *smell* the water, it was so close.

Sand crusted the surface and Kadesh went to work scooping out the dirt and rocks. He moved with a speed that surprised me.

"Maybe you *are* of the desert," I told him. "You know exactly what to do."

Kadesh gave me a grin, making me dizzy. "Now that's a compliment I'll gladly accept. With all my travels, I've probably uncovered a few hundred wells in my lifetime."

Quickly, I fetched the waterskins, and for the next two hours, my father and Kadesh took turns pulling up water to fill the buckets for the camels to drink.

It was fresh water, clear, clean, and cool. I could have

jumped right into the well itself and not grown tired of drinking and swimming and bathing for hours. Sitting back on my heels, I wondered if my thirst could ever be quenched, but by the time I was finished, my stomach was so swollen I wasn't sure I'd ever eat again.

One by one the camels gorged on the sweet water and then wandered off, bellies distended. They picked at the ground, nibbling on roots or a bit of grass. Scrub brush and grass were beginning to bloom. A good sign that the bounteous northern lands were getting very close.

I pulled up one last bucket and dipped my hands into the exquisite liquid, splashing my face to erase the days of dust and heat. It was so marvelous I started laughing with the pleasure of it. After I finished washing my hands, I poured the rest of the bucket over my head to wash my hair and dress, then poured a second just to be sure I was completely clean again.

I hauled a third bucket of water for Leila to wash as she lay in the shade at the canyon wall. Leila was becoming frightfully thin. It would be wise to rest next to her, but after drinking and bathing I became restless and started wandering the trail, my mind turning toward the relief of seeing Aunt Judith and Grandmother Seraiah soon, as well as Hakak and her younger sister Falail. But I also dreaded giving them the bitter news about my mother and Isaac and Sahmril.

Soon, I found that I had wandered far from the well. I was alone in a narrow alleyway of stone, so long I couldn't see the end of it. Only twists and turns of red cliff walls everywhere I looked, the sky a sliver of blue canopy overhead.

I touched the pink and violet colors embedded in the flat rock corridor, running my fingers along the cracks. The rocks were cool. Hardly any heat seeped into these tightly enclosed spaces. At one point, the two walls of rock were so tight and narrow, sunlight barely managed to worm its way through. It was dizzying and wonderful.

Near the end of the passage, the path opened up into a large space, like the courtyard of a palace. In fact, the solid wall in front of me looked just like a gate to an ancient world.

I was slowly walking, taking in the beauty of my surroundings, when the sound of a male voice made me gasp. "It's stunning, isn't it?"

I turned to find Kadesh standing behind me. I placed a hand against the stone wall as it sloped upward to a series of caves, trying to keep my balance on the uneven path. Kadesh reached out to help me cross the broken stones. I shook my head, an unearthly pounding taking place inside my chest at the sight of his sun-browned fingers, the way the rich weaving of his cloak fell in folds along his arm. "Will you never get tired of frightening me?"

"Actually, *you* startled *me*," he said. "I've been sitting here admiring the rock formations when I heard you coming."

"Then I've interrupted your solitude."

"I don't mind at all. I'm ready for some company," he said, gesturing for me to sit.

I shook my head, acutely aware of how close he was. His hands were on his knees, dark hair falling in waves along his shoulders. I wondered how soft his hair would be if I were to touch it, and I shivered in the shade of all that stone, my own hair still damp from its washing.

"How can I enjoy the magnificence of this spot while you stand there like an awkward gazelle?" he asked.

"So I look like a gazelle?"

"That's a good thing," he added with a teasing smile.

"I'll sit, but only for a moment." I sank to the rock, inching as close to the edge as I could manage, but I could still sense each one of his breaths next to me. Still smell the spicy fragrance of his skin. I pointed up at the gate-like cliffs. "Do you think it's possible to climb up there?"

The stone facing of the inner courtyard looked as though somebody had etched patterns into the red sandstone. Cracks and swirls decorated the smooth surface. On both sides of the high wall there were small, dark openings, as if another series of caves lay above.

"Why don't we find out?" Kadesh suggested.

I jumped upright, shaking my head. "Aren't you still healing?"

"It's been nearly two weeks; I'm doing much better," he answered, holding out his hand to help me navigate the rocks.

He had touched me several times over the course of the journey when I needed help. Perhaps that's all Kadesh was offering now, but I brushed past, my head reeling, unsure of myself. He followed me across the courtyard, and I was excruciatingly aware of his presence as we climbed in silence to the top of the rock gateway. Miraculously, there was a series of rough steps cut into the rock, which made the ascent easier.

I slowed down as we reached another area high along the stone facing. The space wasn't very large—just another long, narrow passageway—but it was cool and dark and mysterious under the overhang of rock. My skin rose with an eerie chill.

I peered down at the large, open courtyard below, and it appeared small and insignificant from this height. Intimidating and thrilling. I took a step backward, fighting a strange urge to throw myself off and see if I could fly.

"Do people live up here?" I asked, thinking out loud. "The Edomite nation or those awful men? Do they actually have families?"

Kadesh nodded. "It appears as though this place is in the beginning stages of a new city. This is the face of what will probably be a temple or the palace of their king. Some of the caves could easily become comfortable dwellings. Or burial spots. I noticed there are roads being excavated in the outlying areas, as well as a main thoroughfare."

"You must know what to look for," I said, adding, "This is all being done by those two dozen men we just encountered?"

Kadesh shook his head yes and smiled, attempting to wrap his cream-colored scarf more securely around his neck, but failing as the ends of it fell loosely across the richness of his cloak.

I clenched my fists together, tempted to reach out and fix the scarf for him.

"Those thieves were a motley bunch of rebels, probably

just passing through, and we happened to get unlucky today. On the other side of these fortress cliffs and rocks are village settlements. Sheep and goat herders that tend this large valley. I'm sure if we were to keep exploring we'd run into a temporary camp town, with families and children, merchants and a marketplace. And many stonemasons and craftsmen brought here to build this place into a city."

"You seem to know so much about it," I told him.

"I've been here before. We sell frankincense everywhere."

"How much of the world you know," I said with wonder. "How very much of it you've seen and traveled. Have you been to the Great Sea, or the kingdom of Egypt? I've heard that nobody is as rich as Pharaoh or lives in such vast wealth."

"Except, perhaps, for the king of Babylonia," Kadesh mused.

"You mean King Hammurabi?"

"The same. He has extended his reach from Ur on the tip of the Persian Gulf as far north as Nineveh, I've heard. He would like to rule Damascus and spread his dominion west to the Great Sea as well."

"That would mean he would infringe on Egypt's shores!"

Kadesh nodded solemnly. "King Hammurabi is a visionary man. None of his predecessors has spread the world rule of Babylon like he has succeeded at doing."

"How do you sell frankincense to the far eastern shores of the Mesopotamian world?" I asked him. "Wouldn't your caravans be forced to spend weeks in the middle of the Empty Sands to reach it?"

"You are very astute, Jayden, daughter of Pharez," Kadesh said, his eyes on my face.

"Nobody survives the Empty Sands, I've heard," I said.

He laughed. "We wouldn't survive either. We don't use camel caravans for the Babylonian trade routes; we use ships that go up the gulf of the eastern seaboard."

"Do you know how to sail a ship, too?"

His lips quirked up into a smile. "Not yet. We hire sailors and keep a fleet of ships docked at the seaports."

I shook my head in disbelief at all he was telling me. "Your business is large and complicated."

"It is, but my uncle has many businessmen to help him. I'm still learning so many aspects and getting to know our foremen for each branch. That's why I need to return as soon as possible. I'm healing quickly after your care, so I know it will need to be soon."

When he said that, my breath caught and I jerked my chin up. He would be leaving soon—and I'd never see him. I'd only known him a few weeks, but already he was a steady, comforting spirit in my life, a boy who thrilled me deep inside my soul, and I couldn't imagine never seeing him again. His eyes searched my face, but we didn't speak. Finally, I lowered my head, my mind racing to think of something to break the intensity between us.

"I heard a story once about the frankincense lands," I said, my voice wobbly. "And I've always been curious if it's true."

"What is that?" He moved toward me, and the hair on my neck rose, all my senses jumpy and alert.

I stepped backward, inching open the space between us. "I've heard there are mystical snakes that guard the frankincense trees, not letting anyone near, so the resin cannot be stolen."

"These mythical creatures sound interesting," Kadesh said as he leaned against one of the stone outcroppings to watch me. "What do they look like?"

"The snakes are said to be red and fierce and leap into the air to inflict a deadly bite on any intruder who gets too close to the trees."

"Ahh, not only interesting but dangerous. Assassin snakes."

I tried to suppress a smile, but it came out as a laugh. "So you're telling me it's only a story?"

"Perhaps you should come to the frankincense lands and see for yourself."

"I would probably die before I reached the halfway point."

"No, you wouldn't die," Kadesh said, shaking his head. "I would protect you."

"You talk of impossible things," I murmured. "I'm sure you have a family waiting for you."

"Only a large, noisy, meddling family of aunts and uncles and cousins and sisters. Plus an array of nephews and nieces."

"What is your uncle's name? Does he have a title?" I spoke flippantly, not expecting the answer I received.

"His name is Ephrem," Kadesh answered, his head inclining. "Uncle to me, but King Ephrem to our city and all the lands between the Queen of Sheba and the Irreantum shores."

My hand went to my mouth as I tried to cover up my astonishment. "The Queen of Sheba! You live near *that* kingdom!" I was awestruck. "They say she is the richest woman that walks the earth. And the most beautiful."

"I might debate your last point," he said, with a glance at me. "Our caravans pass through her kingdom on the way to my home," he added, his feet crunching on the stone gravel as he closed the gap between us once again.

"What does Irreantum mean?" I said, trying to change the subject.

"The name means 'many waters.' A sea that rolls beyond the horizon, farther than a person can sail. An ocean that takes a person past any land known to man."

"It sounds mysterious and magnificent." I paused, trying to imagine his life, his land, this wild sea.

"See, you've saved the life of a potential prince," Kadesh went on, his eyes never leaving my face.

"Surely, someone like you—" I broke off, embarrassed, wavering on my feet, wanting to run down the stone steps but wanting to know more about him, too.

"I'd expect no less from a girl who is in line to become a princess herself, as your father tells me."

I shook my head vehemently, and then realized I shouldn't be potentially betraying my dislike toward Horeb. Although Kadesh had said nothing about Horeb. Perhaps he didn't know about my betrothal.

Abruptly, I turned to pace the stone walkway, my heart racing.

"What were you going to say a moment ago?" Kadesh asked, pressing forward.

"It doesn't matter. Nothing matters." I stared up at the blue sky, so deep and clear above the red, lofty cliffs, and wished I could crawl into one of the caves and start my life all over again. I was fairly certain that Kadesh didn't know I was betrothed to the prince of my tribe, or he probably would have said so outright, despite his saying I was in line for the role of princess. My father would not confide the details to a stranger. Only that our families were connected to the ruler of Nephish, to show our tribal standing.

"It matters to me. Don't be afraid, Jayden. You can tell me, I promise."

He hovered close, and I knew he wouldn't let me run back down the stone staircase until I finished my sentence. "I was only going to say that surely someone like you, in line to inherit the frankincense and business of your uncle, is—is already married—or betrothed to the most beautiful girl in your kingdom. I'm sure that's why you're so eager to get back home."

Kadesh looked startled. Then his face clouded over as he snapped his cloak, striding away. He stopped at the edge of the stone precipice, and then turned to me with such an expression of dismay and frustration, it caught me off guard.

"Don't speak of things you know nothing about," he said quietly.

"I've said something wrong," I quickly apologized. "I'm so sorry. I'll go now."

No sooner did I move to head for the stairs than Kadesh darted forward into my path. We bumped into each other and I wobbled, not expecting him to be there.

Without speaking, he gently steadied me, placing a hand on the stone parapet so I wouldn't lose my balance and fall forward. The touch of his hand on my arm caused my stomach to rise into my throat, and yet it saddened me, too. His pensive, melancholy reaction spoke to the fact that there *was* someone else in his homeland. Someone his heart must be missing. Another girl, a princess meant just for him, and yet he didn't confirm or deny it.

Kadesh's eyes were black as a well of water, with depths I couldn't even begin to fathom. We stared at each other, mere inches away, not saying a word. I needed to move, to walk away, but I felt rooted to the ground, unable to compel myself.

"Jayden—" he began, and the sound of his voice speaking my name seemed to engulf my soul with something peculiar and magical and wonderful.

"No," I said with a small shake of my head. Taking a shallow breath, I stepped toward the staircase, my thoughts careening in a thousand different directions.

"Jayden, I only—"

I shook my head. "Please don't say my name like that."

He looked at me, confused. "And how am I speaking your name?" His voice was so tender, so gentle, so complicated.

I trembled, dizzy from the intense focus he was directing at me. I wanted to sit down, but I was certain that sitting would be much too dangerous.

"You mustn't look at me like that," I whispered, my eyes locking onto his.

His gaze was like fire on my face. "I can't tell you what's in my heart?"

I put up a hand to touch my hot cheek. "No, Kadesh."

"But," he said. "I think you feel it, too."

My throat was thick with unspoken words, but I finally tore my eyes away and ran, jolting down the steps back to the courtyard below.

"Jayden, please come back!" His voice made me ache all the way to my toes, but I hurried across the expanse of the earthen courtyard and slipped inside the tunnel crevice that would take me back to my family at the well.

Overhead, black rain clouds concealed the sun where there used to be blue sky. There was a sudden white snap as lightning flashed. Thunder roared next, rumbling the earth under my feet.

I put my hand up on the wall of stone and felt the vibrations deep inside the rock. It was the sound of a fury coming straight at us, but I had no idea if it was a storm or an earthquake. At the moment it didn't even matter, I was so sensitive to the atmosphere that Kadesh created around me.

My heart slammed into my ribs when I turned to see that Kadesh had followed me. He was right on my heels, and before my heart could beat again, his hand closed over mine, locking me to the wall. I turned my head away, aware that I couldn't gaze into his face and not betray my fascination toward him. He mesmerized me, filled me with an intense longing I couldn't even define.

His hand was warm as it engulfed mine, his strong fingers

grasping my own in his, entwining us together. I couldn't move; I couldn't breathe, every one of my senses shivering and vibrating like the rocks around us.

Before I could say a word, Kadesh lifted my hand from the cold stone and turned me toward him. We stood inches apart and I gazed, enthralled, as he brought my open hand to his lips and gently kissed my palm. I knew I should pull away, yet I had an urge to lift up my other hand so that he could kiss it as well.

"Jayden," he said softly. "You're trembling. Please know that I would never hurt you, or your heart."

"I think I know that, but—"

He cut off my protests by quickly kissing my other hand, holding it to his mouth, his eyes closed. The touch of his lips made me want to burst out of my skin.

"As a man who spends his life directing caravans for whole seasons at a time, you know I have great patience," he said as he bent to whisper in my ear. He was so close; if I merely took a new breath, I would melt right into him.

"Sometimes the seasons pass too quickly," I whispered. Horeb and my impending marriage were in my mind, never far away. But Kadesh knew none of that, and I couldn't bear to tell him. The words would break me apart. I didn't want this moment to end. If only I could stop the sands of time from slipping through my fingers.

Kadesh tightened his grip, and a strange joy stirred in my belly. "There's plenty of time. Don't worry, Jayden."

I didn't answer, knowing there was so much to worry about. And I was running out of time. But I couldn't tear my eyes away from his face, his lips, and the wonder of his hands holding mine, the caress of his skin, his fingers, so exquisite, even as tears swam behind my gaze.

The narrow tunnel suddenly fell into shadow as afternoon became evening. When the wind rose, fat splashes of rain fell through the narrow ceiling of sky overhead. Within seconds, a torrent of rain began to fall, dribbling down my face as though the clouds had split open.

"Look," Kadesh said, pointing to the ground. "The rain is coming down fast. This is going to be a big storm. Not a good sign."

Puddles were forming right where we stood—and growing larger by the second.

He looked up, rain running in rivulets down his face, soaking his hair and clothes. "We can't stay here," he said, nudging me forward. "We need to leave, and quickly."

I nodded and glanced back at the narrow passageway from where we had originated. Had I really wandered so far? The entrance to the corridor still loomed a great distance ahead, the path hidden by twists and turns of the narrow, sheer rock walls. Within seconds, the water was rising so rapidly I wasn't sure we'd make it back to the entrance before we were engulfed.

"It's a flash flood!" Kadesh suddenly shouted. "Run—as fast as you can!"

I obeyed, my knees pumping, feet stumbling across the rocky ground, hair whipping into my eyes.

The rain continued to quickly fill the passageway. Too quickly.

"I don't think I can outrun it!" I gasped.

Within moments, the water level was halfway up my legs, making it hard to even walk. My hands scraped against the rough sandstone as a sea of reddish-brown water pulled at my feet. I fell, banging my knees into the stony ground, swallowing a mouthful of dank water.

Kadesh lifted me up by the waist and I coughed so hard my lungs burned. "Are you all right?"

I nodded and started forward again, willing myself to keep moving. Kadesh stayed right behind me, urging me forward, but by the time we reached the end, we were sloshing through water as high as our waists. The last few feet were painful, as though the ravine had created its own undertow, desperate to suck me down. Slogging forward, I burst out of the passageway, free at last, but the current was still strong and fast, although not as deep. My legs were on fire by the time we struggled up the steep slope and were safely out of the high water.

Finally, I turned to look back.

Behind us, the narrow gorge kept filling as thunder smashed overhead. Roaring floodwaters flowed down the cavern like a river had suddenly been created. If we'd stayed inside the passage a moment longer we would have surely drowned.

"You aren't hurt?" Kadesh asked. I shook my head, gulping in blessed air as rain soaked my skin, and I could tell his relief was immense.

I sensed that he wished he could sweep me up and carry me onto even higher ground, but we both saw my father at the same moment, standing in the pouring rain scanning the horizon. As we ran, I purposely widened the space between us.

"Keep going, Jayden," Kadesh told me tenderly. "We still have to get to higher ground."

I was exhausted, but managed to keep climbing even though the red dirt had become a slog of mud, sucking at my feet.

A puzzled expression crossed my father's face when he saw us together, and he gripped my arms as soon as I reached him. "Did you know that people have drowned in that crevice when there are floodwaters?" he asked, his arms enclosing me. "As soon as it began to rain you should have left."

I shook my head, my teeth beginning to chatter. "Kadesh found me in the narrow ravine. He knew. That it wasn't safe, I mean. With the rain, the flooding." I stopped. I was beginning to sound guilty, like I'd done something wrong. But I wasn't guilty of anything, was I?

The rain continued to pour. Leila hung on to the harness of one of the pack camels, the shawl over her head dripping forlornly. The camels stood stoically, unfazed by the sudden inundation of the storm. My father and Kadesh rallied the animals, tying them together in their dwindling line as I mounted Meela.

The sensation of Kadesh's fingers gripping my hand lingered as I stared down at my own. As if his skin had imprinted onto me forever—his lips searing my palms, his eyes reading my soul—as though we would forever remain in the narrow crevasse, living that moment over and over again.

My mind reeled with desire I'd never felt before, accompanied by the despair that I was betrothed to someone else. I shouldn't be daydreaming about any other boy this way, but I only wanted him to touch me again, even as a shadow of guilt crossed my conscience.

I held on to the memory of Kadesh's lips against my palms, the burning in his eyes that told me he was thinking about me just as much as I was thinking about him.

$\mathcal{11}$

Several days later, we entered the summer lands near the city of Tadmur, a week's journey from Damascus.

When I saw it coming over the last ridge of sand dunes early that morning, I was sure we'd found paradise. The large oasis pond reflected the sun while groves of palm trees, heavy with dates next to wild grapes, circled the ring of water. Grass and shrubs and flowers spread like an intricate carpet before formidable mountains in the hazy distance.

Familiar black tents dotted the oasis valley, the most welcome sight of all.

We quickly rode into camp and when we got to the tent of Abimelech, Horeb's father, Aunt Judith ran out, her face streaming with tears of relief to see us at last. She wiped at her eyes, laughing at herself, and then clucked her tongue. "Every day I thought we would see you behind us, but never were my prayers answered."

"We had some delays along the way," I said wearily. "But we're here now and that's all that matters."

"You girls are skin and bones," Judith went on. "We'll have to feast every night to put you back together again."

Uncle Abimelech eyed my father's shrinking herd. "Three camels lost. You've suffered on your journey," he said simply.

My father nodded without speaking. There was nothing much to say, but eight camels was a pathetic herd, even for a poor man, when the rest of the clans had many dozens, even hundreds of camels for food and trade. As tribal chief, Abimelech owned close to a thousand camels, and yet he wouldn't shame my father by giving him any. He could only help my father get his lost herd back by organizing a raid to retrieve them from the Maachathites, who had stolen from us over and over again.

With Kadesh's help, my youngest cousin, Chezib, ran around the camels, untying them and giving them lush flowers to eat straight from his cupped hands. I could hear the pair of them chattering and laughing together. I wanted to sit and watch as Kadesh patiently listened while Chezib instructed him on camels and travels and the next hunting expedition.

But as I looked over at the fire hearth in front of Abimelech's tent my stomach dropped, the relief on my face quickly erased. Horeb lay on a mound of pillows, sipping coffee and eating from a basket of ripe fruit.

I walked over, but my betrothed didn't get up. "You're

dirty, Cousin," he said matter-of-factly.

"Most people are travel worn after more than two weeks on the desert," I replied, not trying to keep the tone of annoyance out of my voice.

He laughed, inching back into the shade. "Your sister's grown," he added, staring at Leila.

I jerked my head, seeing Leila through his eyes. Grown? Not in height. Only in womanly attributes. I gave a snort as Horeb rose up on one elbow, examining Kadesh. "Who's the stranger?"

"A man named Kadesh from the South," I said shortly.

"Where did you find him?"

"He found us, actually," I said curtly, trying to cut off the conversation.

"Where? After you left our last camping site or on the road?"

"Before we left. We were—my mother—" I couldn't get the words past my lips.

"That's right. Your mother was about to give birth. Did she finally manage a son for your father?"

I closed my eyes and wished Horeb would disappear from my sight. He was so unfeeling, so insensitive. "There was a son, Isaac. He died. And a twin sister. My mother—" I still couldn't say it, and I couldn't move until our conversation was deemed over.

Horeb sat up from his rug and swished a stick through the hearth fire's embers, where water was boiling for coffee later that evening. He studied my face without any emotion of his own, but surprisingly read the pain in my eyes. "You had to bury her before you left. That's why you never caught up with us."

I nodded and bit at my lips.

"And your father trusted this boy, this stranger? You're lucky you're all still alive."

"He was wounded by enemies," I answered, making sure my voice was devoid of any sentiment. "My father and Shem tended him. He'd lost his caravan and had to come with us until he can buy more camels in the market at Tadmur and get back home."

"I see," Horeb said, appraising Kadesh from a distance as he and Chezib led our tired and hungry camels out to a field of flowers and shrubs.

Silently, I watched my father move the bundles of tent and stakes to an empty camping spot several hundred paces away from Abimelech's camp. "I need to put up the tent," I said. "My father is weary. It's been a terrible two weeks since my mother's loss."

Horeb pursed his lips, nodding. "You'd better hurry before the sun sinks."

I stared at him; he wasn't even moving to help me. A moment later Hakak was at my side. "We'll help with the unpacking," she said, kicking a foot at her older brother. "Just because you stayed in the city all night with your friends at the drinking houses doesn't mean you can be lazy all day."

"Yes, it does, little sister," Horeb said, leaning back again. "I've been cleaning and sharpening my tools and weapons, as well as preparing for this evening. We're having a tribal council meeting after all you girls go to bed."

"It's nothing but boring talk. But you're good at that, dear brother."

"Is that a compliment or a critique of my negotiating skills?"

"The former, I suppose," Hakak teased in return. She paused and added soberly, "I know you will make a fine king one day for the tribe of Nephish. Already you are forming alliances, making us stronger. Not everybody can do that."

Then Hakak slipped her arm through mine. "And when you and Jayden marry and settle into the finest tent, I picture you holding court and solving problems and using your wisdom to keep us strong and safe."

Horeb inclined his head, gazing at me again. I wished I'd had a bath and combed my hair. I looked every bit the poor and dirty peasant. "Thank you for your confidence, dear sister. I just hope that Jayden will understand the good life she will have with me," he added meaningfully.

Hakak gave a snort. "Of course she does. We all know how fortunate and blessed your union will be."

Horeb picked up a bowl of sliced melon and popped one into his mouth. He offered me a piece, and as hungry as I was, I shook my head in refusal. I didn't want to get so close that he could grab my arm. "She can be assured on that account. I'll be gone a lot or have visiting dignitaries from other tribes, so Jayden will need to run the camp alone, but I know she's capable. And she will live like a queen once we're anointed. A chest full of jewels will be hers. A herd of camels she won't be able to count. And so many servants, she'll never put up a tent or draw water again."

It was strange to hear them talking about me like this, even complimenting my household skills, but I couldn't say a word.

Hakak tugged at my arm, stooping down to get our woefully empty food baskets that had been left on the ground after unpacking the camels. "No more talking, Horeb! Jayden's exhausted and we need to bathe and dress her and help her get settled. We will see you at dinner."

Hakak led me away, looking healthy and beautiful even though the tribe had to have arrived at the oasis only a few days earlier. Her marriage to Laham was getting close; perhaps that accounted for Hakak's radiance.

As we walked, I knew I had to tell her about my mother. The words were on my tongue, but I couldn't bring myself to say them. My throat closed up as Hakak embraced me.

A moment later, Falail and Leila came up the road, carrying fresh water in a large clay jug from the oasis well between them. "I'll help you girls with a bath," Falail said. "Now that we have water. You can borrow some of our clothes until yours can be washed."

"Now tell me," Hakak said, squeezing my arm. "Where is your mother? I haven't seen her yet. Did she slip by us all, and she and my mother are catching up on all the gossip?"

At that moment Aunt Judith hurried around the camel carriage that was now sitting empty on the ground. "Jayden!

Leila!" she shrieked. "Where is your mother—the litter is empty!"

I held myself tightly, forcing myself not to fall apart in front of everyone.

Aunt Judith read my face and clasped me in her arms, then pulled Leila close as she herded us into her tent for privacy. She began to weep. "It's true, isn't it? She's gone. Oh, dear God, it isn't possible! Rebekah, dear Rebekah. When did this happen?"

"The day the valley emptied. She went into labor that morning."

Judith pulled back in surprise. "But the baby wasn't supposed to come until we got here. Where is the child, the infant? Let me see him!"

Tears slipped from my eyes and I tried to brush them away, but there were too many. "There were twins, Aunt Judith. My brother, Isaac, is buried with my mother. Sahmril survived, but she's with Shem's family, who left us at the crossroads to go to Mari." I stopped, not wanting to recount that terrible day of the journey. It was too painful, still too fresh. "Dinah agreed to nurse her."

Aunt Judith groaned and wiped at her face.

"Nalla did all she could, but there was no way to stop—" I broke off, weeping as that terrible morning swept over me all over again.

"I pray Rebekah didn't suffer too terribly." Aunt Judith shook her head, disbelief etched in her eyes. "Then, her last night alive was your betrothal celebration—only—weeks ago.

It doesn't seem possible that she's gone. She was my dearest friend in all the world."

I buried my face into my aunt's neck, wanting to give her all the grief and anxiety I'd been holding in for so long.

"Where is the grave?" Judith whispered.

"Under the bluff," I said. "Father dug it deep and we covered it with rocks. I—I danced for her. To say good-bye."

"What a good daughter you are, Jayden." Aunt Judith traced a finger against my empty collarbone as she raised her red, streaming eyes to mine. "Where's your jewelry? The necklace, the earrings—they're missing."

"Payment to Dinah for saving Sahmril," I choked out.

Shock filled my aunt's eyes. "That wicked woman!" She hugged me tightly, and I leaned against her, unloading all my grief of so many weeks.

Leila was weeping again, too, and Falail and Hakak sat her down, embracing her and murmuring condolences. Then Hakak and Aunt Judith bustled about, getting us bread and camel's milk to eat and drink. My sister was so thin I worried about her. But it was a relief to sink into the rugs of someone else's tent and let myself be cared for.

A few moments later, the tapestry partition was pulled aside and I saw my grandmother Seraiah standing in the doorway; the folds of her wrinkled face were almost as dear as my own mother's.

"My girls," she said, holding out her hands.

I jumped up to run to her, fresh tears bitter on my cheeks. "Oh, Grandmother!" I cried, burying my face into her neck.

Seraiah was tiny and frail, but her soul was like a rock, firm and immovable, and she loved me unconditionally. She was the one person I'd wanted to see more than anyone else.

"Ssh, ssh," she hushed me, kissing my cheeks and stroking my hair. "No need to speak. Your father has told me all that has happened." She embraced me again and I wept into her for everything I had lost.

A few hours later, after my father and I erected the tent, laid out our rugs, and unpacked the pots and jugs, we fell into our beds. More tired than hungry. But Judith and Abimelech wouldn't let us keep to ourselves for long. Two nights later we sat with them for dinner, enjoying a feast we hadn't had in almost a month.

Surely the terrible time was over, I prayed as we feasted on a huge platter of roasted meat and mounds of rice and dripping fat to celebrate our safe arrival.

There were stories of the desert crossing and laughter and relief. And all the while, from across the fire, I felt Kadesh's eyes on me. After those secret, intimate moments between us in the flooding chasm, I tried not to let my own eyes linger, but it was impossible, and it wasn't long before Horeb noticed the attention Kadesh was giving me. I blushed, always aware of the heightened excitement Kadesh caused in my belly, but I worried over Horeb, who was watching me too, observing everything Kadesh said and did—as well as my reaction. It was worse than if he'd smirked and laughed. As if he'd caught me cheating, and was enjoying it. And yet, I could say and do nothing.

At the end of the meal, Kadesh rose to his feet, holding out his cup. "You have all been endlessly kind to me. I honor the House of Pharez for rescuing me, healing me, and giving me a home on my solitary journey. Thank you, Abimelech, for this feast. If I may give a small token of my gratitude." He untied one of the leather bags at his side and pulled out a rectangle of fluttering lavender silk, then bowed to Judith and laid the beautiful silk at her feet. "Thank you for your hearth and home."

Hakak leaned close to Leila and me, her eyes dancing. "He's very generous and courtly, isn't he?"

Stepping across the rugs, Kadesh kneeled to kiss my father on both cheeks. "You saved my life and no gift can equal that, but when I return to my uncle and finish my business there, I intend to bring back fifty camels to help heal your herd."

My father bowed his head and murmured his thanks. Camels were a fine gift, and expensive, but it could take months for camels to arrive and my father needed them now—especially when the oasis became overgrazed and it was time to leave for the winter rains, when we wandered from valley to valley following the rain clouds that brought food for our camels.

"Before I leave I will inspect the swordmaker shops in Tadmur," Kadesh added. "And bring back a sword as a token of my devotion."

My father looked pleased. The only weapon he owned was the short sword given to him by his father when he turned twelve and went on his first raid. But it had always been more like a long dagger rather than a true sword. Nothing like Kadesh's weapons.

"You may not have an *extra* sword for gift giving, stranger," Horeb said, standing up to circle the fire like a restless lion. "But you have at least one."

"That's true," Kadesh said, nodding.

"An expensive sword, is it not? From the city of Damascus?"

Kadesh's only response was another brief nod.

Abimelech clapped his hands on his knees. "Let's see this great weapon, young stranger."

"Girls," Aunt Judith said smoothly. "Time to clean up and let the men talk of weapons and alliances and raids."

Leila gave me a nudge. "Will they be comparing the size of their weapons or each other?"

I rolled my eyes. Scooping leftover rice into a pot, I watched the men huddle around Kadesh's sword, discussing its intricate pattern, the strength of the brass, the well-crafted hilt.

Horeb gazed at Kadesh. "Where did you say you purchased it?"

Kadesh held the blade flat against his palm. "Actually, I didn't. The sword was a gift. Purchased in the city of Babylon, but originally crafted in Damascus, where swordmakers are experimenting with various metals and styles."

"A fine gift, indeed," Horeb said, hinting that he'd like to know who the gift giver was, but Kadesh didn't take the bait. "These etchings are interesting. What do they represent?"

I watched Kadesh stiffen and then force himself to relax.

"Merely family markings of ownership."

Horeb was clearly annoyed at the nonanswers. Then he glanced at me, catching me gazing at Kadesh. I averted my eyes and began to sweep crumbs from the rug. How many other secrets was Kadesh hiding? Then it came to me. Kadesh's closed mouth had everything to do with frankincense. His uncle had probably given him the blade to defend himself on this journey *because* he carried frankincense. I wondered if the etchings were the personal markings of frankincense grove owners. A secret that must be kept at all costs.

Sudden clarity washed over me. Kadesh had trusted my father and me, to tell us of his family business and the attack that wounded him. As far as I was aware, he'd said nothing to Leila, even if he did give her a peculiar look every now and then, which I still had not figured out. Tonight he was being purposely evasive, and after the way he'd brought his lips to my palms back in the canyon, I knew I would keep his secret until I died.

Before I could remove another empty dish, Horeb pulled his sword from his belt and whipped it through the air, letting the evening sunset glint off its bronze surface. "Let's see how sturdy your sword really is, stranger."

"You may call me Kadesh."

Horeb shrugged, as if calling Kadesh by his actual name was too much bother.

Before Kadesh could answer the call to raise his own sword, Horeb ran forward, swinging his sword straight at him. I gasped as Kadesh fell to the ground to avoid a direct hit.

Scrambling to his feet, he grasped the hilt of his weapon with both hands, returning the thrust with one of his own. There was a ringing sound as the two weapons made contact.

Abimelech clapped his hands. "Excellent. You've got a quick adversary, son."

My father didn't speak, his face disapproving as he crossed his arms over his chest. I was sure he didn't like that Kadesh and Horeb were fighting, even if was supposedly just for sport.

Before I could leave the area and disappear into the tent with Judith and Hakak, Horeb turned on his heel and came at Kadesh again. Their swords clashed a second time, slamming so hard I thought their arms would snap. I let out a cry, wanting to look away, but I couldn't. A strange force compelled me to watch, even as I swayed on my feet, my sense of dread growing.

Dust kicked up around the campsite as the sparring grew more serious. Horeb was huskier, wider in the shoulders, thicker in his arms, but he wasn't as tall as Kadesh, and he couldn't move with as much speed. The two swords struck repeatedly and the high-pitched sound vibrated the air with such a clanging I clapped my hands over my ears.

The other girls hurried out of the tent again. "What's going on?" Leila came up and slipped her arm through mine. I tried to be nonchalant and purposely made an effort not to grip her hand too tightly. It would show that I cared too much, and I didn't want to betray my true feelings for either boy.

Hakak shook her head. "I suppose they have to make sure

their swords actually work—and find out which man is the better fighter."

Aunt Judith tried to end the match. "I have fresh-ground coffee beans. Let's return to the fire." The men paid no attention and Judith stuck her hands on her hips, motioning to my uncle Abimelech to stop the fight.

Horeb seemed to grow impatient to strike Kadesh to the ground, but Kadesh was too quick and lithe. They circled each other with such intensity it was clear this had become much more than a friendly sparring match.

"If your sword is truly a magnificent blade from Damascus," Horeb called out, "you should have already taken me down."

Kadesh merely smiled, which seemed to infuriate Horeb even more.

I shuddered as Horeb attacked again, but this time, instead of one or two thrusts, he continued to lunge forward, his sword swinging wildly as he slashed at Kadesh, as if he was trying to plunge his sword straight into his chest.

I gasped, shocked at his aggressiveness. "He fights as though he wants to kill Kadesh!" I whispered hoarsely as Leila gripped my arm, as if she, too, was surprised. Only Judith seemed to take pride in her son's fighting ability, her eyes alight with excitement every time Horeb got the upper hand.

Sweat dripped down both the boys' faces as Kadesh deflected Horeb's blade, but it was obvious Kadesh hadn't realized how hard and fast Horeb was going to attack, and he barely managed to keep his face from getting sliced to ribbons.

The sun sank farther, and the fight moved out of the fire's light and into the shadows as the two young men continued on.

"Why don't they stop?" I whispered.

"Someone *will* get hurt," Hakak murmured. "This is silly; what's the point?"

Falail spoke up next. "How can they stop when their pride is now at stake?"

"It was supposed to be a friendly sparring for entertainment," I said, beginning to get angry. And yet I couldn't tear my eyes away. My heart thrashed against my chest in worry for Kadesh. Though another part of it beat in furious terror for Horeb's life; if they did not stop, Kadesh would be blamed for ending it.

Regaining his footing, Kadesh suddenly stepped out of range of Horeb's next thrust. Catching Horeb off guard, he twisted his opponent's arm behind his back, which forced Horeb's sword to fall to the ground.

Grunting and furious, Horeb swung his free arm across his body to punch Kadesh in the face. The blow found empty air as Kadesh ducked. "This wasn't meant to be a fistfight," Kadesh burst out.

Before Horeb could throw his fist again, Kadesh threw an arm around my cousin's neck, pulled him tight against him, and then pressed his blade against the skin of Horeb's throat. Immediately Horeb stopped struggling. The move to Horeb's throat was an obvious sign that Kadesh was the winner. My betrothed didn't move a muscle, but hatred filled his eyes.

A heartbeat of silence passed. Next to me, my father began to clap his hands until Uncle Abimelech joined in as well.

"An entertaining game," Abimelech said, shrugging off his son's defeat, returning to the hearth to pour coffee. "Not many have ever bested Horeb. And on another night our visitor probably wouldn't again. It was pure luck that Kadesh gained the upper hand."

I wanted to laugh at his words. Kadesh had obviously proven himself. He was the stronger opponent, not only in swordsmanship, but in strategy and tactics. Horeb was all swagger and boastfulness. He assumed he could knock Kadesh down within a few moves and prove his stature, but he failed. A smile came to my lips, and I ducked my head, hoping to hide my satisfaction.

Judith let out her breath, putting a hand to her chest in relief as the fight appeared to finally be over. "Let's bring out the honeyed cake, Jayden," she said, bringing me out of my thoughts. "As my future daughter-in-law, you may help serve."

Clear across the camp, I saw Kadesh's sudden intake of breath. I cringed at her words and felt Horeb's black eyes bore into me, despite the deepening dusk. Hot tears pricked at me as I ducked my head to follow Aunt Judith.

Before I had taken more than a few steps, Kadesh picked up his sword and placed it back into the sheath at his waist. "A good match and well done," he said to Horeb, bowing.

Horeb wiped the back of his hand across his mouth, staggering as he picked up his own weapon from the dirt. Gripping the handle in both fists, he swung around again as if to attack

Kadesh from behind, and I let out a cry, relieved when my father stepped between the two boys, barely escaping a glancing blow himself.

"I believe our evening is over," my father said evenly. "Even though we've been here for two days my family is still in need of rest. I'll join you for coffee tomorrow evening, Abimelech."

Nothing else would stop Horeb faster than losing his audience.

As I began to walk back to our own tent, Aunt Judith came over and took my arm. "You know this wasn't a real fight, Jayden. You must be assured that Horeb—"

I cut her off. "I know, Aunt Judith. You don't need to say anything. This changes nothing about how I feel about Horeb and our betrothal."

Of course, my aunt didn't understand my double meaning. She embraced me and kissed my forehead. "Of course, Jayden. You are the perfect bride for him. Good night, sweet daughter."

I hurried after my father, following the beam of his swinging lantern in the heavy dusk. The sun was a small, red ball of fire low on the horizon, but the light was virtually gone.

Leila caught up to me and held my hand. "Jayden, what was that fight about?"

"I don't know what you mean."

"I see how Kadesh looks at you. Could they have been fighting over you?"

I laughed at her words, but my stomach clenched. "Why would you think that?" What had my sister observed? I'd been so careful to treat Kadesh and Horeb the same so that no one would be suspicious of where my true affections lay. "Don't be ridiculous."

"It's so romantic."

"You're being silly."

Leila lowered her voice, whispering in the darkness. "You're not fooling me, Jayden. Horeb might be your future husband, but Kadesh is the handsome stranger who can't take his eyes off you."

"Stop it! You'll shame us both with such talk."

"I'm only speaking of what I see. I seem to recall the day in the canyons when you both were caught in a rainstorm. After being gone a long time." She smiled.

I gasped with denial as she giggled into my ear. "Nothing happened during that flash flood. I'd gone exploring and was just returning when the storm started. I was lucky Kadesh knew enough to tell me to run. He helped me get through the crevice safely, that's all. If he hadn't I wouldn't be standing here today."

Amusement played around Leila's mouth. "Maybe so. But while I was resting and Father tending to the camels, I noticed Kadesh disappear into those cliffs and caverns, too. For quite a while. You're saying that you didn't see him at all?"

I didn't want to lie to her, but I couldn't confide the truth either. I couldn't afford Leila whispering secrets to her best friend, Falail, who would go directly to Aunt Judith. "I wasn't with Kadesh," I finally said, cringing as I lied. "I may have seen him wandering from a distance, but I wasn't paying any attention."

"You say that, but I sense something brewing in the air, and I think Horeb does, too. That's why the fight tonight got out of hand."

"Believe me, Leila, this fight wasn't about me at all," I said firmly. "Horeb hardly gives me a second thought, and he probably won't until our wedding. He's too busy training and negotiating and receiving an education about a thousand different topics so he can step into Uncle Abimelech's role one day. Horeb fought because he wanted to prove his merit as the future king of our tribe. He wanted—needed—to boost his own status in front of all of us. It was not about me."

"He is a show-off," Leila assented. "But you have to agree that Horeb's handsome looks are spectacular, and he's so muscular as well. Perhaps Kadesh *was* just lucky. Horeb is definitely the stronger of the two."

I didn't say a word, but it was fascinating to me how we'd both interpreted the same sword contest so differently. Horeb might be handsome in the usual manner, but Kadesh's eyes were so striking it was like he'd appeared from a dream.

"I've seen Horeb fight in competitions before, and he never loses," Leila went on. "See what you've been missing!"

"I'm not going to mourn over what I've missed," I assured her. "I'm more worried that Horeb's embarrassment tonight will fuel his ill feelings toward Kadesh."

"Why?" Leila asked me too quickly. She was suspicious, I could tell. "It was just boys playing. Besides, don't you find it flattering to have the boy you're going to marry fight for you, even if it's all in fun?"

I stopped for a moment in the starlight. Wispy clouds trailed across the full moon and a chill rushed through me. Tonight I was ending my sixteenth year. "Go on without me," I told my sister. "I'll be right there. I just want to look at the sky."

"You're such a romantic," she said, laughing at me again.

Her previous statement left me breathless. *Don't you find it flattering to have the boy you're going to marry fight for you?* But Leila hadn't specified Horeb in her words.

A moment later, I got angry at myself for being so foolish. The desert would have to be covered in ice before I'd have a chance of breaking the betrothal with Horeb. I'd been doomed to that end since I was born. My father and Abimelech would never agree to a renegotiation or contract breach. Now I understood how Leila felt when she said that she wanted to run away.

I'd crossed the threshold into womanhood, but it had been the longest weeks of my entire life. My mother's last night alive was like a dream to me now. How I wished I'd talked to her before the party.

If anybody could have helped me break the betrothal, my mother could have.

I was running out of options.

12

E very task I performed during the first weeks of summer in Tadmur reminded me of my mother, especially unpacking, when I placed her wedding chest in a corner of the tent where it would be safe from the cooking fire or spilled grease. Each time I glanced over, the chest brought back her last night—my betrothal ceremony—and the jewelry she'd kept there as a special gift just for me.

And now, two weeks into our stay here, baking the morning bread brought my mother's memory to mind yet again. As I knelt at the hearth, flattening a ball of dough, a shadow passed over me. I looked up to find Kadesh, watching me. He'd grown stronger as the days had ticked by—as his departure grew near . . . and as my wedding to Horeb inched closer.

"Jayden," he said softly, and I shivered at the sound of his voice.

"Stop. Please," I said, quickly glancing up at him and then back to my work. "We can't be seen speaking to each other."

"No one is around," he replied, leaning in closer. "I know your secret."

I sucked in my breath. "I have no secrets," I replied. "Everyone here in camp knows everyone else's gossip."

"I know you're afraid. And I know you despise Horeb. I've been watching both of you these past weeks."

I shook my head as tears began to well up. Horeb and I had minimal interactions, but when we did speak, I always felt uncomfortable, wary, never sure how he would react. "Please. You must not talk like this."

"Look at me, Jayden. Please know that I won't let him hurt you."

I stared at the pattern of the rug. One of my tears dropped onto the hot dome of the stove and sizzled from the heat. "I can't. If I look at you, I know you will put a spell on me."

"But you have already put a spell on *me*," Kadesh said, his voice low. "I will be under your enchantment forever, and there is no going back. I only want to wipe away your tears."

He reached up to touch my face and I shook my head, knowing that if I let him do that, I might let him do so much more. "No one can do that," I said hopelessly. "It's too late."

"Jayden, it's never too late. Trust me. Have faith that we will find a way."

"If only it were true! But the betrothal—the ceremony—it's done. It's finished."

He shook his head decisively. "It's never too late until the vows are taken, the contract signed, and the dowry accepted."

Without meaning to, I raised my face when he said that, gathering hope in his words. He was closer than I expected, and a rush of longing rose from my toes to my chest.

Tenderly, Kadesh put his hand on my hot face, and my heart filled my throat, my body about to float off in a haze of fog, when he suddenly said, "Your bread is burning."

"Oh!" I jumped back, and Kadesh tossed the blackened loaf into the sand.

"Your father will think you're burning his tent down." He retrieved a bucket of water, cooled down the stove, and waved at the billowing smoke with a small rug.

"Now go, go!" I said, flapping my hands.

He laughed, and I couldn't stop myself from laughing in return.

"You're dangerous, Jayden," he said, gazing at me, his cloak swirling around his feet. "I fear you need to be kept under surveillance or you'll set us on fire while we sleep."

"I will if you keep distracting me from my tasks!"

As Kadesh backed out the tent door, he gave his characteristic princely bow and I tried to catch my breath.

Lying on my bed later that afternoon, I stared up at the ceiling, thinking back to that morning. If Horeb learned of our conversations, or had knowledge of the way Kadesh had clasped my hands and kissed my palm in the canyon—I could be accused of infidelity. Another reason never to confide in anyone, but nobody could intrude on my thoughts, or stop my daydreaming.

That night my sister didn't come home for dinner. I worried about what antics she might be up to as I cleaned up the evening meal, peeking over the tent partition between the main room and the women's quarters to listen to my father and Kadesh.

"How is your wound healing now that we're settled?" my father asked.

"I feel completely well. And, sir, I'm afraid that I must speak with you about returning home to my family. I'd like to go into Tadmur and find a caravan to send a message to my uncle. Then I'll spend a few days purchasing camels and getting supplies for the journey."

"I think it would be wiser to find a caravan you can travel with," my father told him.

"That's true, and I plan to do exactly that, but I'll still need my own animals and supplies."

My father frowned as he stared out the tent door. I suspected he wasn't ready to lose Kadesh. That he'd come to depend on him to help with some of the heavier labor, as well as company for the quiet nights now that he was a widower and alone.

"I will need help on our next raid," my father said thoughtfully, changing the subject. "We plan to attack the Maachathites and get back the camels they stole from us. I could use a good swordsman like you. And a scout. You would be the perfect riding companion, as well as a negotiator if we need one."

"Thank you, sir, but is it wise to go raiding so soon after the hard journey?" Kadesh asked, pouring my father another cup.

"Abimelech doesn't plan to leave until after Hakak's wedding, but Horeb has already sent out spies to scout the Maachathites' location. We're taking stock of our weapons. Discussing our routes. Fattening the camels."

I threw the dregs of the teapot into the small fire behind the women's curtain. There was a good chance Horeb, Abimelech, and my father would arrange the final wedding contract and dates while they were out on the desert—without my knowledge.

Perhaps I was only fooling myself when I hoped there might ever be a chance for me and Kadesh.

Stooping to scrub the pot, I gazed at the fires flickering across the valley of tents. The hearths had always symbolized home and comfort and peace. With my mother gone, so much of the comfort and peace had been replaced by loneliness and sorrow.

When the two men went off to join one of the neighbor's hearths, I took the opportunity to slip away, too, heading out onto the moonlit path.

The air was cool in the evening and felt good on my skin as I walked. Images of my mother, Kadesh, Sahmril, and Leila and Horeb swirled in my head. So much had changed in so little time. Two new moons had come and gone since that tragic day. We had four months left of our season here at the Tadmur oasis, and before we left, I'd be married and chained to Horeb for the rest of my life.

There was gossip that my father could find a new wife by next year. *I must find a time to speak with him, alone.* There were always too many relatives within earshot. I continued walking, pondering my dilemma, but voices from within Aunt Judith's tent brought me back to reality.

Hakak spotted me and darted out to grab my hand. "I'm trying on my wedding jewels, Jayden! Come and see!"

I walked into the brightly lit tent. White linens had been laid out on the carpet. An array of jewels and beads and silver spread across the fine cloth. "They're beautiful, Hakak," I told her. "You're going to be the most beautiful bride in all the tribe this summer."

There was a pang in my chest, knowing how plain I was without my jewelry. How bare my neck felt—how empty my ears and wrists! My fingers hovered over a particularly sheer indigo piece of silk. I pictured myself wearing it, the material slipping over my shoulders, my thick hair falling down my bare back, the shadow of Kadesh hovering close by.

When I raised my head again, Aunt Judith was watching me as I stared at the wedding finery. "When you marry Horeb, you will have so many jewels and dresses, you won't be able to pack them when it's time to move."

Hakak giggled and pulled me next to her, whispering, "As soon as my wedding is finished, we need to start on your trousseau. We can spend the rest of the summer sewing—and you can marry Horeb before we leave for the winter grazing."

Aunt Judith brushed a hand against my cheek. "I will stand in for your mother, dear Jayden. You needn't worry about being without a mother to watch out for you and help you plan all the details. Timnath and Hakak and Falail can all cut fabric and sew, too."

I smiled wanly, but no words would leave my throat.

"You know every girl is envious of you," Hakak added. "Even if he is my brother, I have to admit that he turned out to be quite gorgeous."

"No one can deny that," I agreed lightly as I rose to my feet. "I actually need to find Leila now."

"She and Falail are inseparable," Judith mused, threading a needle to sew the ivory beads to the wedding gown. "I believe they've gone to visit my sister's home. With Hakak's wedding, I think Falail feels neglected."

I wasn't sure if that was actually true. The two girls had sneaked off to the tamarisk groves at our last winter camping spot, and now here at the oasis they were disappearing more often than ever. Perhaps this was Leila's way of grieving for our mother. Or searching for a way to escape the desert life.

"They're probably flirting with potential husbands," Hakak said.

"I suppose I can't do that, can I?" I added jokingly.

"You'd break my brother's heart!"

"Not to mention this old mother's heart," Aunt Judith said as she jabbed her needle into the white linen.

I kissed Hakak and Judith good-bye, then slipped out the door, heading for the far side of the pond. A thick forest of trees grew beyond that, closer to Tadmur, but less than an hour's walk. The meadow forest was probably deserted, but I had to know for myself that Leila wasn't there.

The murmur of men's voices sitting around hearth fires

floated on the still air. I ducked my head as I passed the women's back-door entrances at several tents, not wanting anyone to recognize me and call out. It would be rude not to stop, and I didn't want to sip tea and chat tonight.

Cool grasses tickled my feet. The earth was heavy and lush here. In fact, the water from the oasis underground springs was so deep and clear and fresh I could kneel at its edge and drink straight from it. Ahead, I could see the black hulking shapes of willows, tamarisks, and date palms.

I walked on, getting closer to the groves of palms and olive trees. My stomach fluttered with anticipation, wondering what I'd find. An empty forest—or my sister?

It wasn't long before I heard the sound of laughter, faint music, and mysterious singing. Leaves rustled overhead, mimicking the sound of chattering women, as if the forest was trying to bewitch me.

The sound of a drum came next, and a few steps farther on, a small clearing came into view. I stopped, grabbing the trunk of the nearest tamarisk. Girls I didn't recognize formed a circle, holding hands. Trees grew tall and close together, keeping the women hidden from view, like many-armed sentinels guarding them.

The girls wore flowing silk dresses with low necklines and no sleeves. Bare legs twirled. Under the moon's silver light, their arms appeared ethereal and ghostlike.

The color of their costumes became a translucent gossamer, but underneath the flimsy, sheer dresses, the contours of their figures and bodies could clearly be seen. I shivered at the sight.

The clothing was completely different from the modest dress of the desert women. It was shameful for them to be dressed so provocatively, but it was also thrilling and beautiful, and I felt the same stirring in my body that I'd felt the night of my betrothal ceremony.

And then I saw Leila. My sister stood out, her dancing dramatic and passionate, her beauty unmatched. Falail was next to her, and I watched the silvery material of her dress flow like water about her bare legs.

The girls stepped to the right, then to the left, sweeping their arms like silent snakes. Their feet were so light it looked as though they barely touched the ground, as if at any moment they might float off into the stars.

Hips and thighs quivered as they performed staccato hip thrusts, their fingers fluttering through the air like raindrops drizzling to the earth.

One by one the girls took turns in the center to perform. I found myself sinking to the earth, unable to tear my eyes away. I wanted one of those dresses. I wanted its sensuous delicacy against my skin, reminding me of the silks spread out for Hakak's trousseau. I wanted to adorn myself in one of those lovely gowns and dance for Kadesh in our very own private tent.

My sister stepped to the center, and the other girls trilled their enthusiasm. Soon Falail joined her and the two of them danced together, mirroring each other. The drumming grew louder and wilder. As the tempo increased, Leila and Falail shook their hips in isolated tremors. My sister raised her arms above her head, closing her eyes in the attitude of prayer.

My breath left me. Leila's silhouette looked just like the wooden idol hidden in the camel litter weeks ago.

Now the entire circle shimmied in the final beats of the drums. The singing became a haunting, mesmerizing chanting in my heart and my bones, deep under the earth below my feet. It took every ounce of willpower I had to stop myself from running across the grass and dancing with them.

When the drums struck a last powerful thrum, low and deep like a mountain lion growling from within the earth, every girl dropped to the ground, flinging her long hair across the grass in a vision of color and breathlessness.

That's when I noticed a peculiar flat stone lying in the middle of the meadow. The girls had been dancing around it all this time. I'd been so entranced by their dresses and flying hair and shimmying moves I hadn't paid any attention.

My jaw dropped as I realized the stone was an altar of worship, and on the altar stood the wooden statue Leila had with her on our journey north.

Most disturbing of all, lying next to the statue of the naked, dancing woman was my mother's alabaster wedding box. The sight of it was like a punch in the stomach. So that's where Leila had hidden the statue all this time. My mother's most precious possession lying on a stone idol altar. A knot of anger and confusion rose in my stomach. I imagined our mother devastated, weeping if she knew. "How could you, Leila?" I whispered into the night air.

Before I could move, my sister rose from the grass and

approached the altar. Reverently, she picked up the statue. Holding the figure up to the moon, Leila twirled on tiptoe, then lowered her arms and pulled the statue close to her heart.

The rest of the girls giggled as Leila dropped back onto the grass. She passed the idol to the girl next to her and while the drumming and singing continued, the statue went from hand to hand around the circle.

My face was hot as I lowered my head. This went against everything I'd been taught my whole life.

The drums gave a final beat, echoing back from the trees as the girls rolled onto their backs, giggling and chattering. The murmuring voices were an intimate sound, and I was lonelier than ever. I wanted my sister. I wanted girlfriends, I wanted to be part of them, but if I wore a dress such as these girls wore and danced and prayed as they were doing I would be betraying all that my mother had taught me.

A lone owl hooted overhead, emphasizing the melancholy that swooped through me. Careful not to stir the leaves under my feet, I began to back away.

Unfortunately, this life was what my sister wanted. Even if it meant deserting me and her family. Leila leaving the tribe was terrifying and inevitable, but I needed her help when it came to Horeb, and I needed her to stand up for me when I talked to my father. Without her, I was completely alone in this world. Fate had given us a blow when we'd lost my mother to death. I couldn't lose my sister to the temple, too.

The darkness closed around me as I returned back through the forest. The breezes lifted my hair and cooled my neck, and

I wondered about the life that I wanted, despite my desire to be loyal to my parents and tribe. But what would I risk to get it?

Tripping over roots and stones in the high grasses, I kept my eyes on the distant hearth fires so that I wouldn't get lost. Somewhere in front of me was the pond of water, and I hoped I didn't fall headlong into it.

I listened for the sound of the stream, but all I could hear was my own heavy breathing—or someone else breathing behind me.

The next instant I was facedown on the ground.

A dozen arms held me; legs ran circles around me. Soft giggles floated on the air.

"Leave me alone! Let me go," I demanded, just as a girl clapped a hand across my mouth.

Leila stood over me. "You were spying on us! You sneaked through the trees to watch us."

"You should have been home hours ago," I told her, pushing the hands off of me.

Falail came into view, her long, black hair in waves over her shoulders. "We were safe enough. My mother thinks we're at the tent of Asa."

"Now you're lying to your own mother?" I asked her.

"You're so predictable, Jayden," Leila said, kneeling on the grass beside me. "Do you plan on spilling all our secrets to our parents?"

"Why were you dancing here in the trees?"

Gasps of indignation fluttered like moths.

Another girl came closer, older than the rest. "Next time,

do you want to dance with us?"

"Who are you?"

She was annoyingly serene. "I'm Esther. Though our clans may be different, we still belong to the same tribe—the tribe of women."

"But your dresses—you shouldn't be wearing such flimsy fabric."

The girls laughed at me and I felt silly and prudish. Like I'd turned into an old grandmother when I was only sixteen.

"Dancing with your friends in the moonlight is not immodest," Esther said. "Where else are we going to practice? During the summer months, the tents are always open to catch the breezes. Tribesmen and children constantly walking by all day. There's no privacy at camp, but here we can do whatever we want, wear what we want. We can wear the style of dresses that we'll adorn when we marry and dance for our husbands."

Esther had a point. It probably was more modest for the girls to dance at night in the tree-filled meadow, away from prying eyes and the men around their hearths.

"Jayden," Leila said. "The dancing that Esther teaches us is no different from the women coming to our tent to dance for womanhood or marriage."

"But you wear almost nothing!"

Leila laughed.

"Who's watching but only ourselves?"

"And spies like Jayden," Falail added, poking her finger into my arm. The girls' laughter trembled in the night air.

Their words made me feel completely silly. "I wasn't spying!"

"Oh, but you were," Esther said. "You were also enchanted by the moves and wondered if you could dance with us."

She was so smug I wanted to pull her hair out. The circle of girls' eyes glittered under the moonlight. They discerned that I wasn't being completely truthful. And they were right. I had wondered what it would be like to dance unhindered by long dresses and sleeves. I imagined what it would be like to perform hip drops wearing only a layer of fine silk between my skin and the warm night air, and I shivered just considering it.

But the purple and silvery dresses I'd seen them wearing had disappeared. The girls were wearing their normal clothing once again.

"Where are the dresses you were just wearing?"

Falail lifted the hem of her cloak and I could see the shimmering silkiness hidden underneath.

"Promise you won't tell the rest of the women about our dancing out here," Falail said.

"No," Leila interrupted. "A promise is not good enough."

"You're right," agreed Esther.

I studied her, wondering why I'd never noticed her in the tribe before. Esther was at an age where she should have already been married, and wives had no time for dancing in the groves with girlfriends. There were babies to tend, work enough to keep a woman weary so that she dropped into bed each night.

Kneeling down, the girl took my hand in hers. Her fingers were surprisingly cool and soft. I tried to pull back, but she didn't let go. "We'll let you return home when you swear an oath that you won't reveal the secrets of the grove."

"That's just silly," I said.

"Would you want your clansmen to learn about us and hide in the trees to watch?"

"Of course not," I said quietly.

"There's no rule that we have to dance only with our mothers and grandmothers," another girl called out.

Esther's expression became contemplative. "The freedom and moonlight of the groves is ideal, but perhaps we need to find a place that is even more private. Like the caves in the hillsides closer to Tadmur."

"We should post guards," someone else said. "We don't want our fathers and brothers to come looking and find us."

A chorus of voices began to discuss where it was safest to dance.

"No more talking, girls," Esther said at last, but her eyes were on me. "It's for your own protection that you keep what you've seen tonight to yourself."

"It's settled, then." I pulled my ankles free from the hands that were keeping me pinned to the ground, and lifted my chin.

"Can we trust her?" someone asked.

"Of course we can," Esther said firmly. "She knows there are consequences if she doesn't keep our secret."

"And what will the consequences be?" Falail asked.

The other girls moved in closer, wanting to know what Esther would say, and that's when I realized that there was no formal oath of secrecy; they were only trying to protect themselves. But Esther was formidable and daunting.

"One day I'll take you to visit the Temple of Ashtoreth in Tadmur and watch the priestesses dance. It's like nothing you've ever seen before."

"Don't tell them that!" I told the older girl.

She smiled. "Why? Are you afraid?"

I shrugged, trying not to let her get to me, but I wished I'd left the groves sooner, run faster. "Of course not. But I don't want to see my sister and cousins disappear into the city and never return."

"Even if they will have a better life? An easier life where they'll never be hungry or cold again?"

"How would you know?" I asked her. "What is your father's name? What clan are you?"

"I'm not part of your tribe at all, Jayden," Esther said, her perfumed breath on my face. "I'm from Tadmur. I live at the temple."

I stared at her, unable to hide my shock. Then I grabbed Leila's hand. "You knew all along who she was, and never said a word."

"Your expression is priceless, Jayden," Leila said, teasing and laughing.

Her delight in deceiving me made me go cold. "I feel like I've been purposely lied to."

"That makes two of us," Leila said, reaching out to grip my hand in hers. "I can keep secrets, too."

"Why would a girl her age live at the temple? Where is her family?"

"I have no family anymore," Esther answered. "My parents

are dead, and I'm in training to become a priestess."

I swallowed hard. "Leila's family is not dead," I said pointedly.

"Oh, Jayden." My sister sighed. "You don't know anything about the temple or life there or of what you speak."

I turned to stare at her. "Do *you*? Truly?"

"I know enough, and I will learn more." My sister at least had the decency to look guilty and as I stepped closer, she backed away. But I wouldn't let her go. I put my arms around her neck and whispered, "Please don't leave me. I couldn't stand it."

Leila's arms tightened. "I'll just have to take you with me, dear sister."

"You know I can't. Father needs me. And so does Sahmril."

Leila let out a choked sob. "Jayden, stop saying that. You know Sahmril is gone forever. You *know* that. Don't torture yourself with hope."

A flicker of anger flared in my chest. "I *will* find her."

Leila shook her head at me. "You always talk of Father and our sister, but you never mention Horeb."

I bit at my lips, pretending to brush off her comment.

"You don't want to marry him, do you?"

I shrugged casually, denying her words. "I don't want to discuss it right now."

"Of course you don't," Leila said with a sigh. "I can see right through you, Jayden."

"Tonight isn't about me. It's about you."

"Jayden, I don't think you will ever understand how I feel about being trapped on the desert. Trapped in a life I don't want. Wanting to fly away, to dance, to live as a real goddess, not a myth from a thousand years ago. It's not a dream. You hate your life, you're stuck with a man you don't want to marry, and yet you will do it anyway. But *I'm* going to have the life I *want*."

There was a bitter taste in my throat as we stared at each other.

Finally, Leila said softly, "I know you don't love Horeb. You love someone else."

"I do *not*—"

My sister put her finger to my lips. "I know who it is, and I promise to keep your secret, Jayden, if you keep mine."

There was no more denying it, and protests were useless. I chewed on my lips as she gripped my hand, stepping even closer so all I could see were her dark eyes in the moonlight.

"Your secret for my secret," she whispered.

Finally, I nodded, embracing her, not wanting to let her go. When I stepped back onto the path, I watched with envy as the girls linked hands and ran back to camp.

My feet sank into the soft grasses while the implications of the promise I'd made to keep Leila's secret sank into my mind. Dancing in the groves was just one more step closer to my sister leaving our family forever.

As much as I hated the confidence I was being forced to keep, I also hated being thrust out from these girls—and banished to the torture of my looming marriage with Horeb.

I raced through the grove toward home, my head swimming with the images of the dancing girls, and how much I yearned to be a part of them. My loneliness was childish. All I needed was my cousins, my aunt, my father, and our camels. But I was lying to myself. There was something else I wanted. *Someone* else. And I couldn't have him. Every other girl was living the life she wanted, dreaming her dreams, marrying the person she adored.

I now carried a terrible secret, and if anyone discovered my dreams of Kadesh, I'd be ridiculed and shunned from my family. My family had always been the most important part of my life, and I could not disappoint my father.

As I ran, the image of the sculpted female carving floated before my eyes. Leila's statue of the goddess, arms raised in prayer, her figure sensuous and unearthly as she silently danced. An image of the beautiful woman every girl wanted to become.

"I need you, Mother, oh, how I need you!" I whispered into the grim darkness. "I don't understand what I'm supposed to do! Tell me! Please help me!"

My face was burning as I pressed my hands against my cheeks. I wondered how far my sister would go to worship the goddess idol.

13

It was a week later, and the tent of Abimelech was crowded with friends and relatives for the bridal dressing of Hakak. Her wedding day had finally arrived, and seven embroidered dresses and veils were waiting for Hakak's dances, the seven dances she would perform for the guests and Laham tonight, just before midnight. The dresses that told a girl's life story, and ending with the final dance to show her love and devotion for her new husband right before he carried her off to the marriage tent.

Leila and I gathered with the other women. I swept a hand across the silks and linens that made up the beautiful wedding trousseau and shivered at the silken indulgent splendor of it all. Last summer, Aunt Judith and Hakak had shopped the markets of Tadmur for the silks and beading and jewels they would need when my cousin became engaged to Laham.

And now, Hakak couldn't stop smiling, and I realized with a pain in my chest that my cousin was in love with Laham and looked forward to her life with him.

My mind went to Kadesh. I didn't even have to be within sight of him for this inexplicable desire to rush over me. My stomach ached. This hunger for him was wrong, and yet the fever in my heart told me it was right. Marriage to Horeb would be filled with riches and misery. A life with Kadesh would make me smile every day, just like the joy on my cousin Hakak's face whenever she mentioned Laham's name.

Aunt Judith brought out several bowls of henna dye that she'd already mixed for decorating Hakak's body with images of flowers and symbols of the desert.

My older cousin Timnath served tea and the traditional sugared dumplings. Symbols of the sweets of marriage. "May your life with Laham be sweet with love and pleasure, and may you always be blessed with bread and the bounties of life," she said.

"I'm too nervous to eat," Hakak declared, giving everyone another hug before plopping down in the middle to be pampered and dressed.

"Laham will get his fill of sweet Hakak tonight," someone teased, and I watched my cousin blush furiously. The tent filled with gentle laughter as my grandmother beckoned Hakak to come toward her. Seraiah stooped over as she spread out a rug for the bride.

"Lie down," Grandmother Seraiah told her. "And we'll begin the washing."

Aunt Judith returned through the rear door, holding a bowl of sweet-smelling liquid. "We are blessed with the scent of flowers here in the summer lands."

Hakak leaned back while our grandmother Seraiah dipped my cousin's long hair into the bowl to wash it.

"But," Falail, her younger sister, teased, "getting married in the summer lands meant Hakak had to wait so many extra months to lie in Laham's arms."

Hakak tried to suppress a blushing smile, but she wasn't successful. "I'm glad the time has finally come. Whether I smell good or not."

Aunt Judith combed and dried her daughter's hair, then oiled it with perfume.

Hakak closed her eyes while the rest of the girls painted her hands and feet and face with the henna dye.

"I'll decorate your ankles," I volunteered, picking up one of the thin brushes. I dipped it into the reddish-brown dye and created swirls and flowers and tiny rosebuds on each of Hakak's toes. With each brushstroke my own marriage to Horeb loomed closer. If I could stop time and never leave this moment I would. What would happen when it was my turn to be dressed in wedding finery and jewels and silks? What if I couldn't bring myself to dance for Horeb, or ran away from the marriage tent?

"Jayden!" someone cried out as my shaky hands tipped over the bowl of henna.

"I'm sorry," I gasped, quickly mopping up the liquid from

the corner of the rug. "I'm sorry, Aunt Judith. Let me clean this up."

"A little henna stain will only remind us of this joyful night for years to come," Aunt Judith said.

I stepped away from the tent and poured the remains of the liquid into the sand, watching it fade into the earth. It was already early evening and the smell of roasting lamb spiced the air. Heat glistened far on the horizon, marking the boundary between the fertile oasis and the dry desert.

The last of the second full moon at the oasis rose with a ghostly glow, and I finally realized the source of my melancholy. Forevermore, I would mark my mother's death and the beginning of womanhood as one event.

Aunt Judith silently approached and slipped her arm through mine, giving me a squeeze. "You're quiet today, my little Jayden. Missing your mother, yes?"

My aunt's words threatened to bring on my emotions, but I merely nodded and smiled. I didn't want to spoil Hakak's day of happiness.

Judith squeezed my waist. "We all miss your mother terribly, especially on special days such as these. Do you have any word on Shem's family and Sahmril?"

I shook my head. "I pray they are still alive. And eating milk and honey in the land of the Chaldeans. Dinah even took—"

Judith put a finger to her lips. "I know," she whispered. "Don't speak of it. Miracles still happen."

When I thought of Dinah, it was revenge I deliberated, not miracles.

Dusk fell as the wedding guests gathered. Dressed in her finery, Hakak's dark hair shone in the light of the torches as Laham placed his gifts of jewelry on her arms and neck and wrists. She was truly stunning now, dripping with the robes of a perfect bride and the fidelity of a devoted husband. I bit back bitter tears, wishing that my future could hold one single moment of pure joy like this.

Laham clasped a band of gold coins around his bride's ankle as Hakak lifted her dress, her bare foot resting on his knee. The watching women trilled provocatively. Laham took Hakak's hand and led her to the raised chairs on the dais while everyone clapped and cheered. Both fathers had taken care of the marriage contract earlier that day, and now it was time for celebration.

Along the grassy area, long rugs and a mountain of pillows had been placed for comfortable eating. Women had been baking for days. There were sugared cakes and dumplings, dates and bread, mounds of steaming rice, and huge platters of spiced and roasted meat.

The eating and talking went on for hours. I ate slowly, trying to avoid both Horeb and Kadesh. I could sense their eyes following me, watching me from afar.

I was startled to glimpse Esther, the girl from the temple, mingling on the outskirts of the crowd. I wondered if Falail or Leila had invited her. It seemed inappropriate when this was a private tribal affair.

Across the crowd, I watched Horeb stop to speak with her, and they chatted and laughed for several minutes. What were they talking so avidly about? Seeing them together was beyond irritating, and a flush creeped up my face. Was I annoyed because she looked as regal and beautiful as a princess in her exquisite linen dress and hair adornments, or because Horeb was ignoring me?

A few minutes later, he was talking with another girl, and then another. I was humiliated to have my betrothed pay such eager attention to other girls, even if I did hate him. The rest of the wedding guests were sure to notice. In fact, it appeared as though he flirted on purpose, just to provoke me.

All at once, Horeb's face lifted, staring intently at me from across the wedding crowd. The pulse in my neck jumped. My feet were stuck to the ground like I'd grown roots as Horeb smiled and raised his cup of wine. He mouthed the words, "To Jayden, my betrothed."

We stared at each other and then Horeb threw his head back and gulped down his drink, wiping his mouth with the back of his hand. His grin mocked me as he led Esther and two other temple girls to one of the tables loaded with food, urging them to eat and stay for the entertainment.

I slowly turned away, my face hot. Suspicions rushed through my head. How did Horeb know these girls? Did he secretly go to the temple for their rites and ceremonies—after he had spent nights in Tadmur at the drinking houses? Sick to my stomach, I moved away, trying to find a place to hide.

Unmarried girls had to be careful with whom they spent

time, but as our tribe's future ruler and prince, Horeb was free to do as he pleased. If questioned Horeb would merely say that he was being a polite host at his sister's wedding, which only added to my infuriation. He didn't care that he was demeaning me.

After the guests had been dished a plate of food, everyone settled on rugs and carpets to eat and chat. I kept wandering, forcing myself to smile at friends and acquaintances, the excitement of the party surrounding me, the din of conversation rising in the air.

I wasn't hungry, my stomach a bundle of nerves. Instead, I ran errands for the cooks, fetched a blanket for an elderly woman who was chilled, played with some of the babies and toddlers so their mothers could enjoy their meals in peace.

When the drumming began, the crowd moved back to find a place as spectators and make room for the entertainment. My grandmother Seraiah was the first to rise. I sank to an empty rug on the grass, grateful to focus on something new. As my grandmother's hips rose and fell she winked at me with her trademark sly grin.

Aunt Judith and Laham's mother were the next to get up and join Seraiah in the ancient womanly dance. Judith's hip scarf of coins and beads jangled as she circled the perimeter of watchers. Timnath followed, picking up where her mother left off; then Falail and Leila came next.

Hugging my knees to my chest, my attention was caught up in their beautiful hip and arm movements, the intoxicating thump of the drums, the swaying of the musicians, and the crooning of the singer. I was safe in my corner of the crowd, alone on my rug, and that's how I wanted the rest of the evening to continue until I could leave and crawl into bed.

Not moments later, my sister and cousins pulled me to my feet to dance with them. "Come, Jayden, you're next." I shook my head, mortified to dance before such a huge crowd of spectators.

"Oh, no, I can't," I said, pulling my hands back.

"You're part of us now," Timnath told me. "And you can't say no to blessing your own cousin on her wedding day."

"Being timid won't get you a husband either," Leila said, grabbing my other arm.

"But I don't need a husband!"

Falail gave me a stern look. "Even though you aren't looking for a husband, you and Horeb are betrothed. He'll be shamed if you don't dance for his sister. Everyone will notice."

But I want to dance for someone else, I thought, and felt my face heat up.

The drumbeats throbbed through the soles of my bare feet. My ears filled with the high-pitched trilling of the women in the crowd as the girls pushed me to my feet and brought me into the wedding circle with them.

Leila slipped her arms around me, quickly fastening her own silver-and-green beaded earrings into my ears. "For tonight. You shouldn't have to dance naked of any adornment."

A tear sparked at the corner of my eye as I embraced her. "Leila, thank you."

As the drums and dancing surged, the night became a blur

of sparkling jewelry and fiery torches under a huge, bone-white moon. Once I forgot about myself, I became lost in the swirling figures of the women of my family, laughing with them, loving the chance to be a part of the women's world.

Every time I caught Hakak's eyes, I saw pure happiness in her face, even though she spent most of the evening keeping her eyes demurely fastened to the ground as she tried not to show how pleased she was.

The drums slowed and began a new beat. It was time for Hakak to dance for her husband.

Laham's eyes lit up as his bride moved down the steps of the dais. She slipped off her outer robe, revealing one of the beautiful flowing embroidered gowns she'd painstakingly sewn. Her hips began a series of slow, smooth circles. Hakak's hands fluttered like dancing butterflies and the jewelry she wore sang a melody of its own against her neck and arms. It was magical, and I felt my own body yearning to move again.

Over the course of the next hour, Hakak changed one by one into the seven gold-threaded dresses. At times the moves were slow and sensuous, then fast and frivolous, playful and flirting. One day I hoped I could dance like this, and I wondered if my cousin's superb dancing came merely from practice—or were the moves inspired by love?

This was one night when the men were not chased off. I caught glimpses of my father and Uncle Abimelech behind the wall of hanging drapes where the men stood to watch their women dance. I saw Chezib, Aunt Judith's youngest boy, peeking through a crack in the tapestry rugs, his mouth open as the twirling colors and flying hair of his older sister flew past him. I reached out to tickle his toes poking out from under the bottom of the rug, and he giggled.

"Come on," Leila said a moment later. "It's time for the candles."

At the foot of the dais Aunt Judith was lighting dozens of tall, milky-white candles.

"Here, Jayden," she said, handing me two flaming candles. The creamy, white candles twinkled in the darkness, the tallow melting in rivulets.

Holding a candle in each hand, I followed the women as we circled Hakak for the last time. One by one each woman briefly danced with the bride, escorting her a few steps closer to her groom waiting at the top of the dais.

When it was my turn to dance with the bride, I kissed Hakak on the cheek. "May your life be long and forever joyous."

"When you marry Horeb," Hakak whispered in my ear, "we will truly be sisters."

I nearly dropped my candles, and I couldn't even begin to form a reply. The soft, leering face of Horeb caught my eye as he peered over one of the partitions, and I stumbled on the hem of my dress. Hakak's words froze my heart. I could not imagine myself dancing for Horeb. I couldn't imagine my wanting him as she clearly wanted Laham. I felt a lurch of bile rise from my stomach. I couldn't do this, didn't want this. I realized truly for the first time how completely wrong this betrothal was.

"Careful, Jayden," my grandmother said behind me. "Or

you'll light yourself on fire with that flame."

A sob thickened my throat, and my eyes were swimming with emotion. At that moment I would rather have died than marry Horeb.

Seraiah's hooded eyes gazed at me. "Are those tears, Jayden?" she asked softly.

"Tears of happiness for Hakak," I quickly answered, dropping my head.

My grandmother frowned, and I suspected that she didn't believe me. How foolish I was to show my emotions!

When I glanced up again, Kadesh was standing in my line of vision across the grassy pavilion. Hidden behind the folds of his foreign, rich cloak, his dark eyes followed me as I danced and whirled and moved my hips. My limbs trembled as I understood that Kadesh had placed the hood purposely over his face so that he could gaze at me unnoticed by the rest of the guests. I was unable to wrench my eyes away from him, too. I wanted to sink into his soul, melt into his heart, dance just for him for the rest of the night. The heat of the candles made me dizzy. The mysterious connection between us left me breathless.

Envy filled my throat as Laham took Hakak's hand. Together they circled the dancers and guests as the tapestry partitions opened to let them through. The women trilled when Laham lifted Hakak into his arms and kissed her. She wrapped her arms around his neck as the high-pitched clamor, the joyful shouts from the crowd, filled the air with a tremendous, happy noise. The uproar continued as Laham carried his bride into the wedding tent where they would spend their first week together, just the two of them.

I snuffed out the flame of my candles with shaking hands. My insane longing was almost a tangible, palpable sensation. I needed to get away. I glanced quickly at Kadesh, and then caught Horeb staring at me through the crowd of guests. My gut tightened.

I ran, darting through the rugs and empty platters of food and children playing games. Laughter and music roared about me. I was light-headed from the dancing and the heat.

"Jayden," I heard Seraiah call after me, but I didn't stop. I couldn't run fast enough, my legs shaking, my face dribbling hopeless tears.

I finally staggered into the safety of my own camp, catching my breath, horrified at being caught watching Kadesh by Horeb.

Squatting at the hearth fire, I stirred the cold ashes, melancholy sweeping over me. "There are times when a woman's emotions are higher and fuller than any other," I whispered, repeating my mother's long-ago sentiment. Knowing I could never talk to my mother about Horeb made my eyes burn with grief. I missed her smile and her comforting arms more than ever. Most of all, I missed her wisdom and ability to make my world right and safe.

The bushes near the tent rustled and I lifted my head, dropping the stick to the ground. My belly lurched as Kadesh ducked under the tent's canopy.

"You shouldn't be here," I told him feverishly. "There will be talk, and I fear that someone will see you."

"I understand, but please, grant me a moment. I need to speak with you. Because I've come to tell you that I'm leaving." Kadesh quietly dropped to one knee even as he respectfully averted his face.

My head jerked up. "What?"

Kadesh finally lifted his face and gazed straight back at me, his cloak spread about him on the hearth carpet. "I waited until after the wedding, knowing what it means to you and your family. But there's a caravan from Edom camped outside the oasis. They're headed south and willing to let me ride with them. Early tomorrow they depart."

"Edomites? But they robbed us!"

"Not all are thieves. These are good men. I know them. Please try to understand. I must return to my uncle, now that I am well. I'm sure he's presumed me dead by now. There are affairs I must take care of."

I lowered my head, fighting the thousand jabs of sorrow in my heart. "Then you must go," I whispered.

"It might be many months before I can return," Kadesh went on.

"Then I wish you God's safe blessings in your travels," I managed to say.

His eyes, so steeped in mystery, settled on my face. "Is that all you wish, Jayden, daughter of Pharez?"

I wished so much more. Above all I wished I could tell him what was in my heart, even as it tore into pieces at the news that he was leaving.

"May God's faith be boundless in your heart," I added,

choking on the words.

"Nothing more than that?" he asked slowly, and I knew he wanted things from me that I couldn't give, that I wasn't allowed to give.

But suddenly, I shifted forward, throwing away caution in an impulsive burst. "What do you wish me to say?"

His hand reached out to touch my face, and I leaned into the warmth of his palm, my resolve melting. "Just tell me that you will be here when I return."

"You know I've been promised to Horeb."

Kadesh gave an impatient laugh. "Yes. Your entire family reminds me of it nearly daily."

"But betrothals can be broken," I let slip, speaking my greatest wish before I could stop the words. My hands flew to my face, heat rushing up my neck. "I mean—Kadesh, it's so difficult. My entire family is involved—my uncle, my aunt, the dowry herds . . ."

"Let me speak to your father, then!"

I shook my head. "You're still a stranger here, and to talk to my father so soon after we've met . . ." These were not the words I wanted to say.

Kadesh leaned in even closer, and I ached all the way to my toes with his presence, his smell, the nearness of his face just inches from mine. "The moment I saw you that day on the bluff—I knew we were meant to be."

"Kadesh, please don't say these things." Quickly, I put up my hand, afraid. "Someone will hear you."

He caught my hand in his and my heart thudded against

my ribs as he kissed each one of my fingers, then pressed my palm to his mouth. I held still, not wanting the moment to end. When he lifted his head again, he said, "I'm going to come back for you."

"But what if . . . there is so little time . . . Horeb . . . the wedding—"

The sounds of the wedding party fluttered toward us. More drumming, singing. Laughter. I smelled ripe fruit and roasted lamb. Woodsmoke covered the stars like gauzy linen. I should have gotten up and returned to the celebration before I was missed, but I didn't move.

Kadesh's face came closer and his warm, spiced breath rushed across my cheeks. "Let me seal my promise to you with the vow of my love," he whispered, and before I could say another word, he pulled me into his chest, and his lips covered mine with a soft, urgent intensity I didn't think was possible. I couldn't speak; I couldn't move, even though my body was on fire, every part of my skin exploding in a frenzy of pleasure. My eyes closed as he lifted me against him. I rose in his arms, and we were tightly sealed together, kissing fervently as my hands slid along the rich fabric of that marvelous cloak and then wound up and around his neck.

Hot, lovely darkness dipped and swirled. I tasted his mouth and smelled the spicy fragrance of his skin as he kissed me again and again.

All at once, he swept his cloak around me, enclosing us together in a private warmth against the cool night air. When I felt his heart pounding against my own breast, it was as though we had become one person, one soul.

"Please don't leave," I said against his lips. "What if something happens to you? I couldn't bear it."

"I won't let the desert claim me, beautiful Jayden. Not when I know you're waiting for me."

I started to speak again, but he shook his head, drowning the words in my throat as he proceeded to kiss my lips, my face, my eyes, my neck. Time seemed to stop. The stars fell from the heavens. When he stepped back I was breathless, as though I'd been turned inside out.

We stared at each other, his hands tight around mine. His face held a joy I'd never seen before, and I wondered if my expression mirrored his. "Hold out your hand," he whispered. Kadesh untied the pouch at his waist and brought out a handful of the pale yellow frankincense, pouring it into my palm. "Frankincense tears for my love. To pledge my commitment to you."

"Oh, I can't take these, Kadesh!" I said automatically, as my thoughts focused on his words, *my love*.

"Take them. They'll bring a good price. Don't hesitate to sell them if you need to while I'm gone." He gently smiled as if not wanting to worry me. "I hope circumstances will never be that desperate. That instead these nugget tears will oil your hair or perfume your feet, bringing memories of me to your mind. But I have another gift for that purpose."

He pulled a silver anklet chain from the depths of the leather pouch and held it up to the moonlight. Feathery strands of silver dangled like lake fronds. "I brought this from my home. My grandmother gave this chain to me when she left this world. She told me to save it for the woman who would be my wife one day, and then pass it on to our daughter. I give it to you, Jayden, as a promise of our future together."

I held the jewelry, studying the anklet's etched silver. The symbols of Kadesh's mysterious clan had been carved into the surface of the wide silver band. An image of a tree with a myriad of gnarled and twisted branches, silhouetted by the halo of the sun on the horizon of the sea. I'd never seen trees like this before, and I knew immediately what grew on those unusual trunks.

Kadesh bent down and lifted the hem of my dress to tie the silver clasp around my ankle. I was glad my dress was long enough to keep it hidden. When he stood I kissed him again, knowing I was now fully the betrayer of my betrothal for what I was doing, but I didn't care. I had committed an infidelity, but in my heart Kadesh was the choice I should have made. Could have made—if I'd been given a chance.

He kissed me in return, more urgently, as if time was running out. I clutched at his arm, my hands shaking. "I'm afraid for you. For us. Your home is so far away. A whole world away."

"It's a journey I know well, Jayden. One I've taken a hundred times."

"What if something happens to you? What if you *can't* come back?" I stopped the words I'd almost added: *What if I never see you again?*

"Believe what I say, Jayden," he said, lifting my chin so our eyes would meet. "The road will be long as I leave, but short and swift when I return. *Believe it.* Believe me."

Kadesh lifted my hands to his face one last time. His mouth lingered on mine, holding me for that fraction of eternity, as though I could glimpse into the future. "One day, Jayden, you and I will be under the wedding canopy," he whispered.

His words spoke of a heaven I wanted more than life itself. At that moment, I'd risk everything to make that dream come true.

"If I don't return before your family starts the return journey south to your winter lands," he whispered against my ear, "the Edomites of the red canyon lands will know where I am. They will help you find me. Remember that."

Our fingers slowly drew apart, a sob caught in my throat, and within moments Kadesh's beautiful dark robes swirled away into the black of the night.

14

Hardly a moment had passed before Horeb appeared out of the darkness. His face was ghostly and macabre in the campfire's dying light. "It's a sign of insanity to talk out loud to yourself, Jayden," he said to me while my mind roared with the impossibility of his appearance not even a breath after Kadesh's departure. "Does your mind go mad after the long journey under the hot sun?"

I stood there, rigid, terrified. Where had Horeb come from, and why was he here? Most unthinkable was the alarm sounding in my gut at what he might have seen before he made his presence known.

"Please leave," I said, darting inside the tent and hoping he wouldn't follow. "I don't want to speak to you right now."

He shoved his way through the doors of the tent and leaned

over me, his lips curling. "Is that any way to talk to your future husband?"

"You're not my husband yet," I managed to spit out. He took a step closer and I willed myself not to flinch as he grabbed my arm.

"It's only a matter of time," he said, his eyes taunting me. He jerked his chin toward the direction that Kadesh had just taken. "Someday you'll be in my arms, as you were just now in the stranger's arms."

He stared hard at me, intimidating and powerful. It was clear Horeb would never love me, that he wasn't capable of love for anyone but himself. His eyes were full of lust for every girl in camp, even my sister. It was the only explanation for his indifference to the sight of Kadesh's embrace.

"Let me go!" I commanded, trying not to show fear.

"Why? So you can run after the stranger? Your father will not be pleased with the news I bring to his ears, dear Jayden."

"You know nothing!" I bluffed.

Horeb tightened his hold, digging his fingers into my flesh. "I've seen enough. Perhaps I should take care of Kadesh right now—tonight." His mouth turned up into a cruel smile. "It's been a long time since I killed a man in battle. He and I fought once. But this time I will win."

"No!" The cry slipped out before I could stop it.

Horeb laughed, reading my face. "I've got another idea," he said, and his breath was hot against my cheek. "After I slit the stranger's throat, I'll come back and take you into the forest far from camp. After that, nobody else will want you again."

His threat horrified me. "How could you? You, who are supposed to love and care for me."

"You'd better watch your mouth, my betrothed." His fingers pinched me harder and my legs crumpled, but Horeb held me up, his grip bruising my skin. If he tried to force me to do anything, I would kill him first. The realization gave me a peculiar sense of strength as well as terror.

I lowered my chin, worried I'd given too much away. Worried I'd endangered Kadesh's chance at an escape. "He's long gone, so keep your dagger in its weak sheath."

Horeb laughed and pushed me away. "The stranger is a fool to journey into the southern wilderness during the fiery part of the summer. The caravan he travels with is actually a band of escaping thieves. Once the wells finish drying up, they'll all die."

"You're lying," I said, gulping down my fear.

"If you're lucky, you won't have to worry about ruining your father's reputation. You'll probably never see your precious stranger again."

With that, he departed, snapping the doors of the tent shut. I grabbed the center pole to steady myself. This couldn't be happening. Horeb would never release me from the betrothal now, if only to spite me.

15

A drizzling rain tapped the roof of our tent as I lay in bed, my knees pulled tight to my chest, trying to stay warm. A wolf howled mournfully in the dismal night, and I couldn't stop shivering. A bed of dying orange coals gave off the only light in the room; even the moon was hidden behind a bank of gray, smothering clouds.

Hakak's wedding party had concluded at dawn the same night Kadesh had told me good-bye—and Horeb threatened me. It had already been a month, but worry over Kadesh often wakened me in the middle of the night.

Hakak's newlywed happiness with Laham was a sliver of envy in my heart. Sometimes I swore the faint smell of leftover wedding food still lingered, just to torment me.

Rolling over, I buried my head under the blankets as Leila snored softly next to me. While I listened to the familiar rustlings of the tent, I closed my eyes and imagined Kadesh lying beside me, his lips on my neck, his arms pulling me protectively close, keeping me warm, keeping me safe.

A tear snaked down my cheek, a tight band of worry making it hard to sleep, wondering if Kadesh was safe. He'd promised to return, but the hot summer months were treacherous, the Empty Sands as far away as the moon.

Like a serpent, Horeb slithered into my thoughts with his poisonous words, his terrible threats. I wouldn't be trapped by Horeb. I wouldn't allow him to kill the man I loved. Kadesh had told me to believe—and I had to do exactly that if I loved him. I sat up, quietly moving the blanket off my legs. Sleep was gone, and I couldn't put off this task any longer.

I slipped my fingers along the silver chain around my ankle, grateful for this tiny piece of Kadesh, giving me hope.

Cautiously, I crawled across my bed, careful not to disturb Leila. When I reached the hanging partition and pulled it back, I was surprised to see the shadow of my father rising from his own bed in the far corner of the main room. Within seconds, he'd shoved his dagger into his waistband and was out the tent door. Quickly grabbing a shawl, I threw it across my shoulders and followed him into the night.

He crouched over the hearth fire, blowing on the embers. The air was damp and smoke hung over the campsite like fog.

"Father," I whispered.

He whipped around, pulling out his knife, and then quickly lowered it when he saw me. "Jayden! You startled me. What are you doing awake?"

"I must speak to you. Mother—"

He put up a hand and shook his head. "I don't have the strength to speak of your mother tonight."

"But I must—"

"No!" He cut me off. Then he lowered his voice, staring into the fire. "There is too much on my mind, Jayden. Go back to bed. Please."

I stared at him, refusing to obey for the first time in my life. "It's a matter of life and death, Father."

He lifted his head and gave me a sad smile. "Everything comes down to that, doesn't it? My camels. My children. My wife. Death and loss has come to our family in every way imaginable."

"Oh, Father," I whispered, the same sharp ache deep in my heart. "I know, and I'm so sorry."

His eyes seemed to gaze beyond me, pensive, sad. "Go on, Daughter, if you won't return to bed. What is it? What do you look so frightened about?"

"You're going to leave on the raid to the Maachathites soon, aren't you?"

"I'm a poor man, Jayden. I must go and try to reclaim the camels that were stolen from us." He paused. "And sell a few animals to replace your lost jewels." I was surprised he remembered. "They'll need to be replaced if you are to marry Horeb."

"That's what I've come to talk to you about, Father—"

The words stuck in my throat, but I forced myself to say them, all the while ignoring the expression of forlornness on my father's face. "Father, I—" I paused, and then whispered. "I can't marry Horeb."

His head jerked up, and there was shock in his eyes. "What?"

"I don't love him. It wouldn't be proper. I can't, Father. I won't."

My father smiled wanly and touched my cheek with his rough hands. "Jayden, love will come in time."

"No, Father. It won't. I'm sure of this."

I darted a nervous glance into the blackness that surrounded us. Someone could be listening, hidden in the shadows, yet able to hear every word we said. I lowered my voice and leaned close, the brush of my father's beard tickling my cheek. "You don't understand. I despise Horeb."

Astonishment crossed his face. "But he's your cousin."

I shook my head. "No, Father, he's not. In name, but not blood. Despite your and Abimelech's vow as blood brothers."

"My contract with Abimelech is the same as true brothers. We swore oaths to each other. Binding until I die."

"Do you not see the things Horeb does?" I brushed a hand against my eyes, willing myself not to break down into tears. My father only saw black and white, right and wrong. And promises he would never break because it was unthinkable to him. It was an honorable way to live, but surely there were exceptions when people's hearts and lives were at stake? My mother would think so.

The yearning for my mother was like a physical pain. If she were here everything would be different. I ached for her arms around me, her heart of understanding, her words of comfort.

"Has he mistreated you?"

"In words only, but he's made threats."

My father stared at me, bewildered. "I'm sure you misunderstood, my dear. Give Horeb a chance. He's young and headstrong, but ready to marry you and create a strong, kingly family for our tribe. After losing three camels on our journey here, we're in a desperate situation. We can't travel during the rainy season over so many months without doubling or tripling the herd. You know that, Jayden. To go anywhere in the coming year without at least four camels per person, death would almost be a certainty. It's imperative that we receive camels from Abimelech for your bride price."

"I can't." I swallowed past my parched throat, clenching my hands together. "What if I were to tell you that I love another man?"

He frowned and shook his head. "No. This should never be."

My pulse pounded in my ears. I wished we could talk inside the walls of the tent, where our voices would be muffled. But Leila was asleep inside, and I didn't want my sister to hear this conversation.

"I'm sorry, but it's true, Father."

"Who is he? Who is this boy you think you love?" my father demanded.

I was sure that any moment my heart would leap straight through my chest.

"Speak, Daughter. Do I know him?"

"Yes, Father," I whispered. I took a deep breath, not knowing what to expect after I told him. "It's Kadesh."

"KADESH?" He reared back as though struck, and then violently shook his head. "The stranger!"

"He is not a stranger, Father. He saved your life! The Edomites, remember—"

"Silence, child. No, this cannot be." He held up his hand, though his eyes told the truth: he did remember, and he'd trusted and confided in Kadesh. "Has this stranger betrayed my trust?" he asked, his voice low and intense. "Has he violated you, made you say these things to have his way?"

"*Never!* He's a good, honorable man. You know that yourself!"

"But he's not part of our tribe. We know nothing about his family, or his ways, or his beliefs."

"I'm sorry, Father, but"—I clutched the folds of my shawl, very cold and very afraid—"Kadesh loves me and I love him in return." My father shook his head again, not looking at me. "I didn't seek to love a stranger," I continued, "but I've felt it now for nearly three months. We had a connection between us from the first day we met, even though I tried to banish it. And so has he."

"These things do not just happen. Is there some reason he wants to claim you, some scheme?" My father stroked his face, confusion tugging at his brow. "And yet, the stranger has shown nothing but loyalty. He helped us across the desert, forsook his own wealth and business."

I touched his arm, hope rising. "Father, for weeks I've tried to fight my feelings, but they only grow stronger."

"Has he told you he loves you in return?"

I nodded. "A month ago. The night he left."

My father studied my face. "That does not bode well for him. How can a man leave the woman he professes to love? He shouldn't have made promises, and then left."

"But you know that Kadesh was traveling on family business when he was injured, and needs to return to his uncle. He's coming back for me. He gave me his vow."

"Jayden," he said, his eyes softening. "Don't let your innocence get in the way of reality. Many men have promised the same thing, never to be seen again."

I fought to stop the sudden, desperate tears. I hated the doubts he was trying to plant in my heart. "He wouldn't lie, Father. And he gave me this bracelet as a promise of his love for me." I showed him the anklet around my foot, which glittered in the hearth fire.

My father groaned when he saw it, burying his face in his hands. "Don't be taken in by gifts and flattery. Horeb is the right husband for you, and he's willing to give a generous bride price." I couldn't believe my ears, or my father's greed; that camels were more important than my fear of Horeb, or my dead heart toward him. "Besides, you know I can't take back my promise."

I shook my head, frantic. "Is saving your honor worth more than *my* feelings?"

Stunned silence followed and I instantly regretted what I'd said.

"Enough!" The hobbled camels near the tent shifted in their sleep, grumbling at the sudden noise. My father lowered his voice, but it was strained with tension. "This is my final word. The marriage to Horeb must be fulfilled."

"But, Father!" I begged.

"No! My contract with Abimelech is my honor. Kadesh is a stranger from a land I know nothing about. You have no dowry, and Abimelech and Horeb are willing to forgo that. Kadesh might appear as though his family has money, but I can't be certain. And he left without saying a word to me about wanting you to be his wife. Or making any promises."

"But I know he intends to. He wanted to—he told me." The words drowned in my throat. Too late, I realized that I shouldn't have stopped Kadesh from speaking with my father about his intentions toward me.

My father reached out to stroke my hair, and his voice turned wistful. "Even if he does return, it might be without any bride price at all. I can't afford to wait for a promise that is only a dream. I'm sorry, Jayden. Perhaps the marriage to Horeb should be sooner. Once you're married, you'll forget Kadesh and these girlish dreams."

The bag of frankincense bumped against my back where I'd tied it into my shawl. My father wasn't convinced Kadesh could provide a good bride price, but the frankincense proved otherwise.

Opening my mouth, I abruptly closed it again. The spice was a dangerous possession. I had to tread carefully. Kadesh had told me to use the frankincense if I was in danger or desperate, but he trusted me to use it wisely.

My father watched me curiously. "What is it?"

I took a step backward, sobs choking my throat. "Nothing, Father."

Horeb wasn't a thief, but if he could he'd demand the frankincense as part of my dowry. It was time to spend a few of those precious yellow nuggets before they were taken from me.

I turned away from my father's eyes. His words were meant to soothe me, but to marry Horeb before the summer was over sickened me. I staggered around the fire hearth to return to the tent. Kadesh would never be able to make it back that fast. Two thousand miles was an entire world away.

My stomach heaved at the fear that I may only have a few weeks left before I was married, an imprisonment I could only escape by death.

"Jayden," my father called softly. "Please understand my concerns for you. I don't want you to spend months or years waiting for the stranger, only to never see him again. Your mother would be so pleased and happy for you and Horeb. With him as tribal king, it is an even greater honor than we dreamed when you were a babe." His voice grew sadder, and I sobbed when he invoked her name. "If Rebekah were still here, she would eagerly be sewing your wedding clothes. Now go back to bed and let's forget our angry words."

Tears flowed over my face, mixing with the drizzle of rain. I wiped my mouth and tasted dirt on my lips. My shawl was damp and my toes chilled in the grass and mud. I would have to marry Horeb now, but a seed of rebellion began to grow in my belly. And after the confrontation with Horeb, who'd threatened me, I was afraid of what he would do to me.

There was only one thing left to do. I had to go into the city of Tadmur and purchase protection.

16

ays later, I seized my chance. The day was hot
and airless. Leila was gone somewhere with Falail,
Aunt Judith was taking an afternoon rest, still
worn out after the wedding, and Hakak was busy setting up
her household. I rarely talked with my other cousins or old
neighbors. They were engrossed with small children and endless cooking and weaving to furnish their tents.

And my father and Abimelech were spending the day in
raiding plans and strategy.

I made my way through the winding, narrow paths of
the oasis, a long, rectangular area with tents spread as far as I
could see, probably two or three hundred of them baking in
the humid heat after another rain we'd had the night before.

Date palms shaded my head at first, but when I left the fertile oasis and continued on the road to Tadmur, it turned dry

and dusty for another hour's journey.

I fingered the frankincense nuggets I'd buried deep in my pockets, loving the woodsy, pungent scent they released. Frankincense was like owning a secret treasure. After my confrontation with Horeb the night Kadesh left, my fear toward him grew daily. My kitchen knife wasn't enough anymore, and my father would never be able to afford to buy me a long dagger or even a short sword.

I didn't know what treachery Horeb would plan to ruin my reputation or what favors he might demand to earn my silence.

Once I got through the city gates, I went straight to the marketplace.

The stalls were crowded with people, squawking loose chickens, and youngsters running in and out of their mother's skirts. I held back, walking through the maze of shops, looking for the weaponry market where one could buy not only knives and swords, but spears of every size, slingshots, and bows with sheaves of sharp-tipped arrows.

At last I found several knife-and-blade shops in a row, spending a few minutes at each one inspecting their wares from a distance, as though I were just a casual observer. Finally I saw a knife that intrigued me and I pushed my way through the shoppers.

Holding my breath, I ran a finger along the edge of the weapon lying on a spread of blue cloth. The sharp blade of the dagger glittered even in the dim light of the market shop.

"Girl!" a harsh voice rang out.

I jerked my hand back, pinching my finger on the knife's

edge. A drop of blood oozed and I stuck my finger in my mouth.

"Bah!" the shopkeeper scolded, his scruffy beard wagging. "Now you'll warn everyone away, telling them that my shop is dangerous."

I shook my head. "It was my fault, but do you have a bit of rag to bind it?"

He sighed, leaning down to pick up a ragged piece of scrap cloth from a basket and thrusting it at me. "Now go on. Girls have no business in a weapons shop."

I serenely tied the rag around my finger, not moving.

It was strange to be so calm even as I contemplated the purchase of a personal weapon.

I sensed the power of it in a way I never had before. Owning something of value, the frankincense, gave me freedom and choice. The pale yellow-and-white nuggets were like coins, only better, much more rare—even rarer than gold.

The shopkeeper roared again, throwing up his hands. He raised a hairy eyebrow and jabbed a finger at me. "Girls don't buy daggers. I'll get out my kitchen knives for you to look at if you're determined to dawdle here."

"I already own one of those. I'm in the market for a dagger." I picked up the knife I'd been looking at, ignoring his mirth as he fell onto a wooden stool. The knife was cool and smooth in my hand. I closed my fingers around the hilt, welcoming the lightness of it, the rounded edges of the simple handle. It fit my palm perfectly. I thrust my arm forward and the knife sliced the air easily. I felt a sense of immense power wash over me.

There were other daggers in the shop, laid out in rows on linen cloth, two tables' worth. Some of them were more beautiful than this one, knives stamped with etchings or detailed handles, but I couldn't afford elegant or expensive.

The man placed his meaty hands on the table's edge and grinned, showing off stained and rotting teeth that only filled half his mouth. "And do you have money?"

I glanced about to make sure no one was watching, and then opened my palm. "Would one of these suit your tastes?" I said boldly, showing a frankincense nugget.

He gave a low whistle. "Now where did you get that?"

"All you need to know is that it's real."

He didn't refute the validity of the pungent spice as the smell wafted to his nose. "But my knives are worth more than one little nugget."

"How many do you want?"

"Eight pieces."

"The dagger is ordinary and simple," I pointed out. "And the smallest one on the table."

He stroked his face. "But this little dagger is my sharpest, thinnest blade. Five is the lowest I can go."

I shook my head. "You are a thief. The knife isn't worth more than two at the most. My father warned me about shops like yours."

The shopkeeper narrowed his eyes. "Is that so? Where's your father now?"

"He's ill, sir, and sends me in his place," I lied. "But I suppose you have so many customers you don't need my business,"

I said as though it made no difference to me. "I'll go elsewhere. Good day."

Without waiting for a response, I ducked under the tent overhang and took several steps away, shading my eyes as though searching for the next knife merchant.

"Girl!" the man said sharply. "Wait. I'll make you a deal."

I turned back slowly, making sure my expression was indifferent.

"Four nuggets."

"Two," I countered.

"Three. And that's my final price."

I nodded. "Deal."

I opened my palm, filled with the largest three of the ten yellow nuggets Kadesh had given me.

"All right, then." His grubby hand reached out to snatch them up, but I held back, making him wait, staring him down.

One by one I dropped the frankincense pieces into his outstretched hand, picking up the knife with my other hand at the same time before he could change his mind. Placing the dagger inside the band of cloth tied to my waist, I closed the folds of my shawl around it.

Before he could speak again, I moved away, disappearing into the crowd.

As I passed through the crowded market, I wondered if anyone could tell from my face what I'd just purchased. I wanted to gaze at the blade again, revel in the peace of mind it gave me. Briefly, I closed my eyes, dreaming of plunging the sharp, dagger-thin blade into Horeb's heart if he tried to hurt me.

Shouting children played sticks, whacking one another on the shins as they darted down the streets. Somebody bumped into me, trying to pass, and I stepped aside, too nervous to stay in Tadmur any longer. I was growing tired of the noise and commotion and just wanted to get back home. Dusk was beginning to stretch its long fingers across the roofs of the city, and it would be an hour's walk back.

As I made my way to the city gates, I daydreamed that Kadesh was at my side, his voice in my ear, his hand on my back. I wanted to entwine my fingers with his warm, strong, slender ones. I shook my head, knowing I had to stop doing this. If I indulged in this sort of fantasy every day, I'd be insane by the time Kadesh returned. Briskly, I moved forward again, stopping where Tadmur's main road intersected the maze of the marketplace.

Two old men eyed me as they sat in the shade of a palm playing Twenty Squares.

"Girl," one of them called, jiggling dice in his palm. "You'll get the fever wearing that heavy cloth. It's so hot you could roast a slab of lamb on the bricks of my porch."

I tried to ignore them, not wanting to engage in conversation, but I realized how conspicuous I must be, wearing a wool shawl in the heat. I was dripping with sweat, but I wouldn't remove the shawl until I had a chance to hide the knife under my dress.

The man's companion rolled his eyes, snapping his fingers to urge his friend to shoot the dice. "Bah. Just one of those dirty desert people."

The first man let the dice fly across the board. He picked up his tokens to reinsert them into new spaces, and laughed, his gaze shifting away from me.

This was why I hated city life. Perhaps I was poor, but I wouldn't trade my life for theirs, not for a hundred gold pieces. Villages were dirty, noisy, and overcrowded; garbage in the streets, the rank smell of outdoor latrines poisoning the air. It was so completely different from the cleanliness of the desert, the solitude of the sky and mountains, and the utter freedom to do and go wherever you wanted. It *was* a hard life, but I wouldn't trade it for Tadmur or Damascus or Babylon.

Sucking my water bag dry, I trudged toward the public wells. The marketplace crowds were thick and clogged, the place busy with last-minute shopping before the evening meal.

My shawl was getting heavier, the late afternoon scorching and oppressive, but as I made my way through the throngs of people, I looked up and my skin prickled. The Temple of Ashtoreth stood before me, rising up on its mound, its circling walls and gold gates growing immense the closer I got. Astonishment at its beauty overtook my senses. I could see immediately why Leila was so drawn to it.

At the base of the temple, a series of tiered, glazed steps ran upward on three sides, coated with an indigo color as if a splash of the deepest ocean had been painted here. On top of the mound sat the square edifice itself, the sanctuary of the goddess.

Even though I couldn't read or write more than a few simple letters, I recognized the Akkadian word for the goddess's name written across the top of the temple columns. *Ashtoreth*. Seeing it there in bold symbols gave me a sudden chill.

The temple structure itself was a pure, glittering white. Four columns rose against a perfect, dusky-blue sky as the sun lowered. The temple's beauty was in stark contrast to the one-story mud houses and shops in the rest of Tadmur. The road directly surrounding the Temple of Ashtoreth was smooth and hard packed; no swirling dust and beggars here.

The vast temple compound with its high walls stretched down the main avenue as far as I could see, where it connected with the Temple of Ba'al.

For a moment, I rested at the well, watching the flock of women bringing up their buckets, chattering in the late afternoon about supper and children and chores. Two of them were discussing the autumn festival scheduled soon at the Temple of Ashtoreth, and my ears perked up.

"Good crops this year," said a woman with long braids hanging down her back.

"We had more rain than usual, but now it will dry out over the next month," her friend added, wearing a red headscarf tight around her forehead. "My husband said I could take two bushels of melons and apricots to the temple to thank Ashtoreth for a good harvest."

"'Then come right home,' my husband told *me*," the first woman said with a laugh, deepening her voice to mimic her husband.

"And why would he be worried?" the second woman said, lifting her eyebrows to tease.

The first woman lowered her voice, glancing about, her braids swinging. "Don't you wish you could see the gold and silks of the priestesses?"

"Your eyes would burn out of your sockets," her friend laughed, shoulders shaking. "Those priestesses don't wear anything underneath their silks when they dance for the men."

"That's what my neighbor told me! Can't imagine. One husband is enough for me—sometimes too much."

They laughed again and paused to fill a second bucket, pulling on the ropes.

I was thinking about the meaning of their conversation, feeling disturbed, when a hand at my elbow made me jump. I found myself gazing into the brown eyes of Esther, the girl I'd met from the groves. Startled, I said, "What are you doing here?"

Esther shrugged. "Shopping in the marketplace. Like you and Leila."

I blinked in surprise. "What do you mean? Leila isn't here. I came alone."

"Oh, I would have sworn I saw her a little while ago. She was talking to one of the priestesses in the temple courtyard."

Leila hadn't mentioned a word to me about coming to Tadmur today. "I'm sure you're mistaken."

Esther's shiny hair swayed about her hips. She looked clean and cool. She smelled good, too.

I forced a smile to my lips. "Are you headed to the oasis to visit?" I said, pretending to be friendly.

Esther smiled back, an amused expression on her face. "No,

I'm headed back to my temple apartment. If I see your sister I'll be sure to let her know you were here."

"There's no need. I'm sure she's not here," I said, smoothing my sweaty palms along my dress. We parted ways and I watched the girl step through the gates and into a tree-lined courtyard that led to the marble steps. "Oh, Leila," I said under my breath.

My head shot up as I realized the two women I'd been eavesdropping on were now watching me, eyes narrowed under the lowering sun. The woman with the headscarf tsked her tongue and began to walk away. Her friend paused, glancing at me from under her lashes. Under her breath, she said, "You look like a tribal girl, not like her." She jerked her head at the back of Esther stepping gracefully up the marble temple steps. "Go back to your camels. Stay away from the temple."

"But you—" I began.

She cut me off. "We take our offerings like all the good citizens of Tadmur, to appease the government and the goddess in case she brings wrath upon our heads. But you don't want the life of a priestess. You don't want to know the things I've heard."

I frowned. "What do you mean?"

She shook her head, walking away. "Go home to your tribe," she repeated, then hurried off, steadying her bucket as water sloshed over the edge.

"What a strange conversation," I murmured to myself, but it only confirmed my fears about what my sister might be doing, and the warnings from my own mother and grandmother.

After filling my waterskin at the city-center well, I passed through the gates of the city and picked up my pace.

Night was filling in the holes of the world as I skirted the pond near the oasis and made my way along the narrow paths. Tethered camels snorted and stamped their feet as I passed.

When I got to my own tent and ducked inside, the place was empty, the fire cold because it had never been lit. I raced through the rooms to rummage through Leila's personal things. With a sinking heart, I saw that most of her possessions were missing. Her clothes, her sandals, her kohl, her jewelry—gone! I sat down on the floor with a painful thump, my head reeling, an eerie numbness settling in my chest. Esther had been right; Leila was at the temple.

My father's camel was also gone. I'd seen the warriors gathering on the edge of the camp far toward the horizon. Masses of camels and the men organizing, packing, making their plans. My father must be among them. I had no idea they were leaving so soon. Leila had chosen the perfect time to run away.

I couldn't walk back to Tadmur in the dark now; I'd have to return in the morning. It was going to be a lonely night, filled with anxiety and dread. Isolation closed in tight around me. I had to find Aunt Judith. I wasn't going to spend the night by myself.

Besides, I hoped to find my father and say good-bye. Snapping the doors shut, I briskly walked to Aunt Judith's tent. The camp was dark, with many of the women dancing at someone else's tent, or visiting a bride-to-be to admire her trousseau. I'd arrived too late and missed them all.

When I came closer, I heard rustlings up ahead. I stopped to listen, barely breathing, touching the new long dagger in my belt, grateful to own a significant weapon.

There was silence again. The nearest campfire was at least a five-minute walk. As the last to arrive in the valley, our tent and Abimelech's tent were on the outskirts. I could see each fire hearth light twinkling over the sea of tents spread on the valley floor.

I stood rooted to the path, listening, thoughts tumbling inside my mind. As I turned to walk back home, rocks crunched under my feet and I stopped again, ears strained for any sound. Only starlight and a sliver of moon shone overhead. There was nothing but the soft moan of wind and the rustle of rodents somewhere off to my right in a patch of flowering shrubs.

After four more paces, I stopped again. I'd heard that same moan once more. And this time I was certain it was not the wind. "Is someone there?" I asked, my voice sounding timid.

The moans grew louder and I turned, aware now that the strange noise was coming from Aunt Judith's tent.

I retraced my steps and opened the door of the tent, stepping inside the familiar home with its rich rugs and furniture. The smell of newly made yogurt spiced with cinnamon hovered in the air.

"Aunt Judith?" I called. There were no food preparations left out. Everything was clean and tidy, as though the owners had been gone for several hours.

Crossing the floor, I peered through the opening in the wall partition that led to the rear rooms. One was a storage space with food baskets and clothing bundles and camel saddles. The other was Judith and Abimelech's sleeping room.

Hesitantly, I parted the curtain and saw the form of someone lying on the raised bed. "Uncle Abimelech?" Seeing him gave me a jolt. He should be with the raiders, conducting them across the desert with drums and bugles and cheers and wine at the start of their journey. He was the leader of our tribe. It made no sense that he was lying here in his bed on this night of all nights.

Softly, I called out, "Are you ill, my uncle? Can I help you?"

He didn't answer.

I wondered now about the rustling noises I'd heard earlier. The sounds of someone moving stealthily about the tent, but I doubted the strange sounds had come from Abimelech if he'd been asleep all this time.

"Uncle Abimelech?" I said again, more urgently. As I reached out to place my hand on his brow, I knew in my gut that something wasn't right. His skin was cool to the touch. In fact, he was too cool, chilled. "Speak to me," I said into the shadows. "Where is Judith? I'll fetch her and we can find your physician."

Still no answer. The corner of the bedroom was dark without a window and it was difficult to see. I ran back to the main room and found a candle, lighting it with an ember from one of the nearly dead coals.

With the wavering candle, I returned to the back room. The feeble moaning I'd heard earlier had ceased now. Uncle

Abimelech was so unnaturally still I began to tremble as I placed a hand on his arm and held the candle up with my other hand.

"Oh, dear God in heaven!" There were three slices in Abimelech's chest. Three distinct stab wounds. Blood had puddled in a red, dripping mess, flowing down his chest and arms.

A wave of nausea came over me, threatening to knock me off my feet. My eyes swept the bed and his body.

I turned and noticed a cup that had fallen from a table onto the floor.

Someone wanted Abimelech dead.

17

My mind was whirling so fast, I could hardly seize a clear thought. I set the candle on the table and reached down to pick up the cup from the floor. It was empty, but there was residue inside, something other than water.

Chills ran down my neck. A few moments ago, I'd heard his moans. He must have been dying as I'd passed the tent. Were those rustling sounds his attackers leaving?

Leaving when they heard me coming along the path.

Quickly I searched the room again, but there was no knife to be found anywhere. When I lifted my eyes, I saw a sliver of starlight shining through the rear doors of the tent, which were slightly apart. It made sense that the person who had stabbed Abimelech had gone through these doors.

Were they still here, waiting to see if Abimelech was dead? Waiting to see what I would do?

My heart beat wildly as I tiptoed to the doors and opened the flap. It was crazy to stay here a moment longer. I needed to find someone and get help, but my limbs were so heavy I felt like I was dragging myself through a sea of sand.

When I peered out, the light from a lamp shone in my face as Horeb came toward the tent from the opposite direction—from the direction of my own tent. "Jayden, my betrothed," he called out. "I was just at your tent looking for you, but the place was silent as a tomb."

His eyes scanned me, taking in my entire figure, but I couldn't respond.

Instead, I stood in utter silence, my mind racing. Who would want Abimelech dead? Who would have motive enough? Who had the most to gain?

Horeb came closer and reached out to grip my arm. I didn't move, wanting him to trust me, even as I tried to remain coherent. "Don't you want to know why I went to visit your tent?"

I swallowed and nodded feebly.

"I went to your tent, Jayden, so that I could get my good-bye kiss before we depart for the raid."

I smelled the sour scent of wine on his breath, and I recoiled. "You've been in the drinking houses in Tadmur," I said, and he tightened his hold on me. "You're not thinking clearly."

"Oh, I'm quite clear in my mind, and it's clear why you're here looking for me. We're alone," he went on, grinning at me. "We could have a taste of our wedding night right here, right now."

His words made me want to throw up, but I tried to hold myself steady.

"We can have a proper good-bye," he continued, "before I lead the tribe out to face the Maachathites. Nobody will ever know."

I wanted to spit in his face. Instead I said, "I'm just trying to be a good clan leader's wife and bid you a good journey and a safe raid."

He shook his head. "You came to my home because you wanted to kiss me, just like you did your stranger. Am I right, Jayden?"

His tone puzzled me, the voice of someone who wasn't completely sure of himself. Or perhaps the problem was that Horeb wasn't sure of me? Maybe all this time Horeb had been waiting for *me* to come to him. Maybe he didn't know how to woo or court me. We'd both been thrown together by our families and had no choice in the matter. That's why he fought Kadesh: to prove himself not only to his entire family but to me.

Kadesh's attention had caused Horeb to appear weak and inferior. Powerless. Unwanted. Second-born sons always took second place.

"You are the prize, Jayden," he said, his voice rough. "And I will win. Nobody will stop me. No matter who they are."

I allowed him to get closer, to trust me, and I could taste his hot, terrible breath on my face. The smell of Tadmur, but something else, perfumed and womanly, lingered on his clothing. "You've been at the goddess temple," I whispered. "You know you don't have my heart, so you must go somewhere else."

He staggered back, obviously more drunk than he was admitting. "You and my father both," he said bitterly. "He always loved Zenos more. Always bragged about how kind and noble Zenos was. Abimelech reminded me every single day that I should have prevented my brother's death. That I wasn't quick enough with my sword, that I should have been watching our backs. Zenos was the heir and I was not. My father told me what he'd lost, what our tribe had lost. Except that Zenos never had the courage to say he didn't want the position. He didn't want his time taken with government and politics. Hearing people's complaints and settling feuds. I've always known I could be the better king. Even Zenos told me that."

My hair stood on end as the meaning of his words became clear. I tried to take a breath in the stifling, hot room. "What are you saying, Horeb? Did *you* kill your brother on that raid?"

"No!" he shouted hoarsely, suddenly pinning me to the tent wall, his eyes glittering with drunken rage. "I didn't put the sword to Zenos's throat; the Maachathites did. That's the truth."

"But you left him to die on that hellish cliff, didn't you?"

Horeb stared at me glassy-eyed. "I saw my chance to take the role of prince he didn't want—and I—I left him there."

"Was he alone when he died?" I asked, trembling with horror as I imagined the awful scene.

Horeb's voice grew raspy, but there was a cold, chilling edge to his tone. "I couldn't look at Zenos's face as he died, bleeding all over the sand. He begged me for water so I left him the last of my bag and returned to our army—after the Maachathites took off with a hundred of our camels. Mostly your father's."

"But, Horeb!" I groaned. "You could have brought Zenos back to camp for medical attention. Our men followed the Maachathites only half a day's ride into the desert before the battle began. How could you have left him there alone? Zenos might have lived!"

Horeb roared at me, and I flinched, fear running like ice through my veins. "Our tribe will be better off with me as leader. By next winter we'll be bigger and stronger as I carry out my plan to bring the tribes of Jetur and Kedemah as our allies. Richer and safer. Isn't that worth the cost?"

I shook my head, an unspeakable sorrow filling me. "But now you will lead with blood on your hands."

"All desert men have blood on their hands! It's called honor. Many kings kill their brothers or cousins to avoid a coup. Or suffer poison in their food."

"A king can rule wisely and fairly and justly—and with love!"

Horeb swung his head from side to side, holding me fast to the partition wall. I couldn't move. I hardly dared to breathe after his alarming confession. "What a fool you are, Jayden! Maybe it's ignorance. You're a naive girl. But I can teach you to lead with me. You have no problem breaking our betrothal with the stranger. You have it in you to lie and cheat—just like me. We will make a powerful kingship together."

I stared into his eyes, which were blurred by hungry ambition. His words cut me to the core. It was true. I had lied. To my father, to Horeb, to the rest of my family. "No. I am not ignorant." I looked over at Abimelech, and knowing what I did about Zenos's death now, I was certain how Abimelech had just died. "You had a choice on that battlefield, Horeb. A choice I've never had. I was meant to find your murdered father in his bed," I whispered. "Nobody else would want Abimelech dead. Nobody but you *needs* Abimelech dead."

"You're too smart for your own good, little Jayden."

"You don't want to wait until we're married to partake of the marriage bed, either. You want to cheat that. To take what isn't yours yet. You can't even wait until your father dies before taking power. You want it *now*. Is that why you killed Abimelech tonight? So you can lead the tribe to the Maachathites and take all the glory?"

He bent over me and I tried not to recoil as his lips brushed against mine. "You think you have all the answers, but you know nothing. My father's undying love for Zenos is only a small part of it. It doesn't even matter anymore that Zenos died."

My stomach dropped to the bottom of my feet. "What are you talking about?"

"Tonight, before leaving to meet our army, my father told me that this battle would be my only chance to lead out to war. He said he wasn't sure he could trust me to always do the right thing. My father said that *you* were raised to have a sound mind and spirit. Integrity, he called it."

"Me?" My breath caught. I was surprised that Abimelech had said these things about me and my parents.

Horeb snorted with derision over the memory of his father's words, and I could see the pain behind his eyes. "My father told me he'd had several private conversations with your stranger, Kadesh, and recommended that we form an alliance with *his* family. That it could bring us unimaginable wealth. He said that between our two tribes we could rule the desert between Damascus all the way to Sheba and beyond."

"How did he plan to accomplish this?" I replied, struggling to hide my surprise.

"He told me the idea came to him the night I fought Kadesh in our little sword competition. He said if you and Kadesh married it would be an automatic union between our two tribes. He would appoint me as Kadesh's general, but that you and he would rule as king and queen."

"What?" I was so taken aback I nearly fell over. My mind whirled with this new information. "And—and did he speak with Kadesh about this?"

"He'd been deliberating the idea for weeks and making his plans. He intended to begin talks and negotiations when Kadesh returned."

"So that's why—that's why—" I couldn't even speak.

Horeb's lips became a sneer, and his face bore a sheen of sweat in the dark tent. "I told him I wouldn't let him. That *I* would marry you before the stranger returned. The leadership and kingship rightfully belonged to me. To *me*! I've fought for it, nearly died for it, and killed my brother for it."

There was a burning in my chest as I listened to Horeb's devastating and shocking words. After all the guilt he'd suffered over Zenos, and the plans he'd been making to forge other desert treaties and protect our tribe . . . and then to hear his own father tell him he wasn't good enough. That he would dare to give the tribe to me and Kadesh in order to form a bold and brilliant alliance, virtually throwing away his son in the process. No wonder Horeb was wild with resentment over Kadesh and wanted him dead.

"We fought and argued for hours—"

"And you were drunk," I interrupted, pointing to Horeb's blade.

He gave a short laugh. "My father was a fool to confide his plans. He thought I would just bend to his will and let him give my throne to someone else. Well, he was wrong! He was wrong and I am right!"

"You killed your own father," I said, the blood in my veins curdling like rancid yogurt. "Just like you left Zenos, your beloved brother, to die."

"How does blood on my knife prove anything? Who is to say it's not the blood of a hyena?"

"There isn't a dead animal anywhere near your tent," I retorted as I brought out the finely shaped clay mug from my pocket. "But there *is* a cup filled with a sleeping draft so you could come in here undetected and kill him while he slept in his own bed."

Horeb's arrogance died and his black eyes turned to stone, just like his heart.

"And *you* are here at the scene of the crime," I went on. "I am witness to the noises of the night as well as the sight of your father lying on his bed in a puddle of still-warm blood. I have the cup. And I've seen your knife with my own eyes."

"You are here, too. Holding the cup." Horeb's voice was calculating and terrible. "You will be next, Jayden—unless you do exactly as I say."

"If you kill me, everyone will know. It won't be hard to deduce what happened here. Two dead bodies in your tent, with wounds that match your knife."

He gave me a mild sneer, still arrogant about his position in the tribe. More so now that Abimelech was dead. I was the only one who knew the truth. And that was the most dangerous position of all to find myself in. "I don't need to kill you right now, Jayden. But someday, after we are married and I've been given the tribal staff and crown. But first, I will kill the stranger, Kadesh, so you can never leave. I will own you, body and soul. Don't doubt me for a moment."

Fingers of panic snaked down my back as tears flowed from my eyes. "What does Kadesh have to do with any of this?" I said, trying to deflect Horeb's wrath from the boy I loved. But I already knew the answer to that question. Uncle Abimelech had permanently destroyed what was left of Horeb's sanity by telling him he would dethrone him and give the tribe to me and Kadesh. After the torture of leaving Zenos to die, Horeb would do anything to ensure his title and position.

"Your stranger is my blackmail against you. I saw you the night of Hakak's wedding. I heard and saw everything. I could have you stoned at daylight for infidelity. All I have to do is say the word. Instead, I will take your silence. Your silence—or Kadesh's death—and one day your demise as well, when I don't need you any longer." He paused and I felt his eyes raking over me. "I wanted you at one time, but you turned away from me, too."

"Horeb—" The pain in his voice was palpable. I fought to stay upright, knowing he could do everything he'd threatened. I had no recourse, nothing but his word against mine.

"It's too late. Abimelech is dead, and I can decree what I want. Starting right now. I'm our clan and tribal leader by default as of this moment."

"Please don't do this!" I pleaded.

He tangled his hand through my hair, pulling back on my neck so that my face was thrust straight upward at his own. "Kadesh's life for your life, Jayden. That's all it comes down to. A simple decision. You were going to have to marry me anyway. We just do it now."

My mind reeled with the horror of what he'd told me. I had to show this proof to someone, and I had to do it as fast as possible, before Horeb destroyed the cup and buried the pieces in the desert never to be found again.

"No, it doesn't come down to that. I have this as proof of my witness!" I hissed, holding up the cup. Before he could respond, I shoved Horeb back against the tapestry partition, turned, and ran out the door. Cutting around the edge of the tent, I raced headlong down the rocky path.

18

Without a torch, I stumbled along the paths as I weaved around empty tents. The night was dismal. A partial moon hovered bitter and white on the horizon.

Horeb had chosen the perfect night for murder.

I picked up my pace, trying to ignore the stones slicing my bare feet. The snuffling sound of rodents came from the brush near the grove. An owl hooted overhead, wings rushing eerily. Wild dogs barked to my left.

I could hear Horeb behind me, breathing hard. He'd been drinking so much, his reflexes were slow, but his legs were longer than mine so he was catching up. I darted left and he cut me off. I veered off the path and a moment later I was running away from the camp, hoping I could get lost in the brush and sand dunes.

Barely a trail now, the grasses along the path grew taller. I was headed toward the groves of the oasis. Perhaps I could hide in a tree or lie flat in the grasses, and Horeb would run right past me.

My mouth was dry. A terrible ache began to gnaw at my side. I stumbled, falling hard to my knees, and cried out without meaning to.

Behind me, I heard Horeb pause, then turn to come directly at me. I got up and took off again, slamming straight into a tamarisk tree in the dark. The excruciating pain sparked lights in my eyes. Skin scraped off my arms and face. My body began to throb with a mass of cuts and bruises as I slowed, toes burning, blood trickling down my arms and legs. A sudden, deep darkness sat directly in front of me. I'd completely lost my bearings.

Turning once more, I ran up a strange, unknown slope and then rushed down the other side. My very next step took me off the edge and I was falling through air, and then landing with a splash into the oasis pond. Water rushed up my nose and sucked at my dress, dragging me under like hands were gripping my ankles. My long hair wrapped around my neck as if it would choke me. It was deeper here than I expected, and I panicked when I couldn't touch the muddy bottom with my toes.

I clawed back up to the surface, choking on the water, and finally managed to pull myself out, grabbing desperately at the rushes and grasses. Rolling over, I struggled to catch my breath, and tried not to cry. My head was screaming with pain and I couldn't tell if it was blood or water trickling down my cheek.

The next moment a hulking shadow loomed up the rise. A burning torch appeared next, and I let out a yelp at the safety of the light illuminating the darkness.

"Jayden!" a deep voice called out.

It sounded so much like Kadesh that I cried with relief at being safe in the arms of the boy I loved. Was it possible he'd returned? That made no sense—it was much too soon for his return—but my ears were filled with water, my lungs burning from gulping down too much pond water so that I was disoriented. Crawling on my hands and knees, I got up one last time and lurched forward, straight toward the torchlight—and straight into Horeb's chest.

Fear seized me so violently I was sure I would pass out. *"You."*

"Who else were you expecting?" Horeb pushed me back to the ground, and then put a foot on my chest to hold me down.

"Let me go," I cried, but my voice sounded weak and pathetic. My throat was raw and I could hardly speak, let alone scream for help.

"You're my wife," he muttered.

"I'm not your wife," I sobbed. Everything screamed inside me to run, but the fall into the pond had seared my lungs so I couldn't catch my breath, let alone get up and start running again.

"But you will belong to me," he countered, and laughed

again as if I were stupid. "You already belong to me."

Horeb, with knife in hand, tried to grab the cup from the pocket of my dress. Stupidly, I fought him, and the next instant his sharp blade slashed against my neck, slicing a line straight down and along my shoulder. I screamed and felt the spurt of blood. The world turned upside down and I staggered on my knees, holding a hand against my neck to stop the bleeding.

Horeb swayed over me, large and fierce, his eyes scouring my body in the torchlight. My wet dress clung to me, outlining every line and curve. "Take your eyes from me!" I shrieked. "How dare you?"

"I'll dare as I please," he said, his words slurring as he used both hands to grab at my collar and rip my wet dress straight down the middle. "A betrothal is as good as marriage, so I have every right to look at you. And do whatever I want with you."

"No dowry or bride price has been exchanged, only promises," I said hoarsely. "And promises can be broken. Wait until my father hears of this!"

"It'll be too late by the time he does." Horeb's deep, drunken laugh was eerie in the stillness of the night. Before I could tell what he was doing, he reached down and ran his fingers along my belly and hip. I jerked and lashed out with my fists, pounding him in the chest as I tried to push him away.

With both hands, he threw me hard against the ground and my head cracked once more. My teeth slammed together, and tears gushed down my face.

"You're a stupid girl thinking your father can rescue you. You are mine and everyone knows it. Besides, the men have departed, and there's no one left to hear your cries. No one left to tell your lies to either."

"My father wouldn't leave without telling me."

"Scouts came back early with information about the Maachathites. Our enemy is within three days' ride, so they had to leave tonight instead of dawn. And your father is a desperate man."

"Why aren't you with them on the raid, then?" I whispered hoarsely. "Or did you prefer to stay behind and fight a girl half your size? You're a murderer, Horeb! It won't look good for you when the tribe finds Abimelech's body—and I tell them you attacked me."

Horeb slapped the back of his hand against my face, knocking my head into the earth again. My jaw cracked, and I heard myself whimper.

Straddling me so I couldn't move, he lifted the cup stained with poison and crushed it between his hands. Shards of pottery rained down around us, and with it any proof of Abimelech's murder. "I intend to satisfy our clan's revenge against the Maachathites, but I'm playing the part of a dutiful husband-to-be. I leave as soon as I rescue you. At least that's what I will tell our families and the others. You were distraught, you were lost, and I was the only one here to save you. Besides, my camel is the fastest of our herd and I'll easily catch up."

His breath was hot and his body heavy against mine as he continued to restrain me. "Now, Jayden, before I leave for my triumphal raid, tell me good-bye like a proper wife. You owe me a kiss. Like you kissed the stranger."

"No!" I cried, jerking my head away. Kicking my legs, I tried to push him off or knee him in the groin, but he had my lower body pinned. "Let me go!" Reaching up with my free arm, I swung at his face. "I hate you, and I always will."

Just as fast, Horeb slapped me across the mouth for a third time, so brutally I was sure my brains had come loose. The next instant the torch rolled off into the mud, the flame sputtering to nothing.

"You won't have to worry about your fool stranger wanting you after I finish with you here. The betrothal will be binding forever once I take you. I'm king now and I decree it."

I fumbled for the dagger at my thigh, trying to reach it, my last chance for escape, but his chest came down on me, knocking the air from my lungs as he stopped me from grasping the knife.

Horeb grunted, his meaty hand sliding higher on my thigh. Before I could move again, he'd found my dagger and unsheathed it, holding the weapon above my face. The knife glistened under the moonlight as Horeb ran the flat of the blade along my cheek. I went still as cold marble. "My wife doesn't need a knife. I'll take this dagger and keep it safe."

And then his mouth came down on mine and I tasted the bitterness of him and thought I'd be sick. His lips seemed to be everywhere, his sweat slippery on my skin. The odor of cheap wine filled my nose, making me nauseous.

"You should get used to your new title. My scouts brought word of the Edomite caravan," Horeb went on, his mouth moving down my neck to my chest as he held my arms fast.

"When I head in that direction, my men and I will overtake them in a matter of days. The stranger will be dead before the new moon."

"You're a liar—Kadesh will kill *you* first."

I flinched, sure he would hit me again, but instead he held up my newly purchased dagger once more and studied it, smiling like a mad man. "I brand my camels with the mark of my clan to show the world they belong to me. To make sure you won't stray from my bed, I'm going to mark you with the brand of Horeb."

Swiftly, before I could even attempt to yell again, he proceeded to make a series of small cuts across the top of my chest and along each of my arms with my very own dagger. My skin was bloody and raw when he finally finished, and I could barely speak for the pain.

My fingers searched the grass in vain for the torch, for anything I could hit him with, but there was nothing.

"The blood of Zenos, Abimelech, and your own have now bonded us forever," he said, his mouth pressed to my ear, his hands all over me.

Clawing at the grass with a desperation I'd never known before, my hand finally closed around a rock. As Horeb tore at the remainder of my dress, his legs pinning mine, I tried to relax my limbs to trick him into letting his guard down. I felt him ease up on his weight as his mouth moved down my belly. In the darkness he didn't see my arm rise overhead. Swiftly, I hit him as hard as I could in the back of the skull with the rock.

Instantly, my dagger dropped into the grass as he went

limp. I pushed at him, grunting as I slowly rolled his arms and legs off of me. I waited for a sign of consciousness, but there was none.

Heaving myself to my knees, I crawled inch by inch across the grass, eyes watering, grappling for my knife, but I couldn't find it.

Forcing myself to rise again, I staggered to where Horeb lay and searched through the grass. At last my fingers closed around the blade of the dagger, the hard handle in my fist. I'd never felt anything so comforting in my life.

Horeb's lips had fallen open. He was unconscious. It would be so easy. "You wanted to bond us with blood and scars," I said. "Now it's your turn."

Crouching over him, I took the tip of the blade and touched it to his skin. My hands were shaking, and sweat dripped into my eyes. I was terrified beyond reason but wanted revenge more than I wanted anything else.

I began to cut across Horeb's chest and stomach. The knife was so sharp it was easier than I'd imagined. Bubbles of blood left dark streaks on his skin.

With every slash I felt more powerful, in control of my own life once more.

Horeb was now scarred, just like me. At least on the outside. I felt a sense of satisfaction when I sat back and stared at my handiwork, but revenge was short-lived. Because now I wanted to crawl into a hole and let someone bury me alive.

I dropped to the damp grass, my shoulders convulsing as though I might be sick. Horeb had ruined any beauty I might have had. I felt violated to the core of my being.

I lifted the weapon into the air, gazing at it in wonder. One single thrust to Horeb's chest was all it would take. One pierce into the center of his blackened heart and he'd be gone. Could I murder him in cold blood as he lay drunk and sleeping?

I raised my eyes to the heavens, searching for a sign. I had never wanted anybody dead before. I'd never hated like this. But Horeb's death would bring me under condemnation before God, and before my family and tribe.

With my dagger gripped tight in hand, I left Horeb lying by the pond unconscious. Not looking back, I raced through the bushes, swaying with unsteady steps toward the distant hearth lights.

19

The camp was quiet when I finally stumbled back into it. Keeping to the shadows, I slipped through the rear door of my tent and dropped to the pillows, exhausted and now in severe pain.

It was black as pitch. The hearth fire was a pile of cold ashes, and no oil lamp had been left burning. My father was gone, as Horeb had claimed. Crawling across the floor, I eased my arms through a warm, clean robe.

The two young camels left behind by my father for milk and company bumped against the outer panels of the tent, trying to come inside. They sensed something was wrong.

"Now don't knock down the poles," I scolded them, trying to speak in a light voice.

Lifting one of the waterskins, I took a shaky sip. Fear was making me crazy. Any hope of Horeb leaving me alone was just a dream. He wouldn't be content to let things lie. After what I'd done to him, his desire to murder Kadesh—and me—would only be stronger.

Suddenly, a new noise came at the tent door and I backed into one of the dark corners, trying not to make a sound as fresh panic seized my heart.

Seconds later, Seraiah parted the tent flaps and stepped inside. "Jayden, child!" she exclaimed. "You're home. Where have you been?"

Quickly, I turned away to hide the bloody knife marks. "You know that my father and the others have gone, then?" I said, trying to keep my voice steady.

"Yes." She paused. "Jayden, what's wrong?"

My grandmother pushed through the room on slow legs, her hooded eyes missing nothing. Coming closer, she lifted my hair before I could stop her.

"Child, you're hurt."

I pulled away. "I fell while walking home."

"Your hair is wet," she observed, combing the strands of my hair with her gnarled fingers. "Mud and twigs and cob-webs."

"I fell into the pond," I added as I checked over my shoulder, terrified Horeb was about to appear at any moment.

Seraiah put an arm around me. "Jayden, you're trembling. What's wrong?"

My mind spun with dizziness and terror. I was caught in the middle of a tangled web, terrified of the blackmail hanging over my head if I made the wrong move. But I needed to tell my grandmother that Horeb murdered his own father, even though I had no proof any longer. I needed to tell her of Kadesh, of my love for him.

I pushed myself tighter into my grandmother's arms, wishing I was six years old again and cuddled together in front of the fire to listen to her stories and songs. Her hands caressed me as she tried to comfort me. Desperately, I wished I could undo the whole night. I wished I'd never found Abimelech.

My grandmother pressed her lips together. "Those wounds are *not* from a fall. Somebody did this to you. Tell me, *what has happened*?"

"If I see Horeb again, I will kill him," I said, the words flying out of my mouth.

My grandmother's black eyes saw and knew everything. "He's done this to you?"

"Yes. And worse things, Grandmother, you must believe me!"

"You don't have to tell me the details," Seraiah said soothingly. "I am your witness."

The empathy and love in her old, dear eyes just made me cry harder. "Oh, Grandmother, what am I going to do?"

She held me, stroking my tangled, sodden hair. "I don't know, child. But you need to tell me what happened tonight. What did Horeb do besides attack you? Are there deeds you regret?"

"There is so much sorrow I don't know where to begin."

"You're shaking like a newborn camel," she said, holding my hands firmly in her own.

Fear filled my throat so I couldn't even speak.

My grandmother kissed my hands and put her thin arms around me as I buried my head into her neck. "Whatever happens, I will be behind you. Believe, my daughter."

I jerked my head up. "*Believe*. That's exactly what Kadesh told me."

She gave me one of her wry smiles. "Then he is even wiser than I gave him credit."

Sitting me down on the rug, she began to gather supplies for cleaning my wounds. Our baby camel pushed her way into the tent and I curled at her side as she folded herself up and blinked at the world through long-lashed eyes.

In a few minutes, the fire was hot and the large pot of water starting to bubble as my grandmother made sure the tent flaps were secured.

Peeling off the last shreds of my torn dress, I felt as though I were shedding the petals of a wilted, dying flower. Something inside me had died, too. The night had changed everything and I wasn't sure I'd ever be whole again.

When I climbed into the tub, I winced as the hot water covered my wounds. Without a word, Seraiah dipped clean linens into the steaming water and began to gently wash away the blood and dirt.

"Everything hurts!" I moaned as the water turned red. The slash along my neck was still bleeding, oozing along my shoulder.

"Lie back now and close your eyes," she commanded softly. "I think we need to stitch this wound."

"But Horeb!" I cried, unable to relax in the hot water. "He was chasing me, and he could show up here any moment."

"I'll deal with Horeb if he does. Now do as I say."

I wanted to immerse my aching body, but my nerves were on edge, the night full of danger. "I'm so afraid, Grandmother. Horeb will kill me out of vengeance for not loving him. For loving Kadesh instead."

My grandmother nodded, listening as she gently sponged my neck and threaded a needle to make three small sutures.

"I tried to talk to my father about the betrothal," I went on. "But he won't change his mind."

"Without camels, a poor man doesn't have many choices."

"Neither does the daughter of a poor man. What will I do if Kadesh never returns?"

Seraiah's eyes held mine with a fierce love. "If you love this young stranger," she said quietly, "then you can only believe that somehow he will find a way to stay alive."

My grandmother tied my hair on top of my head so she could examine the knife wound and begin to make a dressing doused in turmeric and myrrh. "I knew something was going on the night of Hakak's wedding," she admitted. "I saw those thunderous gazes between you and the stranger. I suspected, but did nothing, thinking you would forget about him when he left. Thinking that was safer for everyone. But I was wrong."

"But will he want me now that Horeb has marked me with all these scars?"

My grandmother pursed her lips. "If Kadesh is the kind of man you could love, then he will forgive the scars Horeb gave you tonight. Not only the scars from his malevolent dagger, but the wounds left on your heart, and the terror on your soul."

Silent tears ran down my cold cheeks despite the soothing hands of my grandmother. From outside the tent came the noises of the snuffling of camels. I gripped my grandmother's arm.

Seraiah's eyes darted about the room. "The night is restless."

I realized for the first time that she was also afraid of the shadows on the other side of the tent walls.

A sudden premonition made me rise from the water.

"Help me out of the tub, Grandmother! We must flee!"

I threw my dress over my head just as the tent doors flung wide. Horeb stood there, blood splattered, breathing heavy, staring at us with slitted, dark eyes.

Seraiah wasted no time in marching directly up to him. "You're not welcome here. Every sane person is asleep."

"Then we must not be sane," Horeb said with a wicked grin. "I came to claim Jayden and take her to my tent. I don't trust her, and she knows it."

"You will not take her from me. Think about your honor, Horeb. Me, an old woman being tended by my own granddaughter, and you barging in here uninvited at this hour."

"Looks just the opposite to me with your medicines and sutures," he countered. "After tonight, Jayden and the kingship are mine. It's done. I officially declare it."

Turning red in the face, Seraiah flung words at him. "You would claim the Nephish throne as our king—and not give your betrothed a wedding fit for a queen! What a shameful beginning to your rule as our leader. Think of your role. Haven't you done enough damage for one night? You could be forced out permanently and banished for what you've done to Jayden, a woman you should honor and protect. I'm ashamed of you."

I turned my back on him, knowing that my grandmother didn't even know the whole story, the loss of Abimelech making me sick. I clutched my hands to my belly, keenly feeling the absence of Kadesh and my father as well.

"Go home to your parents. We will discuss the matter of the betrothal and your wedding later. Not in the middle of the night. And be warned: I will kill you myself if you lay a hand on Jayden again before your marriage."

Horeb took a step forward, his face dark with fury. Pointing his finger at me, he added, "Do not believe everything she tells you. Your granddaughter is a cunning liar."

I whirled around, but before I could say a word, he strode through the tent doors and was gone, like an evil spirit.

My grandmother turned to me. "He has the eyes of a wild man. I fear for the tribe under his leadership. And I can see why you fear for Kadesh. What did he mean by his accusations against you?"

"He saw me and Kadesh . . . before he left to travel with the caravan. My virtue is not at stake, although Horeb tried to take it from me tonight."

"The snake! Trying to blackmail you and me. At least he has time to grow up and be trained by his father."

I shook my head, bitter tears swamping my eyes and throat. "There's more," I added softly.

She grasped my hands in her old, wrinkled ones, her own eyes stricken and wild. "What haven't you told me?"

"Abimelech is dead. Murdered this very night in his bed by Horeb. I saw the evidence myself, but Horeb already destroyed it."

"I believe you," my grandmother said slowly. "The deed is written all over Horeb's face and in his efforts to steal you away tonight to his bed. I fear our tribe is in dire trouble, and you are doomed, my child. Horeb will not let this rest. Not until you've given him what he wants—and Kadesh's dead body."

20

There was no sleep that night.

I lay on my bed with my newly purchased dagger in my lap.

My grandmother polished her own small knife in front of the tent fire where my father usually sat, her frail hands scrubbing the blade across the whetstone to guarantee its sharpness.

There was a raw edge to the world, and as the night deepened, I was as agitated as ever. The moon wavered on the horizon, about to crash into the edge of the world—and with it came the screams of a woman.

My grandmother's chin jerked up. *"Judith,"* she breathed.

Grabbing my dagger, I immediately headed for Abimelech's tent, Seraiah right behind me.

We found Aunt Judith standing under the canopy of her fire hearth, screaming and throwing ashes over her head. Tears stained with black soot ran in rivulets down her cheeks.

Across the valley, women parted their tent doors to peer out into the black night.

"Judith!" Seraiah cried. "Go inside! You're making a spectacle of yourself."

There was an unnatural look in Aunt Judith's eye. "Have you no compassion? My husband is dead! Murdered in his bed this very night! My sons are both gone! I will die now!"

Judith prostrated herself on the ground, sobbing.

My grandmother's sharp brows came together as our eyes locked. "And so it begins. I wonder where Horeb is, and if the snake led his own mother to his father's body."

Cries of grief quickly spread that Aunt Judith had been widowed through the night. That Abimelech, our tribal leader, was dead.

Women hurried over to Judith's campsite, flinging ashes into the air and wailing. I held myself still, willing myself not to collapse. I hadn't slept for a moment and my body ached as if I might have a fever.

Judith's grief was horrible and frightening.

My grandmother whispered fiercely, "You are right to fear Horeb. We all should." Her eyes darted about the camp and I could almost hear her thoughts. "Where is Falail? And your sister?"

I shook my head. "I don't know."

"They were to attend a new baby party with Judith last night, but I see that isn't true. Judith must have come home to search the girls out—and found her husband instead." Seraiah pursed her lips. "I'm sure we can both guess where they are now."

I nodded, not wanting to admit that my sister and cousin were at the temple. I would not be the one to tell Judith that she had lost a daughter to the Temple of Ashtoreth, after losing her husband.

Aunt Judith let out another wail as she smeared ashes across her forehead. She covered her hands with the fine, gray powder and lifted them to the sky. "I need my son, my Horeb! And he is gone, too."

Seraiah tried to pull Judith to her feet. "Let's talk inside the tent."

Judith crumpled into a heap and my grandmother knelt in the fire's ashes with her, trying to soothe her as she had done for me earlier. "God will bring Horeb home. Of that you need not worry. And we will find Falail and Leila. Remember your young son, Chezib. He needs you now as we mourn Abimelech."

After a few moments, Aunt Judith suddenly pressed her lips together, smoothing soot-stained hands on the shreds of her dress as she rose from the hearth. Her calm demeanor now scared me more than the screaming rants. "I can be happy about one thing. That Horeb is not here to witness his father's death. That he will be spared his burial while he's out protecting us and assuring our security."

I flinched at the lies. She would never doubt Horeb, never question her son's loyalty and love.

"There's more to say before we wash and dress my husband's body." My aunt turned to me and gave me a cold stare.

I shrank back, my heart hammering against my chest. "Last night Horeb met me on his way to lead the tribe. We talked about many matters."

"What could be worse than the news we've already shared?" my grandmother murmured, trying to shepherd Judith into the tent, but my aunt wouldn't move. She merely spoke louder, in front of all our neighbors and friends.

Judith turned red and swollen eyes on me, pointing harshly. "Horeb's betrothed, our *dear* Jayden here, has betrayed him."

Her words were stones in my chest.

"What are you saying?" my grandmother asked sharply.

"Your innocent granddaughter is more devious than you know," Judith hissed. "Jayden has given herself to the stranger, Kadesh. Horeb says that she is no longer pure."

My world seemed to explode as I heard the gasps and cries of the women surrounding us. Some were shocked, but a few faces turned ugly and spiteful. I knew I shouldn't have sat up all night with a dagger in my skirt. I should have killed Horeb when I had the chance. I was sure he had left for the desert after coming to my tent and arguing with Seraiah, but instead, he'd gone to his mother and whispered dangerous secrets into her ears.

"Lies!" I moved toward Judith, looking her in the eye, not willing to be disgraced. "All lies!" I sputtered. "What about these cuts? These bruises?" I pulled up my sleeves, wincing as the festering cuts stuck against the cloth and pulled away with fresh specks of blood. "Horeb," I spat, "your beloved son, attacked me earlier—before he talked to you."

"You won't get me to turn against Horeb," Judith snapped. "I've seen you making eyes at the stranger. We all saw it, and were relieved when he was gone so your marriage could take place and secure the safety of the tribe. You've brought shame to us, your family, and dishonor to Horeb, our leader." She clutched her belly, grief overcoming her. Through her tears she screeched, "How could you do this, Jayden—after all our family has done for yours! You don't deserve Horeb. You've dishonored us all!"

Judith dropped to the heap of rugs. She pulled at her hair, her mourning howls piercing the night. The other women of the camp surged forward to comfort her, offering solace while Hakak and Timmath sent me sharp, razor glares as they passed. One woman even spat at my feet.

I was so humiliated, I couldn't even move. Horeb had taken everything from me, and Aunt Judith's words had now condemned me.

My grandmother wiped at her face and then said in her soft, commanding voice, "There's more here than can be discussed right now, despite the horrors of this night—" Her voice broke off as the sound of racing camels roared behind us.

"Horeb!" Judith screamed, running forward.

Horeb and a group of his hunting and raiding companions quickly surrounded the tent. Camels and men were every-where, reigning in their mounts, shouting orders.

I sank to the ground, keenly aware that I'd been caught in a prison—not for my own sins, but for Horeb's treachery. The moments of my life were already slipping away as the warriors' camels spit and reeled in a frenzied circle, trapping me forever in fabricated lies. The scorpion's sting was a dagger to my heart. I'd be stoned at dawn. All because I secretly loved a stranger.

Horeb and his entourage of more than a dozen young men were decorated and ready for battle. Dust swirled about their camels' feet in a cloud-like plume. The animals were packed and loaded with water, rations, and sleeping mats. Swords and curved daggers were strapped to their waists. They were outfitted for a war they were determined to win at any cost.

I pressed a fist to my chest, trying to suck in air, trying not to faint.

"My son," Judith murmured as Horeb leaned down from his saddle to embrace her.

"We ride to avenge my good name, my father's death, and the reputation of my betrothed, the daughter of Pharez," he declared in a loud voice.

My lip curled as I realized that Horeb had just betrayed himself. He'd mentioned Abimelech's death before he was supposed to know about it.

I threw a hateful glance at Judith and the others, but my aunt stared up at her son, enraptured by him, her hands clasped to her breast. My grandmother's eyes caught mine, and she slowly nodded. At least somebody believed me. Someone would help me. But who would listen to an old, feeble woman? Horeb would blackmail her, too. Or toss her aside.

"The stranger, Kadesh, has attempted to strip away her virtue, and for this he will be killed," Horeb went on, his presence commanding as he sat tall on his mount. "We've learned that a caravan loaded with spices from the south is heading to the city of Damascus, hardly a week's journey. We'll take their camels and riches as payment for my betrothed's purity."

The group of raiders lifted their swords, cheering at Horeb's words.

"You are so good, so noble," Judith said, pressing Horeb's hands to her lips, tears rolling down her face. "To think of your betrothed over your own welfare and good name. God will bless you as you take your father's role as tribal leader."

I watched my worst fears realized, and there was nothing I could do. Bile raced up my throat, and I was sure I'd be ill right there.

Horeb smiled down at his mother from his lofty perch, and only I could see the condescension written on his face. "There's only one line of wells, and the stranger's caravan will not leave the trail merely to avoid a raid. They will be impossible to miss. I'll come back with riches for you, and I will return with the head of the stranger called Kadesh!"

I dropped to the cold fire under the canopy of Judith's tent, but immediately elderly hands grasped my arms. "Come, child," my grandmother urged.

The earth shook from the speeding hooves as Horeb's raiders began to depart. New grass and flowers were trampled as the men skirted the oasis and headed for the open desert. The confident war cries of Horeb's men—boys I had known my entire life—rang like death in my ears.

Kadesh would never survive. He was completely outnumbered. Even with a caravan, Horeb would use his army's cunning to separate Kadesh from the rest of the people he was traveling with to murder him. An army against one.

My grandmother tugged at my arm again as Aunt Judith turned to us. Grief had thrust deep etches in her soot-stained face. Her eyes were hollow, her dress torn and ragged as a witness to her dead husband.

"Judith," Seraiah said bluntly. "Horeb knew of his father's death without ever entering the tent to witness his body. Before anyone had the chance to impart the news."

Aunt Judith's eyes came into focus. "You will not turn me against my son and my king. Most likely, one of his men heard the news and informed him. He also witnessed the obvious signs of grief here."

"Judith—" Seraiah started again, but the woman ignored her, throwing up a hand to dismiss her, and leveled her gaze at me instead.

"You've brought humiliation and defamation to my family and to my son. Now get out of my camp."

"Aunt Judith, you must listen, please—" I begged.

She raised both hands as though she would strike me, and I stepped back to avoid the blow. "Deceitful, lying girl! Your father would do well to cast you out forever."

"Judith!" my grandmother cried. "That's enough!"

"Don't defend her, Seraiah! Now get out," she screamed, turning to me. "I don't want to see you again!"

Tears streamed down my face as I stumbled backward.

Horeb had won. With Judith's condemnation as tribal queen, I was officially an outcast. Until Horeb took me to the marriage tent and I could be forgiven.

"Horeb planned my destruction well," I told my grandmother as she accompanied me back to the tent. "He'll still agree to marry me despite the fact that he claims I'm tainted by Kadesh and impure. The clan will believe he's a man of honor and integrity!"

My grandmother was sorrowful. "His prize will be every camel your father brings back from the raid, of course. Your bride price and dowry in one."

Tears slipped down my face. "My father will believe Horeb's falsehoods. Because I already confessed my love for Kadesh."

I pictured Kadesh's caravan ambushed while he slept, Horeb's sword slitting his throat. My father coming home in shame to a daughter who had betrayed him. What if Horeb had plans for my father, too, to ensure that I would never be able to tell him about Horeb's deeds?

"I hope being in my company doesn't taint you now, Grandmother."

She gave a grunt. "*I* will decide who I speak to. Besides, I'm too old to care what people say."

My mind raced ahead. "Leila! I need to find her at the temple. I need to talk to her. What if Horeb goes there and tries to destroy her, too?"

"Oh, Jayden, no," she said sadly. "My worst fears are being realized with Leila and her lust for the Temple of Ashtoreth, but not you. Is there any way to talk you out of going there? I fear you will never come back."

I shook my head, gritting my teeth at the thought of betraying her and my dead mother, but my grandmother nodded, understanding that there was no time to lose if I was going to stay ahead of Horeb. Seraiah kissed each of my cheeks, and then held me in her old, bony arms. "Go with God, my daughter. I pray I'll see you again before I die."

I clung to her and kissed her, knowing there was a strong likelihood I wouldn't see her again.

The night was dark and sinister, but I couldn't wait until morning for the possibility of stoning by Judith's loyal friends. Quickly, I stroked the forelock of the young camels, saying good-bye as they lay asleep, cobbled in front of the tent.

I paused under the canopy to untie the silver bracelet Kadesh had clasped around my ankle, clenching it in my fist to extract its strength, to remind myself of his love. It had been two months since we'd said good-bye. My throat was full of emotion as I touched my lips, trying to remember the feel of Kadesh's lips on mine instead of Horeb's poisonous mouth. He'd taken away my beauty and my peace of mind. He'd smothered the good memories of Kadesh, the ones I clung to when I feared for his survival in the brutal desert.

When I finally stepped outside to leave, the moon was waning. Tomorrow it would be smaller still—a tiny shard low in the sky like one of the broken pieces of the clay cup. The next full moon would have marked the possibility of Kadesh's return.

Hatred grew inside my chest. Perhaps vengeance was a good thing. I'd use my loathing to stop Horeb from succeeding.

He'd driven me from the safety of my home, to the one place that could ruin my reputation far worse than a stolen kiss from Kadesh.

A picture of Kadesh in his cloak flashed before my eyes. An image of him coming home to me. To *me*. I saw the vision clear as day, sharp as lightning. I didn't know where or when, but I would see him again. I had to cling to that hope.

In the middle of the night I left my beloved tent and camels and ran for the city of Tadmur.

My destination was the Temple of Ashtoreth.

21

The road to Tadmur lay beyond the wild groves of olive and tamarisk. As dawn stretched across the sky, I was weeping so hard, I could barely see the road circling the oasis. With each step, fatigue took its toll. My legs burned, heavy as tree stumps, muscles shaking so badly I could hardly stay upright. Sleep and food had been in short supply the past few days.

By the time I'd walked more than an hour, I was lurching back and forth across the desolate road. It seemed as though this day was hotter than all the days that had come before, even though summer was coming to an end.

My eyes dripped with tears and the harsh sun blinded me as it surged over the horizon. Sweat coursed down my body as the escape into Tadmur became a mixture of phantom images and voices.

I replayed the horror of my mother's death on the floor of our tent, burying her in her best dress and jewelry, silver laid upon her eyes. The clang of my father's shovel as he buried her rang in my ear.

When I stumbled over the sand and rocks, a mirage of memories from my betrothal dance spun before my eyes. Leila's and my mother's and cousins' faces blurring as I whirled around Aunt Judith's tent made me dizzy all over again. I was so thirsty, almost nauseous. Every step was a struggle, but every step took me farther away from Horeb.

After another hour of walking, much longer than the journey normally took, I was about to faint from exhaustion when I became aware of people and camels milling about. The stone pylons of the city gates soared like jagged giants above me. Marketplace noises rang in my ears. Children rushed past, kicking a ball. The sounds and smells were overwhelming, making me dizzy and more confused. When I tried to take another step past the gates, my legs buckled and I hit the mud-packed dirt with a jolt that rattled my bones.

Just as I started to wonder if I would die, a woman's voice spoke nearby. "I think she's hurt. She's bleeding."

"Who is she?"

". . . should we get a physician?"

"No, herbs and a healing spell from the wise woman . . ."

". . . one of the desert people."

A hand plucked at my arm and I jerked away, trying to open my eyes, but the lids were sealed shut, burned from the sun and lack of kohl to protect my eyes.

I tried to speak, but my tongue wouldn't work. I needed water desperately but couldn't seem to get myself up and moving forward again to find the city wells. Perhaps there was no more well at all. Horeb had told me that. I would die out here in the desert. I should lie down and rest. Dig for water under the sand.

More hands shook my arm and then a voice roared, "Who do you seek, girl?"

"Leila," I croaked, and then realized that nobody would even know who my sister was. I finally managed to whisper, "Ashtoreth."

All I heard next was a cacophony of voices, and then hands lifted me. I cried out with the pain of my bruises and the knife wound slashed across my shoulder. I must have lost consciousness because the next thing I felt was a strange coolness as my body sank into a downy bed.

Plump pillows. Scented candles.

Soft hands washed my face and hands. The aroma of healing salves wafted on the air.

A silk gown.

Cold, delicious water on my tongue.

Sleep. Sleep. I'd never slept like this before. Perhaps I'd sleep forever.

So many dreams.

So many nightmares.

The light in the room was dusky when I woke, unsure if I'd slept an hour or three days. I turned over onto my side to see Leila lighting a set of sconces on the far wall. A bowl of clear soup and warm bread sat on a table next to me.

"Leila," I whispered, wondering if I still had the ability to speak.

"Jayden! You're awake. I was so worried." Leila quickly doused her torch and came over to sit next to me.

"How long have I been asleep?" My throat hurt as though I'd been screaming.

"Nearly two days," Leila answered. "Esther—all of us—we've been caring for you. Even Armana asked after you and directed the physicians to make every medicine available."

"Armana?" I said and tried to sit up, but I was so weak Leila pressed me back onto the bed.

"She is the Head Priestess of Ashtoreth and runs the temple. But there's plenty of time to learn all of that. You need to rest."

"I'm sure you're famished," another voice said, and I looked over to see Falail rising from a chair. Her hair lay in curls across her shoulders, her dark eyes rimmed in kohl, lips red with pomegranate stain. "Try to drink some of the soup. And I'll fetch some soft, sweet fruit." She smiled and disappeared through an arched doorway.

I stared up at the polished ceiling, at the figures of beautiful dancing women carved into the wood high overhead. Even in this simple bedroom, the beauty of the temple was stunning.

"Jayden," Leila said as I tried to get my bearings. She stroked my hand and there was a strange tremor in her voice. "How did this happen to you? The scrapes and gashes and bruises on your body. All those horrible cuts," she added, wincing.

I gazed at her, hesitating. "Oh, Leila, there is so much to tell you of the things that happened when you and Falail left."

"Is Father well?" she whispered.

"Yes, but nothing else is right." My eyes swept the room, taking in the racks of elegant dresses, the jeweled tables laden with makeup and perfumes. Leila and Falail had filled their lives with beauty and wealth, just as they'd always wanted.

"It almost appears as though you were attacked. Is that true?"

"You never told me you were leaving," I said, ignoring her question.

Leila laid her cheek against mine for a moment, and her skin was cool and scented. "It wasn't intentional. Falail and I came to see the dancing the night of the bridal party. It's the beginnings of the harvest celebrations. Quite dramatic and special, with musicians and food fit for a queen. It got so late; we didn't want to walk home alone, so we stayed here. It—it just got easier and easier to stay." She glanced away, looking guilty. "I know we should have sent a message. . . . Then two days ago a few citizens arrived—with a girl they'd found half-dead at the gates of Tadmur. A girl that kept repeating my name! I've never been more astonished in all my life when I saw you." Leila's voice dropped. "I was terrified that you were dead." My sister's eyes brimmed with tears. "Father is gone raiding, isn't he?"

I nodded, all my worries flooding over me again.

"When I saw you in that terrible state, I knew something was very wrong. Jayden, please tell me what happened."

I clenched my fists as I lay back on the pillow. "Falail will not want to hear what I have to say."

"What do you mean?"

"Horeb chased me and—and we fought."

"What are you talking about?"

"I had proof that he'd murdered his father."

She gasped. "Uncle Abimelech?"

I nodded. Leila's face drained of color as I told her the whole story. When I finished, I said, "You don't have to tell Falail the entire ugly story, but it's the truth. And she needs to know that her father has left this world. And that her mother is alone and needs her."

Leila nodded silently. "The other girls and Armana will help her. They've been wonderful in assisting with the care for you."

"I am grateful," I said cautiously. "Although I never dreamed in my life that I would lie in a real bed in a luxurious room of the Temple of Ashtoreth."

Leila's face was thoughtful. "Our lives have changed so much in just a few months. Our families torn apart . . . Do you still think about Sahmril?"

"Every day I think about her, and you—and our mother." I paused, tears swimming in my eyes. "Leila, I can't go back home, even though Grandmother is there and she helped me, and stood up for me. It's too dangerous, and I never want to see Horeb again. Judith cast me out. I'm officially banished, and not a single woman has spoken to me—not even our cousins. All I could do was find you."

Her eyes studied my face. "And Kadesh?"

I remembered our pact from that night in the groves of tamarisk and terebinth trees. My secret for her secret. "I never thought I could be bound to someone with all my heart and soul."

"I'm happy for you to find such love, but I never dreamed Horeb could . . . it's unthinkable. The man every girl wished she could have." Leila drew in a breath. "To hate so much . . . I don't like hearing the things you say. Your heart will turn black with so much hate."

"Didn't hate bring you here? Hate for the desert? Hate for all of its hardships? And now you're choosing the life you want. When I refused the life everybody else chose for me, it made me lose all the things that I wanted."

Leila reached over to kiss me on the forehead. "One day, Jayden, you'll be a rich woman."

I smiled wanly. "That will never happen. Horeb plans to kill Kadesh and force me to marry him. I have to run away, too."

"Stay here with me, then. With us."

"But our mother and grandmother always warned us away from the temple. . . ." I weakly protested. Even though I felt safe here from Horeb, I was abandoning my parents' beliefs, all the things my mother had wanted for me and Leila.

"Do you see anything terrible happening here?" Leila asked. "We've become friends with the other girls. It's beautiful and peaceful here, and there are such incredible comforts, as you can see. Why would anybody say anything bad about it?

I don't understand. Our mothers didn't know what they were talking about."

I shook my head. "I trust their wisdom. She said the dances were corrupted from the ancient purposes of our first mother. That the women of the temples weren't modest . . . You heard what the women said the night of my betrothal ceremony."

Leila bit her lips, not speaking, turning away to get me another glass of water from the pitcher on the gilded bedside table. I wondered what she had already done here at the temple, and the idea of it made me queasy.

"Even though you and the priestesses have saved my life, I'm uncomfortable here," I whispered. "It's as if I'm betraying Mother and Grandmother. Maybe I should try to get a camel and find Kadesh in Damascus. Horeb mentioned sight of a caravan on its way north from the southern lands. If that's Kadesh, I need to warn him about Horeb, who will follow his tracks after the raid is over with the Macchathites."

Emotion choked my throat, and Leila reached out to hug me. Softly she said, "That idea is insanity, Jayden, and you know it. You have no idea where he is, and you'll kill yourself trying to scour hundreds of miles of empty desert. Horeb and his men are days ahead of you, and have scouts, food, and gold for bribes. You have no camel to ride, no money, and no clan for protection."

I nodded helplessly as tears rolled down my face. "If it's impossible to stop Kadesh from being attacked by Horeb, then I must find Sahmril instead. I miss her. We need our sister with us. She belongs to *us*."

Leila swept back my hair with her fingers just like our mother used to do when we were ill. "For now, just sleep and get strong again. We'll figure something out when it's time."

"What about Falail? Who will tell her the news about her father's death?"

"I will," Leila said at last, and I saw a strength in my older sister I'd never known before. Perhaps she really *was* meant to be a part of temple life.

After several weeks, I was finally strong enough to get up from my bed for more than an hour or two to stroll our balcony or sit on the adjoining porch in the warm afternoons.

"You need to stretch your legs, Jayden," Leila told me, pulling me out the doors of my sickroom after we'd eaten a late lunch. "And I've never given you an official tour of the temple grounds."

I smiled at her wanly, not admitting that I was curious to see more of the temple.

"Falail returned home to be with Aunt Judith. And there is so much to do to get ready for tonight."

"What's happening?" I asked her.

Leila put her arm through mine as we entered the marbled hallways. "The final autumn harvest party with so much food you'll think you're dreaming, and dancing with the temple musicians. Tonight is the night we thank the goddess for the summer's bounty and good fortune."

I smiled at her, indulgent at her excitement. And yet, there was a tug in my belly at the dream of music and dancing. It had been so long since I'd moved my own body and felt the drums in my feet.

"But first, we need baths and then we can choose our dancing dresses."

I bit my lips, knowing that I was woefully underdressed, more like a beggar. "There are days it still feels like I have stray twigs in my hair from falling in the pond—and grass stains on my feet."

"The bathing rooms are heavenly, aren't they? Nothing like our tin bathtub in the tent, although you haven't enjoyed the large luxury baths with servants yet. I confess that I pretend to be the Queen of Sheba herself when getting pampered in the bathing rooms."

As we walked through the corridors, Leila talked nonstop. "The temple isn't just a place of worship, it's part of the local government. People come here to pay taxes, obtain food if they're hungry, receive permission to set up a new shop, or to expand their lands. A hundred reasons. The Goddess of Ashtoreth and the God of Ba'al watch over the people in all things."

I didn't reply as we passed through a hall with towering columns, where throngs of people moved quickly. Maids carrying trays, slaves wearing white loincloths, shouldering bags of grain, produce, or linens.

At the end of the long hallway we entered an expansive inner courtyard. Slick floors, glazed like marble, felt warm under my bare feet. Half columns, painted to give the impression of palm trees, met my eyes, and I stopped to stare at the miracle of the artists' talents. Overhead, the roof was open to the sky, and wedges of afternoon sunlight fell upon the clean sweep of tile.

Across the open foyer, I spotted richly dressed men, obviously city diplomats. Women of all ages on various business errands clustered in conversation, or moved down countless corridors branching in every direction.

I didn't want to appear interested, but curiosity got the better of me and I found myself staring at the bustling crowd.

"On the lower floors are granaries, food stores, and offices," Leila said, interrupting my thoughts. "An orphanage is housed on the floor just below us, too."

My eyes flew to her face. "An orphanage?"

She smiled. "Yes, the priestesses spend a lot of time on charity work when they're not busy with their priestly duties taking care of the goddess."

"What do you mean, taking care of the goddess?"

"The statue of Ashtoreth in the main hall. They bathe and feed and clothe her, taking care of the offerings that are left by the citizens of Tadmur. Priestesses also organize the festivals and worship services during the year."

"So it's not just silk dresses and flowers in your hair and soft beds to sleep in," I said with a smile, glancing over at her.

Leila stuck out her tongue at me and for a moment, it felt like old times, when we were children. A time that was long gone. "Of course, since the population of the temple is fairly large, with people who live or work here, there are many people to feed, too."

As we explored the various wings of the temple, the

population of women increased. Most doors were open and I couldn't help peeking inside as we passed their apartments.

Food was being cooked, beer brewed, jewelry designed, fabric woven on enormous looms. There was even a room filled with cut flowers where perfume was created. Another where black kohl eyeliner sticks were made. I hadn't realized how complicated a temple center could be.

"This way," Leila said as we went deeper into the temple. Here the doorways were lower, and there weren't any windows open to the roofs. It was dark and shadowy after the fierce glare of the sun.

Wall sconces flickered against walls painted a deep red color, earthy like a field of soil. Unusual spirals and swirls decorated the plaster, which was so smooth the walls appeared slick as water. Lapis lazuli winked in coiled patterns on the ceiling, along with carnelian, and orchids created from ivory. Gold leafing embellished the corners and edges of crown moldings.

Tucked into recessed alcoves, I spotted copper and stone sculptures, and statues of women in various poses of the women's dance. They reminded me of Leila's sculpted wooden figurine from the tamarisk grove.

I'd been taught not to worship statues and idols, but I couldn't keep myself from admiring the craftsmanship and the beauty of these statues. They represented the prelude of dance performed before the Sacred Marriage Rite began. The marriage rite involving two people who not only were not married, but most likely didn't even know each other.

When my mother spoke of it I'd been disturbed, even

frightened that girls and women had corrupted the beautiful dance of our Mother Goddess to lure men into their bed in the name of the goddess.

Despite that, the dance was still beautiful, and I realized that *I* needed to dance. It was in my blood. Dancing would help me get strong again. And I wanted to keep my mother's memory alive within me.

Leila stopped in front of the sculptures. "A few of us want more than cooking over hot fires, chasing after smelly camels, and sweeping dirt from the rugs."

I shook my head in disagreement. "Summer at the oasis is the best part of the year. There's always a wedding or a new baby, more food than we can eat, plus endless conversation and visiting."

"Until this year," Leila said pointedly.

I bit at my lips, becoming restless surrounded by exaggerated glamour and polished floors. I wanted to go outside, experience the texture of dirt beneath my feet again. "I hear music," I said, changing the subject.

Leila smiled as I followed her down a staircase of cream-colored tiles. "There's always music somewhere."

The lilting sound grew louder as we walked on, and I recognized drums, a lyre, and a flute. It reminded me of a time when I'd come to Tadmur with my mother and we'd stopped to listen to a group of traveling musicians in the town square.

Soon we entered another room, where two sunken marble tubs took almost the entire width of the space. The tubs were filled with steaming, scented water. Beside the baths stood racks filled with jars of creams, perfumes, and ointments. Plates of fat grapes were ready to eat while bathing, and thick towels lay in stacks for drying off afterward.

Small, high windows had been cut into the upper walls, creating an airy, large room.

An arched doorway at the opposite end opened into a second apartment with more baths. Beyond that I could see sleeping rooms with luxurious beds. Dresses in every color and fabric had been flung over chairs and tables.

"This is where we sleep and dress for the festival," Leila said. "And now that you're well again, you will be able to wear a new dress and attend the ceremonies, too."

I wanted to touch every single one of those silky, flowing dresses and lift each perfume bottle to smell its heady fragrance. "It's so strange to be here." Even as I spoke, I found myself staring at the shining, sunken bathtubs, and the beauty of clear, steaming water. I'd never had a bath quite like this before. The one upstairs in my recovery room was small with only Leila to help me. These were as enormous as a small pond.

"Are you all right, Jayden?" Leila asked, touching my hand. "Your face—"

I tried to shake the images that haunted me from that night when I fled Horeb and the deathbed of Abimelech. Running over rocks, falling into the pond, clawing my way to the bank, and then fighting with Horeb and enduring the slaughter he'd made of my body with my own dagger. "I'm all right," I finally said, trying to appear happy. "The room is exquisite, like a dream."

Leila slipped out of her clothes and stepped into one of the bathtubs, then flung water at me. Droplets sprayed the air, and I had a sudden urgency to run. Temptation for ease, elegance, and luxury warred against my plain desert upbringing. The baths made me long for my mother, when she'd help me wash my hair in our enclosed tent late at night, when all the world would sleep. She'd scrub my neck while crooning lullabies, chatting softly before tucking me into bed.

Before Leila could urge me into the water, Esther was behind me in the bathing room, tugging my old, worn shawl from my shoulders. I tried to snatch it back, but she held it high in the air so I couldn't reach. "Leila, your sister's got a knife in her waistband!"

I turned toward Esther, whose eyes stared at me, cold and questioning.

"Jayden!" Leila hissed. "What are you doing with a dagger?"

"I purchased the knife more than a month ago in the market. You know the men were leaving for their raid, Leila, and I needed something for protection. Even if it's only a wandering hyena," I added lightly.

Esther slowly smiled. "Perhaps I underestimated you, Jayden."

I didn't look at her, focusing on wrapping the knife in my shawl again. "It's really just a big kitchen knife," I said casually, bending over to swirl the water with my hand.

Taking a bath was enticing in the heat, and it would take the girls' minds off my new dagger. With my back turned, I self-consciously undressed and stepped into the tub, instantly submerging myself so they couldn't see the cuts and bruises on my body. Even though they were mostly healed, I still winced at the stinging sensation in the water.

Leila dripped puddles over the glossy floor as she got out and grabbed a towel. "I'll pour fresh water for you, Jayden."

"We'll get the maids to do it," Esther said. "Let's curl your hair, Leila, after it dries. Tonight is the culminating night of the festival, the night of the Sacred Marriage Rite, and we must all look our most beautiful."

There was a pang in my gut when she spoke those words. Leila and I would have to find a corner to hide in after the meal and dancing were over. We could probably return to my bedroom and stay up talking like we used to do.

I sank back in the tub and closed my eyes, trying to clear my thoughts. The huge font of clean water made me think I was drowning until I realized that I could actually stand on the bottom of the tub. Benches for sitting and washing had been built into the corners, making the bath a place where one could relax and daydream. Like a guilty pleasure.

A young girl no more than twelve poured hot water from a pitcher. She leaned over the edge of the tub, sprinkling a bowl of white granules that made the water lush with bubbles and foam, which helped me hide the red slashes on my skin. Next, she took another bowl of soap and washed my hair, scrubbing with more energy than I thought she was capable at first.

"Rinse," she commanded, swishing her soapy hands.

I closed my eyes and went under the surface as if I were swimming in a river. This was the first time I'd washed my hair in something other than a bowl of perfumed well water, and the sensation was oddly sensuous.

Esther and Leila insisted I put on one of the temple dresses while my own dress was taken away to be properly cleaned.

My hair was tied up on my head with a jeweled clip while it dried. A silk dress the color of a maroon sunset floated down over my shoulders. The gown brushed the floor with such lightness, it was almost like wearing nothing at all. So this was how those beautiful dresses the girls had been wearing at the dancing grove felt against their bodies.

Stabs of guilt pierced at me for the desire I had of wanting to experience the wearing of such a dress. For wearing such finery while Falail had just lost her father and Aunt Judith had to bury her husband. It pained me not to be with them. But it hurt more to have been thrust out of the camp. My mother would never have allowed it. She would have believed me about Horeb. Trusted me, just like my grandmother did.

Sitting me at a table in front of a mirror, Esther fixed tendrils of curls at my neck, and then added an extra jeweled clip at my ear.

"Are you training to be a priestess?" I asked her.

She smiled. "Of course. It's a privilege to worship the goddess every day and serve her."

"But Ashtoreth is just a marble statue. A story. A myth."

Her eyes narrowed. "No different than your god of the desert."

I met her steely gaze and shook my head as she continued. It was no use arguing with her; she'd never understand the people of Abraham.

"You'll experience the power and joy of Ashtoreth tonight," she said, putting her hands on my shoulders and speaking softly into my ear. "Now that you're well, you'll get to see the dancing, Jayden. Through the temple dance, we take part in the act of creation and harvest, and through the Sacred Marriage Rite, we ensure continued blessings from our goddess."

I shook my head. "No, I can't."

"Please, Jayden, just this once," Leila pleaded with me. "Tonight I get to be part of it. I get to become part of Ashtoreth's power and divinity." She stared at me with pleading eyes, and I felt myself wanting to please her so she wouldn't run away from me forever. "We haven't danced, you and I, since your betrothal celebration months and months ago. You'll see that there's nothing to be afraid of. There's only loveliness and peace."

My sister took my arm and led me back upstairs into the main temple hall. The drums and the melodies—all the elements of the dance washed over me as I stared at the sanctuary, which was unlike anything I'd ever imagined. Airy, open ceilings gazed into the twilight and early-evening stars. Spacious marble floors caressed my feet.

Sumptuous chairs and torch sconces were wreathed in hot-red roses and tight, pink buds. Elaborate tables overflowed with plums and dates, melons and pomegranates, smoked meats carved into thin slices and laid onto platters. Fat loaves of braided bread fresh from the ovens were piled into baskets, honey and butter ready to slather.

The wealth was overpowering and heady. I felt dizzy,

drinking in everything, my mouth watering.

A stunning woman glided over the polished floor like a cat on silent paws. She was a poem in silk and jewels, thick, ebony hair falling to her knees, glittering as though gold dust had been sprinkled through each strand.

"So this is Jayden," she said. "I'm Armana, the High Priestess of Ashtoreth. Welcome to our abode, my dear." Her voice was hypnotic and lovely. She wasn't as young as the other priestesses, but neither was she old, appearing ageless as time itself. "We look forward to seeing you dance tonight, too."

Nerves clenched at my belly. "I don't think—"

The High Priestess waved away my words. "The dance will soothe you after so much loss and illness. I used to be a girl of the desert long ago, too."

"Oh!" This gorgeous woman had grown up in the deserts? It didn't seem possible.

She glided away as the music began, before I could ask her what tribe she belonged to. I tried to shake off the unnerving foreboding as the gilt-edged doors of the high-ceilinged room opened. Girls and young women entered, dressed in flowing silk and linen sheaths, flowers in their hair, pomegranate color staining their lips. The flutist played a series of high, quivering notes, and then the drumming began.

The music was irresistible and Leila pulled me into the circle. The polished floors felt magnificent under my feet, but I missed the tug of the desert sands sifting through my bare toes. Intoxicating beauty surrounded me, but I couldn't forget the walls of my tent and the intimate smiles of my friends and family, the people who used to love me.

Light from dozens of small windows threw shafts of fading yellow against the walls of the torch-lit ballroom. The life-like statues created from stone and clay sat watching from their pedestals and niches, seeming to dance along with us.

On the far side of the hall stood the Goddess of Ashtoreth on her stone pedestal. Crafted from fine, white marble, she prevailed over the temple, willowy and majestic. Trays of sumptuous food had been laid at her feet. Queenly purple and ruby-red silks draped her sculpted, perfect, and sensuous body.

Shivering with the music thrumming through my own body, I trembled with the pulsing of the beat. At Hakak's wedding, I'd been too self-conscious to dance freely, to ignore all the watching guests around me. Especially because Horeb spent his time leering at me. It had been a long time since I'd felt the sheer power of the dance.

The music filled me with a desire to reach for the heavens, to yearn for eternity. An eternity with Kadesh.

Under the open-air roof overhead, the sky was filled with a shower of dazzling stars.

And I danced. As if I'd never danced before. As though I'd never dance again.

The music from the drums and harp and lyre swept me under, filling my nostrils and lungs with a passion that made me ache in every fiber of my being. Just when I was about to weep with the intensity of the drowning music, I felt as though Kadesh was with me at my side, touching my hand, whispering in my ear. His fingers were sure and strong even as I trembled with the love I had for him.

I closed my eyes, seeing my mother behind my eyelids, and those days in the future when I would teach Sahmril the ancient, beautiful dance. Emotion trickled down my cheeks at my aching, empty arms.

Leila took my hands and we danced with the long line of my ancestor mothers who had come before us. I tried to picture their faces as I circled my hips and lifted my hands to the sky.

Using my fingers, I traced their stories, bringing the beauty of the desert and the mountains into this palace of wealth and perfume. The drums beat faster, and my hips moved into the final quivering shimmies.

When the music slowed and softened, the beating drums no longer quite so wild, I opened my eyes and found myself in the center of the dusky room.

Leila came toward me and brushed at the tears on my cheeks. "Why are you crying, Jayden?" she asked softly. "Isn't it beautiful and exhilarating?"

"As lovely as it is, I refuse to cross the doorway into *this* world," I told her. "I will never worship the idol Goddess of Ashtoreth."

My sister just smiled at me the way she always had. "But you already did! You were worshipping her during the entire dance, and now we will finish our worship with the Sacred Marriage Rite. Ashtoreth and Ba'al will consummate their union and power and divinity tonight. Look at all the worshippers who've come, Jayden."

My stomach dropped as I looked around the dusky marble

hall filled with the watching citizens of Tadmur, who had come to enjoy the final harvest ceremonial dancing. I had no idea the public was invited, that I'd be dancing for strangers.

As I gazed along the walls while the audience clapped their appreciation for our performance, I realized with clarity that the citizens of Tadmur who came to watch the temple priestesses weren't made up of families and friends enjoying a dance on an early autumn evening.

There were only men standing along the walls, applauding the presentation. Shame raced up my neck and face. I'd been stared at by strangers. By a room full of gawking men as they watched our bodies move freely to the music and drumbeats. Gazed at my legs and hips and breasts beneath a layer of maroon silk.

Putting my hands to my face, my skin burned with horror. I was still attempting to catch my breath, my thighs shaking from the final dance, and wondered how I could have blocked out the world so deeply. I hadn't been aware of who lurked in the shadows of the marble-columned sanctuary.

I heard myself let out a moan as I wondered which direction would take me to the exit. There were so many doors. I couldn't move, couldn't hear past the blood pounding in my ears.

Esther's voice whispered behind me, "Armana is pleased with the worship you gave Ashtoreth. There are visitors who want to choose you for their partner in the Sacred Marriage Rite. Would you like to feel the rush of Ashtoreth's divinity in your body and soul tonight?"

I sucked in my breath as tears burned the corners of my eyes. "Oh, please, dear God in heaven, tell me that I wasn't worshipping Ashtoreth!"

Esther merely smiled. I took in her kohl-rimmed eyes and the chains of jewels dripping from her forehead. A man, big and dark-skinned, with rings in his ears and nose, stepped up to claim her for the Sacred Marriage Rite.

I staggered backward. "No," I whispered. "How can you do this? How can you turn your back on a husband who loves you, marriage and babies, and a life with your family?"

Esther shook her head, looking at me condescendingly. "Perhaps a simple desert girl like you can't understand, Jayden. The higher realms are too complicated."

"I'm intelligent enough to know that you're insulting me." I wanted to sink into the floor and disappear forever. Had I surrendered my soul to Ashtoreth? The worst part was I had enjoyed it.

As I lifted my head to get my bearings and escape the sanctuary, I found myself looking straight into the face of one man who was not clapping at all for the dance performance. One man who was silent and still—beautiful and perfect and regal—and I swore my heart ripped out of my chest and fell to the slick marble floors. I instantly recognized that long, dark hair, the deep, bottomless eyes that saw everything.

He stood apart from the rest of the crowd, between two of the elegant marble columns, wearing a swirling cloak of finely woven cloth with unusual foreign markings. And he was staring straight at me.

Kadesh had witnessed me dancing for the Goddess of Ashtoreth.

22

I staggered back a step, as if I'd just seen a ghost.

Confusion devoured me in the chaotic commotion that filled the room. Dancers and people pushed past me, blocking my line of vision. I blinked, trying to get a grip on my senses.

I expected to see Kadesh again at the tent of my father, not here at the Temple of Ashtoreth. Why was he here? How did he find me? When did he return?

More importantly, Kadesh was still *alive*.

For one long, agonizing moment, we stood staring at each other, unmoving. My face burned. Horeb had tortured and humiliated me, but having Kadesh find me here, dancing in worship for the goddess in nothing but a sheer silk gown, seemed so much worse.

I bowed my head, turning to stumble away in disgrace.

Suddenly another man, a total stranger, stepped in front of me, his thick fingers grabbing at my hands, his eyes ogling the curves of my body. "I choose you for the Sacred Marriage," he said, slipping his arm around my waist.

"No!" I cried, jerking away. Immediately, I ran, afraid the stranger would grab me again and take me somewhere against my will.

"Jayden!" Kadesh shouted behind me. The sound of his voice made me want to sink with shame, even as his voice flooded me with memories I'd held close to my heart the last few months.

I kept running, trying to keep my balance as I nearly slipped on the glossy floor right in front of the jewel-draped statue of the goddess.

Ashtoreth peered down her nose at me, her all-seeing eyes gazing straight into mine. Chills ran down my back. I would have sworn that her perfect, frozen smile had turned into a mocking sneer.

A moment later, I reached the long, softly lit corridors; voices drifting from the rooms. Bursts of giggles. Low whispers and moans. I raced past dozens of doorways, not looking into their depths, not wanting to see the marriage rite of the goddess.

The fiery torches wavered from their lofty perches on the walls as though laughing at me. In the ceiling above me, images of the goddess had been carved among the galaxy of stars. I dropped my eyes, then touched the spot on my thigh where I'd strapped the dagger, grateful I'd had the presence of mind to keep the knife with me when I'd left the baths.

The corridor was dark and looped around like a maze, the goddess figurines dancing in the flickering flames of so many wall sconces.

For a moment I lost Kadesh behind me. He was unfamiliar with the temple, and after Leila's brief tour, I had an idea that I was headed in the right direction to reach our private rooms.

My bare feet slapped the smooth tiles. Wind seemed to fill my ears as I ran and slipped and then banged my knee, leaping up again to try to find a door that would let me hide from Kadesh. I'd spent months waiting for Kadesh, yearning for him, and fearing he might be dead, but now I couldn't see him, couldn't face him, let alone look into his eyes.

My first dance for him wearing sheer, lovely silk was supposed to be on our wedding night. In the wedding tent. Instead, I'd flaunted myself before the public, before other men, even as I blamed the High Priestess for her temptations, or the cloying perfumes that made my head ache, the sensuous music that roused me to the very core of my being.

"Jayden!" he yelled again as I turned a corner and tried to hide. "Stop! Please!"

I was lost in a maze of hallways, trying to find the apartments and dressing rooms I shared with Leila. I wanted to burn the temple clothes and change into my normal dress and become the daughter of Rebekah and Pharez again—the desert girl I really was.

Finally, I saw a cracked door and headed toward it, the sound of Kadesh's cloak slapping against his legs as he barreled down the hallway after me. "Jayden, please!" he called again in earnest, and the sound of him saying my name nearly made me halt.

His voice! The voice I'd dreamed of for months. The voice I wanted whispering into my ears for the rest of my life.

Instead, I pushed through the door where a sliver of light spilled to find an escape route—and stopped short.

Candles lit the room, creating hideous shadows. Heavy, red draperies covered the walls, dulling sound and light. I saw an inlaid table of cedarwood. A bed with linen sheets.

I let out a yelp as I saw my sister standing across the beautiful room with a strange man. I watched him peel Leila's dress off her shoulders, stripping her naked. The man jerked his head toward the door and I stepped back into the shadows, holding my hands over my mouth so I wouldn't break down.

Leila snatched up her dress in an attempt to cover herself. "Jayden, what are you doing here?"

"Who is she?" the man said, pouring two tumblers of red wine from a bottle perched on the cedar table.

"My sister," Leila snapped. "Jayden, you're breaking the divine conduit to the goddess, and ruining everything."

"You're mad," I whispered, trembling so badly I was sure I'd collapse any moment. "Please come with me," I begged her. "Please don't do this! What would our mother say? This goes against everything we know."

Leila clutched her dress, but the strange man snatched it away from her body, grabbing her around the waist and bringing her down onto the bed with him. "No, Jayden. This is who

I am. Who I want to be. Mother is gone and I can't bear it, but I'm not a desert girl. Please go away!" She turned her head as the man laughed in a low, deep voice. "Just go!"

"Is there nothing I can say to turn you away from this?" I whispered.

Leila turned her face away from my eyes, vehemently shaking her head.

The man unbuckled his dagger from his waist, pulling out the sharpened weapon while he stared at me. He grinned as Leila pulled a sheet over her bare legs. I backed toward the door, slammed it shut, and fell into the corridor.

I tried to breathe. I couldn't believe what was happening. The dishonor of the entire night bubbled up my throat, choking me. "Jayden!" I turned to see Kadesh coming toward me.

Our eyes locked. "No. Please. I can't face you, Kadesh," I whispered, gulping for air. "Not like this. Not here. I didn't mean for this to happen. I'm disgraced. My mother would be ashamed of me. I've let her down. I've let you down. And I've let myself down. There is no forgiveness."

"No, Jayden, you're—"

I let out a sob as his hand reached out to brush my arm. Stumbling away from him, I sprinted down the corridor, searching again for an escape.

I pushed through another door and stumbled into a small courtyard. Tall palm trees fluttered overhead, shadowy in the night air. I was running so fast, the momentum launched me into a table. Two cushioned chairs went crashing to the brick patio.

Getting up again, I whirled around to find Kadesh right behind me.

"I won't let you get away from me again," Kadesh said as he reached out and spun me around, holding my arms fast. He stared at me, as if searching my face for the girl behind the rouge and pomegranate lips. "Oh, Jayden, the moment I saw you, I knew it was you. That I'd found you at last." He was breathless and his hands gripped my shoulder where Horeb had sliced me with his knife. I grimaced at the brief moment of lingering pain, unable to look into those beautiful eyes.

I thought the wound had nearly healed, and was surprised by the sudden tender throbbing. I swallowed my tears to hide the pain.

"I've traveled hundreds of miles across the desert and never even made it home," he said quietly.

"What do you mean?" I asked, my voice shaking as though I were seeing a mirage in front of me.

"The travel plans of the caravan were not what I expected. First, they went to Damascus and all the way southwest to Salem to dispatch deliveries. They returned to Tadmur at my insistence, even though they wanted to finally take the road south along the Red Sea to my homeland. But I knew I couldn't be away from you for several more months, so I came back to take you home with me. We can never be apart again, my dearest Jayden. When I arrived at your camp today, I nearly went out of my mind when your cousin Hakak told me your father is gone on the raid and you and Leila were at the temple."

All the events of the past few months crashed through my

mind as I sank to the patio, the rough bricks scraping my knees under the temple gown.

I closed my eyes, fighting to hold back the tears, when I felt Kadesh sink to the patio with me, pulling me into his arms.

I bowed my head against his chest. "I've shamed myself before you." My throat was tight with love and sorrow and the exquisite nearness of him.

When Kadesh brought me even closer to him, his cloak brushed against my bare toes, sending shivers up my spine.

"No—" I started to say.

"Please don't tell me no," he said huskily. "I've come too far to find you again," he added, and then that lovely cloak swept around me, enclosing me as Kadesh folded his arms around me.

The softness of his shirt brushed against my face, and the warmth and safety was almost more than I could bear. All the tears I'd bottled up for so long began to spill down my face. Tears of rage and fear, tears of shame and regret. And tears of relief as the dream of Kadesh I'd carried with me for so long finally surrounded me in reality.

Kadesh's voice—so close, so warm—was like an embrace. I could still recall in detail that day in the canyon lands when he first whispered my name and kissed my palms.

"I never meant to come here," I choked out. "Leila came to the temple, and I had to find her. My father is gone, Aunt Judith banished me, and Horeb—he—Abimelech is—I've shamed you. And my tribe. And my father."

Kadesh pulled me tighter. "You haven't shamed yourself, or me," he whispered. "The Temple of Ashtoreth is like the temples of the Sariba Goddess in the southern lands. I understand more than you think."

I shook my head, mumbling into the folds of his beautiful cloak. "I don't deserve your kindness."

"*Kindness?* I found you before it was too late, just when I thought you might be lost to me forever."

Our bodies melded together as Kadesh touched my hair and trailed his fingers down my face. "In the sanctuary, you were a nameless, faceless dancer. Nobody knew who you were except for me. And I will make sure with my very last breath that you never dance for anybody else again—until you dance for me on our wedding night."

Shivers ran down my arms at the warmth of his hands as he clasped mine, lacing our fingers tight. Letting out a shaky breath, I pressed my lips against his palm. Fresh tears streamed down my face.

He cupped his hands around my face and looked into my eyes. "I thank the god in heaven that I found you. And you are still alive and safe."

"*You're* alive, Kadesh. There were moments I feared I'd never see you again, but you're truly here. Tell me everything that's happened the last few months." I stared into his face, sensing something else. "Are you all right?" I asked.

He shook his head, brushing off my concerns. "It's been a long summer. The caravans had trouble on the way to Salem. Robbery, stolen goods, wells that are drying up, which took some of our herd. And then came the news that Horeb and a band of men were pursuing us. At least they were headed for

Damascus when we were already finished with our business there and on our way to Salem."

He glanced up for a moment and I could sense his hesitation, his grave countenance.

"What is it, Kadesh? Tell me."

"I received word that my uncle has been very ill, news that has weighed heavily on my heart."

"I'm so sorry. You should have gone to him already."

Kadesh shook his head. "My family is large and complicated. That's the only way I can explain it right now. But it's nothing for you to worry about. You've had a summer of grief, too, Jayden. And I was terrified that Horeb had already carried you off and you were lost to me."

"Why would you think that?"

"Your family was threatening to move the marriage sooner. And because I visited the Nephish camp this morning, as I told you. I know that Abimelech is dead. For that, I am very sorry. He had spoken privately with me about tribal affairs and hinted at a potential alliance."

"I know," I whispered. "Horeb told me. He's the one that killed Abimelech."

"I suspected as much. Horeb was about to lose his position. That is usually the first suspect when a tribal leader is killed."

"How long ago were you at the oasis?"

"Just a few hours. Instead of you, I found an empty tent, your father gone on a foolish raid, and King Abimelech dead. The last of your camels were taken by Judith."

My stomach dropped at my aunt's audacity, but I had to

know about my father. "Are the men of my tribe safe?"

Kadesh nodded. "So far, yes. And your father is alive."

I sagged with relief. But what would my father do when he learned Leila and I were living at the temple? "I also heard rumors of you pulling a knife on Horeb."

"Who told you that?" I asked.

"Your grandmother Seraiah." He smiled. "She's quite something."

I smiled back at him. "I could never have survived that night without her."

His eyes locked on to mine as I gripped the folds of his tunic, remembering that night of terror, my dagger glinting in the moonlight in Horeb's fist. Softly, I said, "The image of my uncle Abimelech dying stays constantly in my mind. I watched him take his last breath."

He stared deep into my face. "Horeb—he hurt you, didn't he?"

I bit at my lips, not wanting to talk about that night. "Blackmail now hangs over my head, Kadesh, and I've been shunned from the camp. With my father gone, I had nowhere else to turn but come here and find Leila."

Kadesh continued to study me and I dropped my head, as if he could see my thoughts. "But you stayed at the temple, Jayden. . . . Why?"

"When I came I—I wasn't well—"

"I will kill him if he ever hurts you," Kadesh said, his voice low and hard.

I put a hand up to stop him and my fingers touched his

mouth, the lips I'd dreamed of kissing a thousand times the past many months. "I couldn't leave Leila. She refuses to come with me back home. She wants to train as a temple priestess. And tonight, I know exactly what that means." My voice broke off, images of my sister in that bedroom like a searing iron behind my eyes. "I will always feel guilty knowing you found me here."

Using his fingers, Kadesh wiped at the tears trailing along my cheeks. "Circumstances were desperate and unusual. I could never look at you differently, Jayden. Why would I shun you for trying to stay alive? For defending yourself and your sister? Of course you needed to come here when you lost the protection of your tribe. There is no one to blame but Horeb."

"He's gone mad, I fear. In his own mind he has good reasons for everything he's done since he—we—lost Zenos, his elder brother. I pray I never see him again."

He gave me a brief smile. "We think alike, daughter of Pharez."

There was a moment of utter quiet as we looked into each other's eyes and then Kadesh bent his head down and crushed his lips against mine. I wrapped my arms around his neck, opening my mouth, kissing him back so deeply I was sure I must be soaring. As if my soul would leave my body and take flight into the universe of stars overhead.

Even as I savored his mouth on my lips and neck and eyes, his hands tangled in the curls of my hair, what we were doing was forbidden. I was breaking my family's betrothal with each kiss, each stolen caress, and each whispered word.

I was willing to sacrifice my life and my family and my reputation for Kadesh. We were meant to be together, and no one could tell me otherwise. His lips lingered on mine, softly kissing me over and over again, and I drowned in the sensation.

When we broke apart to catch our breaths I gazed into his dark eyes as he brushed my hair from my face. He bowed his head over my hand, kissing each of my fingers, and then finally pressing his lips into my palm as he'd done so long ago.

"If you do not leave to go home," I told him quietly, "Horeb will eventually find you, and he'll kill you without blinking twice. Without my clan and tribe, an outcast, we have no protection, nobody to call on to help us."

"I'm not planning on challenging them, especially not alone. I know how to keep a low profile." His hand slid down my arm and he grasped my fingers to pull me to my feet. "Come here. We need to talk."

Kadesh checked the outer tile paths that circled the temple to make sure we were still alone. Then he led me to the table, where we sank into two cushioned chairs facing each other, inches apart, our knees pressed together as we clasped hands, our grip so tight I thought we might never come apart again.

"I've sent a message to my uncle with the returning caravan that I had business in Tadmur and would return home in a few weeks."

"How did you get here? Surely you didn't walk again."

He gave a wry smile. "This time, I managed to keep my camel underneath me. And I've brought sixty camels for your father just as I promised him long ago. I have them being held by a camel trader I've done business with for many years, right here in Tadmur."

"Sixty! But the original promise was for fifty, which was incredibly generous."

Kadesh shook his head. "I'm buying another hundred camels as a promise for you. More for when we wed."

I stared at him in disbelief. "My father has never owned half that in his life."

"Jayden," Kadesh said quietly. "You are worth ten times that—and a hundred camels is hardly my life's fortune."

The wealth he alluded to was unimaginable. "You are richer than any king!"

He laughed. "My uncle has more than a thousand camels. We run many caravans."

"So it's true," I whispered, still in shock.

"What's true?"

"The rumors of the wealth of the frankincense lands. The gold and camels and castles!"

Glancing around, Kadesh put a finger to his lips and I dropped my rising voice. "I can't wait to show it all to you."

He pulled me out of the chair and into his lap, and his arms were so strong and comforting I felt safe in a way I never had before. I ran my fingers through his long, dark hair, and he kissed me again with such urgency, a strange wonderment that he was mine swept over me.

He finally pulled back, his eyes searching mine. "How soon can you leave?"

"What do you mean, leave?"

"I want to take you to my home, where it's safe. I want my uncle to meet you."

His words took my breath away. "Despite all the suffering of the last months," I said softly, "I'm worried about Leila. I want to make sure she really is safe here at the temple, and that they will take care of her. And Sahmril—" My voice choked as I pictured her with Dinah.

"I want to take you to a place where Horeb can never find you or hurt you again. In the southern lands, we can await word of your father's return from the desert, and then we can officially marry. Your family is welcome to come with us to my home, and you will never be apart again."

Hope rose inside me, but I shook my head. "My father will never leave his tribe or clan, despite my uncle Abimelech's death. In fact, he will be motivated even more to help Judith and see Horeb rise to his rightful place. I'm sure he will take Horeb under his wing as his own son now. My father doesn't see the bad in others. He never has. But perhaps when he learns of what Horeb did to his father, and to me?"

We fell into a moment of silence.

Kadesh said, "As long as Horeb is out there, I won't leave you alone."

I leaned forward and kissed his lips. "As much as I want to, I can't go with you to your wonderful frankincense lands until I find my sister Sahmril. I need to rescue her first before I can move forward with my own life. Sahmril needs to be with her real family: me, Leila, and my father. I promised my mother on her deathbed that I would watch out for her."

"Have you had any word since Dinah and Shem parted at the crossroads?"

"Nothing at all. But that day was one of the worst of my life, watching them disappear across the desert toward Mari."

"Mari?" Kadesh's face turned bleak as he recalled their destination. "Jayden, have you heard about what's happening in Mari?"

I shook my head, puzzled at the strange expression on Kadesh's face.

He hesitated. "The place is in chaos. King Hammurabi of Babylon has invaded, determined to take Mari under his rule. Thousands of soldiers occupy the city. There are curfews, rebellion, fights that break out daily. Very little commerce comes in and out of the city right now, and the tribal people are avoiding it at all costs."

"No," I whispered, feeling my hope for finding Sahmril fail me.

"Hammurabi's plan is to topple the government and take over the city. He wants to rule all of Mesopotamia."

Misery washed over me. "But Sahmril is there. With Hammurabi's invasion, Shem's family might have left. Or—or, if they didn't escape before the siege, they could all be—"

"Don't think that. You must stay hopeful."

A cold chill settled in my belly. Searching for Sahmril in a city under siege was risky. Was any of Shem's family still alive? Perhaps I was foolish to even consider it.

"But what if I can help her?" I whispered. "How can I live my life not knowing her fate? How can I break the promise I made to my mother? I should have kept Sahmril with me. I should never have let her go."

"No, Jayden. Sahmril wouldn't have lasted another two days with us on the desert. You did what you had to."

Kadesh's expression was sober. Gripping his hand, I murmured, "I've seen young children—toddlers, even—in the temple orphanage. Children who have lost their parents to war or illness. The little girls remind me of Sahmril. If I don't find her, she will never know her true family. I know Dinah won't raise her as her own, that she'll only keep her as a servant." My eyes welled up.

Kadesh kissed my hand. "Jayden—"

"Leila always says that memories of Sahmril will kill my heart. That she probably already died from lack of milk on the desert before Shem's family ever reached Mari. But I have to know for certain, or I will never forgive myself."

"Jayden, we *will* find her. And I will protect you with my life and all that I have."

"But how can we travel together? Not—" I broke off, embarrassed.

"I already have a plan. Since we can't marry until a contract is arranged between your father and my uncle, we will travel as brother and sister."

"Can we do this?" I whispered.

Kadesh held me tight, and I closed my eyes against the richness of his cloak, breathing in his smell. "Have faith in me."

I looked into his eyes and we gazed at each other without speaking. I always thought my faith was steadfast and immovable, but life had become so uncertain and dangerous, I found myself faltering. "I do have faith in you, more than ever," I said as he tenderly kissed my palms.

Later that night, as I stole along the outer balcony walls, the moon waned, barely lighting the stone stairs. Torches glowed by the doorways, but the sentries had just looped around to the east. Now was my chance.

I crept up the stairs, inserted the key into the apartment door I shared with Leila and the other girls, and slipped behind the floor-length draperies. The large, airy bathing room was quiet. Hours had now gone by and the festival of Ashtoreth with its dancing and banquet and rites was officially over.

My neck felt clammy, my stomach sick as images of the Sacred Marriage Rite continued to race through my mind. I slipped through the sitting room and made my way to Leila's bedroom, tiptoeing past several sleeping alcoves.

"Leila," I whispered, touching her arm. She rolled over sleepily and I slid under the sheets, snuggling my face into her silky hair and smelling the familiar musky perfume she usually wore.

On the soft temple bed, we lay side by side, reminding me of so many cold nights on the desert when we bundled up in our blankets under the stars.

"Jayden, what are you doing here?" she whispered. "Can't you sleep? Sometimes I get a little homesick. Sometimes I dream about Mother."

"Me too," I whispered back, biting my tongue at all the

things I wanted to say. I wanted to shake her until she cried and abandoned the temple lifestyle. Instead I said, "I miss Father terribly. And the tents, and the camels and our cousins." My voice broke as memories of home and all that I'd lost living here at the temple the past several weeks rushed over me.

Leila let out a sigh. "I don't miss any of that, only our parents."

I watched her in the dark, holding her hand, drinking in her voice, thinking of the dangerous trip to Mari and then to the southern lands with Kadesh, that there was a very real chance I might not see her for a long time.

Softly, I told Leila that Kadesh had returned and of our plan to find Sahmril. I could see her dark eyes staring at me, hear her gasps of astonishment as I related our plans of traveling under cover of false pretenses.

"I can't leave Sahmril in a city that could be destroyed. Especially by enemy tribes and customs." I paused, then said, "Leila, come with us, please."

Adamantly, she shook her head. "Never will I cross a desert again. That last trip nearly killed me. This decision is not my choice, Jayden. It is yours. This place"—she glanced around at the lovely rooms of the temple—"is my choice."

"Leaving you here at the Temple of Ashtoreth isn't what I want for you, Leila. Please, go back to Father. It would destroy him to know you are living here worshipping the goddess. Let our grandmother take care of you. I keep thinking of our mother and her watching you and that man—"

"Stop trying to make me feel guilty!" Leila said. "I may

have been born into a tribal family, but my heart belongs with the women of the temple, the lifestyle of the city, and the work I've found here in the orphanage. This is what I want." She buried her face into my neck. "I'm sorry, Jayden, but this is where I belong now."

We stared at each other in the dark as we lay on the soft pillows, and Leila didn't say another word. No explanation about what I'd seen her do with that strange man after the ceremony. No regrets. But I saw her eyes glisten as she swallowed hard. "I'm not alone. I have the other girls. Please don't worry about me. I'm safe here and have everything I need. But I'll see you soon, won't I? You'll return to the tribe with Sahmril, right?"

I gulped back all my fears for Leila. "The time is getting close to return to the winter lands. I won't make it back from Mari in time. And—and you know I can never go back. Not until Horeb—" I stopped, not wanting to say how much I wanted to see him dead. Unable to tell her the truth.

"What about Horeb?"

"Whatever happens, Leila, *please* do not tell him where I am. He is not who he appears to be. I've broken the marriage contract by coming here. And now I'm running away with another man. Even if that man is helping me find Sahmril. Horeb and the rest of the tribe will see it otherwise, and I can't risk it. If we ever meet again, he will kill me."

My sister's eyes widened. "What are you saying?"

"He branded me, remember? He thinks he owns me."

Leila shuddered, tracing the more than dozen small, white

scars that ran along my chest and arms. "I'm so sorry, Jayden. I promise you my silence."

I took in the beautiful, graceful room. How surreal that I'd actually lived here for a time. I gazed at the ringlets in Leila's hair, the beaded combs and silver jewelry spread across her dressing table. The brushes and pots of rouge and kohl. The silk dresses hanging over every chair, stuffed into drawers and chests.

"Sometimes a person's path in life is hidden," I said softly. "Every day I wake up, it's as though I can only see a few feet in front of me. I must do what is right for this moment."

Leila embraced me, her tears on my cheeks. "Please survive this journey, Jayden. I can't lose you either!"

I nodded, choking back a flood of fresh tears. "I must go. Kadesh waits for me out in the hills with the camels."

After Leila fell asleep, the moon set, leaving cold, brilliant stars in a charcoal sky. I shivered as I slid out from under the linen and crossed the bedroom for the last time.

The scent of musk stirred the air as I opened the wooden chest next to Leila's bed. I lifted dresses and veils, and finally spotted my mother's beautiful alabaster box. I snatched it up as a wave of homesickness washed over me.

Quietly, I lifted the lid and studied the statue of the dancing woman with her long, carved hair, arms reaching for the heavens. The figure reminded me of my mother, her gentle beauty and faith as she taught me to dance.

Now I understood why Leila treasured the figurine and carefully hid it in our mother's wedding box. When I returned it to the chest, I knew that I may never see my mother's prized possession again either.

Pausing at the doors to the balcony, I hid behind the curtains to see if guards were still making their sentry rounds. I should have told Armana I was leaving. I should have officially asked for permission to leave after partaking of their generous hospitality, but there would be arguments and I didn't have time or heart for that.

Peering around the temple walls, I thankfully saw no one. Even the torches were almost burned out. Clutching my old, worn cloak, I ran down the cold, stone steps of the temple and raced across the dark paths toward the distant hills.

23

I met Kadesh near the city gates of Tadmur as dawn crept along the horizon. He was waiting for me with four camels: two to ride and two already packed with water and food supplies. The journey east to Mari on the Euphrates River was less than two weeks' time.

As he and I rode in the opposite direction of the oasis, swells of dust billowed like puffs of smoke behind us. It appeared as though my tribe was on the move to follow the rains over the desert. It was hard to believe that we'd left the winter desert almost eight months ago now.

My head was filled with memories of home, my clan, and my cousins. I wondered if my father had survived the raids, and what his emotions were when he returned to an empty tent.

"What are you thinking about, quiet Jayden?" Kadesh asked when we stopped for a brief midday meal. He smiled as he pulled me next to him.

I chewed my bread in small bites. "Wondering where Horeb is right now. Hoping he is still west of here in Damascus, thinking that's where you are."

"We can only hope," Kadesh said as we shared a bowl of milk.

We fell silent as I wondered where Sahmril was and what she looked like after all this time. "I'm also thinking about how Timnath and Falail are doing—and my grandmother. I worry about her in her old age. I think about Hakak's happiness and if she is with child now. How many camels my father brought back from the raid. If he despises me or thinks I'm dead."

Kadesh held my hand in both of his. "I worry, too, but there's nothing you can do to help them. The journey to Mari isn't a hard one. We'll be there in ten or eleven days if we ride hard."

I tried to smile. "I had no idea the Euphrates was so close. I've never gone this far east. My tribe stays more to the west, along the range of mountains north of the Red Sea."

"Once we cross through the crevice of those hills up ahead, we'll be in the river valley."

I nodded and paused. "I worry we could be in danger from warring foreign tribes in this region. Or if Horeb is actually ahead of us, searching for us in Mari. Constantly, I wonder what he's doing, what he's thinking, and what he's planning."

"There's no reason for him to believe we've gone to Mari.

He doesn't know our information about Sahmril. I'm sure he's far to the west."

A shiver came over me as we sat in the warm sun on a bed of flat rocks at the mouth of the mountain trailhead. The riverbed was bone dry after the hot summer. Soon the winter rains would come and this ravine would trickle with water.

I turned back. "Kadesh, I know deep in my soul that Horeb is looking for me. If he's back with my tribe, and I'm not there . . . He would quickly learn from Judith or Falail that I've been living at the temple. If Horeb were to discover that I'm with you in Mari . . . He could have me executed, and everyone in the tribe would stand by him."

"But you know the truth about Abimelech's killer."

"Nobody will believe me because I have every reason to lie about it. They all know I want to be with you. I'm a shamed woman. Horeb looks like a hero, marrying his poor, misguided betrothed, despite the way he ruined my reputation. The people of my tribe will hail him as a kind and most forgiving man."

Kadesh came closer, but didn't touch me, even as he kept one eye on the valley for other travelers in the distance. "You must put him out of your mind, Jayden. I promise you'll never have to see him or deal with him again."

Tears burned my eyes and I brushed a hand across my face. "You don't understand. I don't think Horeb will try to hurt *me*. He's going to try to kill *you*. That is the one thing that will confirm his heroics before the tribe. He'll be hailed for helping to restore my good name. Please be careful. Please stay alive. I couldn't bear to live in this world without you."

We stood there, so close, and I could see the muscles in his jaw clenching with the effort to keep his distance. Finally I broke away and hurried to the camels, untying them quickly before I lost my mind with the longing to throw myself against him.

Kadesh ran after me, catching the reins as I climbed onto the camel's back. "Jayden," he said. Before I could stop his impulsiveness, he gripped my hand. "I promise I will stay alive. I promise you that one day you will be with me at my home in the frankincense lands. Do you still have the nuggets I gave you all those months ago?"

I nodded, keenly aware of the secret bundle hidden beneath my dress.

"Then let's get to Mari as quickly as possible and find Sahmril. Focus on that, because there's nothing you can do for Leila or your father anymore."

Kadesh swung up onto his camel, double-checking our leather bags of water. He kicked at his camel as we headed for the narrow, rocky trail, and his dark brown eyes met mine. "Our future together cannot come fast enough, my lovely Jayden."

A strange, tender joy filled my heart as his camel took off, and I urged my own animal into a gallop to catch up.

Our pace soon slowed as the hills grew steeper. When we stopped after sunset that night, we built a small campfire and ate quickly.

I headed straight to my blanket, staring up at the

never-ending stars in the black bowl of sky, focusing my thoughts on finding Sahmril.

After a week we progressed through the mountains, and then days of desert sands and saltbush later, we galloped down the final slopes into the plains of Mari.

"It's breathtaking," I gasped, drinking it all in as we approached the valley. The world before us stretched like an expanse of gold silk, the Euphrates River wide and thunderous as it wove through harvested lands of grain and corn, orchards of fruit trees and vineyards of grapes.

"Have you been here before?"

"Of course," Kadesh said, smiling at me. "I know a safe inn where we can stay, if we don't find Dinah and her husband right away."

Our camels stood side by side as we stared out at the enormous valley. In the very center was the city of Mari, like an enchanted mirage before my eyes. The city had been built in a circle with high stone walls surrounding the entire perimeter, and the river winding through the center.

"On either side of the wall are two sets of gates," Kadesh said, flicking his reins to start our camels up again. "That straight line of water cutting the city in half is a canal. They've built levies and retaining walls to steer the course of the Euphrates directly into the city for easy access. No need for digging wells and creating cisterns. No going outside the safety of the city to get water. Brilliant, isn't it?"

I nodded in awe, steering my camel over a patch of rocks

and back onto the trail as we hit the sloping foothills. "It looks quiet, not like there's a siege going on at all."

"From a distance, it can be deceiving. But do you see those camps?" he asked, pointing to the north. "Those are the troops of Hammurabi."

"Why did he invade? My father told me once that Mari's King Zimrilim and Hammurabi of Babylon were allies, so this war makes no sense."

"That is all in the past. Now Hammurabi wants to control the entire state of Mesopotamia—and Zimrilim isn't strong enough to keep him out. Just like his father, who was assassinated in a coup several years ago, King Zimrilim underestimated the need for a bigger army. He spent more time building his palace than his protection."

Kadesh pointed down below. "See those shining pools of water and the maze of stone walls surrounded by the biggest cluster of trees—right in the middle of the city? That is the royal palace compound."

Our magnificent view disappeared as the trail descended out of the hills and we drew closer to the city. All I could see now were the high walls and battlements and the specks of soldiers surrounding the fortress city. "What if we can't get in?" I asked softly.

Kadesh's face appeared calm, but I could see a touch of worry in his eyes. "Even though Mari has been under siege for several months now, it appears as though people are beginning to move in and out more freely."

When we approached the gates, I made sure my face and

head were covered and didn't speak a word, but I caught the grim tension of the soldiers as they examined our camels and inspected our packs of food and supplies. When they questioned Kadesh about our business, their tone was brusque. After telling them we were visiting relatives, the guards fell silent when Kadesh supplied them with coins. The massive wooden gates, studded with brass, finally opened, and we entered the occupied city of Mari.

As we rode through the streets, an edgy atmosphere filled the air, giving me an unsettling sense of trepidation. Street after street was filled with shops and inns and drinking houses. The marketplace bustled with people and trading, just like Tadmur, but the neighborhoods were much more subdued, as though people were afraid of being stopped and questioned.

"Mari has always been the biggest trading post along the Euphrates," Kadesh said quietly. "People come from up and down the river, from as far south in Babylon, or from the north beyond Nineveh to buy, sell, and trade goods and animals."

Even as he spoke, I watched scraggly chickens and mangy dogs roaming the poorer alleyways. When the streets narrowed even more, Kadesh and I climbed down from our camels and walked beside them, holding tight to the halters.

"Let's find a place near the canals to water our animals," Kadesh said. "The plaza should also be close by, within sight of the Temple of Inanna. We'll get information about Mari's citizens more easily at the plaza. If Dinah is here, we'll find her. And Sahmril."

Kadesh's instincts were right. While I watered the camels

at the wells, dragging bucket after bucket up with the hand crank, I watched him under the hood of my cloak as he made careful, guarded talk with the older women who came to the canal. Women who'd lived in Mari their entire lives, and knew their neighbors and all the gossip.

The soldiers on horseback marching the streets made me uneasy. Guards and sentries were posted along every corner, watching the citizens for any uprising.

Babylon was rumored to be the largest and most dazzling city of the ages, but no one knew how ruthless King Hammurabi might become to achieve his goals of total Mesopotamian domination. Mari had become a tense and dangerous place.

I sat on a stone near the well as our animals drank. Kadesh disappeared into the crowds. A chill crept over me and I tried to focus on the camels, petting their noses, keeping them out of trouble.

"Kadesh," I whispered, terror striking at me when he didn't return for an hour.

Trickles of perspiration dripped down my face. He'd probably stepped into one of the shops, but it was hard not to panic. I pulled at the camels' tethers, trying to get them to obey me, but they were stubborn.

"Come!" I yelled, finally getting them to move from the well. I stood with them for nearly another hour in front of a rug and brass merchant, trying to ignore the patrolling soldiers with their swords and clubs.

I felt the edge of my own dagger under the belt of my skirt, and my gut tightened. Kadesh had told me that the citizens' arms had been confiscated with the invasion.

He was suddenly at my elbow, and relief flooded me. "Where have you been?"

"I think I've found them," he whispered.

Instantly, I went still. "Are you sure?"

"My stores of silver are dangerously low. I'm nearly broke from all the bribes I've been passing out."

"Looking for someone?" the merchant suddenly said behind us, shrewdly studying the signs of Kadesh's clan on the decorations of his camel. "I can help you. Business is slow."

"Thank you, sir, but I believe I've found my long-lost aunt and cousins."

"That girl your sister?" the man asked, staring hard at me.

I pulled my shawl closer and didn't say a word. My accent was different from Kadesh's and would give me away.

"Yes, sir, she's been ill. We lost our small herd to raiders and have been searching for our relatives, who headed this direction at the end of the spring season."

The man pursed his lips and spat on the ground. "If you need anything, just ask for me, Romuel. My price is good."

"Thank you for your kind offer." Bowing his head, Kadesh clucked at the camels, pulling them to a crossroad of streets and alleys. I was careful not to look back.

In the midst of the crush, I said, "Tell me! What do you know?"

Kadesh kept his face forward. "Nothing's certain yet, but one of the women at the well took me to her sister, who has a neighbor who knows everybody. There's a section of town for new immigrants. Within that area, there's a group of tribal people. That's our best chance of finding Shem and Nalla and your cousins."

After we found the neighbor of the sister, Kadesh asked about the newer residents. I stood again with the camels, closing my eyes against fatigue, swaying on my feet.

"I've got some leads," Kadesh said when he came out of the door of the tiny house. I crept closer, tired of the crowds, weary after two weeks of travel, and worried that we'd come all this way and learn that Shem's family had fled the city before the siege.

It was twilight when Kadesh knocked on the tenth door, each one leading us closer and closer, but never quite the correct house. "This is the last for today. We need to find a place to sleep."

A platoon of soldiers clattered down the street, swords clanging. They were yelling something I couldn't understand, so fierce I wanted to jump out of my skin. "What's happening?" I cried softly.

"There's a curfew," Kadesh said. "We need to get off the streets or we'll be arrested. Come this way!"

We darted down another alley, and I lost count of how many twists and turns we'd made. At last, Kadesh knocked on a door at the end of a row of single-story buildings with low roofs and sagging doorframes. Two soldiers spotted us and galloped forward. Kadesh knocked harder and the door finally creaked open.

"What do you want?" a woman's voice muttered. "It's after

curfew. We'll all be arrested—go away!"

Kadesh's voice was strong despite the nervousness of the woman. "I'm looking for the house of Shem. It's urgent that we find him."

"How do you know the family of Shem?" The woman's dark eyes were all we could see as she started to close the door again.

I pressed forward, recognizing the voice. "No, don't shut us out! Nalla, is that you? Please, Nalla, let us in! The soldiers are upon us."

I heard the woman give a startled gasp and the door creaked open a few more inches. "Jayden?"

"Yes, yes, it's me!"

The soldiers began shouting at us and drew their swords as we tumbled into the house and Nalla slammed the door behind us.

I blinked into the dimness of the quarters. The room was small and close and hot. A smell of rotting vegetables and smokiness permeated the tiny house.

Nalla stared at us; then she embraced me quickly and pulled back again. "Setting eyes on you is like seeing a ghost, Jayden. Where did you come from?"

"From Tadmur, the summer oasis."

She shook her head, sinking to a stool. "But Mari is a long ways from Tadmur. Isn't the tribe on their way south back to the winter lands by now?"

"Yes," I said softly. "They probably are."

"And you're not with them?" Suspicion lined Nalla's face.

"Where are your father and Leila? And why aren't you with your husband, Horeb?"

"Much has happened, Nalla," I said quietly. "Horeb and I are not married . . . yet. I haven't seen him or my father since they left on a raid months ago. And Leila . . . She is living at the Temple of Ashtoreth."

The woman's expression crumpled with shock and pity as she grasped my hands. "It's been a hard year for your family, Jayden. I'm so sorry. You have changed, too. You look so much older, wiser somehow. And even more beautiful, just like your mother."

I tried not to weep at her words. "That means so much to me, Nalla. Thank you."

"But why are you with the stranger from the southern lands? Your father will disown you, and so will Horeb."

Politely, Kadesh bowed, murmuring, "Please believe that we mean you no harm or trouble."

"It's not right to travel, unmarried, with another man, Jayden. Your reputation is ruined, your future destroyed."

"We are traveling as brother and sister. Kadesh accompanies me so that I can find my sister safely and bring her home. I'm looking for Sahmril. Where is she? I'm here to take her back with me."

Nalla flinched and turned away, poking at the small fire, adding a few sticks to the blaze. The rest of the small house was so dark I had no idea who might be lurking in the back rooms, and the unknown put me on edge. Kadesh paced the floor, glancing into the back hall, his fist on the hilt of his sword.

"I've been so desperate to get her back, you know. I promised my mother I would raise her."

Nalla raised her head from the fire. "My husband, Shem, was conscripted to Hammurabi's army. I only see him once a week, every ten days. Dinah's husband"—she stopped, and I could tell that grief was overwhelming her—"Dinah's husband—was killed in the first raid on Mari. Mistaken for one of King Zimrilim's soldiers."

I barely had time to register my stunned shock at the terrible news when the rear door flew open and Dinah herself strode through. She looked exactly the same as I remembered. Pinched, thin face, greasy hair pulled away from her brow. "So it's *you* my mother is talking to," she said, staring at me coldly.

My mouth went dry. Grief pervaded the thick air of the house. A sense of anger and hopelessness. "Please accept my deepest condolences. I'm so sorry, Dinah." I paused. "So you are now two women alone, trying to survive in a war-torn city."

Dinah's voice was severe. "I don't expect you to care a bit for *our* loss."

"Of course I do—" Then I noticed the jewelry hanging from Dinah's neck, the feathery silver earrings dangling from her ears. *My jewelry.* The jewelry that my parents sacrificed to purchase for me. I wanted to rip it from her neck, but instead I became dizzy. It was too warm in here. The day had been much too long and frenzied after our weeks of travel. The floor seemed to rush up toward my eyes and I trembled with fatigue.

Kadesh's arm was suddenly supporting me, keeping me on

my feet. "Sit here," he said.

"Yes, please sit," Nalla said, bringing two stools. "I don't have much, and we have no extra beds."

"I will sleep with my camels," Kadesh assured her.

"Sahmril." Her name burst from my mouth. "I want to see her! It's been so long and we've come such a long ways. I've missed her so. Thank you, Dinah, for all you've done for her. I want to take her with me. You'll be able to focus on your own child, and not worry about Sahmril any longer."

Dinah licked her dry lips. "I don't know where Sahmril is."

"What—what do you mean? In the desert, did she—" I stopped. The words wouldn't come out of my mouth.

Dinah shrugged. "I didn't think I would see you again."

The room swirled around me as though she'd punched me in the chest. "You left my sister to die in the desert! How could you, after I gave you all that I owned?"

"No!" Dinah snapped. "No, Sahmril is alive. It was *my* son who died in the desert. Because I was sharing my milk with your sister. And then my husband was killed. I've lost every-thing—everything, you ungrateful girl!"

"*No, no, no.* Oh, Dinah, what you have suffered is too much to bear." Tears rushed down my face. "I'm so sorry, so very sorry! But where is Sahmril? I must see her! I'm desperate to hold her."

The expression in Dinah's eyes was callous. "She's alive, but I sold her to pay for my husband's debts and burial."

"What?!" I screamed. "You sold her into slavery?"

Nalla rushed over to shake my arm. "Silence! In Mari, even

the walls have ears! And our neighbors are much too close. We had no choice, Jayden," she hissed in a low, fierce voice. "We would have been put into prison or hung for debt. Sahmril was all we had left to barter for our own lives."

"You sold a baby? An innocent child? To be beaten or worked to death, or—or worse!" I groaned with the horror of it, and Kadesh placed his hands on my shoulders to keep me from lunging at the woman. "How could you? You—with my jewelry around your dirty neck! You could have sold that instead! Or the camel!"

"The camel is our only milk."

"You could have traded for a lesser camel instead of selling Sahmril. You selfish pig."

Dinah reached out and slapped my face with the back of her hand. "*I* am the one who has lost my family, not you," she spat at me.

The roaring in my ears drowned out the rest of her words. I'd lost my mother, my sisters, and my father would disown me now that I'd lived at the temple. I'd sealed my fate when I traveled to Mari as an unmarried woman with a man of another tribe. And she dared to tell me that she had lost more? I wanted to tear the room into pieces, throw their belongings into the streets, and scratch out their eyes.

"Who did you sell her to?" I hissed. "Who bought her?"

Sullenly, Dinah folded her arms and didn't answer. Finally Nalla said, "A traveling merchant paid us enough for our funeral expenses. All we know about him is that he was on his way to Salem."

"Salem?" Kadesh said sharply. "That's four hundred miles southwest from here. Near the Great Sea!"

All my hopes and dreams of holding Sahmril in my arms had shredded into a thousand pieces. I'd come all this way for nothing. She was farther away than ever. How would I ever get to Salem? I had no money, no time, no camels. My baby sister was truly lost to me.

24

"I'm going to help you search for the location of the Salem merchant," I told Kadesh after two days of sitting with Nalla and Dinah, tending to the tasks of their household in payment for a sleeping mat. "I can't sit inside that hole of a house another moment and listen to my jewelry tinkling around her neck."

With only a name on the ticket of receipt, Kadesh and I set out to search for more information. The days dragged on. We'd been gone from Tadmur for three weeks now. The autumn season was full upon us, winter biting at our heels.

On our fifth day in Mari, Kadesh and I sat on a bench near the Temple of Inanna, seeking new people to ask our questions to.

"The city has a different mood to it," I said, noticing furtive conversations, people more hurried than usual. The soldiers seemed even more grim than usual.

"It's dangerous, Jayden," Kadesh told me, frowning. "I fear we don't have much more time to get information before the city shuts down."

"But we can't travel to Salem not knowing where the merchant lives—some sort of address or directions. All we have is a name."

He nodded slowly. "I have learned that the man dealt in weavings, but there are two streets in Mari with weaving stores."

"I can visit the shops, too, and ask questions. It will save us some time."

"After every shop we'll meet and check our information," Kadesh said. "But we need to keep in sight of each other."

The day was long and wearying as we visited every shop, pretending to buy a rug or a new loom or a shawl or a skein of yarn. Eventually asking questions about a merchant who had closed up shop and left for Salem with a young child.

I talked to women, to children, and when I didn't make a purchase the shop owner usually became impatient with me.

Every hour I met Kadesh in the street to report our findings, which were nothing.

There were only three shops left when I stood at a table looking at an array of cloaks with various grades of wool. I was so weary; I felt dazed, numb. The search seemed fruitless.

"Girl, I'm about to close up shop," a male voice said. "You need to leave now."

I jerked my head up, taking in the merchant's haggard face.

"I'm sorry. How much is this?"

"You've been standing there for a long time contemplating how to steal that scarf, and I do not believe you have any money to make a purchase."

"Steal?" I repeated, blinking at him. "I've never stolen anything in my life."

The shopkeeper shook his head. "You're a desert-tent girl, I can tell. And desert people steal all the time."

I was about to argue when I saw Kadesh coming slowly down the street. I could tell he had no news. Our time had run out. I'd failed.

I cleared my throat. "I'm looking for a merchant who owned a shop here in Mari. A few months ago he was going to sell it and go to Salem—"

He cut me off. "People move all the time. And with the city under siege, more have left than usual. If you were smart you'd go, too. Life is going to get uglier. Hammurabi has rejected the king's latest truce."

His words meant almost nothing to me, and this was my last chance. So I forged ahead. "This merchant bought a little girl he planned to sell in Salem. I've been trying to find her."

The man's eyebrows knit together. He looked me up and down. Out of the corner of my eye I saw Kadesh pause and wait, his hand on his belt.

"A girl, you say, eh? More like a baby, a toddler?"

"Yes," I whispered. "Do you know who that merchant was?"

"You might be referring to my brother. He wanted to leave

due to the political situation here and his ill health. I took over his shop, which I'm now regretting myself."

"Do you know what part of Salem he went to, or who the slave trader was? I will gladly pay for any information."

"He bought the girl but eventually found a better buyer right here in Mari. So he never left, and he may not survive this siege, either. He's living in my house now."

I whispered, "You are too kind, sir."

"You're too young to be on your own here. Do you have family?"

"Yes. Relatives."

"Go home. The city is more restless than usual tonight. I fear there will be an outbreak of violence against the soldiers."

"But, sir!" I cried. "Who did your brother sell the child to? Do you know? Can I talk to him?"

The shopkeeper shook his head. "A married couple bought the girl. Paid double. They're one of the fortunate ones who still have any money. A nobleman who went into hiding at the palace. A longtime friend of the king's."

"The palace," I breathed, my eyes widening. "Is she going to be raised as a slave for King Zimrilim? What will happen to her now that Hammurabi is overthrowing Zimrilim?"

"I don't know, but the palace citizens may not survive. Zimrilim has been pretending to negotiate a treaty before he actually exiles himself to Damascus. Meanwhile his generals are arranging the biggest attack yet on Hammurabi. We need to leave the city before the gates are locked. The danger has been escalating and there are rumors something will happen tonight. It's no longer safe for any of us. I implore you to leave while you can."

I lurched out of the shop and nearly fell into Kadesh. The street was suddenly thinning in the late afternoon. "Did you hear that?" I asked him.

Kadesh nodded. "Our search has finally proven fruitful. We'll go right now to find your sister."

I felt the color drain from my face. "This very moment? It's like a miracle, Kadesh!"

I followed behind him as we maintained our pretense of a sibling relationship, hurrying out of the weaver's market and heading to the main plaza. "Let's go to the palace immediately," he suggested. "The city is not safe tonight. As soon as we find Sahmril, we need to depart."

We hurried as fast as we dared, closing in on the palace courtyard gates as the sun began to set.

"Jayden." Kadesh spoke my name, and we halted. Beyond the gates in front of us, trees grew denser, shade covering our heads. He lowered his voice. "You must prepare yourself for whatever happens."

"What do you mean?"

"I'm fairly certain Sahmril is healthy and has been taken care of, but seeing her is going to be hard for you."

"We can buy her back, right? Take her with us tonight? We have enough coins and frankincense, don't we?"

Kadesh nodded but didn't say anything else, which left me troubled.

I was nervous and queasy as Kadesh spoke to a man at

the small, golden gates of a courtyard on the north side of the palace. Past the spires of the gate, my eyes became lost in the sight of gardens, pools, statues, and shrines. The scent of roses and orchids perfumed the air. Luscious grass grew along the winding stone paths, and pools of clear, blue water shone cool and inviting.

A breeze rushed through the air, and I sensed the smell of smoke and incense wafting down from the temples on their hills as the palace guard unlatched the gate and let us slip inside.

When we stepped along the narrow courtyard paths, dusk settled over the gardens, but the outer torches stayed unlit. Darkness enveloped the grounds and dread settled in my belly. I didn't speak even though I had a hundred questions about how Kadesh had managed to get us inside.

We approached a door, were led down a hallway to another door, and the guard gave a light rap, speaking quickly and furtively, and then disappearing.

The door opened and we were ushered inside. I was suddenly aware of my travel-worn cloak, my tangled hair, and the absence of any adornment. It was obvious that I was a poor camel herder's daughter. The people who had bought Sahmril had titles and wealth and education. I had nothing to offer them. I feared they would laugh at us, but Kadesh had obviously bribed the guard well to give us an appointment with them.

The space where we stood was a small waiting room, lit by candles in tall, brass holders. The windows overlooked the apartment gardens and a greenish pond of water lay flat under the rising moon. Shadows flickered everywhere and my nerves jangled; I was so eager to see Sahmril.

We waited for what seemed like hours.

I paced the floor, sure I would faint by the time the door across the room finally opened, and a middle-aged man with a gray beard entered.

"I'm Thomas, a retired diplomat of King Zimrilim." He studied us, taking in my destitute appearance, and turned to Kadesh, whose manner and cloak were far superior to mine. I felt the hair on my neck prickle when our eyes met and the nobleman quickly glanced away, but I tried to stay calm.

"We understand that you want to speak to us about our daughter, Ramah," Thomas finally said.

I gasped, tears burning the back of my eyes. Their *daughter*! The words were so unexpected.

"As you know, we've traced an infant girl to you," Kadesh said. "A baby purchased several months ago through a rug merchant named Limhi."

Thomas nodded slowly. "We're aware of this."

"And you still possess this child?"

"She's *in* our possession, you mean," Thomas corrected.

My legs trembled beneath me. The man's demeanor and words were coming together in my mind, and I was having a hard time taking it in. "Kadesh," I whispered as I sank to the floor.

Thomas rang a bell and instantly a servant appeared with water and cups. I took one gratefully and sipped, the cool water clearing my head.

Thomas cleared his throat. "Perhaps I should explain how we found Ramah. I've known the merchant Limhi for many years. He travels through Mesopotamia—Egypt as well as Ethiopia and Babylon—purchasing a variety of things for the king. Treasures, sculptures, works of art, animals. I oversee this process. My wife and I are childless and it has always been our greatest dream to be parents. When Limhi heard of the girl child who had been bought by a Salem slave trader, he immediately purchased her and brought her to us. She was the baby we've wanted all our lives. Our daughter is beautiful, an answer to many prayers."

Silent tears trickled down my face, and Kadesh reached down to hold my hand. I no longer cared what anyone thought of our relationship. I would never see these people after tonight.

"Where is she?" I asked, gulping back my tears. "May I see her, please?"

Without answering me, Thomas strode across the room to a set of windows overlooking the courtyard ponds and water-falls.

"My wife and daughter are in the garden," he said. "Zarah was going to bring her inside so you could see her, but now she has changed her mind."

"But she's my sister! I've come so far, please, I beg of you."

The nobleman pursed his lips and made no reply.

Kadesh stood next to me as we watched a servant holding a little girl in her arms appear through one of the garden gates, handing her over to the woman of the house, Zarah.

The toddler had rosy cheeks and a mass of black curls. I

recognized the baby's eyes instantly. They were my mother's: the same shining pools of dark water; the same fringe of lashes against her cheeks. Her perfect skin was Leila's, her tangle of black curls mine.

I watched as the toddler took several tiny steps, holding on to the servant's fingers as she wiggled toward Zarah, who finally swept up the beautiful child—my sister—into her arms.

My throat ached as Zarah nuzzled Sahmril's neck and kissed her soft baby cheeks. I wanted to touch my little sister and hold her. I still remembered that sweet baby skin, the smell of her, and the fragility of a newborn infant. "Oh, Sahmril," I cried, sagging against Kadesh. "She's even more beautiful than I remembered. But it's her—it's truly her! We've found her at last."

Thomas turned to me. "So you think Ramah belongs to your family?"

"I'm positive she's my sister. The child of my mother, who died giving birth."

"Your mother is dead?" Thomas asked, staring out at his wife and the little girl as they fed bread crumbs to the ducks in the pond. "How did Limhi the merchant come to own her?"

The lump in my throat grew bigger. "The woman who sold her was the wet nurse who kept her alive on the desert after we buried my mother."

Understanding flooded Thomas's face, and then a brief flash of empathy. He watched me for several long moments. "I can tell that she looks like you," he said rigidly. "Our daughter is going to be a beauty."

"Just like my mother," I added. I recalled Judith telling me the very same thing the night of my betrothal celebration. A lifetime ago. A lifetime of pain and sorrow. "How long have you had her?" I finally asked, watching Zarah run her fingers through the silky, fine hair of my sister, nuzzling her neck and making her giggle.

"Since she was about two months old. I estimate that she's about nine months old now. She's walking early."

I took a step forward, jerking out my hands. "Please, may I hold her?"

Thomas shook his head. "She's the child we always wanted, and we paid dearly for her."

I tried to stay calm. "I promised my mother on her death-bed that I would care for her, that I would make sure she was always safe."

I sucked in my breath when, through the windows, Zarah turned to meet my gaze straight on. I could tell that she wanted me and Kadesh to leave.

Thomas cleared his throat. "You fulfilled your mother's wish, then. Your sister is well and healthy and happy with us."

"But I always planned on returning for her. When I arrived in Mari, I fully expected Sahmril to be with Dinah and Nalla. That was the original plan."

"Plans change, don't they? Good and bad happens to all of us, and it's our turn for something good."

I stared at him, tempted to slap him. This man who had such a fine home, a title, wealth. Instead I quickly said, "I will pay you the same sum you used to buy her from the merchant.

Plus more. In fact, double that amount for the cost of taking care of her."

Thomas's face closed up. "I think you misunderstand. I wasn't caring for this child for *you*. She's my daughter, and I care for her because I love her. Ramah is mine and will be raised as my daughter in the household of the palace, with everything she ever needs or wants. One day she'll be educated and will have a good marriage to a nobleman's son. Which, I may add, you cannot give her."

Blood pounded in my skull as I quickly withdrew my bag of six frankincense nuggets. "You may have all of these for her."

Thomas snorted, clearly insulted.

I frowned, knowing I'd blundered somehow, but I wasn't sure.

Kadesh stepped forward, his great cloak snapping the air. "And there are hundreds more of those where they came from. I can guarantee them from my personal groves. And as much silver and gold as you want. We're not insulting you. We just want the child. She belongs with her blood family."

Thomas's expression became severe as he stepped away from the windows. "*We* are Ramah's family. We paid for her honestly and saved her from slavery. She is ours and *not* for sale."

"Then let me triple our offer," Kadesh said, pressing harder. "And I will also give you one hundred head of camels and cattle and horses as well. This should be very welcomed, since King Zimrilim and the city of Mari may fall soon."

Thomas gave me an angry glare. "Why would my wife and I ever turn this child over to you? To be dirty and hungry and poor. She will never be for sale again, no matter the price. We've gone to the legal authorities and done the paperwork as her permanent parents. There is no price you can name for her. Now go!"

I reared back as though I'd been slapped. My eyes spilled with a thousand tears and Kadesh pulled me close. "Come, Jayden," he said softly. "Let us go and leave these good people in peace."

"No, no, I can't!" I was frantic, desperate. "Please let me hold her just once. Please, I beg you again!"

I ran to the window, but Zarah was already shepherding Sahmril out of my sight, far on the other side of the courtyard into a different wing of the house.

"I do not plan to take her," I said, the pain in my chest sharp and excruciating. "It's just that I've come such a long ways to find her—"

Suddenly we heard the sound of screams, yells, and shouts from across the palace grounds, and then the dreadful noise of pounding feet.

The door to the nobleman's apartment rattled violently. A servant quickly opened it.

A guard stood outside, sword drawn. "You must leave at once!" he commanded. "Hammurabi has stormed the palace walls and everyone must evacuate or be killed. The traitor's soldiers are swarming the place, and the palace is burning even as we speak."

The smell of acrid smoke permeated the room.

Thomas began to shout orders to the servants, then he fled, casting a final glance at us over his shoulder.

I started to run after him, knowing they would escape with Sahmril right before my eyes, but Kadesh held me back. "We have to get out of here, Jayden. Now!"

"Thomas!" Kadesh yelled, stopping the older man in his tracks. It became apparent that Thomas was prepared for a full-blown attack on the palace. His servants had their belongings and food packed and ready to go.

"Where do we go?" Kadesh asked him, his eyes boring into the older man's face. "You know we have nothing to do with this and came here in good faith. Please tell us the safest exit!"

Thomas flicked his eyes to another servant, a burly man with a sword and dagger at his waist. "This man will lead you out of here. Once you're off the palace grounds you're on your own."

Kadesh nodded, and pulled me out the door with him. Smoke filled the courtyard and ash drifted into the beautiful pools of water, blocking out the starry sky. I could hear the chilling roar of flames in the distance even though I couldn't see them.

As we raced down corridors and then outer garden pathways, the screams of the night grew worse. The bedlam of palace noblemen, employees, and servants filled every inch of space as people ran carrying baskets and trunks of belongings. We were tossed and pulled and pushed and shoved. I gripped

Kadesh's arm as we followed Thomas's servant to the outer palace wall, and he pointed to a door farther down set in the stone. Other citizens had already flung the door open and were streaming through to safety.

"I suggest you head for the desert through there," the servant said brusquely.

"I already planned to," Kadesh told him, but before he finished his sentence the servant had disappeared into the madness of the night and screams and smoke.

While Kadesh and I ran toward the crush of escaping people at the open gates, images of Sahmril filled my eyes. I was pummeled and jostled and elbowed for what seemed like hours, but I couldn't get her out of my sight.

The streets of Mari were in chaos. Everywhere soldiers on horses, people running, carrying baskets of food and bedding. Shouts and screams became a roar, the sight of fighting, swords ringing together until my ears hurt. Women screamed and I saw men staggering and bloody. It had all happened so fast. In the last light of day, as people were eating dinner and unprepared.

On Kadesh's heels, I kept my hand clenched tightly to a fold of his cloak so we didn't get separated as we entered the city from the palace compound. I focused on getting out, finding our camels, and leaving Mari forever.

What would happen to Nalla and Dinah? Shem was fighting for Hammurabi, so perhaps they would be spared. Or they would surrender to the Babylonian soldiers when they went door-to-door to ransack and arrest.

"Where are the camels tethered?" I asked Kadesh when we turned a corner.

"In the back alley behind Nalla's house. We'll get the saddles and gear and our belongings, then head as fast as we can for the north gate and the desert."

"But we came in through the south gates."

"The northern gates are much closer to Nalla's house. We'll fill our water bags in the river and flee to the desert as fast as we can."

Kadesh whipped around another corner and pressed me into a tight doorway just as a company of soldiers on horseback clattered down the street in full gear. They were headed for the palace, and I found myself praying that Thomas and Zarah and Sahmril had made it out safely.

Burying my face into Kadesh's chest, I tried to become just a shapeless mass in the darkness of the doorway. No torches were lit in this poorer part of the city, and we stood still and utterly silent, barely breathing. This close to Kadesh, I could hear his heart beating beneath his tunic as he closed his cloak around me and kept us from the soldier's view.

"We're safe," he finally whispered as the street quieted. Quickly, we stole down the street, racing toward safety. Our footsteps were muffled by the sounds of the chaos in the city, and at last, I could see Nalla's doorway. I breathed a sigh of relief. Hopefully, we would be out of Mari within the hour.

Just beyond the tiny house, I spotted a large grouping of camels standing saddled in the darkness. Dozens of men were talking, their voices bouncing off the walls and doorways so that it was hard to tell exactly how many there were.

"Are those soldiers?" I asked.

"I don't think so, but they may be men of Mari in the process of being forced to fight. I don't want to get caught in it. If they grab me and force me to join them, hide with Nalla until you can escape back to Tadmur."

"No!" I cried softly. "Don't say that!"

The night grew colder and I shivered as we made our way down the street, slithering around door frames so we wouldn't be spotted. But my broken heart yearned for Sahmril. I never once considered that I wouldn't be able to buy her back. Now that we were back at Dinah's doorstep, the night felt surreal, as if I was moving in a trance.

Under cover of darkness, Kadesh pulled me to the doorway. Finally, we were safe. I just wanted to collapse before the fire. Kadesh pushed open the door, shoved us both inside, and slammed it behind him.

The room went eerily silent as I realized that Nalla and Dinah were not in the sleeping room in the back as I expected. Instead, they were sitting upright and stiff in chairs as Kadesh and I rushed through the door with breaths of relief.

The remains of a fire smoldered in the grate. A man stood leaning against the hearth, and at first I thought it must be Shem stealing a moment with his wife and daughter.

But when he turned around, I almost died when I saw that evil grin and those sinister eyes.

Horeb was standing before us.

25

Kadesh grabbed my hand and shoved his shoulder into
the door to escape back into the street, but we were
instantly surrounded by the very men we'd seen earlier. Not Mari soldiers or King Hammurabi soldiers at all, but
Horeb's men, my tribal brothers.

"Welcome, please come in," Horeb said with an eerie smile
as I was forced back into the house.

"What are you doing here?" I burst out, and then stopped,
coughing. My throat had gone raw from the acrid smoke of the
fires around the city.

Horeb gave me a scornful stare, but he didn't move from the
hearth. He didn't have to; his men were keeping me enclosed
in a tight circle in the center of the room, which now smelled
of sweat and fear. "My raids brought me north to the wonderful city of Mari, where my men and I have joined with King

Hammurabi to secure the city."

"The Babylonian is not king yet," Kadesh said.

"Oh, he will be. Have no worries there, stranger." Horeb laughed, sending chills down my spine. The hard-edged planes of his face in the firelight made me want to crawl into a hole and never come out. "The royal family of Zimrilim is probably dead by now. Zimrilim was a weak king and didn't deserve such a fine city."

Kadesh studied him coldly. "I question Hammurabi's intelligence if he burns the very city he wants to rule."

"Cities can be rebuilt. Practically overnight." Horeb snapped his fingers and drew closer, his bulk threatening as he laughed at Kadesh. "You must not understand how to conquer and rule a kingdom. It's a good thing no one is looking to *you* for help or direction."

Kadesh didn't respond to Horeb's taunting, but his men loved it, laughing and snorting behind me.

"Why would you want to help Hammurabi conquer Mari? Aren't you needed as leader of your own tribe?"

Horeb curled his lips. "I've had a busy couple of months destroying and then negotiating with the Maachathites, as well as hunting you both down, but the council of Nephish elders awaits my return. With my bride. It seems I'm not officially their leader or king until I'm a married man. The wedding ceremony is planned for the night I get back with Jayden."

Dinah stared at me stonily, but Nalla shifted uncomfortably in her chair.

"I will never marry you, Horeb," I told him, my voice

shaky. "The contract is broken. After all, your own father is dead."

His smile was sinister. "Actually, the contract stands stronger than ever. Abimelech's death sealed it with his blood, never to be broken. I also have a written decree from Pharez to bring you back with me. It's legal and binding and will not be seen as kidnapping. You're an unmarried girl and I'm acting on your father's behalf in your best interest. He and I also have an understanding upon our return that all your father plundered during the Maachathite raid will be mine. His payment for bringing you back home. The tribe's leadership needs to be settled, and you play a key role, Jayden, as my queen."

I wavered on my feet and I felt Kadesh silently standing behind me, giving me strength as Horeb ranted on.

"When I arrived in Mari and learned that Shem was a soldier in Hammurabi's army, it made it easy to learn where his wife and daughter were living. I came to pay a visit to the members of my tribe, and you drop right into my hands. I don't have to search any longer. You've made it so easy."

He started to laugh, and there were chuckles around the room from the rest of his men. My only consolation was knowing that my father was still alive. And that he must have brought back more camels—many camels—if he could offer them to Horeb.

"Haven't you been hunting me or Kadesh all this time?" I shot back.

"True," Horeb admitted, "but you always knew you couldn't get away from me. We're tied together for life, and my reward for patience is you running straight into my arms once again."

I shuddered at his words. Kadesh and I should never have returned to Nalla's house. It was the biggest mistake of our lives.

"You will have the most envied life of every girl in the tribe, Jayden. As an ally to King Hammurabi and with the other tribal alliances I'm forging, we will be wealthy and secure. I can offer you a better life than this wandering stranger."

"Except love and honesty," I whispered to myself, but Horeb heard me, and my face burned as the room broke into amused laughter. Even Dinah narrowed her eyes, a sneer on her lips. Only Nalla looked miserable and helpless as she sat unmoving by the fire hearth.

"Who needs love when you have power and wealth and status?" Horeb said, challenging me. "As well as the admiration of all you meet."

"Subjugation, you mean," I said, despising him.

"There's only one problem, Horeb," Kadesh spoke up. "I won't let Jayden go."

Horeb put his hands on his hips. "You're surrounded! You don't have a choice. I've outwitted and outnumbered you." He paused. "But if you'd like to fight me for her, I'd welcome the sport of another sword contest. Then she will have no choice but to go with the winner. There are many witnesses here to attest to it."

"We'll duel at dawn," Kadesh told him, stepping in front of me. "Alone."

"I'm ready to fight you right now. I'm taking Jayden tonight, stranger. You must die so that her standing in the tribe can be repaired. You see? There's no decision or choice here. You have to die. And I am the one who must do it. With the help of my men, if needed."

"You need your men to help you win your battles?" Kadesh said evenly.

Horeb advanced across the room, his face dark. "I *will* kill you. Make no mistake about that. And if a sword thrust into your heart helps make that happen, so be it. Shall we begin now instead of waiting?"

The next instant, Horeb's long sword came out of his belt and he slashed it through the air. I reared back, but the sharp tip sliced down the front of my dress in a clean, swift tear, and I screamed, backing up into the door and crashing into Kadesh.

"Get out of my house!" Nalla screamed at Horeb, leaping from her chair. "There will be no blood spilled in my house. Get out, or I will have Shem report this to his captain."

Before I could move again, Kadesh had unsheathed his own blade and clashed it against Horeb's weapon.

"No, no, no!" I screamed at them. In the tiny house, Horeb's sword barely missed my head and I fell to the ground, cowering, sweat streaming down my neck.

Their swords whipped against each other, and the clang of steel rattled my teeth. Nalla braced herself against the stone hearth and I crawled away as Horeb sliced the air, inches from Kadesh's face. Kadesh struck again at Horeb's blade, so hard Horeb nearly fell over, but he fought to stay upright. The two men were face-to-face, grunting as their swords braced against each other in a momentary deadlock, keeping the other from advancing or being able to strike a fatal blow.

Months ago, Kadesh had won the sparring match in front of my family, but I could tell that Horeb had been practicing. He was better now, more forceful and surer with his thrusts, although still not as light and swift on his feet as Kadesh. The power behind Horeb's arms and chest made me shudder as I watched them circle each other.

A split second later, Kadesh threw Horeb off, spun around, and raised his sword to cut Horeb sideways across his chest, but Horeb managed to nick Kadesh in the arm first, sending him hard against the wall. Blood trickled down in spurts, turning his hands red. Horeb's men roared with the thrill of the brawl, and the din was unbearable.

"No!" I screamed, lunging toward Horeb with my dagger so he couldn't plunge his sword into Kadesh while he was down.

Kadesh jerked to his feet, shouting, *"No, Jayden, no!"*

Horeb's sword cut through the air as he knocked his body against mine, throwing me off just as I'd been about to shove my knife into his side. My dagger went skittering off into a dark corner.

Before I could go after it, the front door swung wide open. Horeb's men had grabbed Kadesh and were dragging him into the dark streets. He fought hard, legs and feet thrashing, but he didn't have a chance with so many of them. Quickly, two of the men wrenched Kadesh's sword from his hand as they dumped him on the gravel road.

The dreary night was black as pitch, choking smoke swirling through the air from the palace fire on the other side of the city.

I ran screaming into the road. "Kadesh!"

All I could see was his form being yanked over the rocks, a dark river of blood running down his tunic and fingers, the flash of silver from so many swords pointed down at the boy I loved.

Surrounding me on all sides were Horeb's men, the men of my tribe and my youth. They were loyal only to Horeb, who would be tribal chief and make them clan leaders, for the rest of their lives. They would kill for him—and die for him. Anything I said would mean absolutely nothing. I was Horeb's possession and he could do what he wanted with me.

"Stay back, Jayden!" Kadesh yelled at me. "No matter the outcome, you already know what to do."

"Kadesh!" I shouted again, not understanding his words. Horeb cut me off, knocking me down as he strode toward Kadesh. My body hit the hard ground, rattling every bone, my head scraping across the wretched gravel.

"Nalla and Dinah, take her back inside," Horeb flung over his shoulder, his face indifferent as he gave the order.

I flinched as the two women grabbed my arms and forced me back into the house. I fought them, hanging on to the door frame and kicking with my legs and feet. I screamed over my shoulder. "This is no fight! It's a massacre!" I tried to squirm out of the grasp of their hands. "Let me go! You know this is an execution. Get the authorities of Mari!"

"You fool!" Dinah mocked me as she threw me across the floor of the house and Nalla slammed the door. "There are no city authorities to call upon. Every man is fighting somewhere, either for Zimrilim or for Hammurabi."

She was right. There was no order left in this metropolis. We'd become victims of Mari's destruction as well. The city had gone mad.

"Open the door!" I shouted. "Don't you understand? They're going to kill him!"

Nalla held me back. "Yes," she said in a dull, flat voice. "They're going to kill him. Kadesh is sorely outnumbered, and you and I cannot stop it. There is nothing we can do. We are strangers here, and have no friends. Many of our neighbors have already fled. We only stay because of my husband, Shem, and the hope that he has chosen the right side for our loyalty."

My insides heaved. "Then I will kill Horeb myself!" The thought of Kadesh dying within steps of where I was, within moments, was more than I could bear. I began to shake like I had a fever, utterly and completely trapped. "Let me go!" I screamed at Dinah, kicking at her.

Dinah's eyes were like flint. "You think you can kill him, with ten of his men right there? Don't be such an idiot! You are destined to be Horeb's wife and you don't deserve it! You understand nothing!"

With one final burst of strength, I shoved her aside and flung open the door. A half moon appeared behind the red clouds of smoke and I spotted Kadesh lying flat on his back, pinned to the ground by at least eight of Horeb's men. Standing tall, Horeb straddled Kadesh, his sword raised in a stance reminiscent of mine when I nearly plunged my dagger into Horeb's chest that terrible night at the oasis pond.

"No!" I moaned, and all at once, Dinah wrapped her arms around my stomach and pulled me from behind with such force my hands ripped away from the door and we fell together to the floor in a heap. Quickly, I rolled over, kicking at Dinah and screaming at her, but before I could lunge forward again, Nalla slammed the door shut for the final time. Her chest heaved, her face a ghastly pallor.

"It's done," she said, her bloodshot eyes staring past me. "The stranger from the southern lands is no more."

A wail rose up from deep inside my belly. "No!" I stared at her wildly, in shock, not wanting to comprehend her words. Screams tore from my throat and I pushed Dinah to the floor, threw over the table and chairs, yanked at the curtains, smashed the dishes lying on a side table, and then fell to the floor in a grief so terrible I thought my soul would flee my body that instant.

A single moment of silence hung on the air, and then the door to the tiny house opened again. Air rushed in, and boots stamped across the floor to where I lay shivering and sobbing. I looked up through my snarled hair and saw the black, sunken eyes of Horeb glittering in the shadows.

He stalked toward me, and I crawled backward to get away from him, stumbling into another table and knocking over a ceramic mixing bowl, which fell, breaking into jagged pieces.

When he reached out a hand, I flinched. "Don't you dare touch me!" I fumbled for my knife, which was no longer on my thigh, but I couldn't see clearly where it had been thrown earlier while fighting Horeb, and my hand was slippery with blood.

"Don't you want to see the gift I've brought you?" Horeb's voice was deep and obnoxious. Breathing hard, he roughly picked me up and shoved me into a chair so I could see him better. I flinched and jerked backward, the touch of him so despicable I thought I'd be ill.

Then Horeb pulled a bundle from under his arm and rolled open the cloth, spreading it out full-length so that I was sure to see it clearly.

The ground under my feet shifted, and I felt myself crumple.

Horeb held Kadesh's dark brown cloak. The cloak he was never without. The fine, swirling cloak he had gathered me into when he'd whispered his love to me. The cloak he'd protected me with so many times. I heard myself groan like a wild animal as Horeb tossed the garment to me as though it were a dirty rag.

My reaction was slow and the heavy cloak fell to the ground before I could get to my knees. Quickly, I snatched it up, afraid that Horeb would take it back, but when I touched the rich, familiar cloth, my strength left me and I slid back to the ground in a heap.

"It's proof of his death. I saved it for you. As a wedding gift. Unfortunately, his blood stained the expensive cloth. He was wearing it when I plunged my sword into him. Kadesh screamed until he died. Didn't you hear him?"

"You lie," I moaned. I buried my face into the cloth, tasting the blood of Kadesh, the smell of his skin lingering in the folds. For a fleeting moment I felt Kadesh's arms around me, heard his voice in my ear.

I pulled the cloak around my shoulders and staggered to my knees, spotting my dagger just beyond the chair's legs. Slipping my hand down, I grabbed the dagger and advanced toward Horeb, holding out my arms as if I would embrace him.

His black eyes glinted. "Now you've come to your senses."

Nalla shrieked when I raised the knife and lunged at Horeb's chest. Immediately, he blocked my arm with such force the knife exploded from my fingers and fell back to the floor. Then Horeb twisted my other arm behind my back and I was certain he would snap my bones. But instead, he kicked my dagger off into a dark corner of the house, then laughed and released me. I fell to the floor, banging my knees with an excruciating crunch.

"Save your passion for our wedding night," Horeb said with a laugh. "I will come for you in the morning. Have her ready, Nalla." He strode out the door and I heard his men mount their camels and gallop off.

I lifted my swollen eyes, the world a haze of pain. The eerily red moon hovering at the horizon seemed to reproach me as it sank below the mountains. Mountains that would have led me home. I belonged to Horeb now, and there was nothing I could do.

"Nalla," I whispered hoarsely. "I want to see Kadesh."

Nalla wouldn't look me in the face. Instead, she knelt beside me and held me in her arms. "He went down quickly after Horeb stabbed him. Horeb's men took the body into the desert to get rid of it. Everything happened so fast. Let it comfort you, Jayden, that Kadesh died quickly. I'm sure he didn't suffer very long."

"But I want to see him!" I cried into her neck. "I should have been allowed to see him!"

"Horeb will never allow you to mourn him," Dinah snapped. "To make a spectacle of yourself like this. In the eyes of the world, your betrothed avenged your good name. You can go home now with your head held high."

I lifted my head to stare daggers at her. "I've done nothing to hide my head in shame. *Nothing!*"

"Girls, stop!" Nalla ordered, anguish in her voice, but I didn't care any longer.

My hand darted out, my fingers like talons as I grasped my mother's jewelry from around Dinah's neck and pulled it off. "You sold my sister, and now you sent the man I love to his death. You could have warned us that Horeb was here, but you did *nothing*! You're an accomplice to murder."

Dinah screamed, clutching at her bare neck. "Give them back! They're rightfully mine!"

Instantly, Nalla towered over us. "Jayden, you will take your mother's necklace, and Dinah, you will keep the earrings you're luckily still wearing. And I never want to hear either of you speak of this again."

Clutching the silver symbol of the evening star hugging its full moon, I saw blood trickling from my fingers, just like the blood that had dripped from Kadesh's hands. I would never forget that image for as long as I lived: Horeb's men standing on his arms and legs, Horeb's sword held high in the air as he laughed right before plunging it into Kadesh's heart.

I curled up into a ball and put my hands over my ears, trying to keep out the sound of shouts and taunting from Horeb's men, the memory of their clanging swords. Sobs heaved at my chest and I was sure I must be dying, my soul slipping away into oblivion.

I spent the night wrapped in Kadesh's cloak, not sleeping. I'd lived on hope these past weeks. In the time it took my heart to beat, all that was gone.

When I finally slept, exhausted, I dreamed that my grandmother was stroking my hair, whispering her words of wisdom.

"Evil won't win forever," she told me. "There is so much more than the world we see with our mortal eyes, Jayden. Don't give up your faith, my daughter. Never give up. . . ." The strange dream faded and I pressed Kadesh's cloak against my face, desperate to feel him one last time.

I relived my moment seeing Sahmril in the palace courtyard and cried bitter tears.

My mission now was to destroy Horeb. To take my revenge and make sure the tribe knew who he really was. It was the only way to make things right again. I had to stow away my grief. I would never submit to him or to defeat. He'd declared war on me by killing Kadesh. And that meant Horeb's defeat.

His death. Somehow I would find a way.

I touched my necklace and the silver bracelet around my ankle that Kadesh had given me, taking courage and hope from them.

I refused to be Horeb's wife. Not even if they dragged me to the marriage tent and pinned me to a pole. I had to escape to the hills before he returned in the morning to take me.

The fire was cold when I rolled over to get up in the still dark void of morning.

Nalla lay beside me as my guard. But when I tried to rise, I realized that someone had tied my leg to the table so that I couldn't escape.

The rope was thick and rough and the knots complicated. Even though I helped my father set up our tent stakes each time we moved and I was familiar with these knots, I couldn't manage to get them undone. I worked quietly so as not to wake Nalla, but within minutes my fingers were badly scraped.

I let out a ragged breath as my arm brushed my thigh. Nalla hadn't thought to check me for weapons. My knife was strapped to my leg, where I'd found it in the corner and replaced it before the house fell asleep.

The good fortune seemed like an omen of hope.

I carefully unsheathed my knife and began sawing at the thick rope. Several times I stopped to listen to Nalla's breathing, but she was sleeping. I knew if I woke her she would do everything to keep me from leaving.

Anxiety made my hands sweat. The light in the room changed. Dawn was coming. I had to hurry.

Finally, I got through the rope and untwisted the last knot, pushing the hateful bundle away from me.

Promptly I rose and crept through the tiny house. I stole a loaf of bread and some fruit and dried meat from Nalla's stores, stuffing the inner pockets of Kadesh's cloak.

After tying the cloak strings around my neck, I carefully opened the door, praying it wouldn't creak. I had to get away from the city before the night sky lightened too much.

The hour before dawn was quiet and hushed. The sounds of fighting between the armies of Zimrilim and Hammurabi had come to a stop for the moment. My nose and throat still burned from the acrid smell of the palace flames.

My plan was a drumbeat inside my head. A camel. The Euphrates. And then west. Kadesh's camels were tied up outside. And our water bags were still tied to the animals, too. That's all I needed to get back to Tadmur—and the safety of the Temple of Ashtoreth. It was my only refuge now. I would live in the basements, never dance again, and be a mother to the orphan children of Tadmur while I made my plans to kill Horeb.

I slipped through the front door, closed it without a whisper of sound, and darted around the side of the building, passing by the alleys and side streets of Mari until I came to the enclosed pen of camels used by travelers. The pen was more than half-empty. People had been fleeing since yesterday morning and taking their animals with them.

I scurried around the remaining camels, but it didn't take me long to realize that Kadesh's camels were gone. Stolen by

Horeb and his men. Tears of frustration filled my eyes. Quickly, I untied one of the empty water pouches from another camel. Breathing a sigh of relief, I could escape now that I could get water.

Leaving the camel pen behind, I fled for the western gate, skirting Nalla's neighborhood—to head for the safety of the hills. There, I could form a new plan. Wait for Horeb to leave. Fend off hyenas and wolves. Perhaps I wouldn't survive. But at least now I had a chance.

26

For the next three weeks, I navigated the hills above Mari, watching its citizens flee the city, endless smoke plumes rising from the king's palace compound as it smoldered. Winter was coming on fast, and the wind gnawed at my fingers and toes. Each night I moved locations, sleeping in hollows under trees and bushes, or in small caves, never far from water in the Euphrates or gathering greens or nuts from along the river to survive. I was used to being hungry, tightening my belt. I couldn't leave the vicinity. I needed a camel to travel back to the Temple of Ashtoreth, and I hadn't figured out how to do that yet, not while the city was still in chaos.

One night well into my fourth week, the smell of pungent woodsmoke drifted across my face, and the memory of Hakak's wedding sprang before my eyes. Strange what a mere smell could do to my mind. That was the night I'd longed to dance for Kadesh. The night he'd kissed me for the first time, and declared his love.

I fell to my knees under the stars, the sharp edges of my broken heart tearing me to pieces. As I stared at the path on top of the hill, I was positive I saw a candle flickering before a couple standing there.

Tears rolled down my face. The wind whispered, like an echo of a future that was never to be. *To Jayden and Kadesh, may you live long and joyfully all your lives.* Those would have been my grandmother's words to me on my wedding day.

There were no cheers from the members of the phantom wedding, of course, and no Kadesh to carry me into the marriage tent. Only a blustery wind that chapped my face, and sharp stones that cut my bare feet. I pressed the rich folds of the cloak to my face, a wave of grief crushing me.

"I can't do it," I whispered. "I can't bear this any longer. Kadesh, is your ghost out there? Can you feel me from beyond the veil of spirits? Please come rescue me and take me with you!"

A moment later, shrubs crackled above me and then a stone skittered past me down the hill.

A child's voice said, "Why is that girl crying?"

Pushing back the hood of Kadesh's cloak, I gaped into the darkness.

Two children, shadows under the moonlight, stood at the top of the trail, watching me. I caught a glimpse of wispy, flyaway hair and dirty knees on a boy. The girl wore a scarf around her braided hair, and her skinny ankles under her shift reminded me of myself when I was eight or nine.

"She must be very sad," the girl said to her younger brother.

I swallowed down my tears, wondering if I was truly seeing a phantom—or still dreaming. "Who are you?"

"He's Benjamin and I'm Anah. I'm older. Of course."

I whipped my head around to examine the hills. As far as I could see, they were empty, silent. Were these children from Mari, perhaps the orphanage at Inanna's temple? Was the city still under siege? I'd had no news at all, no sense of what was really happening in the valley below me.

"He still sucks his thumb," Anah added, twisting a finger around the bead in her ear. "And he hurt his arm."

The boy had a linen bandage wrapped around his left forearm, but it looked clean and didn't appear to pain him.

"How did Benjamin get hurt?" I asked.

"He fell from a big rock. It happened during the new moon, when it was too dark to see. Mama told us not to play there, but Benjamin did anyway."

I found myself smiling at the girl's tattling. "Are you from Mari or are you lost?"

"What's Mari?" she asked me.

"Those tiny pinpricks of lights far, far out on the plain. By the river. But where are your parents?"

"Over there," Anah answered, turning her head.

I walked to the crest of the hill and looked down. In a hollow of earth, a campfire flickered, barely three hundred paces away. My phantom woodsmoke was actually real.

"You're not from Mari at all, are you?" I said, realizing that they were desert people.

"Anah! Benjamin!" a woman's voice called.

"Your mother is worried," I told them. "Run back to her."

Before they could go, I saw a woman standing on the hillside, opening up her arms for her children. Her smile dropped when she saw me. "Who are you?" she said, gathering her children protectively.

"My name is Jayden. I'm a daughter of Pharez of the tribe of Nephish. Please don't be afraid. I'm alone."

The woman peered at me through the gloom, pulling her black shawl tighter. Benjamin continued to slurp at his thumb, and his sister, Anah, jerked his hand out of his mouth, rolling her eyes. The expression on her face reminded me of Leila when she used to roll her eyes at me.

"Aren't you from the city?" the woman countered, as though suspicious of my story.

"I was at Mari during the burning of the palace, but I'm a desert girl, truly," I said quickly. "My family is gone and my home has been taken from me—I'm alone—" I choked on the words, realizing how desperate I was to talk to someone. "Please."

The dried dung on the campfire was pungent, crackling in the evening chill. A burly man speared roasted lamb and placed it on a dish. Fresh-baked bread was pulled from the coals and my eyes brimmed with tears as I felt transported to my old life.

The woman paused, clearly wary of me. But after a moment, she said, "Come. Have some food."

Gratefully, I followed her, sitting down to take in the

warmth of the fire. She offered me a bowl of camel's milk, which I drank greedily. As I wiped my mouth, I realized this was the most food I'd eaten in one sitting since Kadesh's death.

"Don't they feed you in the city?" the man asked, filling my bowl again.

I didn't admit that I'd been living in the hills for weeks. "There is no other meal like this one. I'm so grateful. Thank you. Let me help you clean up."

As we scrubbed the bowls with sand, the woman's eyes were filled with questions. "How long have you been hiding out in these hills?"

"I—" I was startled that she'd already come to that conclusion. I looked down at myself, seeing myself in their eyes, dirty and unkempt. "I don't know exactly. Weeks. I've lost track of time." I paused. "It's—it's dangerous for me to return." I looked at the woman helplessly, but she didn't prod me. "My betrothal went badly. I would tell more, but it's . . . complicated. I need to get back to Tadmur, to my sister there, but my camels were stolen and my kinsmen are gone."

"Mari has been dangerously occupied for months now," she agreed. "But you're going to starve out in these hills before long—if you haven't already. You do not look well."

The unspoken question of me traveling with her family was left dangling in the air. I wouldn't ask, and the woman wouldn't offer until she knew me better and discussed it with her husband.

She bent over her work, but I could sense her studying me. "I can't help noticing that you only have one simple necklace.

Your family, I mean—" She stopped, a flush rising up her cheeks.

I touched my throat and pulled the collar of my dress higher. "My jewelry was given to save the life of my baby sister."

The woman shook her head in sympathy. "Sometimes life is hard on the desert, isn't it?"

"Where is your husband's clan?" I asked.

"We plan to meet my husband's family at the next well on the way to Tadmur. For the winter we continue heading west, past Damascus and then south until we get to the land of Isaac's twelve tribes."

"Then we are distant cousins."

She bit at her lips. "I can't help noticing that the rich cloak is such a disparity with the rest of your appearance. Plus it's a man's cloak."

"It belonged to a dear friend who is now dead." I turned away so that I wouldn't weep in front of them.

"What's this?" Anah asked, her small hands tugging on the leather pouch tied to the back of the cape.

"Please don't touch that!" I sounded more alarmed than I should have, and tried to cover it up. "It's only a few mementos from home."

Too late, the bag's ties had loosened and the leather pouch tumbled to the ground. Two frankincense nuggets fell out, exposed in the fire's flames.

The woman stared down at the fallen items as I snatched up the pouch, sweeping my hand over the spice-fragrant teardrops to hide them.

She took a hesitant step toward me. "Where did a poor girl get such riches?"

"I—it's—" I was at a loss to explain. "You know what these are, then."

She nodded, staring at me with astonishment. "That's frankincense. From the secret southern lands."

Disquiet rose in my gut. "How do you know about the secret lands of the South?"

A brisk wind cut over the hill, and I tugged the cloak over my arms, pulling up the hood.

Her eyes swept over me. "That cloak wasn't even remade for you. It's much too large."

I nodded, longing to confide in someone who wouldn't judge me or misunderstand. "It belonged to the love I lost. My cousin—the boy I was betrothed to—gave me this cloak stained with his blood—as proof of his death."

Understanding filled her face. "This boy, the love you speak of—he gave you the frankincense, didn't he?"

I nodded at her astuteness. "It was to help me in case I was ever in trouble."

"I'd venture to say that you're in a great deal of trouble right now," she said, gazing at me.

"I've been hiding in these hills, trying to figure out how to steal a camel in Mari. Whether I should try to find my tribe. Go back to my sister at the temple. Or go south to find my dead love's family. But with the city under siege I haven't dared try to get back inside the city gates."

"Those are hard decisions. But you cannot do this alone.

It's impossible to travel any of those distances by yourself. You need more than one camel, too."

"I realize that I might die," I said slowly. "But any of those decisions are made with one goal in mind."

She cocked her head, scrutinizing me. "What do you mean?"

"I plan to kill the man that killed my love."

She stepped back in alarm. "You speak of evil deeds. Please tell me no more."

I bit at my lips and looked her in the eye. "He has murdered before, and any redemption inside him has disappeared. Now he lives only to torture me. Unless I marry him, he will kill me, but I've vowed to kill him first. I must, in order to survive."

"That's why you're hiding out here in these hills."

"That's right," I whispered, recounting the last seven frankincense nuggets in my bag and securing the string tie around my waist.

"You are a determined girl," she said, watching my careful actions with the frankincense. "I'm sorry for all you've lost." And then her next words astounded me. "We saw frankincense like this on our journey up to Tadmur before we came east to Mari. A man from the canyon lands had a bag of frankincense nuggets. He took a piece and ground it up, making a paste to rub into the bleeding gash my son, Benjamin, suffered when he fell."

I pictured the nugget I'd ground up for Kadesh's wound in his stomach and felt faint with the memory. So many months ago. So much had happened, it was nearly impossible to grasp all that I'd been through and all that I'd lost. My eyes burned with unshed tears as I wrapped Kadesh's cloak around me, hiding the bag of frankincense once more.

"Anah told me her brother fell playing on some rocks. Did the frankincense help to heal his wound?"

"Yes, it did, and we were so grateful that he helped us. Having frankincense close at hand was like a miracle. I've heard of its medicinal use before but never witnessed it."

I felt myself begin to shake. "Why didn't he use the desert people's turmeric or henna?"

"He told us the frankincense would work more quickly and better. I've never owned it because it's much too costly. It's rare for any tribal person to possess the spice, much less use it for healing. Frankincense is only for temples and wealthy families or the Egyptians, who must embalm their citizens." She lifted her arm in a gesture of awe. "To give it away like that, for a poor desert boy like Benjamin? Unheard of."

There was a peculiar roaring in my ears although the night was still, ten thousand stars a carpet of glittering lights above us. The fire crackled and snapped, dying down to coals for sleeping. "You said you were in the canyon lands, but there are many canyons all over Mesopotamia. Were you that far south? Were you near the frankincense lands?"

"Oh, no," the woman said, shaking her head with a brief laugh. "I've never been that far south. Nowhere close. They say it's like traveling to the ends of the earth, past the Empty Sands, even. And nobody survives that desolation."

I nodded, and then shook my head. I was so tired and sick, and I'd been close to starving in these hills that my mind was now playing tricks on me. For a moment I'd hoped that perhaps this family might have met some of Kadesh's family, but of course not. That was completely ridiculous. The southern frankincense lands were mysterious and foreign and too far to get to on my own. Besides, even if I could manage to make the borders, I might not be let through. They were kept secret for a reason.

The woman stirred the fire as I wrapped my arms around my knees, the precious nuggets bumping against my legs. She added, "We were just north of the red canyons when this happened. Benjamin got into trouble on the rocks and cliffs—we could hardly keep him contained." She laughed softly, and I envied her family and good husband and children.

"What part of the world do you mean? I've only ever been through red canyons in the land of the Edomites."

She lifted her head. "That's where we were. In the canyons of the Edomites. They have a good well there—for a price. Fortunately, we had sold some of our herd and had enough coins to pay their water tax."

Inwardly, I'd begun to shake with my memories of Kadesh in those same rock canyons. The first time he'd touched me, held my palm to his lips, spoken my name in his extraordinary voice.

"It's a beautiful place," I said softly. "The city will be remarkable when it's finished."

She nodded. "We were so lucky to arrive at the same time

this man was there with his healing frankincense. I understand that he doesn't usually make his home there. He was a stranger, too. Our path crossed at just the right moment. One of God's tender mercies."

A slow pounding started in my head. My breath caught in my throat. "A blessing indeed. But he knew these Edomite people?"

"He had a friend that had taken him in."

I tried to stop my voice from shaking. "Why is that?"

"I don't know any details, but it seems he had been badly hurt. Near death even when he was brought there, and the Edomites were nursing him back to health."

I could hardly ask my next question. "What—what was this man called?"

She shook her head. "We never knew his name, but when he heard about our son's accident he offered to help, even though he was still recovering himself. I'll never forget his kindness and generosity."

I couldn't breathe. It was as though she described Kadesh. Surely the frankincense was only a coincidence. The man who had doctored Benjamin's arm was someone else entirely. Kadesh was dead and I had to accept that. A lump of anger filled my throat. I didn't want to hear any more. It was only the mention of the frankincense that brought Kadesh's face to me, saturating my mind and heart.

Waves of grief and memories crashed over me. I rose, holding up my hand, wanting her to stop talking, to stop torturing me, but she was staring into the fire, completely unaware that I was standing there, frozen to my spot. I feared that in a moment, I might fall straight into the hot coals.

"I told my husband that he seemed different from the other Edomites. The men of Esau were unfriendly and demanded high payment for their water. This healing man was very kind and generous. Oh, and he owned the most beautifully decorated sword. Benjamin was quite in awe."

My legs turned to liquid and I sank to the sand, gasping for air.

"Are you ill, dear girl? Please, come sit by the fire and I'll get you some tea."

My mind screamed. I tried to figure out how much time had passed, how long it had been since Horeb killed Kadesh that terrible night in Mari. If a caravan from the South had passed through and taken his body, there would have been time to leave him with the Edomites before heading to Salem or Egypt with their load, but I pushed down the hope. Nalla had said Kadesh was dead. They all had.

Still, I kept asking questions, almost as if to torment myself. "You say he kept his face covered. Did he have a cloak?"

"No, he only wore a headcloth wrapped around his face."

An image of Kadesh crouched on the bluff watching me at my mother's grave flashed through my mind. His face scarf had been the color of camel's cream. I fought back a flood of burning tears. "Do you know why he wouldn't show his face to you?"

"I actually suspected he was deformed or diseased, but his hands were clean from leprosy. I didn't know what to make of him. Such an unusual person. Tall and holding himself quite regally."

I could barely get the words out. "When did you say you were there and Benjamin was hurt?"

"It was during the new moon. From there we came straight through to Mari, pushing ourselves with winter coming so quickly this year."

The new moon. Long after Horeb had given me Kadesh's bloodstained cloak the night of the ambush.

Overcome with grief—and hope—I took leave to lie down. But I didn't sleep at all that night. I simply lay in my beautiful cloak and stared at the sky. Listened to the rustle of the wind in the brush. Could it be possible Kadesh had survived? So many details about the kind man with the frankincense matched Kadesh; it was uncanny. I tossed and turned, the idea of him surviving keeping me restless and foolishly daring to hope.

The next morning, the husband and wife offered me a place with their family—to ride with them south along the Euphrates to Babylon.

I was probably foolish, but I turned down their generous offer, the story of the healing man playing over and over again in my mind. If there was a possibility Kadesh was alive, I had to try to find him.

I was given a supply of dried meat and bread, and the husband filled my leather water bag, giving me a second one from their own stock.

"Thank you," I whispered. "Thank you for everything."

I headed down the rocky mountain path. My thoughts raced, tumbling over one another as I began to make plans. I'd need to travel now before the winter grew even colder and the ground froze at night. I also needed to travel lightly, without a tent or cook pots so I could move as quickly as possible.

I'd be traveling by myself into the Edomite nation, with its potential raiders and thieves. But Kadesh was well acquainted with a particular Edomite man in the red-rock canyons. Someone who might help me. I remembered Kadesh mentioning a name that day we were ambushed by the men on their horses, and our camels taken for water. Maybe by the time I reached the canyon lands more than four hundred miles southeast of Mari, I'd remember who it was.

I gazed up into the sky, enclosed in Kadesh's cloak. I finally had the answers I'd been searching for. Meeting the family after weeks of seeing no one, hearing their story of the frankincense man hiding in the hills, and the last precious nuggets I'd been saving. All the pieces fell, strangely, into place.

The camel market on the outskirts of Mari was bustling, the place wild with clamoring noises. Summer raids and new camel calves had netted new and plentiful herds, and every tribesman wanted to trade and sell before leaving for the winter migrations. It was getting late in the season and no time to lose.

Men shouted and gestured, arguing their camels' traits and qualities. The beasts brayed and spit and stomped the earth, sending up so much dust the air was a haze of brown.

I was careful not to get my toes smashed as I worked my way through the crowd. The buyers and sellers paid me no attention, assuming I was there with my father or a husband.

I only had enough frankincense for one camel, so I had to purchase the best I could get. If illness or death struck my animal, I'd be stranded in the middle of the desert. Certain death.

"Off with you, girl!" a man cried as I strained to lift the hoof of one of his camels. "You'll get yourself hurt." He eyed me, chewing on a green blade of grass, the tail of his salty beard quivering as he spoke. "Women don't know camels."

"Then you don't know women very well, do you? At least not desert women."

"I wash my hands if you get kicked in the gut."

I pried open the camel's mouth and checked its molars and tongue, then ran my hand through the mare's hair for signs of malnutrition. I'd always wanted one of the beautiful white camels from the West, and this one was the perfect size for me.

"Where is her young?" I asked, knowing she'd dropped a calf sometime over the past year.

"We ate him on the desert," was the unsentimental response.

"Why are you selling her?"

The man folded his arms across his chest. "You're a nosy girl."

I smoothed my hand along the camel's flanks, trying to remain nonchalant, even as my eyes darted about the market, hoping Horeb or his men weren't here watching for me. It was the riskiest thing I'd done, coming down, but I had to buy a camel to travel, or die in those hills above the city.

My legs would get sore since I didn't have enough nuggets for a saddle, but so be it. The canyon lands were almost three weeks' journey from Mari. Perhaps less if I rode hard every day.

"Has this mare ever traveled through the red canyon lands?"

"A year ago she came up from the Gulf of Akabah."

Perfect. I was convinced this was the camel for me. "How much are you asking?"

"Ten pieces of silver."

I held out a closed fist. "Would you settle for frankincense nuggets?"

His eyebrow arched upward again. "You bluff, girl. Besides, she's a white camel and worth a great deal."

I opened my palm to show him six pale-yellow chunks.

The man eagerly picked up one of the pieces of spice and smelled it. "It's real."

"Of course it's real," I said soberly. "And I want this camel."

"You have yourself a deal."

I emptied the contents of the pouch into his hands. Six pieces of frankincense: just what I'd hoped to pay, and no more. I shook the bag so that he could see it was empty and there was nothing left to ask for—or rob me of later.

The last nugget was bound to my chest, saved for the other supplies I would need.

I untied the rope that kept the animal cobbled to the ground, and she groaned as she rose to her feet, spraying a mouthful of saliva into my face. Exulting in my purchase, I led the camel through the crowd, keeping a hand on her neck.

At the edge of the marketplace, I made an abrupt stop. The camel's chest bumped into the back of my head and my palms began to sweat. In the middle of the haggling throng, I spotted a couple of Nephish men.

My sweaty fist clenched the halter and the cord took a bite out of my hand. I wanted to run, but I couldn't bring any attention to myself. Laying my face against my camel's haunches, I swung away from where the men stood, holding on to the bit in her mouth so she wouldn't bolt.

Making sure Kadesh's hood covered my face, I softly clucked to my new camel and moved past, fear thudding inside my chest. Keeping my head low, I gripped the rope and kept going, but not before spying someone with a familiar gait, and a tunic and cloak I knew well, made from my mother's own hands. My father was here at the camel market, standing almost directly in my path.

My throat turned thick, aching as tears bit at my eyes.

A lifetime of memories swept through me. The many days we'd spent raising our camels, making the hearth fire, telling stories and singing. His beard tickling my face as he taught me to make knots, or milk or saddle the camels.

My heart crumbled as he turned away, not seeing me. I wanted to speak with him so badly, I was shaking. He must be here searching for me and Leila.

"I love you, Father," I whispered as I tugged at my camel's

halter. When I glanced backward, my father had already disappeared into the throng.

It was nearly dark when I made it through the range of low-lying dunes and knolls, dropping close to the desert on the other side. I stopped for the night, praying I wouldn't see Horeb and his men on my tail, but I couldn't ride at night and I didn't trust my camel not to get us lost.

I made a small fire to warm my hands and feet before I crawled into my bedding for the night, chewing on a few dates and a day-old loaf of bread. Then I stamped out the flames until they were coals. The moon rose, glowing a bright, silver hue.

I went through a checklist in my mind. Food, water—everything was in place.

I had plenty to reach the cold, clear water of the Edomite well, as long as I didn't spill any or spring a leak in my water-skins.

I'd made an irreversible choice. I was destitute again, except for my camel. But she was so beautiful and perfect, I felt rich. As she chewed her cud, I finally gave her a name. "I will call you Shay, and you will be my surrogate mother."

At the memory of my beautiful mother, my throat closed up, but I flung my hood over my head and pushed down the fear that spiraled up my chest. Water, food, safety, family. I'd left comforts and security behind when I didn't speak to my father. Loneliness, cold, and terror possibly awaited me.

Even if I survived this trip, there was a chance I could end up back at the Temple of Ashtoreth with Leila as I mourned Kadesh's death all over again.

Or I'd be forced into becoming Horeb's bride.

But I would make this journey, even though unanswered questions dangled before me. I possessed Kadesh's bloodstained cloak, and the witness from Horeb's men that he'd died, but I wondered if I was embarking on a foolish quest.

"Am I merely hoping against hope?" I whispered into the cold night air. Many people watched him die. They'd taken his body away and left him for the vultures. What made me think he could have survived a blade run through his heart? Horeb would have made sure he was dead.

Wrapping my arms around my knees, I stared out over the dark valley. There was a long, lonely road out there with little water, dangerous hazards, and wild animals. Maybe I was headed into a peril too great to survive. But Kadesh had once told me to find his Edomite brother if I needed help.

And something fierce inside me told me that I had to have hope. I had to believe, just like Kadesh had told me to.

I pulled his warm cloak tighter around me. My longing for him rushed up through my belly until it reached my heart and sank into my soul. I would never settle for the temple or being Horeb's queen, no matter how dangerous the next few weeks were to reach the Edomite lands. If I gave up the sliver of hope I had, I'd lose myself forever.

My mother was gone, but I still had the knowledge of what she'd taught me. If she were here she would want me to choose my life, my soul, and the boy I loved, even if it meant facing death to be together.

I wept tears of loss as my mother's presence suddenly came to me. I sensed her spirit close, the touch of her fingers brushing my cheek as she whispered love into my ears.

My mother's ghost warmed me, as though she held me in her arms. A moment later, I found myself rising to my feet. I would dance with her one more time, as she and I had danced in our tent since I was a young girl, and as I had danced for her at her grave to say good-bye.

Digging my feet into the earth, my body swayed in the wintry evening twilight, my hips circling the familiar, comforting movements. My arms reached for the stars, pulled down the moon, and then I whirled my toes on the cold dirt as I enfolded Kadesh's cloak around me, homesick for him all over again.

My mother had always empowered me, and the dance now filled me with a surge of strength and wisdom.

War was coming. War with Horeb. A battle between good and evil. Integrity and deceit. Life and death.

I danced for Kadesh and his mighty sword, and for his victory.

I danced for Horeb's defeat.

Last of all, I danced for Leila and Sahmril. I would find my sisters and save us from Horeb's long arm of vengeance. I danced everything in my heart and soul until I dropped, exhausted, to the sands.

My mother caught my hands in hers as the music of the desert ended. The world stopped spinning when she kissed my cheeks and pressed her lips into my palms. Then my beautiful mother breathed her spirit deep into mine to keep her with me always.

"There are times, Jayden, when a woman's emotions run higher and fuller than the waves on the Akabah Sea, threatening to drag her to the bottom and drown her."

My mother's words had been true nearly a year ago, and they were still true, but I wouldn't drown. I would rise above the waves of danger and death and fear.

"You have become one of a long line of goddess women at last, Jayden," I heard her whisper as the wind swept over the hills and across the Assyrian plains. "Just like the ancient goddess who gave us life and power and womanhood so long ago. Nobody can ever take that away from you."

Danger and uncertainty twisted deep in my belly as the universe around me shifted. Images of my ancestors danced before my eyes; unseen spirits of the ancients pushed against my back, and I felt as though I were being flung across a new threshold. But it was a doorway I wanted to enter, a life I wanted to live. I was creating my own time now, apart from the women's circle of my tribe and my mother, separate from my father and my grandmother and Leila and all that I'd known.

I wouldn't see the people I loved for a long time, if ever again. The desert was a harsh master and never held any promises. But this was a step into a world *I* had chosen. A world I would fight for, a clan I would die for, and I knew that my life would never be the same again.

Acknowledgments

I t's almost surreal to be writing the acknowledgments for this novel. The setting and time period and people of the ancient Middle East have been a love interest and passion of mine for close to twenty years. I purchased, borrowed, and read stacks of books and researched until my eyes went blurry. It's been ten years since I wrote a messy draft of the first chapter of *Forbidden*. The story has gone through countless configurations—too many to keep track of over a decade, but my love for the story's roots and its themes of family, faith, dance, and courage has never diminished. Publishing this novel, which is close to my heart and soul, is a deeply satisfying event and honestly I'm thrilled to pieces.

Even though a writer sits alone with her paper, pencils, keyboard, and imagination, no writer's journey to publication is ever solitary—thank goodness, or we'd be certifiably nuts by the time we reached The End! I'm thankful and indebted to Jim and Carol Gee and our Jordanian tour guide, for taking us to all the behind-the-scenes wonder that is the ancient glorious city of Petra. It was a thrill to travel the ancient King's Highway and visit their Bedouin friends in their tents and caves. The deserts and mountains of Jordan are stark and magnificent and awe-inspiring. Riding jeeps through the scenery of Wadi Rum was like a dream and literally took my breath away. Memories never to be forgotten.

I am blessed with many friends who read with enthusiasm from the very beginning when the story was awkward and gangly in its infancy. First, the Fems: my long-ago critique group of dear friends and talented women: Carolee Dean, Kris Conover, Nancy Hatch, Marty Hill, and Neecy Twinem. Thank you for always lifting me up when I brought a new chapter and giving me terrific advice.

After four years when I was lost and wondering if I was on the right track, Shutta Crum generously read the manuscript and nearly burned her dinner because she couldn't put it down. Shutta, you gave me the impetus to write a new draft and keep going, thank you!

Still, the story needed new plot oomph and it was Lisa Ann Sandell who provided inspiration and a push when I rewrote the manuscript again two years ago. Her comments and insight pushed me to think harder and deeper, and many parts of the story came alive in new ways. Thank you so much, Lisa!

Two women have recently come into my life and become my new best friends: Jackie Garlick-Pynaert and Martina

Boone, both brilliant writers and story analysts. You adorable gals have played a huge role this past year in helping me bring Jayden's story to new heights. I will be forever grateful.

My incredible agent, Tracey Adams, stuck with me through some major ups and downs with *Forbidden*, but never wavered in her belief in this book. Thank you from the bottom of my heart, plus a deep well of gratitude to the entire Adams Literary team!

Tremendous appreciation also goes to Karen Chaplin whose enthusiasm and love for this project carried me through hard revisions and delays and lots of personal angst along the way. Our first marvelous phone conversation on the day you made the offer for the entire trilogy will remain in my memory forever. I'm grateful to the entire HarperCollins team of assistants and copy editors and cover designers for their hard work and dedication to *Forbidden*. Working with you all is a dream come true.

Finally, I am always grateful to my husband, Rusty, and our children, Aaron, Jared, Adam, and Milly, for letting me spend time with my imaginary world and characters and for indulging me in those revision nights when I begged for take-out burgers to keep me sane.

For pictures and photo albums of the Middle East and the friendly Jordanian Bedu people, please visit my website, Pinterest pages, or Facebook photo albums.

www.kimberleygriffithslittle.com

Author's Note

My fascination with the ancient time periods of Mesopotamia began more than fifteen years ago when I heard a magical story about how the Arabian horse was bred and raised on the deserts by the nomadic tribes. After researching the roots of the story and publishing a version of it in *Cricket* magazine, the first flicker that originally sparked my imagination became a bonfire of intrigue and passion.

I spent the next several years reading everything I could find. The writings of early explorers and adventurers daring to cross the Empty Quarter of Saudi Arabia, Yemen, and Oman on the Arabian Sea Peninsula, as well as the writings of nineteenth-century historians, researchers, and members of various Bedu tribes who have written personally about growing up on the desert with their tents and camels. A lifestyle and culture that has remained virtually unchanged over thousands of years.

I've also been fascinated by the historical figure and prophet Abraham and his posterity that has virtually spread throughout the world over the last 4,000 years. I chose that era for my own since I would not be held accountable for errors in a history that is unwritten except for the Old Testament (written several hundred years after Abraham's lifetime). But I've written enough historical fiction and novels about other cultures over the last fifteen years that I painstakingly strive to make my books as accurate as I possibly can.

We don't know the exact dates when Abraham lived; historians put it anywhere from 2000 to 1800 BCE. I split the difference and chose approximately 1900 BCE. We know from Biblical records that he lived 175 years. He and his wife Sarah had a son they named Isaac. His son, Jacob, had twelve sons of his own, who are well known as the Twelve Tribes of Israel, some of whom are the ancestors of the Hebrew people of Moses (who lived approximately 500 years after Abraham).

Abraham's second son by Hagar was called Ishmael. His offspring of twelve sons/tribes spread throughout the deserts of Arabia and became known as the Arab people. I chose one of the lesser known sons' progeny, Naphish (sometimes spelled Nephish) to depict in my story.

The tribes of the modern-day Middle East descend from the Twelve Tribes of Ishmael. Four thousand years later, the Islamic people still revere Abraham as a prophet and their ancestor. In the time period of my story, his descendants, those twelve sons/tribes of Ishmael, would have tried to follow Abraham's teachings and way of life while other local city dwellers worshipped the deities (gods and goddesses) of the local temples and religions.

In 1759 BCE, King Hammurabi was the king and ruler of Babylon and actually did lay siege to the ancient city of Mari on the Euphrates River, as he conquered many nations to bring them under the Babylonian Empire.

The Queen of Sheba is mentioned in this story as well. This is not the same queen who visited King Solomon in Jerusalem (called Salem in the time period of *Forbidden*), since that queen lived in approximately 960 BCE. But the Kingdom of Sheba existed in the far reaches of the modern-day country of Yemen on the southern borders of Arabia and was ruled by various kings and queens through the centuries. The name "Sheba" was not the given name of the queen but refers to the name of the land, or the Kingdom of Saba/Sheba. The people of Saba are called Sabaeans. Archeological excavations continue in Yemen, unearthing palaces and dams from thousands of years ago.

Interestingly, after the death of Abraham's wife Sarah, he married an Arab woman by the name of Keturah. Their son, Jokshan, fathered two sons he named Sheba and Dedan. But before Abraham's grandsons, there were also two grandsons named Sheba and Dedan through Cush, Noah's son. Their descendants spread south into the lands of modern-day Yemen, also known as Arabia Felix, more than a thousand years before the Queen of Sheba who is linked to King Solomon in 960 BCE.

Kadesh, who is from the southern frankincense land of Oman, is a descendant of Noah and Abraham through the tribes of Dedan and Sheba. More about Kadesh, as well as the Dedan and Sabaean tribes'/kingdoms' return, will be explored in the second book of the Forbidden trilogy.

Discerning readers might notice a mention of the country Ethiopia, in the horn of Africa. In Biblical and ancient Egyptian texts, it was called Kush or Nubia. It was also known as Abyssinia over the last several hundred years. I used Ethiopia so readers would have an easier time determining the geography of the story.

I also purposely stayed away from specific physical descriptions of my characters, except in hair and eye color. Researchers still debate what ancient people in Egypt and the Middle East thousands of years ago actually looked like. I didn't think it was necessary to mention skin hue or to say he/she was "olive-skinned," etc., because I don't think it matters. Readers can picture the characters however they want to. Some people would have been lighter or darker skinned, depending on where they were from—or how much time they spent outside. In addition to modesty and religious traditions, a prevailing reason people wore—and still wear—clothing that covers their limbs, including head and face scarves, was to protect themselves from the brutal sun, wind, and blowing sand.

The ancient dance depicted in *Forbidden* is founded in the roots of dance that predate written history. The descriptions of the dancing statues mentioned in the story are based on stone and wood statues found in archeological digs around the Middle East. Often called Oriental Dance or *Raqs Sharqi*, (an Egyptian term developed a hundred years ago to depict tribal folk dances), the dance is now called by its modern-day term, "belly dance." The dance was used as exercise, preparation for birth, entertainment, weddings, women's private social gatherings, and in the ancient goddess temples.

If you have any further questions about the historical aspects of *Forbidden*, please email me at kglittle@msn.com or visit my website, www.kimberleygriffithslittle.com.

TURN THE PAGE FOR A SNEAK PEEK AT
THE HEART-POUNDING SEQUEL!

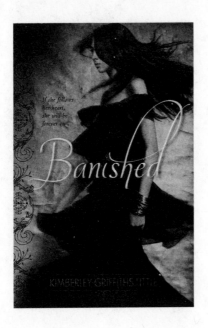

1

A dirty, callused hand slapped down over my mouth and the stale breath of a man hissed in my ear. "Don't move or I'll slit your pretty little neck."

I clawed at the stranger's cloak, trying to push him off, but he was too heavy. A moment later, I realized my ankles were tied together. I couldn't run, couldn't even move. Shrieks gurgled in my throat as if I was drowning, his hand cutting off my air.

Last evening's fire was nearly extinct and a cold, wretched moon shone a pillar of silver across the hollow I'd nestled myself into. This was my last night in the hills of Mari before I headed into the desert with my camel.

Only one day into my journey to find Kadesh and I was already dead.

The sharp tip of a blade pressed against my neck, and I whimpered.

I'd planned to be gone by dawn. Leave behind the city of Mari, and Sahmril, my baby sister who was lost to me when her adoptive parents refused to give her back. The promise I'd made to my mother to keep her safe was broken.

"Give me the frankincense of the stranger we killed." The man's foul breath dragged across my face. He was referring to Kadesh, the boy I loved, who'd been murdered by Horeb, the prince of my tribe. I'd watched Horeb plunge his sword into Kadesh and then order his soldiers to drag his body off.

Shock flooded me when I realized who my attacker was. I wrenched his fingers away from my mouth and with a raw voice said, "Gad? What are you doing lurking about the cliffs of Mari?"

This man was a childhood friend of Horeb's and one of my own tribesmen. His body pressed against mine, and I writhed in disgust.

There was only one reason Gad was in the foothills of Mari, far from the oasis of Tadmur where my tribe camped for the summer. He was a member of Horeb's army.

Horeb, my betrothed. The man who'd attacked and scarred me. Blackmailed me for the murder of his father to hide the fact that he'd killed Abimelech so he could steal the tribal crown. He thought the kingship gave him the right to murder Kadesh—because Kadesh had stolen me away. Horeb was the boy I knew as a child, ran foot races with, fought with stick swords, and tended baby camels with.

He was now the king of the Nephish tribe, and he'd been hunting me for weeks. If he found me he'd either kill me or lock me up in chains as his wife. Guarded by soldiers so I wouldn't slit my own wrists.

Nausea rose up my throat as Gad's beard grazed my cheek. He smelled vile and filthy. "Tell me where the frankincense is," he murmured, his hand hovering over my face. "If you refuse, I'll shove my dagger into your heart—then strip you naked to find the nuggets myself."

Flashes of that night when Horeb tried to rape me at the oasis pond crashed through my senses. I couldn't relive such an attack again.

Gad grinned and I knew he was thinking the same thing. "It's too bad Horeb's paying a ransom to get you back. If not, I'd be doing more than just stealing your frankincense."

I tried to swallow. "But I have nothing!"

"Liar! You were seen at the camel markets in Mari. You had frankincense and now I want the rest of it."

"I spent everything on the camel—I can't walk to Tadmur on foot!"

His fingers slinked along my waist and hips, fumbling in my dress pockets.

"Touch me and I'll kill you," I threatened, shifting as he searched, which freed my arm to reach the knife strapped to my thigh.

An amused smile spread across Gad's face. "There's a rumor that you're fairly adept with a knife."

I shuddered. So Horeb was bragging about the fact that he'd

branded my body with a knife to claim me as his so nobody else would want me.

"Where is Horeb?" I asked to distract him. "I thought he and I would travel together."

Gad's laugh was scornful. "You're a terrible liar."

"And when I see him next," I continued, "I'll tell him *you're* a deserter and a thief—and tried to attack his betrothed."

Surprise streaked his ugly face. He obviously didn't expect me to fight back.

"I know you're on the run. Give me the wealth."

"I don't have anything!" I said, spitting at his face. He slapped me, and my head slammed the ground. My eyes swam with tears. I could only insult him so far. For all I knew, Horeb was already here in the Mari hills, only a shout away.

My camel was on the far side of the boulders, looking skittish and uneasy. Her fur glowed white under the pink light of dawn.

Gad's grin cracked his face, showing stained brown teeth. He snatched up my cloak next, still sitting on top of me, and greedily searched the folds and inner pockets.

Of course, I was bluffing. The last nugget of frankincense, the one I'd saved for medicinal purposes or an emergency, was tied to my chest, but so small it wouldn't buy much.

With Gad's attention on my cloak, I slid my hand down to retrieve the dagger strapped under my skirt. My fist curled gratefully around the hilt.

The morning sun hit the horizon, and a blazing dawn streaked the sky.

"Nothing!" Gad muttered. After checking the rope around

my tied legs, he jumped up to tear apart the campsite.

While he searched my rations pack, I began to quietly saw at the rope around my ankles. I spoke out loud to hide my task. "See? I have no frankincense. You've climbed into the hills for nothing."

Ignoring me, Gad grabbed the halter of my camel and swung her head around. She bellowed and stomped her feet. Then he proceeded to hunt through her blanket and decorative tassels, even peering into her ears and mouth.

"Leave her alone!" I shouted.

"Damn!" he yelled when Shay bit him on the shoulder. Without hesitation he hit her head with his fist. Fury boiled in the pit of my belly at his treatment of my well-bred camel, but I tried to focus on freeing myself.

Just as the rope began to fall into pieces, Gad raced toward me with a roar. Before I could crawl away, he threw me flat on my back again, the dagger falling to the ground.

His touch made me sick. Instinctively, I shoved my knee into his soft belly, but he had more leverage and began to rip at the folds of my dress, breathing heavily. "The frankincense is strapped to you!"

"No!" I screamed, flailing my arms and legs, trying to maneuver my dagger to stop him. There was no other way out of this.

Suddenly, Gad stopped and swung his head around. "What's that noise?"

Low, hideous growls came from the cliffs above.

My camel screamed in fright, galloping across the campsite

to the head of the desert trail.

A striped gray hyena slinked along the cliff above us. Saliva dripped from its teeth. The animal's ribs showed; it was obviously starving and sick. The coarse fur on the back of its neck rose in attack mode, teeth grinning as it howled at us.

Fear soaked my body in rivulets of sweat. "I think he just found his dinner."

Gad fumbled for his sword. Before I could take another breath, he slashed at my dress and spotted the frankincense bound to my chest. "You sly girl." He grinned with pleasure just as the hyena launched itself from the edge of the cliff.

My breath came in terrified spurts. "No, no!" I moaned. "Get off me! The hyena's going to attack us both!"

But Gad was determined to steal the only thing of value I had left—and steal my virtue with it. Panting, he ripped at the cloth binding the frankincense to my chest, his face lighting up with greed and lust. Before I could form a coherent thought I gripped my dagger and thrust it straight into his soft stomach.

The sensation was sickening. Bright red blood dribbled down his cream-colored shirt into the waistband of his trousers, the hilt of the knife still tight in my fist.

My chest convulsed in horror at what I'd just done. "I—I never—"

Gad stared at me, terror in the whites of his eyes. He tried to speak, but only a trickle of red slipped through his lips.

Scrambling backward on my hands in the dirt, I screamed, "Shay, come!" My camel's ears pricked up, however, she hesitated at the sight of the hyena slinking along the earth in stalk mode. But a moment later, she came hurtling toward me. Sweat trickled into my eyes as I swept up my blanket and satchel. I lurched to my feet, and then clawed my way up onto Shay's back, wrapping the halter around my wrist to keep from falling back down in the process.

When we raced out of the small clearing, I stole a glance behind me. Clutching at the wound in his belly, Gad fell to his back, groping for his sword. The hyena paused and sniffed at the scent of fresh blood pouring from the hole in his stomach.

"Oh, dear God in heaven," I moaned. I'd wielded my knife out of pure desperation. But even if Gad managed to fend off the wild hyena, I knew he didn't have long to live.

Burying my face in my camel's neck, I shuddered with sobs. Not a moment later, Gad let out a chilling, unnerving scream. I could hear the hyena's fierce teeth crunch down on bone, imagine the slobbering mouth and powerful body pinning the Nephish tribesman so he couldn't fight back.

"Go, go!" I urged the camel, closing my ears to the man's agony. I couldn't have fought both Gad and the hyena and stayed alive, but I was flooded with guilt.

After weeks of fear and loneliness in these hills while I crafted my plans to search for Kadesh, I'd just survived my first deadly encounter.

Tears of terror were cold on my face, wind smearing the salt across my cheeks. My camel tore headlong down the rocky hillside. I swore the ride jolted the bones from my skin. Every ounce of strength washed away, leaving me limp as a worn rag.

When we slowed at the bottom of the hill, the words of

Hannah, the desert woman I'd met many days ago, echoed through my mind. I latched on to them as though I was a child again, clutching my mother's nightgown when I had a bad dream. Hannah and her husband, Gedaliah, with their young children had traveled through the Edomite lands three moons ago.

They had told me the story of a man who wouldn't show his face, but who healed their son's arm with frankincense. Frankincense. Such an unusual possession. Not many people in these poor deserts owned the expensive nuggets.

The woman's voice came to me again: . . . *and he owned the most beautifully decorated sword.*

Instantly, I had pictured Kadesh's Damascus sword with its etchings and the imprinted symbol of his frankincense tribe. The man Hannah described had to be Kadesh. Somehow he'd survived Horeb's attack and ended up back with the Edomites. Not the wild men who'd tried to kidnap Leila and me and stolen our camels on our migration to the summer lands, but someone he trusted. A friend I had forgotten Kadesh mentioning long ago.

Once we were out of the Mari hills, I urged Shay forward to find the southern trail and start our journey for answers. If there was only a small chance Kadesh was actually alive in the Edomite city, I still had to know the truth—even if the perils of the desert tried to destroy me.

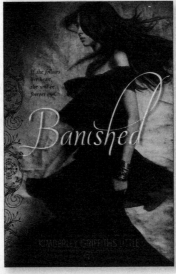